# Undressed

## KRISTINA COOK

## ZEBRA BOOKS
### Kensington Publishing Corp.
www.kensingtonbooks.com

ZEBRA BOOKS are published by

Kensington Publishing Corp.
850 Third Avenue
New York, NY 10022

All Kensington titles, imprints, and distributed lines are available at special quantity discounts for bulk purchases for sales promotion, premiums, fund-raising, educational, or institutional use.

Special book excerpts or customized printings can also be created to fit specific needs. For details, write or phone the office of the Kensington Special Sales Manager: Attn. Special Sales Department. Kensington Publishing Corp., 850 Third Avenue, New York, NY 10022. Phone: 1-800-221-2647.

Zebra and the Z logo Reg. U.S. Pat. & TM Off.

ISBN: 0-8217-7980-X

First Printing: June 2006
10 9 8 7 6 5 4 3 2 1

Printed in the United States of America

## Praise for *Unlaced*

"Sexy and entertaining!"—*Booklist*

"*Unlaced* is a fast-paced, exciting story with all of the elements that make a good read."—*Affaire de Coeur*

"I was totally charmed . . . This reviewer gives *Unlaced* my highest recommendation."—The Road to Romance

"The breath of fresh air that I have been waiting for!"
—Roundtable Reviews

"*Unlaced* is undeniably a fabulous debut for Kristina Cook."
—Romance Junkies

"Not only do you fall in love with the hero and heroine, but the secondary characters are also very well developed . . . fast paced and compelling, with an ending that kept this reader enthralled . . ."
—Fallen Angel Reviews

"*Unlaced* is a very auspicious start for newcomer Kristina Cook. Winning characters and strong storytelling are the reasons for much of its appeal."—Romance Reviews Today

## Praise for *Unveiled*

"Happily, the promise so evident in Cook's debut, *Unlaced*, is fulfilled . . . mesmerizing as once again Cook provides thoroughly enjoyable entertainment."—*Booklist*

"*Unveiled* is touching and tender, with just enough pathos-tinged humor to win our hearts."—*Romantic Times*

"A totally charming tale . . . sexy and delectable."
—Historical Romance Writers

"Certain to gain a place on historical readers' list of favorites . . . a firm keeper."—Fallen Angel Reviews

"Witty and charming!"—Romance Reader at Heart

## Also by Kristina Cook

*Unveiled*

*Unlaced*

Published by Zebra Books

*For Danny,*
*for always pushing me to be better than "good"*
*and for making it possible for me to chase my dreams.*

*And for Vivian and Ella,*
*just for being your wonderful little selves.*

# Acknowledgments

I would like to thank astrophysicist extraordinaire Dr. Neil deGrasse Tyson, Director of the Hayden Planetarium, for so generously and cheerfully answering my astronomy questions. All errors are, of course, entirely mine. I would also like to thank the fine folks at the Fort William/Lochaber Online forum for sharing so much information about their favorite Scottish region, and especially Colin (I swear, that's really his name!) for sending me the lovely photos of Ben Nevis for inspiration. Lastly, I'd like to thank Charlotte Featherstone—not only for her friendship, but for being the best critique partner imaginable. Her unique perspective and dead-on suggestions never fail to strengthen a book, and this one is no exception.

# Prologue

"Och, woman, is it done?" As the coach door swung shut and the conveyance lurched off, the florid-faced man squinted at the squirming bundle the woman clutched to her bosom.

"'Tis done, husband." She gently pulled down the plaid that covered the bundle, revealing a damp thatch of fine hair—auburn intermingled with gold—curling against tiny ears. Pale aqua-colored eyes stared balefully up at the faces hovering above. The babe yawned and began to suck its fist with loud, slurping noises.

"And what of the wet nurse?" He looked to the woman with a scowl.

"'Tis all arranged. We will collect her at the coaching inn. Now, Donald, look at the bonny lad. What do ye think of 'im?"

The man's eyes, deep set in his craggy, lined face, misted over. "He's bonny, indeed, Ceilie, just as ye said. Now they willna say that Donald Maclachlan canna sire a son, will they? Nay, I've a fine son, indeed." He reached for the child and, laying him down on the worn leather bench, began to unwrap the swaddling layers. One chubby arm appeared, then another. In a flash, a small hand reached out and grabbed a handful of the man's beard.

"Och, ye canna do that, my lad." Gently, he disentangled the fingers from his beard. "There now, my son. We've a long journey ahead of us. Best get some sleep now." He smoothed down the auburn curls across the child's forehead while inquisitive eyes peered up at him curiously. "Iain he shall be called," he said, his voice almost a whisper.

"Check his linen," the woman said. "A dry bairn is a happy one, me mam used to say."

The man reached down to feel the carefully folded linen, his brows drawing together in confusion as his movements became brusque. "Devil take it, woman!" The linen fell away, and both pairs of eyes goggled at the sight before them.

"Dear Lord!" The woman made the sign of the cross. "'Tis . . . 'tis—"

"A lass," he supplied, his round face flushed scarlet. "The bairn's a lass."

"But . . . but . . ." she sputtered. "How can that be?"

"Ye canna ken the difference between a lad and a lass, Ceilie?"

"I . . . I dinna ken how this happened! The lassie was still upstairs with the nursemaid; only the lad was sent out for an airin'. I dinna ken how—"

"Ye didna check, woman?" he roared.

Her bottom lip began to tremble. "Check? Why I . . . Nay, I didna check. There wasna time," she wailed. "All the preparin' gone to naught." She sobbed into the folds of her cloak.

The child, still lying between them on the bench, began to whimper. The man waved one hand at her small form in dismissal. "Take her back, then. I've no use for a lass."

"Take her back? We canna do that. We'll be hanged for sure! Nay," she sniffled. "Nay, we must follow our plan and make haste to the border. We havena a choice." Her voice rose shrilly.

For a moment, the man simply stared out the coach's dusty window. His eyes narrowed; his jaw muscles tensed. A vein in his temple throbbed visibly. At last, he nodded his assent. "Aye, I suppose ye are right. We canna risk it. But what in God's name am I to do with a daughter?"

As if she understood the words, the child began to wail pitifully. The woman gathered her into her arms and glared at her husband across the top of the babe's head.

She reached down to stroke the child's hair, murmuring softly as she did so. "There now, child. Dinna cry. A lass ye are, but a bonny lass, indeed. It isna your fault. There now."

At last the babe quieted and round, blue-green eyes—seemingly full of understanding—met hers. The wee lass stuck her thumb into her mouth and began to suck enthusiastically, her eyes never leaving the woman's face until she could hold them open no longer, and, at last, her tiny lashes fluttered shut.

Only then did the woman allow her own tired eyes to close, the rhythmic rumbling of the carriage soothing her jangled nerves. 'Twas done. She had a child, no matter that the child was a lass. She was beautiful, perfect in every way, even if English blood did flow through her veins. There wasna help for that; the child must come from far enough away that no one would come looking for her.

She shifted in her seat, sighing deeply. Moments later, in the peaceful gloaming between wakefulness and sleep, she felt her husband's movement beside her and opened her eyes just wide enough to see him awkwardly pat the sleeping babe's head.

"Sleep now, wee tinker," he whispered. "All will be well in the end."

The woman closed her eyes once more, a smile slowly spreading across her face. Perhaps it would.

# Chapter 1

*Lochaber, Scotland, May 1819*

"Bloody bastards!" Brenna Maclachlan pushed her chair back from the table and stood on unsteady legs. "Burning them out of their homes—women and children. Forcing them to leave with naught but the clothes on their backs. How can they treat their own people so vilely, so cruelly?" She glared at the page lying before her on the roughly hewn trestle table. The Clearances had begun long before Brenna had been born, but never had the removal of tenants been accomplished with such violence, with such lack of humanity, as was now happening in Sutherland. She shook her head fiercely, barely able to believe the words she'd read. "Can it possibly be true?"

"Aye, I have no doubt it is true." James Moray, the Maclachlan land steward for nearly two decades, frowned and reached for his hat. "Isna the first I've heard of such atrocities. More sheep mean more money to fatten their purses, and Stafford cares for naught else."

Brenna reached a hand up to her temple. "But those families have worked that land for generations. Who is he to turn them out now? When will it end? When there are naught left but sheep in Sutherland?"

"He claims to be improving the lands, the bloody sot."

"Improving? Bah." Brenna waved one hand in dismissal. "'Tis butchery, nothing more. Fueled by greed. To think that a Scot would do this to another Scot."

"Stafford is no Scot, and the countess spends most of her time in England. She has little or no regard for her subjects. She's a Gordon, ye know. Not even a Sutherland."

"And what of our own crofters, Mr. Moray? Have they heard this latest news from the north? Do they fear a similar fate here at Glenbroch?"

"Of course not, milady. Your own crofters know ye to be a generous and just landlord, as your father was before ye. They know they remain safe so long as a Maclachlan is at Glenbroch. But the same canna be said of our neighbors on Lord Hampton's estate." He moved to the window and turned his gaze east. "An absentee landlord with no interest in his property, save collecting his dwindling rents. . . ." He trailed off, shaking his head. "'Tis likely he will soon decide in favor of sheep. Indeed, some of Hampton's crofters have already chosen to emigrate, but many cannot. Only a matter of time, your father said, just before he fell ill and—"

"Stop." Brenna held out one hand, her fingers visibly trembling. "I canna listen to more." She closed her eyes and inhaled sharply, the pain of losing her parents still too fresh to bear. Hot tears burned behind her eyelids, but she would not let them fall. Not today.

Hera jumped into Brenna's lap, and she reached down to stroke the cat's silky fur. In response, the animal began to purr loudly, her intense green gaze locked on her mistress's.

"Oh, Hera, 'tis awful, is it not?" Brenna murmured, comforted as always by the animal's soothing presence.

With a meow, the cat stood, arched her back, and then rubbed the side of her face against Brenna's chin.

"My Lady Maclachlan?"

Hera leapt from her lap as Brenna looked up in surprise to find the housekeeper standing in the doorway, her stout body filling the small space. As always, it took her a moment to realize that the servant was addressing her and not her mother. "Aye, Mrs. Campbell?" she managed at last.

"If ye'll pardon me, there are strangers at the door, mum, inquiring after ye." The housekeeper wrung her hands. "I dinna ken what to tell them."

"Strangers?" Brenna's eyes narrowed.

"Another English lord and lady, mistress. And a man of the law with them."

"Is that so?" Coming to offer her a bonny price for her land, no doubt—land that was not for sale. She'd had two such visits in the past fortnight alone, and she'd had just about enough of it. With a swish of her woolen skirts, Brenna strode out of the dining room and headed for the front door. "I'll see to these Sassenachs straightaway."

Indeed, there were strangers at the door. A stocky

man wearing a monocle stood on the front steps, rocking back on his heels as he checked his watch. Behind him stood a man and woman, likely in their mid- to late-forties, with their heads bent together, whispering in hushed tones. All three pairs of eyes turned on Brenna as she appeared in the doorway, her fists planted firmly on her hips.

She tipped her chin in the air and boldly met their questioning gazes. "I am the Lady Maclachlan. What business have ye here?"

The man with the monocle turned to look at the pair behind him. The woman nodded, and he turned back to face Brenna once more. "Is it true, my lady, that you were born on October ninth, in the year of our Lord seventeen hundred and ninety-two?"

The odd question sent Brenna's heart racing. What was the meaning of this? She fought to steady her voice before answering him. "'Tis true, but I must insist on your name, sir, before I continue with this unwanted address. I dinna like to speak with those who know my name but do not provide me equal knowledge."

The man bowed sharply. "If you'll forgive me, my lady. Mr. Jonathan Wembley, of Bow Street. I am in the employ of Lord and Lady Danville and am at their service." He turned and bowed obsequiously to the couple behind him.

Quite formal, wasn't he? Brenna wished he'd quit his scraping and get on with it.

At last returning his attention to Brenna, he cleared his throat and removed a folded sheet of paper from his breast pocket. Squinting through the monocle, he peered at the page and cleared his throat once more.

"And is it true," he continued in a booming voice, "that you were born in England, on the aforementioned date?"

"I was, indeed, but I canna see what difference it makes to your lordship there. My parents traveled to Lancashire before my mama realized she was with child, and they were forced to remain there until after my birth."

"Four months, I believe?"

Brenna arched one brow. "Four months? I dinna understand your question, sir."

"I believe you were four months of age when you arrived at Castle Glenbroch?"

"Aye," she muttered. She'd heard the oft-repeated story of her untimely conception and subsequent birth in Lancashire many times over but never heeded the details. Besides, what should it matter to this stranger? Her annoyance grew a measure. She had work to do, and she'd had quite enough of this already. "I suggest ye quit speaking in riddles, Mr. Wembley, and state your business at once."

The plump woman broke free of her husband's grasp and dashed forward, reaching for the runner's sleeve. "The birthmark," she insisted with a breathless wheeze. "Ask her about the birthmark."

Mr. Wembley nodded solemnly and squinted at the paper in his hands once more. "You must pardon the indelicate question, my lady, but is it possible that you have a birthmark on the inside of your right . . . ahem, upper limb, in the shape of a . . ." He trailed off, shaking his head. "Lady Danville, it says here in the shape of a fleur-de-lis. That simply cannot be."

All breath left Brenna's body in a rush, one hand involuntarily moving toward her right thigh. "However did ye know—"

"It *is* her!" the woman exclaimed with a sob, tears coursing down her cheeks. "I knew it, the moment I saw her hair." She reached up and untied her bonnet, tossing it to the ground by her feet. She hastily pulled the pins from her hair till it spilled across her shoulders.

Brenna could only gape at the woman's uncovered head glinting in the sunlight. Deep auburn tresses generously intermingled with gold fell in soft waves about the woman's shoulders. Hair the exact same color and texture as her own.

"After all these years of searching," the woman continued, sobbing into her handkerchief. "At last, Mr. Wembley. At last you've found our daughter."

"Daugh . . . daughter? Are ye daft?" Brenna's gaze swung from the smiling Mr. Wembley to the couple beside him. "Is the woman daft?" she repeated, her voice rising.

Over the woman's head, the man—Lord Danville, Mr. Wembley had called him—looked up and met her gaze, his eyes the same blue-green as hers. "I can barely believe it," he said, a smile spreading across his face. "I never thought I'd live to see the day. Our daughter. Margaret."

Margaret? *They must be mad, all of them,* Brenna thought. The ground beneath her began to tilt, her vision narrowing. She suddenly became aware of a deafening roar in her ears, and then, with a small gasp of surprise, she slipped to the ground in a swoon.

*London, June 1819*

Colin Rosemoor winced as his boots tapped the cobbles in an angry staccato. He reached one hand up to his throbbing brow, clutching his walking stick more firmly with the other. His stomach lurched uncomfortably. *Damn Mandeville and his brandy.* Though in all honesty, he'd needed the drink—most desperately—after last night's debacle. A fiery rage surged through his veins, propelling him forward, back to the scene of his ruin.

He had no idea how that blasted card had found its way into his coat pocket, but he most certainly had nothing to do with it. That anyone should think him a cheat was laughable; he lost far too much blunt at the tables. But it had seemed he'd finally found his winning streak. In a rare turn of events, he'd won several hundred pounds and the deed to some profitable land in Scotland from the Marquess of Hampton.

And then, after Colin's second big win of the night had significantly lightened the Duke of Glastonbury's purse, that bloody bastard Sinclair had called him a cheat and forced him to turn out his pockets. And there, tucked neatly away, had been a four of hearts. No doubt put there by Sinclair, but how could he prove it?

Glastonbury had called him several choice names and then had him tossed out on his ear. Colin winced at the memory. Mandeville had happened upon him in the street and dragged him away before he'd had the chance to reenter White's and call out Sinclair. Of course, once they'd reached Mandeville's study and Colin had recounted the evening's unfortunate events, Mandeville, a sworn enemy of Sinclair's, had vowed to set things straight at White's on Colin's behalf. But dammit, Colin couldn't let him do that. No, it would seem cowardly and weak, having the Marquess of Mandeville fight his battles for him. He would take care of this disagreeable business himself, by God, or die trying.

Colin hurried his step, turning down St. James's Street. Glastonbury enjoyed his port at his club each afternoon at precisely two o'clock, without fail. Colin fished out his watch and checked the time. A quarter past two. He snapped shut the watch, stuffing it back into his pocket as he narrowed his eyes against the glittering afternoon sun. He would speak with the duke, assure him that the hand in question had been won fairly and honorably. And then he would find Sinclair and deal with *him,* once and for all.

It was obvious enough that Sinclair had set him up—he was Colin's chief rival for the hand of the fair Miss Honoria Lyttle-Brown, and by all indications, Miss Lyttle-Brown was soon to accept Colin's suit. She'd indicated as much not three days past, even allowed Colin a forbidden yet chaste kiss in a darkly shadowed lane at Vauxhall Gardens.

He stormed up the steps of number 37 and threw open the doors with vengeful determination, doffing his hat and handing it to the footman along with his walking stick. The footman accepted the items without meeting Colin's gaze, his eyes darting about nervously instead.

The porter behind him cleared his throat loudly. "Pardon me, Mr. Rosemoor, but I must ask that you wait here. Tillson"—he motioned toward the footman—"summon Mr. Montgomery at once." The club's manager. The footman scurried off.

"Is something amiss?" Colin drawled, struggling to rein in his ire and maintain a calm demeanor.

"I'm afraid so, Mr. Rosemoor. I was told to summon Mr. Montgomery at once if you chose to—"

"Mr. Rosemoor," Montgomery called out, striding purposefully down the stairs with two burly attendants following close at his heels. "I'm afraid I will have to ask you to leave these premises at once."

A coldness settled in the pit of Colin's stomach. "I'm sure I don't understand, Montgomery," Colin said, hedging.

"Oh, I think you do, Mr. Rosemoor. We don't take kindly to cheats here at White's." The reed-thin man gestured for Colin's hat and walking stick, and the footman hurried to hand them over. "We are a *gentleman's* club, you see. Effective immediately, your membership is revoked. I'll have to ask that you remove yourself at once."

The two attendants moved forward menacingly, and Colin involuntarily took a step back. "Why, my father won't stand for this," he sputtered. "He'll have a word—"

"Tell Lord Rosemoor to have a word with the Duke of Glastonbury. I'm sure the duke will be happy to explain his position on the matter. Good day, sir." He dismissed Colin with a nod and turned back toward the staircase.

In stunned silence, Colin watched the man's retreating form. The porter and footman shuffled their feet, refusing to meet his gaze as he donned his hat and took up his stick, his heart racing at a dizzying rate.

Turned out of White's? Without being allowed to defend his honor? *No,* his mind repeated over and over. It couldn't be true.

"This is not the last of it!" he roared. Blind with rage, he turned on his heel and stormed out.

Damn it to hell. He would not accept this so easily. He would find Sinclair this minute and call the man out; that's what he would do. But then he thought of Honoria, Miss Lyttle-Brown, and stopped short. He took several deep, calming breaths, attempting to think rationally. Had the news yet reached her ears? With a sick feeling of certainty, Colin realized that Sinclair had no doubt gone straight to her with his lies, attempting to divert her affections and wheedle himself back into her favor. What other purpose could he have in ruining him?

*Not now,* his mind screamed. Not when he'd come so very close to finding happiness, to securing love. He'd seen both Lucy and Susanna married off in the past two years—seen them find love and companionship, watched them gaze adoringly into their husbands' eyes—and he'd selfishly wanted the same for himself, wanted someone to gaze at him with such longing. He'd turned into a bloody romantic fool, but so be it. And after all these years, all this time searching for just the right sort of woman, he thought he'd finally found his match in Honoria. Would she still have him if Sinclair got to her first with his lies?

With a groan of frustration, Colin made haste for the Lyttle-Brown residence, just off Berkeley Square. He only hoped he wasn't too late.

# Chapter 2

Brenna swallowed hard and raised her eyes to the man standing before her. *Her brother.* Her mind repeated the words over and over again. She had a brother. A twin. Was it truly possible? She blinked back tears as her gaze searched his face, scouring it for some sign of recognition. Wavy auburn hair curled against his collar; round, blue-green eyes stared back at her, surveying her just as curiously as she surveyed him.

All at once, his mouth curved into a grin, his eyes dancing with obvious delight. "Dear God, you *are* my sister." He shook his head. "I rushed home from Sussex as soon as I received the news. I can barely believe it, though my heart tells me it's true." He opened his arms and gathered her in his embrace.

A single tear slipped down Brenna's cheek. There was something so familiar about this man, this complete stranger. Hugh Ballard, heir apparent to the Earl of Danville. *Her brother.*

He was the reason she'd finally capitulated to Lord and Lady Danville's demands that she accompany

them to London. Not because she felt any obligation
to these people who had ordered her about as if she
were a child, who had called the only family she'd
ever known *thieves* and *kidnappers,* but because they
told her she had a twin brother in England.

She had grown up with no siblings, no childhood
companions. So many of Glenbroch's tenants boasted
loud, boisterous broods that made Brenna's quiet,
solitary existence within the manor's walls seem dull
in comparison. While other children her age played
blindman's bluff and skipped stones on the loch,
Brenna whiled away her afternoons in her papa's
study, watching, learning, helping with the ledgers
once she proved herself clever with sums.

On nights when the seemingly ever-present mists
rose, she would climb the steep stairs up to the observatory they'd built her in the south tower. There
she would gaze through her telescope for hours on
end, carefully charting the skies above Castle Glenbroch in her leather-bound books—her most prized
possessions, save the telescope itself. It had been a
happy childhood, yes. But a lonely one. How she
had longed for a brother or sister. She'd always felt
as if she somehow didn't quite belong, as if something vital was missing from her life.

And now that the man they called her brother
held her in his arms, she knew with all her heart
that she was bound to him by blood, no matter the
years they'd spent apart. A sigh escaped her lips as
she pressed her cheek against his coat.

There had been no denying the pressing curiosity that had lured her away from Scotland when
she'd learned she had a brother, though she had
been terrified to leave Glenbroch and the only life

she'd known for the unknowns of London. Yet, through discreet inquiry into Lord and Lady Danville's lives, she'd learned that they frequented the same social circles as the Marquess of Hampton, absentee owner of Glenbroch's neighboring estate. If only she could gain the man's ear, she could learn his intentions toward his Highland estate, perhaps convince him of the evils of the Clearances. At the very least, she could use her time in London to raise awareness of the brutality being perpetrated so coldly and ruthlessly in the far north. Yes, she would stay in London, at least until autumn. How could she not?

"Let me look at you again, Margaret." Her brother stepped away from her, still clutching her hands in his own. "Pinch me so I might believe I'm not dreaming this."

"'Tis not a dream, I assure ye. But ye must call me Brenna."

"Brenna? Is that what those people called you?" he asked with such evident disgust that Brenna could not suppress a shudder.

"Brenna Margaret Elizabeth Maclachlan. And 'those people' were my parents, Mister . . . Lord . . ."

"Hugh. You must call me Hugh."

Brenna nodded. "Hugh, then."

"But those people were not your parents," he continued. "Surely you know it to be true? You heard the evidence Mr. Wembley presented. And now, standing before me, can you deny it?"

She sighed, shaking her head. Nay, she couldn't deny it. As dreadful as the revelations were, as painful as they were to hear, she could not deny the truth when faced with such overwhelming evidence. "Aye, I accept the truth, though it is with great difficulty. My parents . . . the people who raised me, they loved me dearly, as I loved them. They were the best sort of parents, and . . ." Her voice faltered, thick with emotion. "And I won't hear them spoken ill of."

"But they stole you from your home, your family." Hugh ran a hand carelessly through his hair, mussing it. "They raised you in the uncivilized wilds, away from proper society and—"

"They loved me with all their hearts, educated me as well as any man, and raised me to take my position one day as Lady of Glenbroch. How many English girls can make such a claim?" She raised her chin in the air, glaring at him defiantly. Her hands skimmed across the folds of her fine lawn skirts, and her heart ached for her familiar, practical woolens. *I dinna belong here,* her heart cried.

"You are six-and-twenty and still unwed. My parents found you in a drafty old manor, nearly in rags—"

"Rags?" Her hands clenched into angry fists. "Because I wore garments more serviceable, more practical, than this?" She spread her arms wide, indicating the silly, ribbon-bedecked frock Lady Danville had insisted she wear. "And 'twas caution on Papa's part, allowing me ample time to choose a proper husband, rather than accept the first fortune hunter who came my way. Besides, a bonny price was asked in tochradh—"

"Tochradh?"

"The English say *dowry.* In clan tradition, the dowry comes from the groom, to compensate the bride's family for their loss. That drafty old manor, as ye so derisively call it, is a lucrative estate, and I am its sole heir, by right of Papa's will."

"Come now, Margar—Brenna," Hugh corrected himself. "Must we bicker? I only want to get to know the sister I've been deprived of all these years. No more of this. Will you allow me to escort you to Lady Brandon's soiree tonight?"

"Have I a choice? Your mother didna make it seem as if I did."

"*Your* mother as well as mine," Hugh said, his tone near insolent.

Would it ever seem so? To lose a mother and then gain another in so short a time. . . . Tears welled in Brenna's eyes, and she willed them to remain at bay. Would anything in her life ever be the same again? Be right again?

"I'll go," she said at last. "If it will please you."

Hugh nodded. "It will please me greatly." He reached for her hand and gave it a squeeze. "But I must say, I hope you've a strong constitution." His mouth curved into a mischievous grin, and Brenna couldn't help but return it with her own.

"And why is that?" she asked.

"Your appearance will surely set the *ton* on their collective ear. We'll set many tongues wagging, I wager. My long-lost sister, home at last."

Brenna sighed. She had never felt as far from home as she did at that very moment.


Sinclair had gotten to her first, the bastard. Just as he'd expected.

Colin's steady gaze met Mr. Lyttle-Brown's wavering one as the man told Colin that Honoria was not at home. He was lying, of course. Colin had watched Honoria glance out a second-story window as he walked up the steps to her family's town house not ten minutes ago, her pale blond head framed in the glass for a fleeting second before the drapes fluttered shut.

"With all due respect, sir, I believe your daughter is indeed at home, and I implore you to allow me to speak with her at once. It is a matter of utmost urgency."

"I'm afraid I cannot allow it. I made a grievous error when I told you I'd be willing to consider your suit. In light of recent events, I'd say that your marrying my daughter is now entirely out of the question, and I'll ask you to leave off where she is concerned. Good day." He dismissed Colin with the wave of one hand toward the door.

"Sinclair was here, wasn't he?"

"I've no idea what you speak of."

"Oh, I think you do. I thought you a better judge of character than this, Mr. Lyttle-Brown. I suggest you have a care where your daughter is concerned."

"It would seem I'm a far better judge of character than my daughter. I knew all along that you were reckless and wild, Rosemoor. That you should be a cheat, too, comes as no surprise. I should never have listened to Honoria's pleas on your behalf in the first place. Silly chit. I'm only glad the truth came to light before the contract was drawn up and her life ruined. Now, sir, I will give you two minutes to vacate these premises, and then I will have you forcibly removed. You will henceforth steer clear of my daughter or there will be hell to pay. Have I made myself clear?"

"Perfectly," Colin bit out, smarting at the insult. Without another word, he quit the man's company. Nearly tripping over the butler in his haste to depart, he retrieved his hat and stormed down the front steps. He climbed into his curricle and took up the ribbons, refusing to acknowledge the blow he'd just received.

He slapped the backs of his matching grays with a growl, and the conveyance sprung forward. Did they think he would simply slink off with his tail between his legs? That he would accept his fate and disappear into the countryside without a fight? No. Oh, no. He would face them all—tonight. With his head held high. He would declare his innocence to Honoria, scold her for believing Sinclair's lies. They could elope, travel to Gretna Green before the week was out and be done with it. He nodded, pleased with the plan.

After all, he had to do *something* before all was lost. His life was swiftly spinning out of control, making him feel powerless, impotent. He could tolerate neither.

He resisted the urge to head toward London's seediest district and find a gaming hell where his name held no blight, desperate as he was for a stiff drink and a hand of cards. No, he needed to think clearly tonight; he could not have his mind muddled when he faced Honoria. He couldn't go to his own lodgings, either, he thought with a scowl as the curricle continued on at a brisk clip. No, nothing to do there but drink; again, not a good idea in his present state of mind. Nor could he go to Rosemoor House or Mandeville House, where he'd be forced to endure a severe dressing down from either his father or Lucy. It wouldn't do. But where to, then? His mind frantically searched for a solution.

*Ballard.* His most level-headed, rational friend leapt to mind. Yes, of course. He'd see if Hugh Ballard could offer him a single brandy—no more—and a sympathetic ear. With a satisfied nod, he turned the pair of horses toward St. James's Square.

A half hour later, Colin stood uneasily in Lord Danville's front parlor, gazing out on the busy street while his presence was announced to the earl's son. Colin watched uneasily as an elegant coach and four rattled by, an elaborate coat of arms on its door. A pair of mounted soldiers in regimentals followed, shiny gold buttons reflecting the afternoon sun. Just as the clip-clop of their horses' hooves died away, Colin became aware of a tapping of heels against marble, gaining strength, moving toward the parlor's open door. He turned toward the sound, expecting the housekeeper, perhaps, but instead found himself staring into the roundest, most extraordinary pair of aquamarine eyes he'd ever seen.

Brenna stepped into the parlor and stopped short, a small gasp parting her lips. An uncommonly tall man stood facing her, looking as startled as she felt. "Pardon me, sir. I was looking for Lady Danville and I thought . . ." She trailed off, unsure of what she meant to say. Her gaze absently flitted over the room's furnishings before returning uneasily to the man before her.

He blinked but said nothing. His eyes—neither gray nor blue, yet somewhere in between—widened a fraction, and then he bowed before meeting her gaze once more.

Brenna swallowed hard, feeling shy and unsure of herself for the first time in all her years. How did a proper English miss correctly greet a gentleman? She wasn't entirely certain. But this man was no doubt a gentleman; everything in his dress and manner exuded wealth and breeding, perhaps a touch of arrogance to boot.

Like Hugh, he was similarly attired in a fashion that struck her as far too formal for midafternoon— fawn-colored trousers, striped gray waistcoat, and a dark blue coat, finely tailored and without a crease or rumple. The only hint of dishevelment was his cravat, lying slightly awry against his linen, as if he'd just tugged on the folds. Brenna raised her gaze to his fair hair, which fell in soft waves across his forehead and against his collar.

He looked elegant, yes. Refined. As if he led a life of lazy indifference and genteel leisure. As was probably the case, Brenna decided. Suddenly she realized how rude she must appear, sizing him up like livestock. A blush infused her cheeks with sudden warmth as she reached for the door, prepared to flee. "Ye must excuse me, sir."

"Wait," the man called out, and she forced her feet to still.

Reluctantly, she turned back to face him. For a moment, neither spoke.

"I apologize for startling you," he said at last. "Allow me to introduce myself. I'm Colin Rosemoor." He bowed again, more exaggeratedly this time.

And how should she identify herself? Brenna? Margaret? She barely knew who she was anymore, and the uncertainty left her more than a little off balance. "I am Brenna, Lady Maclachlan," she said at last, the familiar words rolling off her tongue. "From Castle Glenbroch," she added, simply to fill the silence.

"Scottish, eh?" His full lips curved into a smile, and Brenna noticed a faint cleft bisecting his strong chin. "I should have known. Pleased to make your acquaintance, Lady Maclachlan. I say, though, you look so familiar. Have we met before?"

"We havena met before, I'm certain." As always, her brogue thickened when her emotions ran high, as they were now.

"Are you visiting Lord and Lady Danville, then?" he asked, his tone conversational.

"Aye, I am. For . . . for the Season."

"Splendid." He looked past her shoulder, to the empty hall, then retrieved his watch from his waist-coat and flipped open the case.

Brenna took two steps back but stopped when he raised his eyes to hers again, returning the watch to his pocket.

"And has your husband joined you here in Town?"

"Husband?"

"Here on business, perhaps?"

"Ye misunderstand, sir. I have no husband." Why ever would he think she did?

"Oh, pardon me. I just assumed that, well . . ." He waved one hand in a dismissive motion. "And have you yet made the acquaintance of my sister, Miss Jane Rosemoor?"

He thought her too old to be unmarried, she realized. She tipped her chin in the air, her pride pricked. "No, I havena made her acquaintance. I've only arrived within the fortnight," she answered, her voice cool.

"Well, then, you must have Lady Danville make the introduction. Jane's the best sort of girl. Quite popular, too. I'm sure she'd enjoy dragging you about Mayfair and making the proper introductions."

Brenna arched a brow. "Indeed?"

"And I'll wager she won't hold your Scottishness against you."

He was teasing her, of course. Still, the comment piqued her temper. Was that how everyone would see her? An aged, Scottish spinster, fit for nothing save parading about drawing rooms, engaging in naught but idle chatter and frivolous entertainments?

She could do long columns of sums in her head, keep ledgers, plan crops, and buy livestock. She was solely responsible for the livelihood of Glenbroch's tenants, people she'd known her entire life— people who depended upon her; people who cared about her. And she'd left them—left them all—in the hands of her steward, capable though he was. And for what? To come to London where she'd be judged as uncultured, uncivilized, should she let her true self show; where she knew no one save strangers. Strangers who shared her blood but not her life, till now.

"Good day, sir," she choked out, turning toward the doorway. She dashed to the stairs, nearly blinded by the tears that had suddenly welled in her eyes.

*Home.* She wanted to go home.

Damnation, was it something he'd said? Colin watched in surprise as the woman fled from him as fast as she could—with tears in her eyes at that. He shrugged, retrieving his watch once more. Where the hell was Ballard? Colin's patience wore thin. He'd give him two more minutes, no more.

He returned his gaze to the now-empty hall. Something about the woman had intrigued him. No doubt she was pretty enough, though not the type he usually found himself attracted to.

This slip of a woman—Brenna, she had called herself—barely reached his shoulder, and she looked fresh from the nursery. Until he studied her face, that is. Her hair, an indescribable mix of red and gold, had been pulled back into a coil on the back of her head in an almost matron-like arrangement. And her eyes, the color of the sea, seemed to reflect a degree of knowledge and experience that most English misses lacked. Beyond that, there was something so very familiar about her. Yet he could not quite put his finger on it. He slapped his gloves against his palm, growing more impatient by the moment.

"Rosemoor, old boy, what brings you here? Thought you'd be at White's by now, enjoying a hand or two."

Colin looked up as Hugh Ballard strode into the room at last. "I went to your lodgings, and your man told me I'd find you here. Don't tell me you have not yet heard the news?"

Ballard's brow rose. "News? No, I'm afraid I've only just arrived here from Sussex and have been preoccupied with news of my own. Wait, let me guess," he said with a grin. "Miss Lyttle-Brown has at last accepted you."

Colin scowled. "Quite the opposite, I'm afraid."

In response to Ballard's look of astonishment,

Colin quickly apprised his friend of the recent happenings at White's and Mr. Lyttle-Brown's subsequent refusal to let him speak with Honoria.

Ballard let out his breath with an audible rush. "Bloody hell."

"Well said. Now what am I to do? He'll have me entirely discredited by suppertime." Colin began to pace before the window, his hands fisted by his sides.

"Perhaps I should have a talk with Miss Lyttle-Brown and plead your case," Ballard suggested.

"Would you?" Colin stopped pacing and turned to face Ballard. "No doubt she'll attend Lady Brandon's soiree. If you speak with her first and smooth the way for me, I'll be able to set things to rights with her tonight."

"Very well, then. I'll do it straightaway. But wouldn't you like to have my news first?"

*Not particularly*, Colin thought. But he decided he'd best be gracious. "Of course. What news have you?"

"A sister," Hugh said, smiling broadly.

"What do you mean, a sister?"

"Haven't you heard the oft-told tale of my twin sister, snatched from our home when we were but infants in the cradle?"

"I suppose I have. I thought the child was long presumed dead."

"And she was. My parents hired an investigator after the kidnapping, but their man found nothing. The kidnappers' trail went quickly cold. The case was closed. Very recently, a deathbed confession—from a wet nurse, if you can believe it—reopened the investigation, and the child, now a woman, has been located and brought to her rightful home."

"After all these years? That's astonishing."

"Isn't it? She has my mother's hair and my father's eyes, even the Ballard nose."

"You must be beside yourself, then," Colin offered.

"Well, old boy, it's both a blessing and a burden. She's well past the marriageable age, so I suppose she'll be left to my care for the rest of her days."

"Surely your parents will generously dower her? If they're so sure of her identity."

"They are, but I'm not certain any gentleman of breeding will take her off our hands, dowry or not. She's coarse and stubborn, not at all schooled in ladylike charms or behavior. Nor is she the least bit grateful for being discovered and rescued from her deplorable situation, and I'm afraid she's far too intelligent for her own good. And I've left out the worst of it—she's a Scot." Ballard spat out the word as if it were distasteful.

Colin looked toward the empty doorway in surprise. A Scot? Of course! That was why she had looked so familiar. He recalled her face—full, rose-tinted lips, a fine nose, round aqua-colored eyes under finely arched reddish-gold brows. No doubt she was Ballard's sister. The likeness was striking, now that he reflected upon it.

"But . . ." Colin sputtered at last, "but she's not really a Scot, not if she's your sister."

Ballard strode to the desk under the bookshelves and picked up a clear-glass paperweight. "She might not be a Scot by blood, but she's all Scot in disposition. My mother has an arduous task ahead of her, if she's to civilize her in any manner fit for the drawing room. But it shall be amusing to watch her try, won't it?" He set down the paperweight with a *thunk*.

With a yelp, some sort of creature leapt out from behind the desk and streaked by, nothing but a silvery blur.

"Whatever was that?" Colin asked.

"The wretched cat my sister brought with her," Ballard answered with a sneer. "Nothing but bad luck, I say." He shook his head, his frown giving way to a wry smile. "Anyway, society will get their first glimpse of my sister tonight, at Lady Brandon's soiree."

Colin's scowl deepened. Dear Lord, he'd only engaged the poor girl in conversation a minute or two before she'd fled in tears, and he was nothing compared to the dragons of the *ton*. Lady Brandon was perhaps the cruelest, most critical of the lot. What were they thinking, taking the girl out in society so soon? A shudder snaked up his spine. If they meant to ruin her prospects, then this was the surest way.

Colin shook his head. A wave of pity washed over him, temporarily distracting him from his own desperate plight. Blast it, the girl was Ballard's sister; where were his protective instincts? Colin's own brotherly sensibilities were affronted.

"You must speak to your mother," he said. "You cannot allow this sister of yours to go to Lady Brandon's soiree. Surely you must see that?"

"Don't be a spoilsport, Rosemoor." Ballard reached up to draw one finger across a dusty tome's worn spine. "She must go. It'll be amusing, I assure you." His voice held an unfamiliar edge, and Colin felt his own jaw tighten in response.

Something did not seem quite right about his

friend today. He seemed restless; his face looked strangely pinched.

Colin forced himself to shrug off the sensation of unease. He had worries enough of his own to occupy his mind without involving himself in Ballard's problems. He would think on it no more. "I should go to my lodgings," Colin said, suddenly wishing to remove himself from Ballard's company.

"Very well." Ballard clapped him on the back. "I'll go at once to Berkeley Square and have a word with your Miss Lyttle-Brown. You've really gotten yourself into a bind this time, haven't you, old boy?"

"I've done nothing wrong," Colin protested, chafing at the injustice of it all. He liked to gamble, yes. But his misdeeds went no further. One might call him a bit reckless, perhaps, but he was a man of honor and integrity above all else.

"If you say it's the truth, then I believe you," Ballard said with a smile. "I'll do my damnedest to convince the lady of your innocence." He reached up to straighten his cravat as he strode toward the door.

Colin hesitated briefly before following suit. For a moment he considered telling Ballard not to trouble himself, that he'd convince Honoria of his innocence himself. No, he wavered, retrieving his gloves and hat. What harm could come of it? Perhaps she'd listen to Ballard.

Besides, the situation couldn't possibly get any worse than it already was.

# Chapter 3

"There now, Margaret. You look lovely." Lady Danville patted Brenna's hair in place. "That's all, Celeste."

"Yes, your ladyship." The harried-looking lady's maid bobbed a curtsy and hurried out.

"That gown is simply stunning, isn't it? Madame Vioget works wonders."

"'Tis lovely, indeed. I thank ye for your generosity, Lady Danville." Brenna swallowed hard, barely able to believe that the young woman staring back in the looking glass was her. Never in her life had her hair been dressed so intricately. She glanced down at the emerald-green silk gown she wore, its bodice generously encrusted with seed pearls. She felt like a stuffed pigeon, trussed up for a feast. Worse still, the cut of the neckline was positively indecent, and she could barely breathe, tightly laced into a rigid corset. She was terrified of exposing her breasts, small as they were, if she *did* manage a breath. Did they truly expect her to go out in society in such a state of undress?

Apparently they did. Lady Danville reached for her hand and helped her to her feet. "Come now, Margaret. I hear the carriage. Promise me, dear, that you'll remember what I've taught you. And do your best to rid your voice of that awful brogue. I won't have my daughter sounding like some barbarian."

Brenna resolved at once to make certain her accent sounded as Scots as possible for the remainder of the evening.

"And you must call me *Mama*," the woman added, patting Brenna's cheek with a gloved hand.

Brenna tipped her chin in the air. "Only if ye will agree to call me *Brenna*."

"But . . . but," the woman sputtered, "your name is Margaret, after your father's mother, God rest her soul. You were christened Margaret Elizabeth Ballard, right before my very eyes. You cannot expect me to call you anything else."

"But I was rechristened Brenna Margaret Elizabeth, and I've answered to that name for six-and-twenty years now. Ye canna expect me to suddenly answer to another."

The woman's eyes narrowed. "I shall speak to your father about this."

"As will I," Brenna challenged, refusing to lower her gaze. Lady Danville was a stubborn woman, indeed, but Brenna could be equally stubborn if she chose to be. They had that much in common, if nothing else.

The maid reappeared in the doorway. "The carriage is here, mum."

"Thank you, Celeste. Tell Lord Danville we will be down directly."

"Very well, mum." Celeste bobbed a curtsy and disappeared back down the hall.

Lady Danville turned back to face Brenna. "I hope you will make us proud tonight, Margaret. I've waited many years for this." Her mother reached for her hand and gave it a squeeze, tears shining in her eyes. "My only daughter, at last taking her rightful place by my side."

Brenna returned the pressure, instantly regretting her ill temper. These people had suffered so dearly. "I promise I will do my best to make ye both proud." And she would, as best she could. She owed them that at least.

"Very well, dearest. After all, it will be difficult enough to secure you a husband, given your age and your, well . . ." Her voice trailed off, and she waved a hand in dismissal. "But I do *so* want to see you married well and happy."

Married well by *her* standards, of course. To some insufferable English gentleman who looked down his noble nose at Highland Scots, who would have no interest whatsoever in Castle Glenbroch and its inhabitants. Brenna shook her head carefully, ever mindful of her hair's elaborate arrangement. No, she did not need them to choose a husband for her. She did not need a husband. She especially did not need an *English* husband.

With an inward groan, she followed her mother out to the waiting carriage.

"Well, man, what did she say?" Colin stepped up to Ballard, his brows drawn. His friend looked uneasy, unable to meet his eyes as the two men ducked behind Lady Brandon's ebony pianoforte.

"It seems you were right, old boy." Ballard clapped him on the shoulder. "Sinclair got to her first. I did my best, but I'm afraid she wouldn't have it. Miss Lyttle-Brown is a stubborn chit, if ever there was one. Sinclair managed to completely convince her of your guilt."

"Damn him." Colin shoved his fists into his pockets.

"And if that weren't enough, her father has threatened to remove her to the countryside at once if she so much as glances in your direction."

Ah, but they'd be long gone to Gretna before her father had the chance. Colin almost smiled at the thought. "Is she here?"

"Shall we take a look? It's quite a crush tonight, isn't it?"

The two men stepped around the pianoforte and began to make their way across the cavernous drawing room.

"Ballard, a word, if you will." Lord Barclay's imperious voice halted them.

"Lord Barclay," Colin said, acknowledging the venerable old marquess with a bow. "Good evening, sir."

Lord Barclay's eyes met Colin's for an instant before he averted them. "A word, Ballard," he repeated, his voice as flinty as steel—as if Colin weren't standing there; as if he weren't worthy of the man's notice.

Colin's hands began to shake with rage.

Ballard looked to Colin with a shrug. "Sorry, old boy," he whispered before turning his full attention to Lord Barclay. "Of course, sir," Ballard said, and then followed Barclay out.

With an oath, Colin began to shoulder his way across the room. Bloody hell, where was Honoria? She would hear him out, and she would know he spoke the truth. Unless he'd misjudged her. *Seriously* misjudged her. Had he been blinded by her beauty and practiced charm? Quite possibly, he realized, stunned by the thought. He reached for a glass of champagne and gulped it down in one long draught.

He pushed his way across the room, increasingly aware of scornful glances directed his way. A trio of debutantes whispered behind their fans, their eyes flashing maliciously above the pleated silk. A pair of gentlemen sneered and turned their backs to him as he passed. No one spoke his name in greeting, not one single soul.

Increasing his pace, Colin accomplished the far side of the room at last and flung open the pair of doors leading out. As soon as he stepped into the warm, humid night, he froze, staring blindly up at the bright moon. He inhaled sharply, discerning the cloying scent of roses over the earthy smell of freshly turned soil. *The garden.* He would go to the garden and take a moment to compose himself, he resolved as snippets of conversation floated on the breeze from the drawing room behind him.

"Rosemoor . . . He's done it this time . . . won't be welcome in a fashionable drawing room in Mayfair by morning . . . a shame, isn't it? His family is so lovely. . . ."

Dear God, he was ruined. *Ruined.* The knowledge hit him with an almost-painful force. With a roar of frustration, Colin stormed down the single flight of stone stairs and across the small square lawn below.

Leaning against the trunk of a linden tree, Brenna looked up at the moon and sighed, hoping the familiar sight would bring her comfort and slow her racing heart. Her eyes skimmed across the inky celestial canvas as she mentally cataloged the stars' positions. There was Leo, to the right of the moon, and the brilliant, twinkling speck that she knew was the planet Jupiter.

She sighed again, more deeply this time. Tonight had been a disaster. The young ladies of the *ton* were so lovely in appearance, such dazzling beauties like Jupiter itself. Yet she was unexceptional, the faintest star, barely visible to the naked eye. She'd felt awkward and coarse among them, completely incapable of joining in their conversations about painting and music and fashion. She'd been mostly ignored once the initial curiosity had worn off, and she'd been happy to fade into the furnishings.

But then Lady Brandon had taken out her quizzing glass and held it up to one eye, appraising her without the slightest bit of pretense.

"A Scot, are you?" the woman had said at last, her voice as cold as ice.

"Of course she's not a Scot," Lady Danville answered. "She's my daughter."

"But raised where, my dear?" the woman pressed, her pale, watery eyes flashing angrily despite her overly polite tone.

Lady Danville's cheeks reddened. "It does not matter where—"

"Let the gel answer, Harriet." Lady Brandon silenced Brenna's mother with an imperious glare. "The poor child *can* speak, can she not?"

Brenna felt a flush climb up her neck. "I assure ye I am fully capable of speech."

"I'm pleased to hear it. Perhaps you can sate my curiosity, then, and tell me where you were raised."

"In Lochaber, just south of Fort William," Brenna answered, her voice cool and composed despite her discomfort. "At Castle Glenbroch."

"Lochaber? The Highlands, then?" Lady Brandon asked.

"Indeed." Brenna raised her chin and met Lady Brandon's disdainful gaze. "'Tis the western Highlands. Lochaber has fared well since the Butcher's ravages following Culloden." As Brenna paused for a breath, she noted the wide-eyed, scandalized expressions surrounding her.

"Jacobite," someone to her right whispered vehemently.

Lady Brandon leaned forward in her chair, her blue-veined hand clutching her cane so tightly that her knuckles turned white. "Is that so?" she finally said in reply, all pretense of politeness now gone. "The 'Butcher,' eh? Well, some find the Highlands charming, I suppose, but I've never seen the appeal of such a barbaric place. Everyone so ragged and unattractive; the landscape so barren and bleak." She waved one thin, claw-like hand in dismissal. "It's positively depressing. I hear that Lord Stafford is taking great pains to improve the land in Sutherland."

"Improve the land?" Brenna's voice rose a pitch. "You call burning roofs over the elderly and infirm an improvement? 'Tis murder!"

"Oh, don't be so dramatic, gel. How old did you say you were?"

"I dinna say, my lady. But if ye must know, I am six-and-twenty."

"Hmmm." Lady Brandon's thin lips curled into a sneer, and the woman swept her gaze from the top of Brenna's beribboned head to her dainty silk slippers. "Six-and-twenty and not yet wed? I'm not at all astonished, given your impertinence." She turned her attention back to Brenna's mother. "Well, Harriet, you'll have quite the time of it, civilizing her, won't you?"

Brenna could only stare at her own hands, clasped tightly in her lap, as a titter of laughter followed the woman's outburst. Fearing what she might say if she remained another moment in the dreadful woman's presence, she rose unsteadily, her head held high. "Ye must excuse me, Lady Brandon. Could ye direct me to the ladies' withdrawing room?"

In reply, the woman tipped her ostrich-plumed head toward the doorway. Brenna bowed stiffly before sweeping off in that direction with as much dignity as she could muster. She had no intention of going to the withdrawing room, of course. Instead, she had headed toward a set of double doors at the far side of the crowded drawing room. Before she knew it, she had found herself crossing a lawn and entering an ornamental garden laden with fragrant roses.

The muffled strains of a harp reached her ears as she moved away from the linden tree and sank onto a nearby wrought-iron bench. Why ever had she agreed to come to London? This was madness; she didn't belong here. Yet these people were her blood, her kin. How could she deny them? Especially the brother she'd always longed for?

The breeze stirred, balmy and velvety against her much-too-bare skin, and Brenna shivered despite the warmth. She glanced down at her gown in irritation. Why, she might as well be out in her nightclothes. She knew she'd been gone far too long, that she should force herself to return to the party. Yet she was loath to leave this peaceful spot where the moon and stars kept her company, as they always had.

The sharp crack of a snapping twig startled her, and she sprang to her feet. Pounding footsteps seemed to appear from nowhere, gaining speed, and Brenna took two long strides toward the house before slamming into something solid. The breath knocked from her lungs, she tumbled to the lawn with a yelp.

"Oof, what the devil?" a decidedly male voice ground out beside her.

Brenna blinked hard, attempting to regain her equilibrium.

"Dear Lord, it's *you* again," the voice said.

Brenna raised her gaze to find the very same tall, blond man she'd encountered earlier that day in the parlor now standing before her in the moonlight.

"I say, miss, are you hurt?" He crouched down beside her, his brows drawn in obvious concern. "You must forgive me. I didn't see you there in the shadows."

She shook her head. "Nay, I'm not hurt. Just a bit winded is all."

"Thank God." His gaze drifted down, toward the broad expanse of her décolletage.

With a gasp, she tugged up the neckline, fearing

she'd exposed far more than decorum allowed. *Ridiculous frock.*

Mercifully, he lifted his gaze. "Here," he said, reaching for her hand, "let me help you to that bench over there." He tipped his head toward the same bench she'd occupied only moments before.

Gaining her feet a bit unsteadily, Brenna swayed against him.

He put one arm about her shoulders, steadying her. "You must sit. No use fainting here among the roses. Thorns, you know. Messy business, thorns."

Brenna couldn't help but laugh. "I assure you, 'tis no chance of my fainting. I'm not so delicate as that, Mister . . . ahem . . . I seem to have forgotten your name, sir." What was it? Rosewood? Rosemont?

"Rosemoor," he supplied. "The Honorable Colin Rosemoor, at your service, Lady Brenna Maclachlan. As you can see, I have not forgotten yours."

A smile tugged at the corners of her mouth. "You've quite a memory, then, haven't ye? After all, it has been what? Seven, perhaps eight, hours since our last encounter? Surely no more than that."

"Ah, you jest. You must be well recovered, then. Here, sit." He led her to the bench, where she plopped herself down rather inelegantly. His gaze raked over her, his eyes full of unmasked curiosity. "You truly *are* his sister, aren't you? Hugh Ballard's, I mean."

Brenna nodded. "Aye, it would seem so."

"Tell me, what proof have they? Besides the striking resemblance, that is."

"Proof enough." Brenna's hand involuntarily moved to her thigh.

"Oh, yes. Ballard mentioned a deathbed confession.

Still, I don't understand how anyone could identify a woman they hadn't seen since infancy."

"Nay, I don't suppose they could. Yet, circumstances seem to prove I am indeed their daughter." The birthmark, of course. How many girls born on the ninth of October in any given year had a birthmark in the shape of a fleur-de-lis on their right thigh? Aye, it was proof enough.

"Your limb, is it injured?" He knelt down beside her, peering at her with knitted brows.

"Whatever do ye mean?" Her whole body tensed. He was only inches away from her—so close that she could smell his masculine scent above the floral notes clinging to the breeze. Tobacco and brandy mingling with sandalwood and leather. Pure male, and it made her a little dizzy.

"There," he said, indicating her right thigh.

Had she been touching her birthmark?

"Are you certain you didn't injure yourself? Perhaps I should carry you back inside." He rose to tower above her, reaching for her elbow.

"Nay, I assure ye I am unhurt. I . . ." She swallowed hard. "'Tis just a twinge, is all. Perhaps ye should return to the house, Mr. Rosemoor."

"Colin," he corrected. "And not till I'm certain of your well-being, Lady . . ." He trailed off, rubbing his chin. "What shall I call you? Is it Lady Maclachlan? Lady Brenna? Lady Margaret?"

"I suppose it depends upon who ye ask. I would say Brenna, Lady Maclachlan, as I supplied ye earlier. But if ye were to ask Lord and Lady Danville, they would insist on Lady Margaret, I suppose."

"But if you aren't yet wed, how can you be Lady

Maclachlan? Wouldn't you be Lady Brenna, just as you would be Lady Margaret?"

"For barbarians, the Scots' laws are much more favorable to women than the English. My father—or the man I always supposed was my father—died without a male heir. He was a younger son, and our land, our estate, is unentailed. When he died, he willed his entire property to me. I am the Maclachlan of Glenbroch now, a position I was raised to."

"You mean to say that your father raised you to inherit his estate? He instructed you in its management?"

"'Tis exactly what I'm telling ye, Mr. Rosemoor. Must ye sound so shocked? Ye canna believe a woman can run an estate as well as a man?"

He shook his head. "I didn't say that."

"But ye thought it, did ye not?"

"Perhaps I did." He leaned indolently against the tree, one boot resting against the trunk. "It isn't a woman's place," he said, carelessly brushing a blade of grass from his trousers.

"What, then, is a woman's place? If ye don't mind my asking, Mr. Rosemoor."

He shrugged. "Well, to run a household, I suppose. To serve as a hostess. And, well . . ."

"Aye, go on. To serve as a decoration? An accessory? A woman should serve no more useful a purpose than that?"

"I didn't say that." He arched one brow, and Brenna saw a muscle in his jaw flicker.

"But ye thought it, no doubt."

"That's an unfair conclusion, based on our limited acquaintance. In fact, I thought no such thing. I can think of several ladies who have earned my esteem and admiration for their intelligence and competency alone, my sister Jane being one of them."

"Then I must apologize, sir." She shook her head, feeling foolish. "Ye must forgive me, as tonight has been rather trying, to say the least. I seem to be a source of disapproval for Lady Brandon, and—"

"Is that why you are out here, all alone? Has that dragon breathed her venomous fire on you already?"

Brenna laughed; the image was fitting, indeed. "'Tis safe to say she does not see me as fit company for her lovely guests. And what of ye? What brings ye out here, seeking naught but the moon for company?"

"It's rather bright tonight, isn't it, for a half-moon?"

"'Tis bright, indeed, but it's not yet a half-moon. Give it two days time."

"Really?" He turned and looked up at the sky beyond the linden branches. "I say, you're right. There, near the bottom half—"

"The lower quadrant. Precisely." She rose to stand beside him. "'Tis beautiful, isn't it? On such a clear night as this."

"It is. Look at that brilliant star above it."

"'Tis a planet. Jupiter."

"Is that so?" he asked, squinting at the sky. "A planet? Fascinating." He shifted his weight, his forearm just barely grazing her shoulder. "Anyway, it would appear that you and I are out here for much the same reason. But instead of the disapproval of one dragon, I've the disapproval of the entire *ton*. In the course of a day, I seem to have lost everything— my reputation, my standing in society, my club affiliation, and the affections of the woman I'd planned to marry." His mouth curved into a frown. "What do you say to that?"

"I say ye must exaggerate. It canna be as bad as all that, I should think."

"I'm afraid it is as bad as all that," he answered with a shrug.

She peered up at him curiously. If it were true, his misdeeds must be egregious, indeed. Yet her instincts told her that he was an honorable man, a trustworthy man. Something about his eyes . . . Yes, she felt safe in his company. Were her instincts so clouded, so marred?

"Whatever have ye done to earn such misfortune, then?" she asked at last.

"I assure you I've done nothing to earn it. Nothing but win a few hands of cards, that is," he added a bit mysteriously, then pointed to the sky. "Look, what of that star there? Seems to be the brightest of all."

Brenna nodded; he had a good eye. "'Tis Vega, in the constellation Lyra. The Harp. See, 'tis a bit like a lopsided box? And look." She drew a right angle with her finger against the sky. "Over here, Vega. Then here," she said, pointing to the tail of Cygnus, "Deneb. And down here"—she moved her hand down toward Aquila—"Altair. They form a triangle, always visible in the summer sky."

"A constellation?" he asked.

"Nay, an asterism." She tilted her head to one side. "You canna even see it in the sky over Glenbroch, the summer nights are so bright." She shook her head and felt a curl escape its arrangement to caress her cheek. "'Tis lovely, though, is it not?" She turned to face him, to gauge his appreciation of the wondrous sight that filled her with awe and amazement.

But he wasn't looking at the sky—he was looking

at her. She held her breath as he reached up to brush back the errant lock of hair, his fingertips softly stroking her burning cheek.

"Lovely," came his reply, spoken so softly that she wondered briefly if she'd imagined it.

# Chapter 4

Devil take it, what was he doing? Colin shook his head, hoping to clear it as he took a step back from the intriguing woman. "I should escort you back inside," he muttered.

Brenna nodded in reply, a faint smile tipping the corners of her rose-tinted mouth. Her eyes, shining as brightly as the stars above, boldly met his. "Perhaps ye should, though I'm finding your company immeasurably more comfortable than that of those inside. Must ye really?"

Colin nodded, a pang of regret startling him. He couldn't help but admire her innocent candor, her guilelessness. She likely had no idea how severely her reputation would suffer were she found hidden away in the dark, shadowy garden with a bachelor, honorable though he might be.

*Honorable?* Colin silently cursed himself, his gaze traveling back toward the house where warm light spilled from open windows onto the lawn below. Blast it, no one in Lady Brandon's drawing room believed him honorable, not anymore. Brenna's reputation would be far more than tattered were she spied out here alone with him—she'd be ruined. *Ruined.*

"On second thought," he said, his voice tight and controlled, "it's probably best that we're not seen in the same company. You've troubles enough without having your name linked with mine. I'd best take my leave from here." He would speak with Honoria another time. Perhaps Lady Brandon's drawing room was not the proper place to question her faithlessness, besides. The last thing he needed was to make a public spectacle of himself. *Again.*

"Verra well," Brenna said at last. "I thank ye for your kindness, Mr. Rosemoor. You've done a fine job of distracting me from my unpleasant thoughts." She tilted her head to one side, and he physically felt her gaze sweep across him, as if she were appraising him.

He straightened his spine and reached up to readjust his cravat, hoping he passed muster. "Yes, well, it's good to be useful at something, I suppose."

She laughed then, a full-bodied, melodious laugh that made him smile despite himself.

"Perhaps ye simply knocked the dour thoughts from my head when ye trampled me," she offered.

"It wasn't as bad as that, was it? In all seriousness, are you certain I didn't injure you?"

"I'm certain, Mr. Rosemoor."

"Your leg—limb, I meant. It isn't paining you?"

"I assure ye my limb is fine, sir. Dinna fash about it."

Colin's mouth twitched. "You certainly are a Highlander, aren't you?"

"Indeed, and proud of it."

"God help Lady Danville. I believe you'll give the woman quite the challenge," he said with a chuckle.

"Do not underestimate her, Mr. Rosemoor. Wherever do ye think I got my stubborn nature? 'Twill be a fair fight, no doubt."

"No doubt it will be." He blinked hard, forcing away the memory of Brenna's silky cheek against his hand. The last thing she needed was him in her life, muddying her name with his association. He took a deep breath and exhaled slowly, then said, "Good night, my lady."

"Good night, Mr. Rosemoor," she answered, then strode purposefully away without looking back.

Colin stuffed his hands into his pockets and watched her retreating form till she disappeared within the shadows, leaving naught but her clean, lavender scent behind.

"Lady Margaret?"

It took several moments before Brenna realized the butler was addressing her. She set down her tea. "Oh, pardon me, Alfred. I do wish ye would call me Brenna, at least among family."

"Humph." The butler cleared his throat, clearly offended. He held out a crisp, white card. "Miss Jane Rosemoor is in the drawing room, and Lady Danville requests that you join them there at once."

"Verra well, Alfred. Tell Lady Danville that I shall be down directly." She smiled brightly at the elegant old man, but he seemed utterly incapable of showing any sign of emotion on his lined face. She shook her head; she would never understand the English.

Alfred bowed in reply and disappeared as silently

as he had appeared moments ago, as if the soles of his shoes were covered with felt.

With a shrug, she headed toward the drawing room, conscious of the clicking sound her own slippers made against the floor. This Miss Jane Rosemoor must be Mr. Rosemoor's sister, the one he'd recommended to show her around. She was curious to see just what sort of woman she was.

Pausing just outside the drawing room, Brenna smoothed her hands down the soft folds of her gown, marveling once again that so fine a frock was only meant for sitting about the house in. She pasted a smile on her face and stepped into the room at last, her eyes drawn to the elegant young woman in yellow silk sitting on the sofa across from Lady Danville. Somehow she had expected the woman to be fair. Instead, chestnut hair peeked out from under her lace cap, and sparkling deep-blue eyes—eyes full of friendly warmth—gazed back at her beneath finely arched brows. She rose gracefully and reached for Brenna's hands.

"Lady Margaret, what a pleasure. I'm Jane Rosemoor." She smiled down at Brenna from a considerable height, and Brenna returned the smile.

"Miss Rosemoor, the pleasure is all mine. Your brother speaks highly of ye. I've been so looking forward to making your acquaintance."

Miss Rosemoor laughed. "Dear Colin. A girl couldn't ask for a better brother. He had several flattering things to say about you as well. I admit, my curiosity was piqued. I was so sorry to miss your introduction at Lady Brandon's soiree, but I'm afraid it was unavoidable. My sister Susanna was hosting a ladies' musicale, you see."

"And how is Mrs. Merrill?" Brenna's mother asked politely.

"Very well, my lady. Marriage suits her well." Miss Rosemoor returned to her seat on the sofa and clasped her gloved hands in her lap.

"I'm glad to hear it," Brenna's mother continued. "Still, such a shame you missed Lady Brandon's soiree. Why, you'll never believe who made an appearance, albeit brief."

"Who? Do tell," Miss Rosemoor asked, leaning forward expectantly.

"Would you believe Hayden, Lord Westfield? Why, I could barely believe my eyes. Rich as Croesus, and single to boot. But one never sees him out in society, except in Ashbourne, near his estate in Derbyshire. A shame, I say."

"Lord Westfield? I don't believe I'm acquainted with him," Miss Rosemoor said, shaking her head.

"Westfield is an earl, and sinfully handsome at that. But with a tragic past, I'm afraid. Why, I remember when—"

"Lady Danville," Miss Rosemoor interrupted, "would you mind terribly if I stole your daughter away? My dear friend Lady Mandeville planned to join me this afternoon on an outing to St. James's Park, but alas, she's feeling unwell. I'd be delighted if Lady Margaret accompanied me in her stead so we might get better acquainted."

"Of course, Miss Rosemoor. I'm sure Margaret would be delighted." Her mother looked to her entreatingly, but she needn't have bothered. Brenna was eager to escape the confines of the house and her mother's constant nagging that she study the etiquette books and ladies' fashion magazines. Truly, she had very little interest in them.

Just that very morning her mother had brought her a well-worn copy of *The Mirror of Graces,* an etiquette primer penned by "A Lady of Distinction." Just *which* lady, no one seemed to know, but said lady was eager to impart her wisdom on the female form, personal decoration, and deportment. Heaven forbid Brenna should commit the crime of wearing red morocco slippers in the morning. And whatever would she have done without the advice that the well-rounded ankle was best displayed in a *plain* silk stocking without any clocking?

She shrugged off the annoying thoughts of such frivolity and met Miss Rosemoor's eager smile with her own. "I would be verra pleased to join ye, Miss Rosemoor," Brenna said. "'Tis nothing better than due exercise on foot to aid in one's shape and complexion," she quoted with a wry grin, earning a nod of approval from her mother. She looked to Miss Rosemoor and saw her suppress a giggle.

Brenna nodded to herself. *Miss Rosemoor and I shall get on verra well, indeed.* In minutes, Celeste had helped her change into an appropriate dress, and she followed Miss Rosemoor to the front hall. Retrieving her shawl from a peg on the wall, she stepped out into the bright sunshine with a light heart.

A half hour later, they reached the park and made their way toward the gatehouse for some refreshment.

"There's Colin," Jane said, motioning toward a table in the corner. "I hope you don't mind, I asked him to join us."

"Nay, not at all," Brenna murmured. In fact, she was pleased to see him again. Much as she hated to admit it, something about him intrigued her, even if he *was* nothing more than an English gentleman of leisure.

"There you are, dear sister," Colin called out, rising.

Brenna stepped out from behind Miss Rosemoor, and she saw his eyes instantly darken.

"Where's Lucy?" he asked.

"Not feeling well, I'm afraid, but look who I've brought instead. Lady Margaret Danville."

"Lady Maclachlan," he said, but did not take her proffered hand.

"Lady Maclachlan?" Miss Rosemoor asked.

"Brenna. You must call me Brenna."

"I thought your mother called you Margaret?" Poor Miss Rosemoor looked entirely confused.

"Oh, she does call me Margaret. Despite my pleas to the contrary, I'm afraid. I've answered to 'Brenna' for so many years now that I'm simply not comfortable with 'Margaret.' When my mother— or the woman I thought was my mother—passed away, I became the Lady Maclachlan. I don't mean to confuse ye. If we're to be friends, then I hope you'll simply call me Brenna."

"Of course, then," Miss Rosemoor answered. "And so you must call me Jane."

"Well," Mr. Rosemoor said, smiling broadly, "now that that's settled, I'm afraid I must take my leave."

"Whatever do you mean, Colin?" Jane reached for her brother's sleeve. "You're not leaving us. First we shall have some refreshments, and then you will escort us out into the gardens."

"I'm afraid I have a pressing business concern, Jane."

"You haven't any pressing business. You said you had no engagements today."

"That's when I thought Lucy was joining you," he said quietly through clenched teeth.

"Lucy?" Brenna asked. He *had* seemed rather disappointed when he'd seen her accompanying Jane. Who was this woman, Lucy, to him? Perhaps the woman he'd hoped to marry?

"Lucy, Lady Mandeville," Jane explained. "My dearest friend. I hope you will soon make her acquaintance."

Mr. Rosemoor cleared his throat. "But you must see that it is rather imprudent of me to remain in your company *now*."

"No, I don't see, not at all, Colin. I only see that you are being rude to my new friend." Jane turned toward Brenna, her gaze entreating. "Isn't he, Lady Margar—Brenna?"

Brenna said nothing. If he were so desirous to be rid of her company, then she had no wish to convince him otherwise. He must be very fond of this Lady Mandeville and far less fond of *her* than she had supposed. Why did that bother her so? She wasn't sure, but it vexed her nonetheless. Quite so. She only shrugged, reminding herself to be more wary where the English were concerned. If their servants were any indication, then they were indeed a closed and difficult-to-read bunch.

*Blast it,* Colin thought. Was his sister so stubborn as that? Didn't she realize that his company put Brenna's reputation in peril? Brenna might not know the reasons behind his reluctance to remain, but Jane bloody well did.

Both women continued to regard him with irritated stares as he reached up to readjust his cravat. No doubt he *had* insulted Brenna, and he was sorry for it.

"Oh, all right," he relented. "But let's be quick about it, shall we?"

"I must apologize for my brother," Jane said, casting him a scathing glare as she took a seat at the table. "He's not normally such a bear."

Colin held out a chair for Brenna. "Aren't I? Well, I must try harder, then."

Brenna met his gaze briefly before settling herself into her seat. He could have sworn he saw a flicker of amusement in her eyes.

"Dinna fret about it, Miss Rosemoor. I had ample time to sketch your brother's character when we last met, and I didna find his manners in any way lacking. In fact, I thought him quite the proper gentleman," she said, her tone light and playful. "But then, I *am* beginning to question my instincts."

"Hmmm, yes, well." No way to answer that one. She was probably right to question her instincts, at least where he was concerned.

"You must tell me more, Lady Brenna," Jane pressed. "I find it most diverting to hear how my brother conducts himself in society when I am not there to witness it."

"Truly, there isna much to tell. Mr. Rosemoor was solicitous and kind, despite the awkward nature of our meeting. We bumped into each other in Lady Brandon's garden, ye know. Quite literally. I fear I made a rather inelegant first impression."

"Fascinating. I do believe he withheld that bit of information in his retelling of the encounter, didn't you, Colin?"

Colin only shrugged.

"Anyway," Jane said with a shake of her head, "do go on. I must hear more."

Colin rolled his eyes heavenward, not wishing to remain the topic of conversation. At the very least, he didn't have to listen to it. "If you'll excuse me, I'll go and fetch us some refreshments." He strode off toward the busy counter, ignoring the curious glances cast his way as he headed across the room. *Best get used to it,* he thought. Speculation and innuendo would likely be his constant companion from now on.

Moments later, he made his way back through the crowd to their table.

"Ye should see the mists rise above Ben Nevis," Brenna was saying, and Colin heaved a sigh of relief at the shift of topic. "'Tis the most beautiful sight in the world. When I was a lass, I was convinced ye could climb Ben Nevis, up through the veil of mist and right into heaven."

"How lovely," Jane murmured.

"Aye, and in the glen between the mountain and the loch is a circle of ancient standing stones. When ye stand in the circle, it's almost as if ye can feel strange currents in the air. If fairies ever existed, then surely they lived there."

"It sounds truly magical," Jane said. "I've never been to the Highlands. I'd love to travel there someday."

Brenna's face lit with a smile. "If ye do, ye must come to Glenbroch. 'Tis not the grandest of homes, more a manor house than a castle, but ye'll not find more pleasing surroundings anywhere."

"I'd like that very much." Jane looked up, suddenly noticing Colin there, hovering over the table with a tray like a manservant. "Oh, Colin, thank you." She reached for a cheesecake. "Brenna was just telling me about her home."

"I heard." He moved aside his coattails and took a seat. "And it does sound enchanting. You sound as if you are counting the days till your return."

"I verra much look forward to my return at the close of the Season." She reached for a cake and took a dainty bite.

"So soon?" Jane asked. "But what of your family here?"

"I'm grateful for their attentions, truly I am, and my affection for them grows daily. Yet Scotland is my home, and I hope to make them understand that. I fear they have great hopes for me, but I canna share those hopes."

"I suppose like every other girl's parents, they wish to marry you off to the highest bidder," Jane said with a frown.

"'Tis true. They canna understand that I've no wish to remain here in England, shirking my duties. What they see as a burden—running Glenbroch— I see as a source of pride and joy."

Jane turned toward Colin with a broad smile, her eyes twinkling with pleasure. "Colin, she *must* meet Lucy, mustn't she?" She returned her attention to Brenna, laying a hand on her wrist. "The two of you will get on so well. She is as passionate as you are about her own interests—veterinary arts, if you can believe it."

"She sounds like a fascinating woman," Brenna murmured, then took a sip of creamy syllabub.

Colin nodded, then quirked a brow. "Lucy is nothing if not fascinating."

Jane nodded her agreement. "So you manage Glenbroch yourself?"

"With the help of an excellent land steward. He's been with our family for many years, and I trust him wholeheartedly."

Colin sat forward in his seat, brushing crumbs from his lapel. "Tell me, are your tenant farms faring well? Or have you considered clearing the land for sheep?"

Judging by the way her eyes began to flash, Colin realized he'd misspoken.

"I suppose ye think the land clearances a fine idea. More sheep mean more money, dinna they?"

"I suppose. I haven't really considered—"

"And what do ye suppose happens to the crofters once they are forced from their land?"

"I confess, I haven't much thought upon it. They take up trade? Emigrate to the Americas?"

"Leave their homeland? Abandon the lands they've worked for generations, oftentimes with no more than an hour's notice, else their croft will burn over their head, Mr. Rosemoor? Have ye not heard of the atrocities in Sutherland? The old and infirm, burned to death in their beds?"

Colin grimaced, shaking his head in disgust. "Good Lord, no. I've heard nothing of that."

"Surely your newspapers carried the accounts of the violence being committed in the name of progress," Brenna said, the swell of her décolletage rising and falling at a rapid rate, her cheeks stained an angry red. The cakes sat untouched, and Jane silently stared at Colin, her mouth agape.

Colin swallowed, then cleared his throat. "I must apologize, Lady Brenna. I did not mean to make light of what is obviously a more serious matter than I supposed." He looked up and saw the eyes of all the shop's patrons upon them. He rose from his seat and offered his arm. "Perhaps we should adjourn for that stroll, ladies."

"What a fine idea," Jane said brightly. "Lady Brenna?"

"Of course." Brenna rose and took Colin's arm. "I seem to have lost my appetite."

In silence they made their way outside and turned onto a pleasant lane, one that led toward an ornamental pond spanned by a wooden footbridge. It seemed a fine destination, away from prying eyes and sharp ears, both of which seemed to follow him at every turn these days.

"Oh, dear!" Jane cried, shaking her head. "I seem to have left behind my reticule. Go on ahead; I'll catch up in a moment."

"Jane, wait." Colin released Brenna's arm and took two strides after his sister, whose lemon-yellow gown fluttered in the breeze behind her as she hurried back to the shop without heeding his protests. "I'll go for it," he called out after her, just as she disappeared around the bend.

"Well, then." He turned back toward Brenna, who was eyeing him with obvious curiosity. "I suppose I won't."

# Chapter 5

"Shall we follow her back inside?" Brenna asked.

"No, of course not." With a tight smile, Colin offered her his arm. "She'll catch up with us eventually. Stubborn girl."

"Your sister is lovely, indeed, Mr. Rosemoor, just as ye said she was. I'm verra pleased to have made her acquaintance." Brenna placed her hand in the crook of his arm and gazed off toward the footbridge. "Shall we continue to stroll? 'Tis a fine afternoon. Far better to be out enjoying the day than sitting inside." She looked over her shoulder, surprised to see a number of ladies milling about behind them, watching them, whispering amongst themselves. She distinctly heard Mr. Rosemoor's name carried on the scented breeze. If he heard them, he gave no indication. Instead, he kept his gaze trained ahead, toward their destination, as they leisurely made their way toward the bridge.

"I'm quite fond of outdoor pursuits myself," he said. "I must say, I'm pleased to see you don't seem to suffer any ill effects from my trouncing you in Lady Brandon's garden."

"Nay, none at all. I'm a sturdy girl, Mr. Rosemoor."

He smiled down at her warmly as they stepped onto the bridge's wide wooden planks. "'Sturdy' isn't perhaps a word I'd choose to describe you. Makes you sound like a tree. A large tree. I'd rate you a sapling, at most."

"I'm liable to lose a few leaves, then, in this breeze." She paused to reach up and steady her bonnet as a particularly robust gust threatened its angle atop her head. Once the wind subsided, she released her bonnet and they continued on, cresting the bridge's arch and moving toward the iron railing at its edge.

Brenna removed her hand from his elbow and leaned against the scrolled ironwork, looking down at the lily pads that dotted the reflection pool below. Her own face, slightly distorted and dancing in the rippled water, looked back. The whisper of soft wool brushed against her forearm, and, keeping her gaze on the waters below, she watched as Mr. Rosemoor's reflection joined her own. He towered above her, the sunlight illuminating his fair hair, turning it into molten gold. He stood so close that, in their reflection, she could not tell where her person ended and his began. His nearness unsettled her, even as it excited her. Her pulse quickened; her hand trembled perceptibly on the sun-warmed iron. She took a deep, steadying breath and forced her voice to assume a neutral, conversational tone. "I must confess, I'm finding the constraints of London a wee bit stifling," she said, unable to tear her gaze away from the pool.

"'Twould seem I'm not allowed to engage in the activities I most enjoy. Instead, I'm encouraged to take up things in which I have neither interest nor talent."

"Tell me, what would you be doing now, if you remained at home in Scotland?"

She looked up, off toward the horizon. "Oh, so many things. Riding the fields with my steward. Keeping the ledgers. Visiting my tenants, perhaps, and making certain that no one was in want of any comfort. 'Tis a beautiful summer day, so perhaps I'd ride out to the glen and bathe in the river."

"Not alone, I hope."

"With no siblings, I've grown accustomed to my solitude."

"But bathing in the river? Alone?" He shook his head. "Certainly not safe for a lady."

She turned to face him, surprised by such a statement. "Why ever not? I'm a strong swimmer. And there's nothing more peaceful than lying on the stones by the river in the warm summer sun, listening to the chatter of birds while waiting for my gown to dry." Brenna sighed wistfully. How she longed to enjoy such an afternoon. She closed her eyes and inhaled deeply, imagining that the golden sunlight that warmed her face shone down from Glenbroch's clear summer sky instead; that the breeze that stirred the hem of her gown and ruffled the trimmings on her bonnet had blown across the loch and through the glen, redolent with the honeyed scent of heather.

In her mind's eye, she could see a single, majestic golden eagle arc across the sky, its wings spread wide as it glided above the loch's dark waters. Her favorite mare would be grazing nearby, tossing her head with a whinny and enjoying the day's freedoms as much as her mistress. Brenna shivered, remembering the feel of a cool, damp shift clinging wetly to her body as the warm rays dried her skin. *Ah, the simple pleasures of home.* She'd taken such days for granted.

At last she opened her eyes, only to find Mr. Rosemoor's blue-gray gaze studying her intensely, an almost wicked smile dancing on his lips.

"You must satisfy my curiosity at once," he said, his voice a low growl. "Tell me, the gown—is it drying *on* your person or off?"

Brenna gasped, heat flooding her cheeks at once.

"I must apologize," he said, his voice returned to its usual timbre and inflection. "I'm afraid I couldn't help myself, not with such a mental image as that."

"Ye must think me terribly coarse and vulgar for saying such things to a gentleman."

"Actually, I find you quite refreshing. And perhaps I'm not such a gentleman, besides."

"Aren't ye, Mr. Rosemoor?" She tilted her head to one side and eyed him quizzically, watching as he arched one brow. A muscle in his jaw tensed.

"The *ton* no longer believes I am." His tone was cool, clipped. "I hope you'll pardon my candor, Lady Brenna. I don't generally go about airing my misfortune to those I'm so newly acquainted with. Still, I feel I must warn you that my reputation has recently come into question. In fact, one might say I've entirely fallen from grace."

"Then ye haven't yet straightened out the misunderstanding ye spoke of? Something to do with winning at cards?"

"No. Not yet, at any rate."

"And the woman ye meant to marry?"

"Miss Lyttle-Brown?" He shook his head. "There's no longer any chance of that."

"I'm sorry to hear it. She must have been a verra special lady, indeed."

"In all honesty, I'm beginning to think I entirely misjudged her character. Perhaps her defection will prove for the best."

Brenna only nodded in reply.

"Still, you might wish to reconsider keeping my company, in light of my current state of affairs. I vow I would not think less of you for it."

"Nay, Mr. Rosemoor. I'm glad ye feel ye can speak plainly with me about such matters, and I admire your honesty. Ye have offered me naught but comfort and understanding regarding my own discontent, and I would do the same for ye."

He smiled down at her, the corners of his eyes crinkling quite pleasingly with the effort. "I do believe we shall be great friends, Lady Brenna Maclachlan of Glenbroch."

"I hope so, Mr. Rosemoor," she answered. "I'd like that verra much."

At the sound of approaching footsteps, Mr. Rosemoor turned toward the path from which they'd arrived. He raised one hand to shield his eyes from the near-blinding sun. "Ah, I see Jane is returned to us at last. Took her long enough," he added under his breath.

Brenna raised a hand to shield her own eyes. "I hope she was able to find her reticule."

As if Miss Rosemoor had read her mind, the

woman raised one arm, the accessory in question dangling from her slender wrist.

Brenna waved a hand in reply, then turned back toward Mr. Rosemoor. "And to answer your impertinent question, Mr. Rosemoor, the answer is *off*."

"Off?" He shrugged, his brows drawn.

"The gown. Off." She couldn't help but smile triumphantly at Mr. Rosemoor's stunned expression as his sister joined them on the bridge.

"Well?" Miss Rosemoor's gaze swung from Brenna to Mr. Rosemoor, who visibly strove to regain his composure. "Whatever did I miss?"

"Verra little," Brenna answered, her eyes meeting Mr. Rosemoor's. His seemed to darken a shade— more steely than blue—and then swept across her form, from head to toe, and back up again. Never one to care overmuch for feminine trappings or flirtations, Brenna suddenly felt more female, more attractive, than ever before. No doubt it was something about the way he looked at her. She glanced down at her frothy, overly ornamented dress and, for the first time since her arrival in London, felt a sudden, inexplicable surge of appreciation. For once, she was glad to be rid of her serviceable woolens, glad to be admired.

Her heart began to race; her palms dampened. She was attracted to him, she realized. Terribly so. And why not? He was surely handsome enough, and he didn't find her interests silly or frivolous. And the way he looked at her—it made her almost dizzy, made her limbs feel weak. Nay, this was nothing like the girlish infatuations she'd entertained in her youth, this was far more physical, more visceral. She shook her head in frustration, forcing a halt

to her indecent thoughts. For they were no doubt
indecent. *Dinna be a fool,* she scolded herself, remembering his careless words about the Clearances.
Nay, nothing good would come of it. He was an *Englishman,* after all.

Colin absently stroked his whiskers, unable to
think of anything save the vision of Brenna lying on
the rocks in nothing save her undergarments. Blast
it, didn't she know what a statement like that did to
a man? Truthfully, she very likely did not. *She's an
innocent,* he reminded himself, struggling to divert
his thoughts.

"Well, ladies," he managed at last, stepping between Jane and Brenna and offering each an arm,
"shall we continue to take our exercise?"

Together they descended the slope of the footbridge and continued their meandering way down
the wide, tree-lined path.

"I still cannot believe I managed to leave behind
my reticule," Jane muttered beside him. "I'm not
usually so forgetful. Lucky for me, it was still sitting right where I left it. I *do* hope Colin was on his
best behavior in my absence. Didn't knock her to
the ground again, did you, Colin?"

Colin ruffled at the insult.

"Not this time, Miss Rosemoor," Brenna said, smiling sweetly. "I assure ye, he was the perfect gentleman."

"See, Colin? That wasn't so very difficult now,
was it?"

"I suggest you hold your tongue, Jane Rosemoor.
Haven't I enough troubles as it is without my own
sister suggesting I'm anything but a gentleman?"
He was only teasing her; still, his chest tightened
at the reminder. He'd heard the tabbies gossiping

about him in the cake house, several of them taking no pains to lower their voices. Some of them had even been so brazen as to follow them out onto the promenades, like lionesses following the scent of blood.

He'd hoped that the business at White's would eventually blow over, that after a few weeks time they'd forget what had happened and move on to the next scandal. Instead, nearly the opposite had occurred. According to Lucy, the gossip grew daily; every past misdeed of his had been rehashed and embellished till the tale began to take on epic proportions. No longer considered simply a cheat, he was now apparently labeled a rake, a reprobate, and even a drunken sot. All of which were entirely untrue, of course.

Yet men of long-standing acquaintance now passed him on the street with nary a word of acknowledgment, and ladies struck him from their invitation lists. The now-familiar flame of anger and frustration shot through him, tensing his muscles uncomfortably.

He *would* prove his innocence and expose those who had set him up. The alternative was insupportable. But he needed time to clear his name and restore his honor.

And what was Jane playing at, besides? She knew his reputation was all but destroyed, that high society no longer received him. Yet here she was, insisting that he squire about Brenna, whose own position in the *ton* was tenuous at best. He should not have offered her the choice to remain in his company. It was far too imprudent. She was not yet familiar enough with the ways of the *ton* to realize the repercussions of such a decision.

"I should go," he blurted out, an uncomfortable sensation settling in his gut.

"Don't be silly," Jane admonished, tightening her grip on his arm. "I hear what they are saying, Colin. Do not let them ruin this fine afternoon."

He said nothing in reply, squinting against the sun as he continued to follow the tree-lined path around a sharp bend, toward the Long Water. "Shall we walk along the canal?" he asked, attempting to staunch his growing resentment.

"A fine idea," Jane answered, her approval evident in her tone. "Oh, look, there's Lady Wellesley up ahead; perhaps I'll pause for a moment as I've something to discuss with her ladyship. But the two of you must feel free to take your exercise and collect me on your way back."

"Subtlety is not your strong suit, is it, Jane?" he said under his breath, leaning toward his sister. She only grinned in reply. "A wasted effort," he added. In truth, his blood began to stir at the thought of finding himself alone in Brenna's company once more, and he cursed himself such weakness.

What else would the naive girl say, furthering his erotic visions of her—visions that he must banish from his mind or he'd go mad? Never in his life had he entertained such impure thoughts about an innocent—an innocent who would return to Scotland come autumn, he reminded himself. Who did not need the blight of his association, besides. And who was in no way the kind of woman he should marry. If she'd even have him; her talk of returning to Scotland and her life there made it seem unlikely.

Bloody hell, he was losing his mind. Little more than a sennight ago he'd thought himself in love with

Honoria, eager to ask for her hand. And now here he was, sniffing around this enigmatic Scotswoman like a hound. And further ruining her prospects in the process. Maybe he *was* a reprobate after all.

For several minutes, they walked in silence. Finally Colin chanced a look at Brenna's face, cast into shadows by the brim of her straw bonnet. The exertion had brought a flush to her cheeks, staining them the faintest petal pink. Her eyes shone, round and wide under a thick fringe of lashes. A smile danced on her lips, dimpling one cheek in a delightful fashion. He supposed her features were what one would consider rather ordinary, except for her brilliantly hued eyes. Surely the fashionable set would scoff at the freckles that dotted her nose. Yet there was no denying that her face delighted him in every way. True, she was not a dazzling beauty, not what the *ton* would call an *Incomparable*. But she was exceptionally pretty nonetheless, in a simple, fresh-faced way. Her countenance bespoke of intelligence and sensibility; how, he could not exactly say. Yet it did. And it was damn bloody appealing, too.

"Are ye finished, Mr. Rosemoor?" she asked, her eyes never veering from the path ahead, the smile never leaving her lips.

He started in surprise, drawn from his ruminations. "Am I finished what?"

"Why, examining me, of course."

"I'm sure I don't know what you mean." Had he been so obvious? Even if he had, most English misses would not have dared to comment on it.

"Hmm, if you say so."

"Yes, well . . . ahem. I say, you must have left many broken hearts behind in Scotland."

"Nay, sir, none at all," she answered honestly, all coyness gone.

"I find that difficult to believe."

"'Tis true, I'm afraid. I hadn't the time for such things as flirtations. I was busy running an estate, ye know."

"Still, most women think of marriage. Far more than they should, from what I've gathered listening to my sisters talk."

"Oh, one day, when the time comes, I'll take a husband. There are several men I respect in Lochaber, men I've known all my life who would be pleased to add Glenbroch to their holdings. Men who work their own land, Mr. Rosemoor, as I do. We haven't had the time or leisure to devote to the frivolities of courtship, as the English are so fond of." Her tone was light, playful, even as she scolded him. "But someday . . ." She shrugged. "How about ye, Mr. Rosemoor? Surely ye have broken many a heart in your time."

"Spend an afternoon in any Mayfair drawing room and you'll hear tales that I have broken dozens." He shook his head. "I should be so lucky. The truth is, most ladies see me as the brotherly type—the type they dance with and confide in while the true objects of their affection, the very rakes and rogues they protest about, look on."

"But why, then, do they tell tales about ye that aren't true?"

"Because the *ton* prefers a scandal to the truth any day. They delight in them; they revel in spreading lies and untruths amongst themselves. It gives them something to do. And at the present, I'm their favorite scandal. I should be honored, really."

She shook her head. "Truly, I'll never understand the English."

"Are the English really so very different from the Scots?"

"Perhaps such intrigues play out in Edinburgh. I wouldna know. But the people of Lochaber—*my* people—are a more industrious lot. We have far better ways to occupy our time and our minds."

"I'm not entirely sure I believe you. Human nature is universal, after all."

"'Tis true, but only idleness and lack of meaningful occupation can nurture such tendencies, I think. And in my opinion, the English are far too idle. At least, those who reside in Mayfair are."

"Those like me, you mean?"

"Nay, I didna mean . . . that is, I'm sure ye . . . well . . ." She'd never appeared so discomposed. "Ye must forgive me, Mr. Rosemoor. I spoke without thought."

"Don't apologize, Lady Brenna. You speak the truth. Would you like to hear how I put my time to use whilst in Town? I rise after ten, some days as late as noon. I read my papers over my coffee, allow my valet to help me dress, spend the afternoon at my club—or at least I did until my membership was revoked." His breathing became fast as his anger mounted, and he reached up to loosen his cravat.

"At five, I might take a ride down Rotten Row, just to be fashionable. My evenings are spent solely in the pursuit of pleasure, attending balls and soirees, routs and musicales, perhaps the opera or theater. And then I might end the night in one gaming hell or another, enjoying a hand or two of cards and a bottle of brandy—well, more like gin these days—before retiring to my lodgings. And if I'm lucky, I might wake in the morning to find some unknown woman in my bed and no idea how she came to be there."

He heard her shocked gasp at his vulgar words, yet he continued on. "That, my dear, is how I spend my days in Town. Lovely, isn't it? Have you a better example of idleness to offer?"

Only then did he notice that they'd stopped strolling and stood facing each other by the banks of the canal. He reached a hand up to his temple, disgusted that his hand shook as he did so. "You must forgive me, Lady Brenna. I had no right to speak to you in such a manner."

"Nay, Mr. Rosemoor. I deserved the comeuppance. Who am I to preach to ye? Ye must think me a self-righteous shrew."

"No, not a shrew." He reached for her hand. "Not at all."

"I shouldna have spoken so carelessly. 'Tis just that I forget . . . That is, ye seem so verra different from the rest, from Hugh and the other gentlemen I've become acquainted with." She swept her gaze from the top of his beaver hat to the tips of his boots. "Despite your appearance, that is." At last, a tentative smile reappeared on her lovely face.

At once the tension in his body seemed to dissipate. A smile tugged at the corners of his mouth. "And whatever does that mean?" he asked, releasing her hand.

"Well, look at ye. Not a crease in your trousers. Your neck cloth is knotted into . . . Well, I canna even describe it, but it looks as if it took hours to accomplish." She lowered her gaze to his feet. "Your boots are like a looking glass, so polished are they. And truly, no man in Lochaber would take his afternoon exercise in both waistcoat and coat, not on a day as fine and warm as this."

"Is that so?" he countered. "And have you taken a look at your own attire?"

She glanced down at her dress, skimming her hands across the folds of the skirts. "I know. 'Tis silly, isna it? A 'walking dress' they call it. There are morning dresses, walking dresses, riding habits . . . a different gown for every purpose. This one *is* bonny, though."

"It is," he murmured. "Made more so by its wearer."

She did not heed the compliment. "And to think, I used to believe that simple woolens were all one needed."

"I must say, I'm glad you changed your mind on that count." Again, he reached for her hand, grasping her gloved one in his, stroking her palm with his thumb through the kidskin.

She kept her gaze on their joined hands, as if mesmerized, but said nothing.

"Brenna?" Her given name slipped easily off his tongue. The sounds of the park receded, becoming nothing but a hum in the distance. He was conscious of nothing save the sight of her tongue, darting out to wet her lips. Then her gaze rose and met his, and the breath seemed to leave his body in a rush.

"Yes, Colin?" she asked, her voice low and husky.

"There you are."

Colin spun toward his sister's voice, dropping Brenna's hand as he did so. He swallowed hard as Jane approached, smiling broadly, with Lady Wellesley by her side.

"I wanted to introduce Bren—Lady Margaret to Lady Wellesley," Jane said gaily, though he saw her eyes dart suspiciously from Brenna to him and back to Brenna again.

What had they seen? Or worse yet, heard? He wanted to kiss Brenna. More than anything, he wanted to take her in his arms, right there by the canal, and kiss her till her legs went weak, till she clung to him in desperation, calling out his name over and over again.

He forced himself to look at her, standing there demurely, clasping her hands in front of herself while Jane made the introductions. She looked like an angel, as unspoiled and untouched as any woman he'd ever met. God's teeth, he *was* a rogue. He would be the ruin of her yet.

"If you'll pardon me, ladies." Without another word, he turned and walked away, wishing to put as much distance between himself and Brenna as possible, yet wanting more than anything to remain by her side forever.

# Chapter 6

"Ye wished to see me?" Brenna asked, stepping into the salon. Her mother sat in a stuffed chintz chair before the fire, her father standing behind his wife with one hand resting upon her shoulder. Brenna's palms suddenly felt damp, and she wiped them across her skirts as her heart fluttered in anticipation. Why ever had they summoned her? Had she done something to displease them?

"Please have a seat, my dear." Her father motioned toward the sofa directly across from them.

Brenna nodded and took a seat, clasping her hands in her lap. She waited expectantly as her mother glanced up at her father.

"Ahem. Well, then. Yes. Your mother tells me that you spent the day at St. James's Park with Miss Jane Rosemoor."

"'Tis true. I like her verra much, sir."

"Yes, yes. Capital. But she also tells me that Miss Rosemoor's brother, Mr. Colin Rosemoor, joined you on this outing, taking refreshments with you and squiring you about the promenades and such."

"Aye, he did." Her hands grew suddenly cold. "We were introduced at Lady Brandon's soiree." It wasn't entirely true, as they were never formally introduced. But she thought it wise not to mention the true nature of their initial encounters, either here at home or in Lady Brandon's garden. She somehow doubted either would be deemed appropriate.

"Well, my dear, first impressions are often misleading. I'm afraid he is not the gentleman he may seem to be. Young Rosemoor has always had a bit of a wild, reckless streak in him, but now he's gone too far."

"Much too far," her mother interjected, her mouth set in a hard line. "Despite his fine family and advantageous connections, he has—"

"But none of it is true." Brenna rose, her hands balled into fists by her sides. "Mr. Rosemoor is an honorable man."

"Says who?" her mother asked. "Miss Rosemoor? Of course she would take up for her brother."

"Nay, Miss Rosemoor has said nothing about her brother. But Colin has said—"

"*Colin?*" her father barked, his face reddening. "Has he trifled with you, Margaret?"

Her mother leaned back in her chair, rapidly fanning her face. "Dear Lord above. I need my vinaigrette!"

"Nay, sir. Of course he has not trifled with me. He is a gentleman in every respect."

"A gentleman? Bah." Her mother sat upright, her fan suddenly stilled in her lap. "Did he tell you that he has been cast from White's? That he was caught red-handed, fleecing the Duke of Glastonbury out

of a fair amount of blunt? That he's no longer received in any respectable drawing room in all of
London?"

"Yes, but—"

"There are no buts, Margaret," her mother interrupted. "What about that business last week in
Covent Garden? Did he tell you about that? About
Lord Mandeville dragging Mr. Rosemoor out of
some seedy public house just before he'd compromised the barkeep's wife? It is only thanks to
Mandeville's interference that Mr. Rosemoor did
not have to face the man the next morning in the
meadow over a brace of pistols. I'm sure he did not
tell you about that now, did he?"

Brenna shook her head, bewildered, as she sank
back onto the sofa. It couldn't be true. *Could it?*
With a sinking heart, she realized just how much
she hoped it wasn't. Why did the thought of him
with another woman make her stomach pitch?
After all, she'd only just met him. It wasn't as if
she'd developed an attachment to him, not in so
short a time. *Had she?* It didn't matter if she had;
the attachment would end now, before it was too
late. Before she made a fool of herself. "Nay, he
didna tell me about that," she said at last, willing
her churning emotions to abate and her voice to
steady.

"Colin Rosemoor is a liar and a cheat, a man
without honor. In short, a rogue." Her father shook
his head. "I do not know what games the scoundrel
is playing, insinuating himself into your life and encouraging you to address him so intimately—"

"I assume her dowry has something to do with
it," her mother put in, her lips curled into an

unbecoming scowl. "He is far enough under the hatches, from what I hear."

Her father nodded in agreement, his face now a mottled red. "Likely so. By all accounts, he's nearly done up. His entire fortune, squandered on drink and debauchery."

Brenna inhaled sharply. Nearly done up? Was it really so bad as that? Could his attentions truly have been nothing more than an attempt to secure her dowry? A heated flush began to climb her neck as she cursed her own naïveté. No, her mind countered. It couldna be true. Surely there was some other explanation.

"You shall cease all association with him at once," her father's voice boomed. "Have I made myself clear on that count, Margaret?"

She could not do what he asked of her. Could she? Had she so thoroughly misjudged Colin Rosemoor?

"Answer your father, Margaret," her mother demanded.

"I . . . I suppose so," she stammered, realizing that she had no choice, not while she remained under their roof and their protection. "But what of Miss Rosemoor? Surely she canna be held responsible for her brother's misbehavior."

Her mother glanced at her father, who nodded. "Miss Rosemoor is a particular favorite amongst the *ton,* and I cannot imagine that her position in society will be affected overmuch. Yes, you may continue your acquaintance with her, so long as you avoid her brother at all costs." Her mother eyed her sharply. "Have I your word?"

Brenna knew she must comply with her parents'

wishes. Even so, she had to swallow an uncomfortable lump in her throat before replying. "Yes, Lady Danv—Mama, I meant."

Her father clapped his hands together, clearly pleased to be done with the discourse. His anger seemed to ebb away all at once, as if the strain of such strong emotion had drained him. "Yes, then, very good. Capital. You'll excuse me, my dears. I'll just be in my study." With a tight smile, he strode over to Brenna and patted her awkwardly on the shoulder, then took his leave.

Her mother rose before her, gesturing for Brenna to follow suit. "Now, Margaret, you must begin to prepare for dinner. Your brother has asked a guest to join us, and you must look your loveliest." She paused to eye Brenna sharply. "Perhaps the sapphire silk gown will do nicely."

"And who is this guest that I must dress so elegantly for?"

"Lord Thomas Sinclair, second son of the Duke of Eston. A very well-bred young man, and Hugh finds him most agreeable. Fifteen thousand pounds a year, Hugh says, and not a farthing less." She reached for Brenna's hand with a smile. "Lord Thomas is eager to make your acquaintance."

"I suppose we shan't disappoint him, then," Brenna muttered. With a heavy heart, she set off to find her maid.

Far too many hours later, Brenna stepped out of the sapphire silk gown with a huff.

"Careful, miss. You'll tear the hem, you will, stomping about like that." With a scowl, Celeste gathered up the soft blue folds and gently shook them out.

Brenna strode to the vanity and, still inwardly fuming, began to pull the seed-pearl pins from her hair. One by one, the pins clattered to the marble as her hair fell softly across her bare shoulders.

"Let me help you, miss." Celeste reached for the silver brush lying on the vanity.

"Nay, I can do it myself." Seeing the maid's face fall, Brenna immediately regretted her churlishness. "Ye must forgive me, Celeste. I dinna mean to snap at ye. I'm just feeling a wee bit out of sorts, is all. Go on to bed," she said gently. "I can get into my nightdress myself."

Celeste bobbed a curtsy. "If you say so, miss."

"Good night, Celeste," Brenna said, rising and reaching for the young maid's hand. Celeste had been some sort of lesser servant, a laundry maid, perhaps, and was only recently elevated to lady's maid. Light blue eyes under pale brows eyed Brenna curiously as she tugged her hand from her mistress's grasp.

"Good night, then, miss." With a shake of her head, Celeste took her leave, softly shutting the door behind her.

Brenna slumped back onto the padded seat before her dressing table. She exhaled in a rush, wishing to forget the evening's unpleasantness. She grasped the cool handle of the brush and began to run it through her hair, staring back at her own reflection as she did so. Her face appeared drawn, her mouth pinched. It most certainly had *not* been an enjoyable evening, and her countenance certainly showed the strain.

Oh, Lord Thomas Sinclair had been polite enough, his manners impeccable and his attentions solicitous. He was no doubt a handsome man as well. Perhaps too handsome for his own good. Yet there was something wolfish about his smile, and his eyes possessed a predatory glint that made her shudder. Several times during dinner she'd looked up from her plate and seen him watching her, his gaze possessive and full of heat. As if he . . . he *owned* her already. And it was clear that that was her brother's intention—that Lord Thomas should own her.

When Lord Thomas had at last prepared to take his leave, he'd reached for Brenna's hand and raised it to his lips while his fingers had stroked her palm. There had been something suggestive about the touch, and when her surprised gaze flew up to meet his, he'd winked at her. Or perhaps he'd had something in his eye, her mind countered charitably. No, she was sure it had been a wink, the rogue.

No doubt Hugh was in collusion with him. She'd watched her brother escort their guest to the front hall, the pair conversing in low, hushed tones, then throwing their heads back and laughing aloud, as if they had shared a most amusing joke. She'd paused on the landing and distinctly heard Hugh say, "Didn't I say she was exactly your type?" At that, Brenna had scurried up the stairs without waiting for the distasteful man's reply.

Brenna smacked the brush back down on the marble, wincing at the sharp sound. *Exactly his type?* Rubbish. What did he know of her? Even her own brother knew very little of her true character, her interests and enjoyments. Hugh wouldn't entertain talk of her years at Glenbroch. As far as he was concerned, her life began the day she arrived at Danville House.

She rose and padded across the room, taking a seat on the edge of the bed. Hera crawled out from beneath the bed and rubbed against Brenna's bare ankles. She reached down and scooped up the cat, depositing her on her lap. After several strokes, the cat was purring loudly.

"Oh, Hera, I do believe Colin Rosemoor understands me better than my own brother does." Spoken aloud, the thought startled her, warming her cheeks. But it was the truth, plain and simple. If Mr. Rosemoor had winked at her whilst bidding her a good night, she would have found the gesture amusing, not disconcerting. It would have been done in jest; it would not have seemed lascivious or indecent in any way, shape, or form.

And then her parents' warning came crashing down on her consciousness. A liar, her father had called Mr. Rosemoor. He'd nearly compromised a barkeep's wife, for God's sake, in Covent Garden of all places. Brenna knew enough about London and its environs to know that a respectable gentleman— a viscount's son—did not wish to be seen patronizing such an establishment. There were enough public houses in London's fashionable districts to serve men of reputation and character. A gentleman only ventured to such seedy districts as Covent Garden when one was desirous of participating in illegal— or illicit—activities. Brenna could only wonder which it was that had lured Mr. Rosemoor there on the night in question. Considering the way in which the night had ended—with the threat of a duel— she supposed it must have been the latter.

She scowled, continuing to stroke the cat's fur. Now that she'd been forbidden to associate with the man, she'd likely never learn the truth, especially if the *ton* truly preferred gossip to fact, as Mr. Rosemoor had suggested. Perhaps it was for the best, she reminded herself. Scratching the cat beneath the chin, she met Hera's steady, green gaze. "Perhaps I *have* let myself grow too fond of Mr. Rosemoor, haven't I, Hera?" No sense in that, especially as she planned to return to Glenbroch come autumn. Taking a deep, fortifying breath, she valiantly struggled to force away all thoughts of Mr. Rosemoor. Setting Hera on the bed, she rose to fetch her nightclothes from the high bureau in the room's corner.

She pulled her chemise over her head and replaced it with a soft, lawn night rail. As she buttoned the tiny pearl buttons at her throat, her mind was involuntarily drawn back to Lord Thomas Sinclair. Just his type, was she? Very well; she would make it her aim to ascertain exactly what his type was, and then fashion herself entirely the opposite.

Shaking her head, she blew out the candle beside her bed and settled herself under the bedcovers, rubbing her cheek against the soft-as-silk linen. Their own linens back at Glenbroch seemed almost coarse in comparison, yet she'd always found them perfectly acceptable before now.

With a sigh of frustration, she sat up in bed and looked wistfully toward the window, its drapes drawn tight against the night sky. Throwing back the bedclothes, she leapt up and hurried across the room, where she drew the drapes and secured them back against the silk-covered wall. Soft, silvery moonlight flooded in at once, and Brenna immediately felt a measure soothed. As her eyes drank in the sight of the bright moon and the twinkling stars, the tension she'd felt bunching the muscles behind her neck eased, if only a bit.

Mr. Rosemoor had appreciated the sky, had listened to her idle talk of the moon and stars with interest. Was he perhaps looking up at the sky himself right now, remembering the words they had shared? Recalling the gentle touch of his hand to her face, as she was? Or did that moment hold far less significance for him than it had for her? For she realized that she had not been able to push him far from her thoughts since that night in Lady Brandon's garden, try as she might. What was she to do? Forget him. She must. She had no choice but to do so. Even if her parents hadn't forbidden it, there was no room for him in her life. She was here in London to become acquainted with her true family, and to raise awareness of the Clearances. Nothing more.

Not removing her gaze from the calming sight beyond the glass, she returned to bed and slid back between the linens, shivering as the fabric skimmed against her bare calves. Hera meowed, then curled herself next to her, the familiar, deep purr filling the room's silence. With a sigh, Brenna glanced one last time at the open window. No, the night sky hadn't changed; it remained as it always had, continuing its cycles uninterrupted. If only she could say the same for her life.

Colin tipped back the tumbler in his hand, draining its contents in mere seconds. He shuddered as the gin burned a path down his throat. Damn the

cheap liquor. His face felt cold, almost numb. With
a scowl, he examined the glass in his hand, noting
the chip on its lip, the stain marring its base. He
glanced wildly about the crowded room, wondering
just how he'd come to be there, drunk as the devil,
in some disreputable East End establishment. The
White Bull? No, that wasn't it. White Boar? Was there
some such creature as a white boar? He hadn't any
idea, nor did he care overmuch.

Here he was viewed as nothing but a rich man, a
gentleman. He didn't have to listen to the whispers,
endure the stares. Certainly far more pleasurable
than anywhere in Mayfair, that was for certain. But
where was Ian Staunton? He distinctly remembered
arriving with the man. They'd played several hands
of faro in the back room before Staunton had disappeared, following a comely serving wench through
the crowd.

Colin set the glass on the table with a *thunk* and
stared unseeing at the far end of the room, which
teemed with bodies crowded in much too small a
space. The stale air reeked of body odor, of smoke.
Of cloying perfume, he mentally added as he felt
something soft brush against the back of his coat.

"'Scuse me, gov'na," a throaty voice said, just
behind his ear and just before he felt her press her
breasts into his back once more, perhaps for good
measure. He reached for the woman's arm and
pulled her around to stand before him. She gig-
gled, tossing her mane of ebony hair over one
shoulder as she did so. A scarlet-colored bloom,
now wilted and browning at the edges, was tucked
behind one ear. Her faded red satin gown clung to
her shapely figure in all the right places, nearly

bursting at the seams—seams that were visibly beginning to pull. Sweeping his gaze across her rouged face, he guessed her to be no more than twenty, perhaps two-and-twenty. Yet her dark, kohl-smudged eyes were dull and lifeless. Old eyes. Worn eyes.

"See anything you like, gov'na?" she asked, raising one brow suggestively. She reached for the empty glass that sat on the table before him, shrugging her shoulders as she did so and giving him an eyeful of round, high breasts crowned by deep, rose-colored nipples. Something in his blood stirred involuntarily at the display.

"I believe I do," he muttered, tossing some coin to the table to cover the cost of the drink.

"Mmm," she purred, licking her lips. "I was hopin' you would, a fine gentleman like yerself." She leaned down to whisper her price in his ear, affording him yet another look at her wares, and he had to admit they were appealing. Why shouldn't he? He was a man with no attachments. No lovers. What difference would it make if he accepted her offer? He could use a warm embrace, after all. A soft touch. It had been far too long since he'd enjoyed such pleasures.

With a nod of acceptance, he rose to his feet and straightened his coat before following the woman through the crowd, around the side of the bar, and up a narrow, dark staircase.

Minutes later, a door shut behind him. Unbuttoning his coat, Colin glanced around the small, drab room. A waning fire burned in the fireplace, sending wisps of smoke curling into the room, over a lumpy brocade chair before the fire and across a bed in the corner, haphazardly made, as if someone had hurriedly pulled up the bed coverings before taking their leave. Gray, shapeless drapes hung across one window, shuttered against the night. A wardrobe stood like a sentinel in the far corner, a chest of drawers beside it.

The woman sashayed across the room, her hips moving sensuously and purposely. Clearly a practiced move. She reached for a candle on the table beside the bed and knelt before the fire to light it. Cupping one hand against the flame, she returned the candle to its iron holder, then turned to face Colin with a sultry smile.

"What's yer name, gov'na?"

"Colin," he answered simply, still rooted to his spot by the door.

"Well, now, Colin, they call me Rosie. I think we're goin' to get on just fine." She kicked off her slippers, then hiked up her skirt and placed one foot on the brocade chair. Colin's eyes were drawn to the curve of her thigh as she rolled down her stocking, inch by inch, purposely prolonging his anticipation. At last she deposited the stocking on the floor beside her slippers, then began the process anew with her other leg. As she did so, her gaze locked with his, as if she dared him to look away from the display.

He didn't. Once the second stocking lay on the dusty floor with its mate, she stood facing him, reaching around herself to untie a single lace that held together the back of her bodice. "Now, Colin, why don't you tell Rosie what brings a man such as yerself here. A fallin' out with yer lady?"

Colin swallowed, his cloudy memory brought

painfully back to the folded missive he carried in his breast pocket. "Something like that," he finally muttered, unbuttoning his waistcoat.

Rosie pulled down her bodice to reveal the bare breasts he'd hungrily admired only moments before. "She don' understand you, do she, love?"

*Oh, but she does,* his mind countered. As no one else does. Not Honoria Lyttle-Brown, not Hugh Ballard, certainly not Lord and Lady Danville. No one save his own family, and he wasn't even entirely sure of *them,* now that he thought about it. He blinked hard, trying his best to focus his gin-muddled brain on the pair of breasts before him. Round and milky white, they stood high and proud even without the support a corset afforded.

Rosie moved across the room on silent feet till she stood just inches from him. With a lusty smile, she let her gown fall entirely to the floor around her feet. Colin's gaze drifted down, across her stomach to the dark triangle of curls where her thighs joined and back up again to her breasts. He reached out to touch one dusty-rose nipple, wondering even as he did so what Brenna's bare breasts would look like, would feel like to his hungry touch. Damn his traitorous mind!

Inhaling sharply, he forced himself to continue fondling Rosie's breasts, taking one nipple between his thumb and forefinger. She was here now. Not Brenna. Never Brenna.

The whore's flesh immediately puckered to his touch, and she tipped her head back, eyes closed. "Yes, gov'na," she purred. "Just like that. Go on, take it in your mouth."

Colin's hand dropped to his side, and he stood motionless, frozen in self-loathing disgust.

Perceiving his hesitation, Rosie opened her eyes and peered at him curiously. "Well? I thought you were up for a good rut, I did. Rosie won't let you down, y'know."

"I'm sure you won't." Perhaps he *did* need a good rut. Perhaps a good rut would permanently erase Brenna from his mind, as her parents wished. As Brenna wished, for all he knew.

He drew Rosie toward him, his mouth slanting across her eager one. He barely felt her roving hands shove his coat from his shoulders and tug his linen free from his trousers' waistband. Valiantly he struggled to focus on her mouth, her lips soft, wet, and yielding. But raucous shouts from downstairs distracted him, drawing his attention away from the woman in his arms. As if she sensed his distraction, she slid her hands up his torso, her nails raking across his skin.

Colin opened his mouth against hers, and her tongue flicked against his in challenge. In response, he pulled her more tightly against his body, her breasts flattened against his chest. He inhaled her scent—cheap perfume, smoke, and stale liquor. Nothing like Brenna, who intoxicated him to near senselessness with her clean, lavender scent. But Brenna was pure, an innocent, a far cry from Rosie, who clearly knew how to please a man, if the hand stroking his mercifully cooperative shaft through his trousers was any indication. Dear God, how he'd wanted to kiss Brenna like this. Not once but twice now he'd thought of nothing save taking her sweet mouth with his own.

Sudden bile rose in his throat, and he pushed Rosie away, staggering backward with a groan. Devil take it, what was he doing? This was wrong. Senseless. He couldn't do it, even if he wanted to. It was clear that bedding Rosie would do nothing to slake his needs.

"Aww, come back now, love. I'm likin' the feel of ye." She reached for the flap of his trousers, but he side-stepped her grasp.

"I'm afraid I've changed my mind," he said, hastily buttoning his waistcoat and retrieving his coat from the floor.

"Oh, no, you don', gov'na." She narrowed her eyes at him. "You agreed to my price, and there's nay goin' back on the bargain."

He reached into his pocket and withdrew several notes that he'd only just won. Money he sorely needed. "Here." He placed the money in her palm and closed her fingers over it. Her scowl deepened, and he wondered if he'd offended her, if she thought his change of heart indicated he'd found her talents lacking. "Here's your price, plus some. I beg you to forgive me, madam. While your charms are tempting to say the least, I . . . I . . ." he stuttered, striving hard to make his voice articulate and respectful, despite the effects of the drink. "I must regretfully decline them."

Rosie's painted mouth curved into a smile, but she made no move to cover herself. "I hope she's worth it, gov'na. She's got you by the ballocks, she does, by the looks of it."

Colin shrugged into his coat, his fingers fumbling awkwardly with the buttons. He had to get out of this place. *Now.*

"If you'll excuse me." He bowed, then opened the door and let himself out into the corridor, cursing under his breath as he did so. What a bloody fool he was. For allowing Staunton to drag him there tonight. For thinking he could enjoy one woman's body while he lusted for another, one he could never have. Damn Danville for bringing his daughter to London and tempting him with something he could never possess.

And damn the man for writing the letter that he carried with him now, the letter that had cut him to the quick and snuffed out whatever hopes had blossomed in his breast against his will, against his reason.

With a groan of frustration, he moved to stand beneath the sconce on the wall, its flame flickering pitifully in the dingy hall. His heart pounding against his ribs, he pulled the missive from his pocket, unfolded the page for perhaps the sixth time in so many hours, and read the now-familiar words:

*I've informed my daughter of your true character and fully explained the details of your fall from grace, including the recent debacle in Covent Garden and the means in which you were extricated from a duel. I have commanded my daughter to herewith cease all association with you and have extracted the promise of her full compliance, which she made without hesitation or regret. If there is any honor left in you, you will cease all attempts to pursue her at once. I will not have my only daughter ruined by association with someone like you, simply because she is far too innocent and trusting to recognize a rogue in gentleman's clothing.*

The letter continued on in the same vein for several more lines, but Colin had no wish to read further. Instead, he held the page up to the wall sconce, watching in grim satisfaction as the corner lit and curled inward. When half the page had been licked away by the flame, he dropped what was left of the missive to the floor and ground the heel of his boot into the burning page till nothing but a pile of smoldering ash remained.

Just like his heart.

# Chapter 7

Brenna followed Jane up the steps of Mandeville House, admiring the grand façade as she trailed one hand along the wrought-iron railing. "It was so verra kind of Lady Mandeville to include me in her invitation to tea."

"Truly, she cannot wait to make your acquaintance. She nearly begged me to make the introduction." The heavy black door swung open to reveal a well-liveried butler standing in the entry hall.

"Good afternoon, Miss Rosemoor," he said, inclining his head.

"Good afternoon, Matthews. We're a bit early, but Lady Mandeville is expecting us. Don't trouble yourself; I'll show the marchioness's guest to the yellow salon."

"But, miss . . ." the butler protested, shaking his head as Jane continued across the marble tiles and into a wide corridor, Brenna trailing helplessly behind.

"Lucy won't mind if we wait in the salon," Jane said once they were out of the butler's earshot. "It's my favorite room in all of Mandeville House and where we always take our tea. French doors open up to a lovely terrace. Here we are." She reached for the doorknob. "Come, you must see the view of the garden from here."

Jane pushed the door open and froze, her fingers still clasping the cut-glass knob. Brenna peered around her, curious to see what had stilled her. A petite, golden-haired woman, surely Lady Mandeville, sat perched on the edge of a moss-green velvet chaise longue, where a man lounged carelessly in nothing but trousers, boots, waistcoat, and rumpled linen. A coat of dark blue superfine lay discarded across the curved arm of the chaise. His face was hidden from Brenna's view, but she could see that he clutched one of Lady Mandeville's hands in his own.

Lord Mandeville, she hoped.

"Colin," Jane said at last, her voice sharp. Lady Mandeville looked up in surprise.

Brenna's stomach pitched. *Colin?* Nay, it couldn't be.

"Colin Rosemoor, whatever are you doing here?" Jane asked, hurrying across the room to the chaise.

Indeed it *was* Colin. In a flash, he rose to his feet, still clutching Lady Mandeville's hand in his own. Dear Lord, whatever had they stumbled upon? Colin and Lady Mandeville in some sort of compromising position? Brenna's heart began to race. *Nay,* her mind screamed. *Nay.* It simply could not be.

"Jane, Lady Brenna." Colin bowed stiffly in their direction. "You must excuse my . . . ahh, casual appearance." He reached for his coat and quickly donned it, his fingers flying over the buttons. "I had some business to discuss with Lord Mandeville, and

I'm afraid I imposed on Lucy's hospitality when I found he was not at home."

"You must be the Lady Brenna that Jane has spoken so affectionately of. You must forgive my manners," Lady Mandeville said, reaching for Brenna's hand and giving it a friendly squeeze. "I did not realize the hour had grown so late."

Brenna found her voice. "I'm only glad to make your acquaintance at last, Lady Mandeville. I hope we did not interrupt—"

"Not at all," Colin said, running a hand through his hair. She hadn't thought it possible, but he looked even more discomposed now than he had before. His eyes never once met hers. He looked . . . guilty. "It's well past time I take my leave."

"You mustn't dash off on our account, Colin," Jane said. "Hadn't you some business with Mandeville? Stay, until he returns. And then you can go do whatever it is you gentlemen do when ladies leave you to your solitude."

His gaze finally collided with Brenna's. "I'm afraid I haven't much of a choice," he answered, his voice suddenly cold.

Brenna knew she ought to be relieved that he was leaving them. Her parents had forbidden her to remain in his company, after all. Judging by the icy way in which he was regarding her, it appeared her father or Hugh had spoken with him, told him that Brenna had been instructed to cease all association with him. Perhaps he thought she had readily agreed to such a mandate.

"Mr. Rosemoor," she blurted out before she thought better of it, "would ye mind verra much if I had a private word with ye before ye take your leave?"

His steely gaze bored through her, making her squirm in discomfort.

"Actually, I would mind," he said at last. "I'm certain Lord Danville would not approve. I've grown quite fond of my limbs, you see. I would not wish to part with them, simply for a moment of your company, no matter how agreeable it might be."

"My father is not here, Mr. Rosemoor, and I dinna wish to leave things unsaid between us."

At last remembering Jane and Lady Mandeville's presence beside her, she turned to find them both wide-eyed, watching the exchange with unconcealed curiosity.

"Colin," Jane entreated her brother in a harsh whisper, tipping her head toward the terrace, "go on."

Colin looked from his sister to Lady Mandeville, who nodded her own encouragement, before returning his simmering gaze to Brenna's. "Have I a choice?" he muttered, striding off toward the French doors that led to the terrace beyond. "Come, Lady Brenna. We'll retire out to the garden. We won't be long," he added as he stepped out onto the flagstones, Brenna silently in tow.

*Perhaps this wasna such a good idea, after all,* Brenna thought as the door clicked shut behind them. She took a moment to study the tips of her half boots as she gathered her courage to face him.

"You realize I've been informed by your father that I am to cease all association with you?" Colin said, watching as she raised her aquamarine gaze to meet his. Damn those eyes. They were beginning to haunt his dreams.

"Aye, I'm aware of it," she answered, her voice

steady. Her gaze locked with his, daring him to look away. "And yet despite what I just stumbled upon—"

"You stumbled upon nothing untoward. Lucy is like a sister to me, nothing more." He folded his arms across his chest as he watched the flicker of disbelief play across her features. She didn't believe him. She truly thought she'd caught him in some sort of compromising position with Lucy. He almost laughed aloud at the absurdity of such a notion.

"Yes, well, regardless," she continued, "I thought it only fair to tell ye that I was displeased by my parents' command that I avoid your company. I . . . I protested against it. Most vehemently."

"How very charitable of you," he drawled.

"Yet they remain convinced of your ill character, despite my protests. I'm verra sorry, Mr. Rosemoor, but as long as I remain under their protection, I havena a choice."

"You can choose to believe whatever you wish about me, Lady Brenna."

"I thought ye to be an honorable man, a gentleman whose name was falsely tarnished."

"But you no longer believe that to be true?" he challenged.

"I . . . I dinna ken what I believe anymore." Uncertainty shadowed her eyes.

"Then we've nothing more to say, have we? I bid you a good day." He bowed stiffly and turned toward the pair of doors leading back inside.

"Wait."

He froze, one hand on the handle. Closing his eyes, he took a deep, ragged breath.

"I must be daft, but I *do* believe ye an honorable man. Despite what they say, despite what I've seen today with my own eyes . . ." Her voice trailed off, and he turned to face her.

A battle raged within him, nearly taking his breath away. Selfishly, he wanted her to believe him, to believe *in* him. He craved her affection with a sharp, near-painful desperation. But what would it cost her? Her reputation. Her father had forbidden her to associate with him, and Ballard had told him that, despite his own protestations, his father's resolve on the matter was firm. What price would she pay if she disobeyed him? What price would he pay at her father's hands?

"I know what kind of man ye are, Colin. A good man, a—"

"You know nothing of my character, Brenna," he interrupted, crossing the flagstones in three strides. He had to do this. There was no alternative.

Brenna took a step backward, her lower back colliding with the terrace's stone railing as his lips descended upon hers. Blindly she clutched at the stones behind her in desperation as his impatient mouth roughly possessed hers, his long, lean body pressed against her. At first she resisted, her lips held firm. Her heart beat furiously against her breast as the delicious sensation of his heat—his power—warmed her, softening her defenses until at last she yielded to his demands, opening her mouth against his.

It was invitation enough. He groaned, a near primal sound, then roughly grasped her shoulders and drew her closer as his tongue invaded her mouth, searching, seeking. His purely male scent invaded her consciousness—tobacco, saddle leather, sandalwood. His mouth tasted of brandy, intoxicating her.

Dear Lord, whatever was he doing to her? She found herself kissing him back, arching herself against him. Her limbs felt weak; her hands trembled by her sides. A strange warmth pooled in her belly, spreading down to her thighs. Of their own volition, her hands stole up to clasp his neck, her fingers tangling in the silky waves that brushed his collar as she drew him closer still, till she could hear the pounding of his heart over the din of her own.

A soft moan of regret escaped her lips when he retreated, his teeth nipping at her bottom lip. A second later his mouth found the pulse that fluttered wildly in her neck, his lips searing her sensitive skin with a moist, wicked heat. A shiver worked its way from the base of her spine up to her shoulders, and she couldn't stop herself from crying out his name.

At once he stiffened, and she felt a rush of cool air as he stepped back from her. Mercifully, he held her shoulders as she swayed against the railing, her fingers once more seeking the stones' support. She blinked rapidly, attempting to regain her senses, to calm her racing heart.

At last Colin released her, one hand moving to wipe his mouth. She could only stare silently as he visibly fought for composure, his changeling eyes darkening to a stormy gray.

"That's what kind of man I am," he bit out at last, his voice as flinty as iron. "The kind who would kiss you senseless, with no offer of marriage to follow. Who would try his damnedest to take what he wants from you, and then walk away without looking back. You would do well to listen to your parents."

Brenna inhaled sharply. "I . . . I don't believe ye," she stammered.

"It's quite immaterial to me what you believe, though I am sorry for deceiving you. Good day." With that, he turned and left her there on the terrace, clutching the stone railing for dear life.

"You seem distracted, Margaret. You've barely touched your dinner. Are you feeling unwell, my dear? Margaret?"

Brenna looked up at her mother in surprise. Whatever had she asked her? "I . . . I beg your pardon. I was lost in my thoughts for a moment there."

"I asked if you were feeling unwell. You look a bit pale, doesn't she, Hugh?"

Hugh set down his fork and examined her across the width of the table. "Hmm, perhaps." He reached for his glass of wine and continued to eye her critically over the rim before taking a long draught of the purplish liquid.

"Nay, I'm feeling well enough," she answered at last. "Just a bit tired, 'tis all. I havena slept well these past few nights." Sleep had eluded her as she lay in bed and remembered the sensation of Colin's lips against her mouth, the feel of his long, lean body pressed against hers. Try as she might, she could not erase his cruel words from her memory. "That's what kind of man I am," he'd said, and with each passing day, she'd allowed herself to believe more and more that he had spoken the truth. Hadn't she seen him only the night before at the opera, in the pit amongst the *demimonde*? Rumor had it that he'd left before the end of the second act with the infamous Mrs. Trumball-Watts, reputed to be the most beautiful, most alluring Cyprian, their heads bent in an intimate tête-à-tête.

Brenna hadn't witnessed his departure herself; she'd refused to allow her gaze to stray his way once Hugh had pointed out his presence directly below their box. Yet every caller they'd received since had prattled on about it endlessly, speculating on his relationship with Mrs. Trumball-Watts and gleefully predicting the man's next misstep. Brenna had finally forced herself to ignore the idle chatter, resorting at last to doing sums in her head to distract herself. It had worked well enough.

"Well, dear, perhaps we should call on the apothecary for a sleeping tonic. This is not the time for your spirits and appearance to suffer now, is it?" Her mother looked to Hugh with a mysterious smile.

Brenna's eyes narrowed suspiciously. "Whatever do ye mean?"

"I'll let Hugh tell you the fine news."

"Of course." Hugh set down his glass, exchanging a smile with their mother. "It seems that you've managed to capture the attention of Lord Thomas Sinclair. Just today he declared his intent to pay you court, and I've indicated our family's approval."

Brenna felt the few bits of food she'd managed to eat pitch about her stomach. Not Lord Thomas, of all people. Despite his charming manners and good looks, he made her more than a wee bit uncomfortable.

"Just think, Margaret," her mother interjected, "a duke's son, even if he *is* a younger son. Truly, we could not have hoped for better. You should be very pleased."

"Just what do ye mean, 'pay court'?" Brenna asked, her voice laced with hesitation.

"Why, escort you to balls and the like, take you riding in the park." Her mother waved one hand in the air. "That sort of thing. I vow you'll find it pleasurable enough. And if all goes well, I'll expect an offer of marriage in a fortnight at most. From what I hear, the man's quite smitten, isn't he, Hugh?"

"He is, indeed. He finds your spirit and intelligence refreshing, and never was I more glad to hear it. I wasn't sure we'd find a man of such means who would find your . . . ahh, unique nature so very acceptable. But, there it is."

"We will be delighted with such a match. Why, only last week your father was lamenting his diminishing allies amongst the powerful Whigs. Think what this connection would do for our family—the Duke of Eston your father-in-law!" Lady Danville's eyes positively glowed with excitement. "And, of course, his courting you will keep Mr. Rosemoor away."

Hugh shook his head. "I just don't understand what's become of Colin Rosemoor. For many years he was a good friend, yet now he forces me to choose sides. I'm afraid I cannot find any truth in his allegations against Sinclair. It would seem that he only seeks to lay blame on others for his own misdeeds. As distasteful as the notion is, I'm afraid I haven't a choice but to sever our friendship."

Lady Danville nodded in agreement. "You must. Your name cannot bear the association. I only feel sorry for his family, such lovely people."

Brenna fidgeted in her seat, wishing the conversation would come to an end. She had heard more than enough.

"Anyway, enough about Rosemoor," Hugh said, as if reading Brenna's mind. "I've some news of my own, fine news, at that."

"Do tell," Lady Danville demanded with an eager smile.

"We shall soon be celebrating my own nuptials."

Lady Danville raised one hand to cover her mouth as she suppressed an almost-girlish giggle. "Hugh, how lovely."

"Isn't it? It's well past time I take a wife, and the most enchanting young lady has accepted my offer."

"Well? Aren't you going to tell us who the young lady is? Wait, let me guess." Lady Danville pursed her mouth thoughtfully. "Lady Amanda Rutherford? No, wait. Miss Cecily Baker?"

Hugh shook his head, clearly enjoying the sport.

"Surely she's a diamond of the first water. Lady Bettina Wallingford?"

"Wrong again, but she is indeed a diamond. Shall I tell you?"

"Please do," Brenna said, finding her voice at last. "We canna stand the suspense."

"Miss Honoria Lyttle-Brown," he answered, his voice filled with obvious pride. "An unexpected surprise, indeed. We've only recently become so well acquainted, but I knew at once that we would suit. No sense in wasting time with a lengthy courtship."

Honoria Lyttle-Brown. The name sounded so familiar, yet Brenna could not place it.

"Oh, Hugh, how positively delightful." Lady Danville clapped her hands together. "Such a lovely, charming young lady she is. And to think, she came so very close to accepting Colin Rosemoor."

Brenna inhaled sharply. So *that's* where she had heard the name. She was the woman Colin had intended to marry, the woman who had withdrawn her affection after his expulsion from White's. And now Miss Lyttle-Brown was marrying Hugh? Very curious, indeed.

"Thank goodness Mr. Rosemoor's true character revealed itself when it did, before an agreement had been reached," her mother continued. "Her parents must be *so* relieved."

"Her father is indeed very pleased with our match, if I might say so myself." Hugh was as puffed up and cocky as a rooster. Something about the whole situation just didn't sit well with Brenna.

Her mother turned toward her with a smile. "Well, Margaret, perhaps I should hope for a double wedding?"

"Nay," she blurted without thought.

"No?" her mother asked with a scowl. "Pray tell me you are not back to that ridiculous notion that you should return to that . . . that dreary pile of stones in Scotland? I didn't think you as ungrateful as that, after everything your dear father has done for you here—after everything we've all done for you, all the sacrifices we have made."

"I *am* grateful, Lady Danv—"

"Mama."

"Mama, I meant. Truly I am. But ye must see that I dinna belong here, that I dinna fit in here."

"You don't fit in because you make no effort to fit in, Margaret. You sit outside and stare at the night sky when you are meant to be in drawing rooms and ballrooms, enjoying the company of others. When a gentleman does manage to engage you in conversation, you speak of crops and livestock, unwomanly topics at best. Worse still, you insist on going about regaling people with outlandish tales of brutality in Sutherland, as if anyone should care about—"

"They *should* care." Brenna rose, her cheeks inflamed.

"Bah. I still cannot believe you spoke of such vulgar matters at Lady Hampton's soiree. I asked your father to have a word with you about it."

"And he has. Aye, I assured him I will be more discreet in my efforts from now on, but I shan't remain silent on the matter, not when the livelihood of so many are at stake on the whim of an English landlord."

"Well, in Hampton's case, you might have saved your breath," Hugh interjected, a wry smile curving his lips. "He carelessly lost his Highland property in a hand of cards, you know."

Brenna frowned. "No, I didna realize that was so."

"Indeed, it is. Perhaps he was simply eager to unburden himself of such unproductive land. Whatever the case, it is no longer his worry. But what you'll find most interesting is the news of who now holds the deed to Hampton's lands."

"Oh?" she asked, near breathless with anger. As if it mattered. One absentee landlord was as bad as the next, particularly if he were English.

"The new landlord is none other than Colin Rosemoor," he answered, his smile near triumphant.

All the breath left Brenna's body in a rush.

"Though whether or not he won the deed fairly

and legitimately is still being hotly debated," he continued. "What *is* certain is that he'll clear the land to fund his debts. A shame, isn't it?"

Brenna sank back onto the velvet-covered chair. While her mind fought to grasp the unthinkable, Hugh and her mother stared back at her with victorious smiles, clearly taking pleasure in her discomfort.

She rose again, this time unsteadily. "If you'll excuse me," she said. *I think I'm going to be ill,* she added silently, then fled to the sanctuary of her bedchamber.

As soon as the door shut behind her, Brenna hurled herself onto the bed. Hera jumped up beside her, licking her arm with a rough tongue. Brenna heaved a sigh, then pulled herself to a seated position, settling the cat into her lap.

"It canna be true, Hera. Can it? Holding Hampton's lands and not telling me? Why ever would he do such a thing?"

The cat stared silently at her in reply, her nose twitching.

"I'm a fool, aren't I? Aye, look at me, talking to a cat." She stroked the soft, gray fur behind Hera's ears. "But you're not just any cat, are ye? You're the only friend I have here, save Jane Rosemoor, and I canna talk to her about her brother now, can I?"

Brenna shook her head. Of course she couldn't talk to Jane about such matters, much as she'd like to. She'd have to find the answers for herself. And to think, she'd wasted her time at Lord and Lady Hampton's soiree, going on and on about the Clearances as if they'd cared. Lord Hampton had rid himself of his estate, passing it to a man more in need of funds than he was. Of course Colin would clear the land. How else would he fund his debts?

"Which is precisely why he never mentioned winning the land to me," she concluded aloud. "He was well aware of my feelings on the matter. Ooooh, the black-hearted rogue. Hera, if ever that man comes near me again, ye have my full permission to scratch out the scoundrel's eyes."

Somehow, she would learn the truth. And then perhaps she'd scratch out his eyes herself.

She set Hera carefully on her feet, then retrieved her leather-bound chart book from her writing desk. "Come, Hera. Let's go to the garden and chart the skies. I think some fresh air will do us both good, don't ye?"

'Twas certainly better than sitting here, allowing Colin Rosemoor to occupy her thoughts.

# Chapter 8

"No, it cannot be true. Come now, Lady Margaret, such violence?" Lady Bertram lowered her quizzing glass and shook her head, the ribbons on her lace cap dancing merrily with the movement. "Sir George would have mentioned it to me, wouldn't you have, dear? He knows I have a fondness for keeping abreast of current affairs. I'm especially concerned about the plight of those unfortunate members of lesser society."

"True, true, indeed," Sir George answered, patting his wife's hand. "Lady Bertram is a true philanthropist at heart. No, I am sure it cannot be as bad as the young lady claims, my dearest. You may rest easy on that count. And even if it were, it isn't really our place to meddle, is it? Haven't we concerns enough of our own, closer to home? The rookeries and such. It's no longer safe for people of quality to venture near the East End."

Brenna felt a flush climb up her neck in response to the ignorant words, spoken so carelessly. If Lady Bertram was a philanthropist, then Brenna was the

Queen of England. She took a deep, calming breath before speaking. "Ye must excuse me, Sir George, but I can assure ye I speak naught but the truth. And if Lord Stafford's own peers won't speak out against such atrocities, who will?"

"Why should the English interfere? It sounds as if most of the atrocities you speak of are committed by Scots, against Scots. Isn't that so?" Sir George asked, stroking his whiskers.

"Aye, in some cases, but Stafford is no Scot. Besides, the English crown has never before hesitated to interfere where Scots are concerned. Why ever should they start now?"

"Well, I never," Lady Bertram huffed. "The impertinence—"

"Lady Margaret's convictions are charming, are they not, Sir George?" Lord Thomas smiled down at Brenna, placing one hand possessively on her shoulder.

"Yes, charming, indeed," Sir George replied at last, clearly not at all charmed.

She certainly hadn't meant to be charming. It was unimaginable that the English remained so blind to the news of the Clearances—so disinterested.

"Lady Margaret, I've yet to hear you entertain us on the pianoforte. Might I convince you to do so?" Lord Thomas moved toward the polished case in the room's corner. "Nothing would give me greater pleasure."

Brenna forced a bright smile. "I'm afraid I dinna play, Lord Thomas."

"Don't play?" Lady Bertram gasped. "Surely you jest. Come now, we don't expect perfection. Just a light tune will suffice."

"Truly, I canna play at all. I'm afraid I havena an ear for music."

"Balderdash," Lady Bertram exclaimed. "Why, even the simplest girl can learn to plunk out a few notes. How *do* you occupy your time, then? Do you paint? Write poetry?"

The evening was beyond hope. She might as well tell the truth. "I enjoy astronomy a great deal."

Lady Bertram's brows rose in astonishment. "Astronomy?" She practically whispered the word, as if it were too vulgar to say aloud.

"Yes, charting the night sky—the positions of the stars and planets and such. I havena a telescope here, not yet, but at Glenbroch I've a tower observatory, and—"

"Speaking of such things, Lady Margaret," Lord Thomas entreated, moving stealthily to her side, "perhaps you'll join me out on the terrace. I confess to sheer ignorance where astronomical matters are concerned. Perhaps you can help set me to rights?"

Brenna sighed, weighing her options. Either she could remain here in Sir George and Lady Bertram's drawing room, suffering their censure while her parents remained obliviously engaged in their own conversation across the room with Lord Thomas's brother Simon, the Marquess of Everton. Or she could accept Lord Thomas's invitation and join him on the terrace. As unappealing as that option seemed, it was far less so than the former, at least at present. Reluctantly she nodded, taking the arm that Lord Thomas offered.

Lord Thomas tipped his head toward his aunt and uncle. "If you'll excuse us."

She could sense the couple's relief as she followed

Lord Thomas across the room, past her parents, who smiled encouragingly at her, and through the open set of double doors. He led her to a bench, then stood opposite her, leaning indolently against the terrace's railing.

Brenna looked past his shoulder, her gaze settling on the moon, but Lord Thomas shifted, blocking her view in an attempt to gain her attention.

"I hope you won't hold my aunt and uncle's behavior against me," he said, his eyes lit with amusement.

No doubt he *would* find it amusing. "Nay, of course not. I'm sure they are lovely people," she lied, feeling suddenly charitable. Truly, their reaction wasn't so different from the rest of the *ton*'s, save the Rosemoors and the Mandevilles—two families that Lord Thomas never missed an opportunity to disparage.

Why, just last night she'd accompanied Jane Rosemoor to dine with Lord and Lady Mandeville. While she still couldn't help but wonder about the nature of the marchioness's relationship with Colin, Brenna had to admit she found the woman exceedingly pleasant, and her husband equally so. After their meal, they'd retired to the drawing room, where Brenna had found herself easily chatting with Lady Mandeville about horses and livestock, and then just as easily discussing crop irrigation and rotation with the marquess. Lord Mandeville himself owned a small estate in Scotland, in the lowlands. Indeed, he spoke of his time spent there with great fondness, and she'd been delighted to hear him talk about the horses he'd bred from Galloway stock.

The evening's conversation had seemed rather

unexceptional, though Brenna could only imagine the vapors Lady Danville would suffer had she heard such "unladylike" talk. Indeed, it had likely been the most enjoyable evening she'd experienced out in society since her arrival in London. She'd said as much to Lord Thomas in the carriage as they'd made their way to the Bertrams' town house in Cavendish Square, and she'd watched in morbid fascination as his handsome face morphed into an ugly, derisive sneer.

"You should choose your friends more wisely," was all he had said in reply. His voice had held a tone of menace, of barely restrained malice, that she had never before recognized. Brenna shuddered even now at the memory. She raised her gaze to his face, wondering just what malevolence lurked beneath the attractive, boyish façade. Only then did she realize he was speaking to her.

"Well, what do you say?" he was asking. "Might I serve as your escort?"

She shook her head in confusion. "Ye must excuse me, Lord Thomas. Pray tell, escort me where?"

His smile disappeared. "My brother's masquerade," he said curtly, glowering at her. "I was saying that it has become an annual tradition and that I would be honored to act as your escort. Ballard suggested it, so your family's approval is already secured."

Was there even any point in demurring?

"You haven't any objections, have you?"

"Nay, of course not." She sighed, feeling defeated.

"I'm glad to hear it. I find masked balls to be highly entertaining, as I'm sure you will. Always a certain . . . leeway of sorts with propriety at a masquerade. Quite liberating, really." He reached for her hand and brought it to his lips.

Brenna fought the urge to recoil. A shudder ran down her arm, causing her hand to tremble.

"Have no fear; I won't ravish you here on my aunt's terrace, not with your parents looking on." His rakish smile had returned, as if he'd misinterpreted her reaction and found encouragement in it.

"I canna say I thought ye would, sir."

"Not that I wouldn't take great pleasure in it. I like your spirit, Lady Margaret. Or shall I call you Brenna? Ballard tells me that is what you call yourself, and I must say, it suits. A fiery name for a passionate woman. I think you'll find we have much in common, Brenna."

"Perhaps," she said noncommittally, snatching back her hand. "Shall I point out a constellation or two, Lord Thomas? Look, over there." She pointed beyond his shoulder, to the cluster of stars above the trees. "'Tis—"

"Oh, I didn't really want to talk about stars and such nonsense. It was simply an excuse to escort you outside. Tell me, what sort of costume will you wear to the masked ball?"

"I havena any idea, sir. Whatever Lady Danville thinks best, I suppose."

"Mmm, a serving wench, perhaps? Or a mermaid. Yes, that would please me immensely." His eyes nearly glowed with heat as his gaze slid across her body, making her feel positively unclothed. "I'd love to see you in a gauzy gown, the color of the sea. To match your eyes. And how would you see me? A pirate? Or perhaps a prince? What would set your blood on fire, Brenna?"

"'Tis a wee bit chilly. I think I'd like to go back inside now, if ye don't mind."

"Of course. How cruel of me, going on in such a vein when we cannot yet act on our desires. It's much too tempting, isn't it? Perhaps at the masquerade we'll find some real solitude, without fear of discovery."

Brenna's stomach lurched. *Not bloody likely,* she thought. She didn't know what games they were playing, her brother and Lord Thomas. Whatever they were, she would play right along, never letting them know she possessed far more intelligence than they credited her with. But she would make it her mission to ensure that she was never alone with Lord Thomas—at least not where there was no fear of discovery. She disliked him, distrusted him, but it was more than simply finding him objectionable or unpleasant. She recognized an aura of danger about him that she thought wise to heed.

And more pressing, just what did that say about her brother by association? Doesn't the company one keep speak volumes about a person's character? If so, Hugh's character just sank a good deal further in her estimation.

Colin glanced both ways before ducking into the alleyway beside the curiosities shop. Sir Nigel Portman stood waiting, cloaked in shadows and wringing his hands nervously, heavy beads of perspiration dotting his forehead.

Colin stepped close to the man, speaking softly. "Have you any news, old friend?"

"Indeed, though I don't think you'll like what I have to tell you. Sorry news. Sorry news, indeed."

"Well, go on, then." Colin grew impatient. He didn't want to risk being seen in Nigel's company. If he meant to gain any useful information, it was imperative that it appear as if their long-standing friendship had reached an impasse, that the two no longer kept polite company. Otherwise, no one would dare speak openly in Nigel's presence. Colin reached for his pocket watch, checking the time.

"Hugh Ballard," Sir Nigel muttered.

Colin froze, the watch clutched tightly in his palm. "What do you mean, Hugh Ballard?"

"If what my man at White's tells me is correct, then there are rumors that Hugh Ballard was involved in your ruination, along with Lord Thomas Sinclair."

Colin shook his head, his insides twisted into a painful knot. "Not Ballard. I don't believe it. Besides, he was away from Town, in Sussex at the time. How could he be involved?"

"Trust me when I say I was equally stunned at the news. Ballard has been our friend for many years, and a good one at that. I wouldn't have thought him capable of it. But my man vows he heard another waiter boasting of his own involvement in the scheme, claiming that Sinclair and Ballard had struck some sort of bargain to ruin you."

"Was he certain he heard them speak my name? God knows they could have been speaking of any number of men, with the way Sinclair goes about making enemies. What reason could Ballard have for wanting to ruin me? I've done nothing against him."

Sir Nigel shrugged. "I do not know the details. Yet my man feels certain that Ballard was indeed involved."

A white-hot rage flowed through Colin's veins. "Damn that bastard to hell."

"I've one more thing to add, old boy, and it's equally unpleasant."

Colin flinched. "It can't get much worse than this, can it? Please, go on."

"Have you heard the news of Miss Lyttle-Brown's recent engagement?"

"Her engagement? Is that all? So Sinclair finally managed to win over Honoria. Well, he's welcome to her, faithless chit."

"It's not Sinclair who has won your fair maiden's hand."

"No?"

"No. It's none other than Hugh Ballard."

Colin clenched his hands into fists. "And there you have it. Motivation. The bloody bastard ruined me for a woman. A *woman*," he spat out as bile rose in this throat. "And not even such a fine specimen, if her easy defection is any indication."

"You needn't give up so easily, Rosemoor. Perhaps Mandeville can aid you in some way. At the very least he could speak with Mr. Lyttle-Brown and tell him our suspicions."

"I will not go to Mandeville for help."

"But with his connections and influence—"

"I will do this myself or not at all. Besides, I've come to believe Honoria not worth the effort."

Nigel shoved his hands into his pockets. "And what of your name? Isn't your name worth the effort?"

"I'm beginning to think it isn't. What's the use? To get back into the good graces of the *ton,* where gentlemen betray one another over a woman? Where gossip is more prized than truth? Ballard was a friend." He almost choked on the word. They'd been boyhood chums, since their carefree days at Eton where they had been housemates—Colin, Nigel, Hugh Ballard, and William Nickerson.

"Ballard *was* a friend," Nigel said, "and there is no excuse for his behavior. I'll admit, I always thought he had a bit of a mercenary streak, though he hid it well. But this? No, I never would have thought any of us capable of this."

Colin's gaze strayed toward the busy street, which was teeming with pedestrians. Unlike the wide streets of Mayfair, the narrower streets of Cheapside were filled with plainly dressed folk, going this way or that with a purpose beyond being seen as fashionable. "I wish Nickerson were in Town," he said, returning his attention to Nigel. "He could be of great use to me right now. If anyone could wrestle an admission from Ballard, it would be him. Everyone trusts Nickerson."

"Where is Nickerson, anyway?"

"Somewhere on the Continent, nursing the broken heart that my sister Jane inflicted upon him last summer."

"Ah, yes, now I remember. Poor chap. I still don't know why she refused him."

"Nor I. My sister seems hell-bent on remaining a spinster. Whatever her reasons, I assume they are sound. Anyway, I should be on my way. No use risking being spied together for idle talk about my sister's lack of prospects."

"True. I'm only sorry my information isn't of more use."

"You've identified who and why, which is significantly more information than I had before. I'm very grateful for your assistance. There are few men left I can trust."

"You're sure you won't ask Mandeville?"

"I'm sure." Colin's chest tightened uncomfortably.

"So be it, then." Nigel nodded, though his disapproval was evident in his expression. "It's your decision, after all. I'll let you know if I acquire additional information that might be of better use."

"Very good. Thank you, Nigel."

"You owe me," Nigel said with a wink, then turned and made his way back to the bustling street, disappearing amongst the crowd within seconds.

Blast it. How could he have been so blind? So stupid? Hell, he'd sent Ballard over to talk to Honoria, to plead his case, just after the debacle at White's. He'd played right into his hands like a fool. Now that he reflected on it, Ballard had seemed a bit edgy, tense, not quite himself that day. Of course he would have been—like Judas, he'd just betrayed one of his closest allies, and not for thirty pieces of silver, but for a faithless woman.

He wouldn't let him get away with it, that was for certain. He would get a confession from Ballard one way or another, if it was the last thing he did.

*Brenna.* Her name immediately leapt to mind, making his heart accelerate. Ballard was Brenna's brother. He spent a good deal of time in her company at Danville House. Colin had agreed to avoid her company, but that was before he had realized that Ballard had effectively thrown him to the wolves. Now all bets were off, especially if he could winnow some useful information out of Brenna. And perhaps he could. Oh, he wouldn't risk her reputation, he wasn't a rogue like her brother was.

He would continue to avoid her in public. But privately?

Everton's masquerade. Surely she would attend. Everton was Sinclair's brother, after all, and Sinclair was now openly courting her. A masquerade would afford Colin the perfect opportunity to speak with Brenna without anyone recognizing him. He would use Sir Nigel's invitation—he and Colin were similar enough in size and build that, in mask and costume, he could pass for his friend. The plan formulated immediately in his mind, and he sighed in relief as he ducked back into the thronging crowd and headed toward his curricle.

It might work. It was bloody well better than sitting around doing nothing. Even if it didn't work, at least he'd get to enjoy Brenna's company, and that thought alone put a smile on his lips for the first time in days.

He took up the ribbons and set off toward his lodgings, his lustful imagination racing ahead as he tried to guess just what sort of costume she would don. Whatever she chose, she was sure to look lovely, and his starved eyes could barely wait to feast upon her. *Soon.* In three days time. He only hoped the waiting wouldn't drive him mad.

# Chapter 9

"Hold still, mum. Nearly done." Celeste took the last remaining pin out from between her teeth and tucked it into Brenna's hair, securing a delicate white blossom into place on the crown of her head. At last Celeste stepped back, allowing Brenna to view herself in the looking glass.

"There you are. Lovely, if I might say so."

Brenna blinked, staring back at her own reflection in astonishment. Celeste had worked a miracle with a scattering of fragrant phlox and some pins. In utter fascination, she ran her hands along the snow-white bodice, across the rough silver filigree adorning the gown's high waist, and down the soft folds of the draped skirts. Fingering the delicate armlets that encircled one arm, she turned slightly, enough to see the silvery feathered wings attached to her back, and smiled. She had thought the siren's costume looked somewhat silly, hanging limply on the hook. But now, as she admired the Grecian-styled gown taken together with her flowing, flower-adorned hair, she had to admit it was truly a masterful piece of craftsmanship.

"Oh, I almost forgot. Your mask." Celeste handed her a matching white-feathered mask, also trimmed in silver filigree.

Brenna slipped it over her face, glad for the anonymity it would afford. If her ball gowns were a bit indecorous, then this gown was positively indecent. It clung to each and every curve, affording one a fairly accurate assessment of her figure. She felt . . . exposed. Vulnerable. Undressed.

Shrugging off her misgivings, she turned to Celeste with a smile. "I thank ye, Celeste. You've outdone yourself tonight. No doubt Lord and Lady Danville will be pleased."

Celeste returned Brenna's smile. "You'd best hurry, then, mistress. I hear the coach in the drive. They'll be waitin', no doubt."

Brenna nodded, then hurried down the sweeping stairs. She only hoped the evening would prove to be far more pleasant than she'd imagined. She did not relish a night in Lord Thomas's company. Thankfully, even acting as her escort, he was entitled to no more than the two dances propriety allowed. Perhaps the ball would not be so disagreeable. Jane Rosemoor would be there, she remembered, brightening at the thought. Jane would see that Brenna was not in want of appropriate partners; it was her nature to see that those around her were comfortable and happy, and Brenna was tremendously grateful for her friend—truly her only friend in all of London.

"There you are, daughter," Lord Danville called out, turning toward the stairs as Brenna approached. Lady Danville followed suit, along with Hugh and

Lord Thomas, their mouths slightly agape as they all stared up at her.

Goodness, did she really look so different? She paused on the landing with one hand resting on the carved newel post, wishing that someone would say something, anything at all. She was being judged, no doubt. Would they find her lacking?

Lord Thomas, wearing a ridiculous-looking frilly shirt, tricorn hat, and eye patch in what must be a pirate's costume, broke the heavy silence at last. "Exquisite," he said, his one-eyed gaze raking down the length of her, and Brenna felt a flush heat her cheeks.

Hugh, like his father beside him, wore a simple dark dress coat—nothing out of the ordinary—but carried a black satin mask in one hand. He eyed her critically, then nodded. "Indeed she is exquisite. Astonishing, isn't it?"

Lady Danville cast a scowl in his direction. "Not at all. Why, it's just as I supposed. That style simply suits her better than the current fashions do." She smoothed a hand down her own colorful gown— a gypsy, Brenna supposed, judging by the kerchief on her head.

"Hmm, so true, my dear. It does suit her well." Her father strode to Brenna's side and reached for her hand. "It's a shame she cannot wear her hair like this every day, isn't it, Harriet?" He placed a kiss on Brenna's knuckles, and the unconcealed pride that shone in his eyes nearly brought a tear to her own eyes. More than anyone else, this man was slowly stealing into her heart.

Lady Danville silently nodded her agreement, her own eyes shining brightly with a hint of dampness.

Lord Thomas cocked his head toward the door. "Well, then, shall we set off? I think we've managed to miss the opening quadrille."

"Yes, yes. Capital." Lord Danville offered his wife his arm as the butler pulled open the heavy door leading out.

The cool evening breeze caressed Brenna's cheek as she took Lord Thomas's arm and followed the party out to the waiting conveyance. As she settled herself inside the coach's dimly lit interior, Brenna's thoughts were unpleasantly drawn—not for the first time—to her unremembered past. How awful it must have been for Lord and Lady Danville to have their infant snatched from the cradle. How they must have suffered.

Still, it was near impossible for her to imagine that her parents, the Maclachlans of Glenbroch, had committed such an unforgivable crime. Had they been so desperate for a child that all rational thought had fled them? What other explanation was there?

"Be mindful of your wings, dear," Lady Danville chided, laying a hand on Brenna's wrist.

*Not a phrase one hears every day.* Brenna slid forward a bit on the smooth leather bench, twisting her torso ever so slightly. There she perched, a bit uncomfortably, but her wings remained out of harm's way.

At last settled, she looked up and saw Lord Danville watching her, a gentle, easy smile on his lined face. Brenna returned his smile, despite her heavy heart. No one deserved such misfortune as a stolen child. She chanced a glance at Hugh, sitting beside their mother and idly polishing his watch with a handkerchief. Had the Maclachlans supposed they were doing Lord and Lady Danville no grave ill, snatching their daughter instead of their son, their heir? Had they perceived daughters to be of so little value to the English?

Certainly English women did not enjoy the same rights and freedoms as their Scots counterparts. The worst of it was the way the English married off daughters without compunction, with no thought to their happiness. Marriage was simply a business arrangement, and daughters were bartered off like livestock. She found the practice appalling, and if Lord and Lady Danville thought to bargain her off in such a fashion, then they'd best think again.

Brenna winced as the coach swayed and Lord Thomas's elbow poked her uncomfortably in the ribs. She couldn't help but cast a scowl in his direction. More than anything, she hoped her parents could see through Lord Thomas's polite demeanor to the man who lay beneath. Lord Thomas might not be a pirate, but he was no doubt a scoundrel. Though the debacle with Colin Rosemoor had caused her to doubt her own instincts where men were concerned, she was certain that she was correct on this count. She sighed, turning her gaze toward the window, watching London's streets pass by in a muted blur.

*Colin Rosemoor.* She hadn't allowed herself to even *think* that name in so many days. Nay, the name alone brought up too many uncomfortable emotions. Confusion, anger, fear, resentment. And desire. Dear Lord, but she couldn't staunch it, not after that kiss. It coursed through her, unbidden, at the mere thought of the damnable man. She was a fool; a silly fool, no better than the giggling debutantes who populated Mayfair's best drawing rooms.

But if it were true that Colin had managed to cheat Lord Hampton out of his Highland estate, if he were truly the rightful owner of Hampton's lands, then she must confront him. She must demand that he act honorably for once in his life and leave the tenants undisturbed. He must *not* clear the land.

Brenna's musings were interrupted when the coach rolled to an abrupt halt before a yellow stone town house. The lilting sounds of an orchestra mingling with a multitude of voices floated across the drive on the breeze. More than two dozen people stood assembled on the walk, craning their necks and standing on their toes in anticipation, awaiting admittance.

"Ah, here we are," Lord Danville said. "A crush, as always."

"Nothing like a masked ball to attract the cream of the *ton* in droves, is there?" Lord Thomas reached for Brenna's elbow and helped her to her feet.

Aye, thought Brenna as she stepped down to the pebbled drive below. And, of course, with the cream of the *ton* in attendance, Colin Rosemoor most certainly would *not* be. Somehow she must find a way to speak with him. If not tonight, then soon. However would she manage it?


Colin handed his card to Everton's butler, then readjusted Nigel's gold signet ring. He was not used to wearing such adornments, and the ring felt heavy and constricting on his finger.

"Sir Nigel Portman," the butler announced, and

Colin smiled behind his mask as he stepped confidently into the crowded ballroom.

This would work. The plan was brilliant, and no one would see through his ruse. He'd arrived in Nigel's coach, wearing the man's ring and carrying his card. The only people who'd perhaps look sharply enough to see past the absurd costume and mask would be absent tonight.

Jane had taken to her bed late in the afternoon, complaining of some sort of malaise, and Lucy had just learned that she was increasing. He did not know the details—did not want to know them, really—but knew she had been feeling poorly the past few days. She would be home, abed, not venturing out into society, and particularly not to the home of Lord Thomas Sinclair's brother, not with her intense, and well-deserved, dislike of Sinclair.

He'd waited till the party was well underway before making his appearance, thinking that the alcohol consumed by Everton's guests by now would aid his deception.

Leaning against a wide marble pillar, he scanned the vast room, searching out his quarry. She was here. He felt it. But where? His gaze flitted across the room's occupants, many of whom were currently spinning about the dance floor in pairs, engaged in a waltz.

A footman brushed past his elbow, carrying a silver tray laden with flutes of champagne. Colin reached for a glass, draining it with one sharp flick of the wrist.

Not the finest vintage, but it would suffice. With a grimace, he pushed off the pillar and moved toward the row of sideboards that lined the far wall, placing the empty glass on the plum-colored satin. When he looked up, he saw a pair of young women headed his way, eager smiles on their faces below their masks. Who were they? Debutantes most likely.

Blast it. He had no need to engage in conversation with anyone save Brenna. He readjusted his hat, further shielding his face from prying eyes, and turned away from the approaching women. He took two long strides back toward the dancing couples, shaking his head in frustration.

And then he saw her. All breath left his body, and he stopped short, rooted to the spot, unable to do anything but simply stare as his heart thrummed against his ribs.

Damnation. She was stunning. A siren, and how very fitting. Even with most of her face covered by a white feathered mask, he was entirely sure it was her. His gaze raked hungrily over her, admiring the way the soft, white folds of fabric clung to her body, concealing little. Even her feet, peeking out from the gown's hem, were nearly bare, encased in nothing save thin silver straps. Her hair, littered with tiny white blossoms, tumbled down her back in soft, reddish-gold waves, brushing against silvery feathered wings, giving her an otherworldly appearance. She looked like an angel and a goddess all at once, and the vision nearly made his head spin.

He took a deep breath, forcing himself to gain control of his lustful thoughts. As he watched, some cowhanded young dandy approached her with an exaggerated bow, then reached for her hand and led her amongst the waltzing couples.

"*Olé,*" a feminine voice called out, followed by a tittering of giggles.

With a groan, Colin turned toward the sound. The two debutantes who'd attempted to approach him moments ago now stood before him, smiling broadly.

"A matador?" the first young lady inquired, quite boldly, really.

"*Si, senorita*," he answered, sweeping into a deep bow.

"Very mysterious," debutante number two said. "Might we know your name, sir?"

He couldn't help but look past the girl's shoulder as Brenna twirled by with the dandy. When would this waltz end? He must somehow engage her for the next dance.

His attention was reluctantly drawn back to the two young ladies before him. Where were the chits' chaperones, anyway?

"Your name, sir?" the second girl repeated, her pale brows drawn into a scowl above her small silk mask.

"That would defeat the purpose of the mask, would it not? No name. Not tonight." He did not risk giving them Nigel's name. "If you'll excuse me." He bowed stiffly, just as two red-faced matrons descended upon the hapless pair, no doubt dragging them off to chastise them for such forward behavior. Deservedly so.

With a sigh of relief, he moved away, distancing himself from the crowd. Searching. The waltz had ended, and Brenna was nowhere to be found.

Suddenly the hair on the back of his neck stood on end. He quickly turned and found himself staring into a familiar pair of round, aquamarine eyes.

They widened in surprise, perhaps recognition. Her lips parted as if to speak.

Quickly, he reached for her hand and placed a kiss on her knuckles, inhaling her scent as he did so. Lavender and soap, so hauntingly familiar.

"Do not speak my name aloud," he said, his voice low.

Something flashed in her eyes—anger, perhaps. Yet she nodded her assent and allowed him to lead her onto the dance floor and pull her into his arms. Where she belonged, his foolish heart insisted. Would he never learn his lesson?

Brenna's heart swelled with emotion—surprise, anger, longing. For more than a full minute, she remained silent, keeping her gaze leveled on his shoulder. "Whatever are ye doing here?" she asked, finding her voice at last. "I didna expect to find ye here tonight."

"No, nor would my host. Perhaps we should adjourn to the rose garden for a brief stroll?"

She shook her head. "I dinna think it wise."

"Nonsense. The paths are well-lit, and there are a fair number of couples out enjoying the night air. It's perfectly within the means of propriety, I assure you."

"Still, I . . ." she faltered. She could broach the matter of Hampton's lands now, in the garden, and be done with it. It was near enough impossible to discuss such a vital matter while twirling about a ballroom, after all. "Verra well, sir."

With near-perfect timing, the waltz ended. Colin bowed, and Brenna dipped a curtsy in reply before taking his proffered arm and following him across

the marble floor and out one of several pairs of
French doors that were thrown open to the night.

Her anger mounted with each step. To think that
he hadn't seen fit to mention to her winning such
a parcel of land, knowing her home was near Fort
William, in the same immediate vicinity as Hampton's estate. Such an omission immediately spoke to
his guilt—he planned to clear the land. To pay off
his debts. Hugh had said as much, and it seemed
likely the truth. Hadn't her father said he was nearly
done up?

They walked in silence, following a path lit by
paper lanterns and perfumed with the heavy scent
of roses. Colin had been correct; no less than a
dozen couples joined them on the path, taking a
turn in the cool night air.

She raised one hand, suppressing a sneeze. The
feathers on her mask tickled her nose most uncomfortably. Would it be improper for her to remove it?
She hoped not, for it was beginning to chafe her,
even if it did lend a comfortable feeling of anonymity.
Without further thought, she lowered it. Perhaps it
would serve her well if word reached Lord Thomas
that she had been seen out strolling the gardens in
the company of a mysterious matador.

"Since I'm not to speak your name, whose company shall I tell my parents I shared, here in the
gardens, if they ask?"

"Sir Nigel Portman. A friend of mine. He was generous enough to allow me use of his invitation. And
his ring as well." He held up one hand, a gold signet
ring on his last finger glinting in the moonlight. "Besides, everyone knows of his great love of all things

Spanish. His mother was a Spaniard, the daughter of a famed bullfighter. Thus, the costume."

"Certainly an interesting choice," Brenna muttered, more closely examining the tight-fitting satin knee breeches and oddly styled coat adorned with rosettes. A wide-brimmed felt hat completed the look, along with a scarlet cloak fastened about his neck and tossed over one shoulder. He should look entirely ridiculous, and yet somehow he did not. Instead he appeared more muscular, more virile than she'd remembered.

She shook her head, refusing to allow her thoughts to stray that route. "Ye never answered my question. Why are ye here? It's clear ye were not invited."

"Because I must speak with you. I realize that our last meeting did not . . . ahem." He stopped, turning to face her, and pulled down his own mask, allowing it to hang against his knotted stock. "Our last meeting did not end on the best of terms. I must apologize for my behavior that day at the Mandevilles."

A flush stole up her neck, warming her cheeks. She did not want to discuss his kiss, or his motivations. It was best forgotten. "There is something I must speak to ye about as well," she said. "Something far more serious than your boorish behavior."

He rubbed one palm against his cheek. "Pray tell, Lady Brenna."

"There is the matter of Lord Hampton's Highland estate."

"What?"

"The Marquess of Hampton. Surely ye know the man. I'm told ye won a parcel of land from him at cards. The night ye were expelled from White's," she added.

"And what if I did? I never expected the man to honor the vowel."

"I dinna understand. Hugh said that—"

"Hugh?" Colin spat out the name. "What did Hugh Ballard say, the bastard? What new way did he find to impugn my name?"

"That you'd won the land and that ye planned to clear it. Hampton's lands border Glenbroch's, ye know."

"No, I didn't know that. Tell me, if I thought myself the rightful owner of such a parcel of land, whatever reason could I possibly have for not telling you about it?"

"As I said, because ye plan to clear the land. Ye know my thoughts on such matters."

Colin visibly blanched. A muscle in his jaw flexed before he spoke, his voice hard. "And this is what you think me capable of?"

"I . . . I don't know what I think."

"Let me assure you that if I had known this land bordered yours, I would have mentioned it to you. I assumed that Hampton would not honor the loss and therefore gave it very little thought."

Brenna's determination wavered. Perhaps he spoke the truth. "According to Hugh, Hampton considers ye the rightful owner. He waits for ye to claim the deed and clear the land. He's happy to be rid of the trouble, Hugh says."

"Hugh is a lying bastard."

"Hugh says the same of ye." Brenna tipped her chin in the air. "And so does my father." Even in the moonlight, she could see the hard glint in his eyes.

"Then why do you remain in my company?" he

asked, his hands balled into fists by his sides. "Surely it's beneath you to converse with me."

"Because I must. I implore ye not to clear the land. I beg of ye, do the honorable thing. Secure the deed. Ensure that the tenants keep their crofts."

A vein in his temple throbbed. "Why should I bother? Let Hampton deal with it."

"Because Hampton was never more than a disinterested landlord to begin with. It's obvious he wants to rid himself of the land, and the next man who finds the deed in his pile of winnings may have no qualms about clearing it. Ye have the opportunity to secure it."

He crossed his arms over the broad expanse of his chest, eyeing her sharply. "I ask you once more, why should I bother?"

Brenna swallowed hard, unable to look him in the eye. Dare she? She took a deep breath, then raised her unflinching gaze to meet his. "Because I'm asking ye to." She held her breath, awaiting his response. Would he do it, for her? Could she offer him anything in exchange that would tempt him, that would ensure his cooperation?

His smoldering gaze swept across her features, never leaving her face. Clearly a battle raged within him—a battle she desperately wanted to win. He was a gambling man, far more experienced at taking risks than she was. She knew she must lay all her cards on the table.

"I'll do whatever ye ask of me, Colin," she said, her voice almost a whisper. "*Anything*," she added suggestively, "if you'll do this for me."

She heard the sharp hiss of his breath and knew she had won.

# Chapter 10

In two long, purposeful strides, Colin closed the distance that separated them. "Does it mean so much to you, Brenna?" he asked, stroking her burning cheek with his thumb as he spoke. "That these people stay on their land? So much so that you'd offer yourself up in return? Do I correctly understand your suggestion?"

"Ye understand correctly, sir," she bit out through clenched teeth. "The Clearances must not come so close to home. I canna sit idly by and let it happen. Ye must understand that." She nearly choked on the humiliating words.

He regarded her silently for several seconds before replying. "And I cannot take what you offer me. You must understand that."

The heat rose in her cheeks.

"But I will do what you ask of me," he added softly, trailing his fingertips across the curve of her shoulder.

Brenna let out her breath in a rush. "I thank ye, Colin."

"But there *is* something I will ask of you in return. A favor. Nothing so demeaning as what you suggested. Still, it is a task you might find unpleasant."

"Tell me," she urged. Whatever it was, this unpleasant task, she would do it.

"A trusted source tells me that your brother, acting with Lord Thomas Sinclair, is responsible for my ruin. A card was planted in my pocket that night at White's. Sinclair's doing, no doubt. The two struck some sort of bargain. Do what you must— hide in the shadows if necessary—but try to learn the nature of their agreement. Help me expose them and restore my name."

Brenna shook her head in confusion. "I dinna believe it. Not Hugh. He might be somewhat . . . disagreeable, but set out to ruin a man he called his friend? Nay. I canna believe it. He's not as bad as that."

"Are you so certain of that?"

"Of course. I can believe anything of Lord Thomas, especially where ye are concerned. It is clear he dislikes ye intensely. But what would Hugh have to gain?"

Colin reached down to pluck a crimson blossom from the greenery. "Perhaps you've heard the name Honoria Lyttle-Brown?"

She gasped sharply as realization dawned on her at once. "Of course. Hugh's betrothed. The woman you'd hoped to wed."

"Exactly." He tucked the blossom into his lapel.

"Ye think he did this to gain her favor? To keep her from marrying ye, so he could have her for himself?"

"That is exactly what I have come to believe."

She wanted to deny that her brother was capable of something so dreadful, yet a nagging doubt kept her silent. Lord Thomas was certainly capable of such treachery; it only followed that his closest associates would be equally capable. She bit her lower lip, considering her options.

Betray her brother's trust and seek to discover the truth, unpleasant as it might be. Or do nothing, remain blindly loyal to a brother who likely set about to ruin a friend, simply to gain a woman's favor. Nay, the latter was unfathomable. She did not owe Hugh fealty. She barely knew the man, and all he'd done in their brief acquaintance was sneer at the Maclachlans, deride the way in which they had raised her, and force her into the company of the unbearable Lord Thomas Sinclair. Hugh had done her no favors. She didn't want to believe her own brother capable of something so dishonorable, so cruel and deceitful, yet she could not entirely discredit Colin's theory.

She nodded to herself, her mind made up. "Aye. Tell me precisely what I can do to aid you, Colin, and it will be done."

"Listen to their conversations when they think they are alone. Gain their confidence."

Brenna nodded. "I'll do my best."

"In the meantime, I'll speak with Lord Hampton and claim the deed. You have my word as a gentleman that the land will never be cleared."

"Verra well. I accept your word, and I shall do my part to help ye."

At once the tension so evident in his countenance softened, and his mouth curved into a wicked smile. "Though I must say, your original offer remains tempting. Perhaps I should reconsider."

Time to change the subject. No use engaging in

a flirtation—not now, not after she'd humiliated herself with such a scandalous proposition, one that he'd been mercifully quick to decline. "We should return inside. No doubt my escort will be searching for me by now."

"No doubt he will, and who could blame him?" Colin's attention was suddenly drawn beyond her shoulder. His eyes narrowed, and then he swiftly returned his mask to its place.

Brenna turned, expecting to see her brother, or worse still, Lord Thomas headed in their direction. Instead, a slight woman, her face hidden behind a peacock-feathered mask, bore down upon them.

"Lucy?" Colin said, his voice laced with incredulity.

"I should have known," the woman called out, increasing her pace. "Jane was afraid you might try something like this. She came by your lodgings today and saw that ridiculous costume of yours. She managed to put two and two together."

"Lady Mandeville?" Brenna asked, peering at the woman more closely. Indeed, it was the marchioness. Lucy, as Colin so intimately called her.

"You should not be here, Lucy."

Lady Mandeville removed her mask, her eyes flashing with anger. "Nor should you. At least I was invited."

"Where's Mandeville?"

"At his club. He had important parliamentary business to discuss with Lord Grey."

"Does he know you are here?"

"Of course not," she snapped. "Do you think he'd allow me out in Lord Thomas Sinclair's company without him?" Lady Mandeville turned toward Brenna and favored her with a tight smile. "You must excuse me, Lady Brenna. It's just that someone must keep Colin from mischief, and Jane was not feeling well enough to mind him tonight."

"Is Jane unwell?" Brenna asked. She had been sorely disappointed when Jane had not made an appearance at the ball.

"It's nothing that a night spent abed won't cure."

"Dammit, Lucy, you look pale. You should be abed yourself." Brows knit in obvious concern, Colin reached a hand up to Lady Mandeville's cheek.

Just as he'd touched *her* cheek earlier. Brenna felt like a fool for having thought the gesture a mark of his desire.

"I must get you home at once," he told Lady Mandeville, his brow knit with concern. "I won't be responsible for you taking such risks to your health on my account."

Whatever was he talking about? Lady Mandeville looked perfectly well. If anything, she looked positively radiant.

"Very well." Lady Mandeville nodded. "I'd hoped you would escort me home. Lord knows I've had a difficult enough time as it is, darting this way and that to avoid Lord Thomas while I searched you out. I should have known to look in the garden."

"In the garden, with a lovely young lady," he quipped. "Where else would I be?"

"You must pardon me for dragging him off like this, Lady Brenna. I assure you it's for his own good. I had specific instructions from Jane."

"Aye, of course," Brenna muttered.

Colin barely spared her another glance, so busy was he with securing Lady Mandeville's wrap about her shoulders. A sharp pang of jealousy shot through

Brenna, surprising her with its rancor. Would she never know what was going through Colin Rosemoor's mind? It appeared the man would forever remain a riddle to her. Perhaps for the best.

"If you'll excuse us, Lady Brenna," Colin said with a nod.

"Aye. Our business here is done. I bid ye both a good night."

Lady Mandeville reached for her hand. "I hope you'll come again to dine with us at Mandeville House, and bring some of your astronomical charts next time."

"I'd like that verra much, Lady Mandeville." Brenna returned the woman's warm smile, even as a million questioning thoughts raced through her mind.

She watched as Colin led Lucy away, back down the path, his fair head bent toward Lady Mandeville's golden one in quiet conversation.

When they'd gone perhaps twenty paces, Colin stopped. Brenna held her breath as he turned, back toward where she still stood. Even in the lantern-lit night she could see his eyes, locked with hers for a fleeting moment before he reached up and removed his hat. In a sweeping gesture, he brought the hat to his heart and bowed in her direction. She blinked hard, thinking she must have imagined the romantic gesture, for once she looked again, the pair had faded into the night's shadows.

Leaving her standing there in the garden, decidedly alone.

For a moment she simply stood there, looking toward the house, listening to the strains of the orchestra that mingled with the flutterings of greenery in the gentle breeze. She did not want to return to the party, though she knew she must. First she needed a moment to collect her thoughts. Just beyond a clump of bushes to her right sat an inviting wrought-iron bench. She would sit for a short spell, clear her head and allow her racing heart to slow. Nodding to herself, she hurried across the lawn, soft and springy beneath her feet. She might as well be barefoot, wearing nothing but straps of fabric on her feet.

Reaching for the bench's curved arm, she lowered herself to the seat, her gaze on the starry sky above. She inhaled deeply, the air warm and redolent with the surrounding blooms. A beautiful night. So much more lovely out here than inside Everton's ballroom. 'Twas good that Colin insisted she follow him out.

Just what was the truth behind Colin and Lady Mandeville's relationship? She couldn't believe that they were naught but the friends they claimed to be. There was something far more intimate about the way they looked at each other, the way they touched each other. Nay, it didn't strike her as sexual, but what other answer was there? And if it were true, why did it seem as though Jane Rosemoor was well aware of it, yet didn't give it overmuch thought?

She mentally shook away her misgivings. Colin's relationship with Lady Mandeville was his own business. All that mattered was that Colin upheld his end of the bargain and secured the deed from Lord Hampton, ensuring that the tenants would retain their homes and their livelihood.

"There you are," came Lord Thomas's voice, startling her. "Come out to look at the sky, have you?"

In an instant, she decided that simply agreeing with him was the safest course of action. "Aye," she called out, careful to keep her voice cheery. "'Tis a lovely night."

"Is it? I hadn't noticed." He reached for her hand and brushed a kiss across her knuckles. "Clever girl, wandering out here in hopes I would seek you out."

The arrogance of the man. She knew she must carefully consider her response. Were she to bristle visibly at his words—administer a severe dressing down, as he so desperately deserved—then he would only applaud her verve, call her "spirited." Instead, she should appear as dispirited as possible, as dull and lifeless as a statue.

Forcing her mouth to form a smile, she looked up to him appealingly. "Nay, I simply grew bored of the ball. I dinna enjoy such merriment, I'm afraid. Dancing, music . . ." She waved one hand in dismissal. "Such frivolous distractions."

"Which activities would you prefer to engage in, then?" His smile was lascivious. Did the man think of nothing save seduction? He was predictable, at best.

"I do like to read verra much," she murmured. "Astronomy, philosophy, the ancient Greek texts." She took a deep breath, prepared to play her trump card. "The Good Book."

He looked sufficiently taken aback, brow knitted, mouth pursed. "The Good Book?"

"Oh, ye know. The Bible. No better way to spend an evening, I always say, than reading a Psalm or two."

"Don't tell me you're a Papist?" For a moment, he looked horrified. Then his mouth curved into a grin. "For a moment there, I thought you might be serious. Everyone knows the Highland Scots are heathens; I shan't hold it against you, you know."

"Heathens?"

"Of course. It's the lack of education, I'm afraid."

She bit the inside of her lip so hard she tasted the faint tang of blood. Was he baiting her? Perhaps he was far brighter than she credited.

"Hmm," she murmured, as if she were carefully considering his words. "Perhaps it *'tis* the lack of education. I dinna ken."

He stared down at her, his eyes narrowing. "I should take you riding in the park tomorrow. I'm willing to wager you can sit a horse quite well."

"Oh, I canna ride. Not well, at least," she lied. She could just as easily ride sidesaddle as ride her mare with no saddle at all. Lord Maclachlan used to say she could ride long before she could walk.

"A stroll in the park, then?"

"I fear I've not the constitution for outdoor pursuits, Lord Thomas."

"Is that so?" He ran a hand through his perfectly coiffed, oiled hair. Instead of mussing it, the gesture only served to make it appear more neat and flawless than before. "I take it you prefer indoor pursuits, then? I'm quite fond of them myself, really. Come here." Taking her hand in his, he pulled her from the bench to stand before him.

Brenna flinched as he lightly trailed a gloved fingertip across her lower lip.

She wanted to strike the smug smile off his face. But she mustn't. "Sir, I must ask that ye do not touch me so intimately." Her voice was flat, devoid of emotion, even to her own ears. *Perfect.*

"Oh? And why not? You've chosen an ideal spot. We're hidden in shadows; no one can see us. I could kiss you now, and no one would know."

She sighed dramatically. "Ye can if ye must. But I willna enjoy it."

"Really?" He inched closer to her, so close she could feel his breath on her cheek. One hand moved stealthily around her shoulder to clasp her neck, as if he were going to embrace her. Instead, he grasped a handful of her hair in an iron grip, eliciting a sharp gasp from her lips.

"Unhand me, Lord Thomas," she hissed.

He only tightened his grasp, nearly pulling Brenna off her feet. "You listen to me, you little fool. I know what games you play. I'm well aware whose company you kept out here, so don't play the role of innocent milkmaid with me. Yes, I watched that amusing tableau unfold. How very sad for you that his little whore came along to drag him away in a jealous pique. No doubt she spread her legs for him as soon as they reached her carriage."

"Get your filthy hands off me this instant, ye bastard," she said through clenched teeth.

"Ah, now that's the Brenna I've come to admire. The little spitfire, not the Bible-reading bore." At last, he released her. Her scalp smarted, but she didn't dare raise a hand to the spot. She wouldn't give him the satisfaction.

He advanced on her, one long, aristocratic finger pressed against her breastbone. "You stay away from Colin Rosemoor, do you hear me? I can make the miserable chap's life a further hell if I take a notion to do so."

"His ruination was all your doing, wasn't it?"

"Do you think me such a fool as to answer that question? Suffice it to say that Colin Rosemoor got exactly what he deserved. You needn't fret over him. Hasn't he Lucy Mandeville for that? Now listen, and listen well. I'm a man who gets what he wants at all costs, and I want you. I *will* have you, with or without your consent. You've proven to be a worthy prize, indeed." He dipped his head, his mouth crushing hers with a bruising pressure.

In an instant, she raised one knee, connecting firmly with his groin.

He pulled away with a roar of pain.

"Mark my words, Lord Thomas. If ye ever lay a finger on me again, ye'll be joining ranks with the castrati."

His face still contorted with pain, he straightened to his full height. Towering over her, his dark eyes stared menacingly into hers. "I *will* tame you, and I'll enjoy every last minute of it."

"Ye might try," she said, her voice calm and cool, not betraying her agitation, "but ye certainly shan't succeed. Of that ye can be sure. Good night, Lord Thomas."

Without sparing him another glance, she turned and walked back toward the house, her head held high, even while her hands trembled violently at her sides.

Perhaps it was time to go home to Glenbroch.

And then she remembered the deal she'd struck with Colin. Nay, she couldn't go just yet. First things first. But soon, once Hampton's lands were secured, she could go home for good. She'd had altogether enough of London.

And more than enough of English *gentlemen*.

# Chapter 11

"Oh, Colin," Jane fretted, moving to perch on the curved arm of the sofa. "How could you be so foolish? Why would you do such a thing as that?"

"No one was the wiser. I have no idea why you felt the need to send Lucy there to fetch me away." He leaned against the window, the noon sun warming his back.

"Don't you think your state of affairs is bad enough as it is? Why risk discovery? What could you possibly have hoped to gain by going to the masquerade, uninvited?"

"I find your sisterly concern touching, Jane. Truly I do. But as much as it pains me to say it, it's really none of your concern."

Jane's eyes narrowed slightly. "Lucy says she found you entertaining Lady Brenna in the rose garden. Perhaps you will be so kind as to tell me what you're about. Lady Brenna is, after all, my friend."

Colin moved away from the window, striding across the room to the bookshelves that lined one wall, reaching all the way up to the moldings.

"Surely you aren't suggesting I was compromising the girl? In full sight of more than a dozen of Everton's guests?"

"I was insinuating no such thing, Colin," she said with a scowl. She let out her breath in a most unbecoming huff. "Must you always be so obtuse?"

"Me, obtuse?" He pulled a thin volume of poetry from the shelf and idly thumbed through the pages. "I don't know what you mean."

"Anyway, Colin, Mama tells me that you've been warned away from Lady Brenna by Lord Danville. Can this be true?"

Warmth climbed up his neck, heating his face. He kept his gaze on the book in his hands, refusing to meet Jane's questioning stare. "I told no one but Lucy, and I can't for the life of me figure out how this information came to be passed around so casually."

"Don't be cross. We're only trying to help you, you know."

"I don't need your help," he snapped, turning back to face her. Immediately he regretted his harsh words. "You must excuse me, Jane. I've been a bit short-tempered of late." He set the book down on the nearest shelf and crossed back to the window.

"You have every right to be short-tempered but no right to such secrecy. I hear what they are saying about you, and I know it cannot be true. At least, it can't all be true," she added wryly. "Anyway, I digress." She rose gracefully and came to stand before him, reaching up to readjust his cravat. "Lady Brenna," she said, her sapphire-blue gaze meeting his. "Have you formed an attachment?"

He shook his head. "No, but if it will satisfy your curiosity, I will tell you why I went to Everton's masquerade.

I needed to speak with Brenna, nothing more. I've come to learn that Hugh Ballard was somehow involved in planting that card in my pocket. He's in collusion with Sinclair. Brenna is Ballard's sister. I wanted to ask her help in discovering the truth, nothing more."

Jane planted her fists on her hips. "You asked Brenna to spy on her own brother?"

"Don't make it sound so nefarious. Besides, she agreed."

"I don't believe it. Why would she agree?"

"Suffice it to say she has her reasons. She and I struck a bargain, and if she wishes to divulge the terms of our bargain to you, then that's her affair."

"Then you haven't formed an attachment?"

"And what if I have? What good will come of it?"

Jane's mouth curved into a smile. "No good at all if you continue to court trouble, lurking about balls you aren't invited to."

"I say, how else do you suggest I gain an audience with the woman? Shall I take my cue from Lucy and sneak in through Brenna's bedchamber window in the dead of night?"

"No," Jane said, her voice rising. "I suggest no such thing. That situation called for desperate measures. This . . . this is altogether different. Perhaps we can figure out something far less drastic. Hmmm," she murmured, tapping a finger to her cheek, "I suppose it's all pointless, anyway, if you cannot restore your honor. Lord Danville will never accept your suit at present."

"Accept my suit? Who said anything about marriage?"

Jane's brow knitted into a frown. "Surely you want to marry her?"

"I think this conversation has gone far enough, Jane. Cease and desist your efforts at once, will you?"

"Are you certain? I could likely arrange some clandestine meetings, you know. Some secret assignations."

"And have you stopped to consider your friend's reputation? She's having a hard enough time as it is finding acceptance within the *ton*. Do you truly think you do her any service, encouraging her to risk her reputation with a man like me?"

"Oh, posh." Jane waved away his protest with a flick of one slender wrist. "A man like you? Not so very long ago you were considered a fine catch. A gamester, perhaps, but nothing worse than that. If you would let Mandeville—"

"Enough, Jane. I do not need your assistance, nor do I need Mandeville's. This discourse is done. Don't you have some pressing shopping to attend to? Important needlework? Anything?"

"Very well, Colin." She sighed dramatically, tucking an errant chestnut lock behind one ear. "I'll leave you to your solitude. But might I remind you, next time you plan to steal into a masquerade ball pretending to be someone else, you should not leave your costume lying about your front hall for anyone to see."

"Point taken, dear sister." He couldn't help but smile. Jane was a gem, no doubt about it. He wouldn't even bother to ask what she had been doing sneaking about his front hall while he was out.

"But a matador, Colin?" She retrieved her reticule and strode to the doorway, where she turned to face him with a grin. "I would give anything to have seen you in those satin knee breeches."

"I wasn't at leisure to be choosy. Besides, I think those breeches were quite flattering."

"Of course they were," Jane replied, her face all seriousness.

Her peals of laughter could still be heard, even after the door swung shut behind her.

Hearing the front door slam shut, Brenna ventured down the stairs, pausing at the landing to look about.

"Oh, there you are, Margaret." Her father appeared in the front hall, startling her.

"Was that Lord Thomas Sinclair?" she asked, frowning.

"Indeed it was. Fine young man. I've some capital news, daughter. Come, let us sit in my study, and I'll tell you before we must leave for Lady Welbourne's musicale."

Her stomach lurched. No news involving Lord Thomas was good news. He'd come to dine with them the past two nights, and it was all she could do to be civil in the man's presence. When would this end? Perhaps she should be more direct and tell Lord Danville frankly that she no longer wished to receive Lord Thomas's calls. On the other hand, his calls did provide her the opportunity to eavesdrop on his conversations with Hugh. She'd yet to glean any useful information for Colin, but, given time, she might. Nay, for now she must allow his calls, unpleasant though they were.

Her feet felt leaden, slowed by trepidation as she followed Lord Danville to his mahogany-paneled study. She took the seat he motioned to, directly across from his massive desk, and waited for him to speak.

"Well now. You've done quite well, daughter. Quite well, indeed. Your mother will be pleased."

"I . . . I dinna ken what you mean, Lord Danville," she stammered, her unease increasing by the second.

He placed his spectacles upon his nose and shuffled the papers atop his blotter. Plucking one page from the pile, he held it aloft, smiling warmly. "A marriage agreement."

She shook her head. Her mouth felt dry, her palms damp. "I still dinna understand."

"No need to be shy, Margaret. Your feelings are known; your young man has told me everything. And soon you shall become Lady Thomas Sinclair, with a duke for a father-in-law. Well, what say you to that?"

Her heart skipped a beat, and she rose on unsteady legs. "Nay, it canna be true."

"I assure you I speak the truth. Here, see for yourself." He laid the page down on the desk before her.

Her eyes scanned the page, her mind scrabbling to grasp the implications of the document. It *was* true. Lord Danville had sold her, like a lamb to slaughter. And for an enormous sum, if the amount named as her dowry was to be believed. She looked up at Lord Danville with newly suspicious eyes. "How could ye do this? Without my consent?"

He drummed his fingers against the desktop. "Lord Thomas tells me he has your consent."

"Nay, he has no such thing. I'd never have agreed to such a thing. *Never.*" Her voice rose a pitch.

"Hmm, well." A frown creased his brow. "No matter. The paper is signed, and I've given my blessing. It's a fine match, Margaret. You'll likely do no better."

"No better than a lying scoundrel? A violent man, a deceitful man? Havena I made my dislike of him—my thorough disgust—evident these past few days? I thought ye, of all people, could see that." Tears burned behind her eyelids, threatening to fall. She took several deep, gulping breaths, refusing to give in to such weakness.

"Nothing but maidenly shyness, your mother says. Come now, Margaret. This is the way these things are done."

"Then they are badly done, sir. 'Tis disgraceful."

He removed his spectacles and eyed her sharply. "I am baffled, Margaret. Most daughters would be delighted with such a match, made so hastily."

"I am not most daughters. I neither want nor need a husband, particularly one of Lord Thomas's character. Ye *must* see that."

"No, I'm afraid I do not. I see only a defiant daughter standing before me. One who would suggest I do not honor a contract made in good faith, a contract that would prove most beneficial to her family in terms of connections."

Brenna straightened her spine, meeting her father's gaze with her own steady one. "I will not marry him."

Lord Danville sighed heavily, his shoulders sagging. "It is possible I've gone about this badly, Margaret. I'll have a word with your mother after tonight's entertainments. Nevertheless, you *will* marry him. You just need time, that's all, to get used to the idea. No need to rush the nuptials. A

Christmas wedding, perhaps." He nodded to himself. "That should do nicely."

She could only stare blankly at the man. Hadn't he heard a word she'd said? No matter; she would be long gone by Christmastime, back at Glenbroch. Where she belonged.

"If you'll excuse me, Lord Danville," she said, raising one hand to her now-throbbing temple. "I'm suddenly feeling unwell."

"Very well. You do look a bit peaked. Perhaps you should go lie down."

"Please give Lady Welbourne my regrets," she said, then exited the room with as much quiet dignity as she could muster.

Hurrying up the stairs, she retrieved her chart book and quill from her bedchamber, then made her way out to the garden, Hera in tow. With a huff, she plopped onto a wide, stone bench. Hera settled herself at her feet, her small, pointed chin resting upon her paws.

Brenna sighed in relief as she listened to the coach clatter from the mews to the front drive, no doubt collecting Lord and Lady Danville. Thank goodness they had not changed their plans and remained home. They would be occupied for several hours at Lady Welbourne's musicale, and she would be left mercifully alone with her dark thoughts.

Sold like a broodmare! She pounded one fist on the bench beside her. She wouldn't stand for it, that was for certain. Lord Thomas had received her father's consent under false pretenses. Surely the contract wouldn't be binding under such deception, would it? Whatever the case, she would convince Lord Danville to reconsider. He must.

And if he wouldn't? Then she would do what *she* must.

Enough thinking of such unpleasant matters. The night was clear, the sky cloudless. She turned her attention heavenward, focusing on the twinkling canvas above.

Aye, this was far more pleasant. There was Ursa Major, the bear. Her gaze followed the line of the tail, up to the bright star Mizar. She squinted, seeking its companion, Alcor. Ah, there it was. If only she had her telescope here.

She reached for her quill, dipping it in the ink with an unsteady hand. Nay, she would not let Lord Thomas Sinclair ruin this fine evening. She began to chart the night's sky, beginning with Ursa Major.

Botheration. Her first attempt produced little more than an imprecise blob of ink. She tore the page from the book with an irritated scowl. *Clear your mind of disagreeable thoughts,* she scolded herself, setting down the quill. *Focus on the heavens.* She closed her eyes and took two deep, calming breaths. At once a sense of peace filled her, calming her jangled nerves. With a satisfied nod, she retrieved her quill and began anew.

This time the results pleased her, and she happily continued on. The scratching of the quill against paper was soothing, comforting. She worked quietly for nearly an hour, when Hera suddenly jumped to the bench beside her, back arched and hair standing on end.

"Dear Lord, Hera, what is it?" She set aside her book and quill. "Ye startled me, silly cat."

Ignoring her, the cat bared her teeth, hissing toward the dark, empty lawn before them.

Someone was there, in the garden. Brenna's heart began to race, her eyes scanning the darkness before her. "Who's there?" she called out, her voice steady and firm.

Colin looked over one shoulder, making certain no one had followed him. No, he was alone. He'd made it through the mews without detection. What good fortune he'd had. Headed toward Rosemoor House in his curricle a half hour ago, he'd passed by Welbourne's town house just as Danville's coach pulled up. Reining in his matched grays, Colin had watched as the earl and countess stepped down, onto the walk. *Alone.* Fate had done him a favor; perhaps he would find Brenna at home, away from her parents' watchful eyes.

Without wasting a second, he'd hastened to Rosemoor House, left his curricle there, and then made his way to Danville House on foot. He'd paused on the front walk, then stepped quickly into the shadows before he was seen. No, he couldn't simply knock on the front door. No doubt their servants had been instructed to deny him entrance. Not quite certain of his plan, yet nonetheless determined, instinct had sent him around through the mews to the back garden.

And there she sat, scribbling away in a book on her lap, a silver and black cat sitting by her side. Only now the blasted creature had stirred, resembling a lion guarding its kill. Time to make his presence known.

He stepped out from behind the linden tree that was shielding him, clearing his throat loudly as he did so to gain her attention. "Would you mind reining in that beast there?" he called out.

"Oh!" she cried, leaping to her feet.

The cat only snarled more loudly, hissing and spitting now.

"Truly, I'm beginning to fear for my life."

"Colin Rosemoor," Brenna said, her voice laced with disbelief. "Ye near enough frightened me to death. What do ye mean by sneaking about the shadows like a specter?"

Colin moved closer, gesturing toward the cat as he would to one of his hounds. "Away," he tried. "Release." Nothing. "By God, that beast is tenacious. I can't say I've ever before seen an attack cat."

"Come, Hera." She reached down and scooped up the animal, holding it close to her breast. "He's a scoundrel, aye, but not a dangerous one."

"What did you call that creature?" He stepped closer still; so close he could smell her scent wafting on the breeze. Deliciously feminine and floral. Intoxicating. Why was it, he wondered, that the scents most ladies favored often made his throat constrict; even the spicy scent that Jane favored sometimes made him sneeze. But not Brenna. He inhaled deeply. She smelled of lavender and sunshine and . . . *Lucy.* Yes, that was it. She smelled like Lucy. He shook his head in amazement. How had he never before recognized it? They were alike in so many ways, Brenna and Lucy, and not just scent alone. No wonder he was drawn to her.

"'Tis a cat, not a creature, and I call her Hera."

"Ah, I see. Your familiar." He couldn't help but make the comparison. She bewitched him. A Scottish witch, perhaps, sent to wreak havoc on his life.

Only his life was already in shambles, long before she turned up, wasn't it?

"Ye didna answer my question." She set the now-calm cat on the ground. As if stalking prey, it wriggled its hindquarters, then leapt at Colin's boots. "Whatever are ye doing here?" she asked. "I know ye didna come simply to accuse me of witch-craft now, did ye?"

"I called on Lord Hampton's solicitors today. You'll be happy to know the deed is now in my name. I had to tell you as soon as possible." The little beast was now rubbing its body against his trousers, purring loudly. Wanted to be his friend now, eh?

"And what if Lord and Lady Danville had been at home?"

"Ah, but I saw them not a half hour ago, arriving at Lady Welbourne's town house. Her annual musicale, I suppose. It would seem I did not make her invitation list this year. A shame."

Her beautiful bow of a mouth curved into a frown. "Oh, dear, I hope you didna give your card to Alfred. He'll tell my parents the moment they return. They've left specific instructions—"

"Of course I didn't. Do you take me for a fool? I ducked around the mews and headed straight for the garden."

"But how did ye know to look for me out here?"

He looked to the sky. "The night is clear, and the moon is full. Where else would I find you but staring up at the stars?"

She followed his gaze, her frown giving way to a grin. "Ye know me well."

"Do I?" he asked, taking a step toward her. He

couldn't help himself; he craved her nearness. "Tell me, what is it you think of when you gaze up at the moon? What puts that lovely smile on your face?"

"Why, I think of home," she answered, her face tilted upward, illuminated by the silvery glow of the moon. "Of Glenbroch, and of my mama and da— the Maclachlans."

"You loved them very much, didn't you?"

"Aye. They were good people, loving people. I canna explain why they did what they did, but I know with all my heart that they loved me as their own. The fever took them both less than a year ago. Running the estate kept me sane after their loss. I couldna have borne it otherwise."

"Hadn't you any family there to comfort you?"

"No one save my former nursemaid, Jenny Cannan. She's been married now for many years, living on Hampton's estate—*your* estate now. She and her husband have a small but profitable croft. I couldna have made it through those dark times without Jenny nearby."

"You must have been lonely."

She nodded, her eyes meeting his. Colin inhaled sharply, the pain in her countenance leaving him breathless. If only he could erase that pain, make it his instead.

And then she looked away, back to the sky. "Lonely, aye, but busy. I was only just getting used to my solitude when Lord and Lady Danville appeared on my doorstep with their outlandish tale. Ye wouldna believe what it was like, to learn that I'd been stolen at birth, that I had a family here in London. All my life I'd longed for a sister or brother, and then, out of the blue, I was given one. I couldna turn my back on them, not after losing everyone who was dear to me. I had to meet this brother of mine, my twin." She bit her lower lip, the warmth leaving her eyes. "What a disappointment he has turned out to be," she said, her voice hard.

He reached for her hand. She wore no gloves, and her bare skin felt warm and soft as silk to his touch. "I'm so sorry," he said, stroking her palm with this thumb.

"Hugh and I share the same blood, yet we are nothing alike in character. 'Tis puzzling, is it not?"

"Perhaps our character is shaped not by blood but by those who raise us. I think the Maclachlans of Glenbroch must have been remarkable people."

She nodded silently, her eyes bright with unshed tears. He suddenly wished she *would* cry. If any female deserved a long, satisfying crying jag, then surely she did. He folded her into his arms, pulling her against his chest. His lips found her hair, and he pressed several kisses into the silky, sweet-smelling tresses.

"Thank ye for saying that, Colin," she murmured, her voice muffled against his coat. "Ye are the first person here who has spoken kindly of them." Lifting her head, she gazed up at him with damp eyes. "And thank ye for securing the deed from Lord Hampton. I will write to Jenny straightaway and tell her that she remains safe, that their livelihood remains secure in your hands. She is not well, you see, and 'twill give her peace until I can return there and tell her so myself."

"You still plan to return to Glenbroch at the close of the Season?" he asked, his chest uncomfortably tight.

"I must return." Brenna swallowed hard, his nearness making her heart flutter. She knew full well she should not let him hold her like this. 'Twas improper at best, dangerous at worst. Yet she could not bring herself to leave the comfort, the security of his arms. "Will you be sorry to see me go?" The words tumbled from her lips before she had the chance to consider them.

He reached for her chin and tilted her face upward, forcing her gaze to meet his. "What do you think, Brenna?"

"I . . . I canna say for certain," she stammered. "At times, I think aye. But other times . . ." She trailed off with a shake of her head. "Other times I dinna ken." *Whenever Lady Mandeville is in your company, for example,* she added silently.

"You have reason to doubt much in your life, Brenna, but do not doubt that I will miss you. Of this you can be sure."

She studied his face, looking for signs of artifice, but she found none. Instead, she saw only honesty, sincerity. Truly, he was beautiful, a mystifying mix of masculine beauty and virility. Soft, gold-tipped waves framed his face, brushing his shoulders, nearly concealing a vertical scar beside one brow that lent him an air of danger. Her eyes scoured his face, taking in every detail—full, sensual lips, strong jaw, faintly clefted chin—before settling on his hooded blue-gray eyes. The raw, primal heat in his gaze nearly took her breath away.

"Please kiss me, Colin," she whispered, suddenly desperate to feel his mouth on hers.

In an instant, he crushed her body against his, his mouth finding hers and possessing it with a masterful assurance. She gasped when his lips parted hers, near ruthlessly, and plundered inside. In response, her whole being trembled, her mind awash in pleasurable sensations. Slowly, deliberately, her hands slid up the hard planes of his back. Her fingers tangled in his hair, cupping his head as she pressed herself against him, wanting the kiss to go on forever.

Her tongue briefly met his. Feeling emboldened, she slipped it between his teeth, exploring the unfamiliar depths of his mouth, tasting him. *Brandy.* He tasted of brandy and smelled of sandalwood, a heady, masculine mix.

He ran his thumbs lightly up the column of her neck, eliciting a shiver of pure delight. She moaned in pleasure, wanting still more. As if he'd read her thoughts, his mouth retreated from hers, his lips trailing a path from behind one ear, down her throat, to her shoulder. His hands moved to cup her breasts, his thumbs drawing sensual circles around hardened nipples that strained against the fabric of her bodice.

Lower still his mouth moved, toward the valley between her breasts. Brenna gasped when his tongue flicked across one sensitive nipple; her back arched in reply, her limbs feeling weak and unsteady. Her heart beat furiously against her ribs.

She wanted to touch him, to feel his bare skin, his warmth, his strength. As he laved her breasts through the thin fabric of her gown, she allowed her hands to roam, to pluck his soft, linen shirt from the band of his trousers. Under the fabric her fingers flew, across the taut muscles of his abdomen, up toward his chest.

At once, Colin wrenched himself away with a

groan, gripping her shoulders so tightly that she feared he might crush the bones.

Guiltily, she dropped her hands to her sides.

"I'm sorry," he muttered. "I shouldn't have—"

"Dinna apologize." Raw, painful disappointment lanced her heart. "'Tis my fault. I shouldna have—"

"It's entirely my fault. You're far too innocent to understand what you're doing to me." He released her shoulders, drawing his hands away as if burned by her flesh. "Damnation, I want you so badly I fear I'm going mad with it. If you keep touching me like that, I cannot promise I won't ravish you right here, right now." He raked one hand through his hair. "I must go."

"Go, then, Colin." She swallowed a painful lump in her throat, feeling like a fool. A wanton. A flush climbed up her neck, no doubt staining her cheeks with shame.

He nodded stiffly. "You'll send word at once if you learn anything from Sinclair or Ballard?"

Was this the true meaning of his visit? To remind her of her part in their bargain? "Of course," she murmured, feeling foolish.

"Very well, Brenna. I bid you good night, then."

"Good night, Colin," she said softly.

In seconds, he disappeared into the darkness like a wisp of smoke. She returned to her seat on the bench, her fingers skimming the rough stone as her heart continued to flutter wildly.

Hera leapt into her lap and began to knead her skirts. Brenna sighed, stroking the cat's back. "I suppose ye witnessed that scene, Hera? Well, 'tis a good thing ye canna speak. 'Twill be our secret, won't it? I've officially gone daft."

Hera only meowed in reply.

*Why didn't I tell him about the betrothal agreement?* she wondered, not even allowing herself to speak the words aloud. *Because he wouldn't have kissed me, had I told him.* And she had wanted him to kiss her. Yearned for it. Despite her confusion about his character; despite her jealousy about his relationship with Lady Mandeville. What a muddle she'd gotten herself into.

"Well, Hera," she said aloud, "'twill likely get worse before it gets better, won't it?"

# Chapter 12

"La, I heard the most remarkable *on-dit* today."
Colin's mother set down her cup, smiling broadly.
She turned toward Jane, who sat beside her on the
sofa sipping her own steaming cup of tea. "Perhaps
you've had the news already, Jane dearest."

Colin poured himself a snifter of brandy, swirling
it around the glass and watching disinterestedly as
Jane arched one brow, peering at their mother over
the rim of her cup.

"I haven't heard any gossip of interest," Jane said.
"Not lately, at least. Do tell."

"I only supposed you might have heard, as it re-
gards your new friend, Lady Margaret Ballard."

*Brenna?* Colin's flagging attention snapped into
focus. Taking his brandy with him, he strode across
the room, leaning against the pianoforte.

"Although," his mother continued, "I don't suppose there's been sufficient time for the news to
travel far. Still—"

"Mama, please," Jane chided. "Do not keep us in
suspense. You must tell us at once."

"Well, I heard tell she's betrothed," she said at last, then pursed her lips thoughtfully. "Hmmm, but I seem to have forgotten to whom. Wait." She held up one finger. "I remember now. It's that odious Lord Thomas Sinclair, of all people," she added.

Colin froze, his snifter poised halfway to his mouth.

"No!" Jane cried out, her teacup clattering to the saucer.

"Yes, I had it from Lady Cowper, who had it from Lady Danville herself. I was more than a little surprised. Isn't Lord Thomas Sinclair the one who caused such a scene at the opera with Lucy the year of her come-out?"

A speechless Jane only nodded in agreement.

"He is the worst sort of scoundrel, is he not? Regardless, I heard that the betrothal agreement was signed just last night, before Lady Welbourne's musicale."

*Last night?* The agreement was signed last night—the same night that Brenna allowed him to hold her in his arms? The same night she all but begged him to kiss him? It didn't signify. Colin's chest felt suddenly tight; his throat constricted. He set his snifter on the pianoforte's polished case, carefully measuring his words. "He is indeed a scoundrel. In fact, I'd favor several choice names for him, names I dare not repeat in the company of ladies."

"Curious, then, isn't it?" His mother shook her head, her lace cap flapping against her ears. "It is not so surprising that Lord and Lady Danville would seek a hasty match, as Lady Margaret—or Brenna, as you call her, Jane—is a bit long in the tooth. Well past what one would consider a marriageable age. Still, she's sufficiently attractive, if a little coarse, and

I found her to be intelligent and positively charming. It would seem they could do better than accepting the first suit offered, especially when the gentleman in question is of dubious character. But I suppose if Lady Cowper had it from Lady Danville, it must be true."

Colin turned toward the window, a fierce rage welling inside him. He needed a drink, badly. Something far stronger than brandy. "If you'll both excuse me, I have something I must attend to."

Jane rose abruptly to her feet. "As do I. Perhaps Colin can drive me. Yes?" She looked to him pleadingly.

He hesitated for a moment. He wished to be alone with his thoughts, not stuck in his curricle with Jane, listening to her prattle on about Brenna's so-called virtues. What sort of virtuous woman would kiss him the way Brenna did, allow him to touch her the way he had, when betrothed to another? The fact that she hadn't mentioned her engagement made her actions seem all the more suspect. Devil take it, what was the girl about?

He looked up and saw Jane watching him closely, a puzzled look darkening her features.

"I suppose I can drive you," he said at last.

"Must you both go?" their mother asked. "Well, no matter. I'll go pay a call on Lucy."

"What a lovely idea, Mama. Please tell her I'll be around in time for tea. I've much to tell her."

"Very well, dear. Go on, then." She waved one hand toward the door. "It looks as if your brother might perish for waiting."

Colin leaned across the sofa and planted a kiss on his mother's warm, wrinkled cheek. "I've much pressing business, Mother. It's unlikely I'll return for dinner." He'd be too far in his cups by then, if the rest of the day went as planned.

"A shame, for Cook has a lovely side of beef today."

"Set some aside for my breakfast, then. I'm partial to cold beef."

"Hmm, if you say so." She waved toward the doorway. "Well, off with you, then."

Jane had retrieved her bonnet and gloves and stood in the front hall, tying the ribbons beneath her chin as Colin crossed the marble tiles and reached for his hat and whip.

"Need I ask where I'm driving you?" he asked as the butler pulled open the door and ushered them out. "Danville House, I suppose?" He handed Jane up into the curricle.

"Of course. Poor Brenna. I can't understand how this happened. What were her parents thinking? She must be terribly distraught."

"Perhaps." He climbed into the conveyance beside her and took up the reins. "Or perhaps you know her less well than you thought. She might very well be satisfied with the match. Sinclair is, after all, the son of a duke. Fifteen thousand pounds a year, I'm told."

Jane shook her head. "No. I simply cannot believe it. Come now, does she strike you as the type to accept an arranged marriage, especially one with a man such as Sinclair?"

No, she didn't. But then, he'd mistaken a woman's character on more than one occasion. In fact, it would seem that misjudging women was his specialty. He sighed deeply, chafing at the injustice.

"Perhaps not," he answered at last. "Truly, I haven't any idea. Just how well *do* you know her?"

A smile tipped the corners of Jane's mouth. "Quite well, I'd say. I've spent many pleasant hours in her company—shopping, taking tea, enjoying a turn in the park. She's spoken often of returning to Castle Glenbroch come autumn. You should hear the longing in her voice when she speaks of home, Colin."

"Then perhaps there's your answer. Perhaps her home is in need of funds."

Jane shook her head, making the trimmings on her bonnet dance in the warm summer breeze. "No, I do not think so. Glenbroch sounds quite prosperous. She said they've turned a nice profit these past few years. There is simply no logical explanation, other than Lord and Lady Danville having a serious lapse in judgment. I will get my answers soon enough, I suppose. No use in speculating."

Colin reined in beside Danville House, his anger mounting as his thoughts returned to his last visit here. Had Brenna played him for a fool? She must have, for he could think of no other explanation.

Scowling at his own stupidity, he leapt from the curricle, hurrying around to hand Jane down.

"Thank you, Colin." She took two steps toward the town house's front steps, then turned to face him once more. "Might I ask just where you're off to?"

"I'd rather you did not."

"Just as I'd supposed." Her displeasure was evident. "There's no reason to earn the reputation you've been burdened with, you know," she chastised.

"No? You'd deprive me of all enjoyment, then?"

"No, but surely you can find a more suitable way

to spend your leisure time than by haunting seedy gaming hells and public houses."

A red-hot, suffocating rage rose in his breast, constricting his windpipe and causing his heart to pound furiously against his ribs. "Oh? Perhaps I should go to my club instead. Ah, but wait." He smacked one palm against his forehead. "That's right, I'm no longer allowed inside those hallowed halls. They've revoked my membership—indefinitely, they claim. Well then, shall I pay court to some respectable young lady instead? I say, I just remembered—I'm no longer received in respectable drawing rooms, am I?"

"Colin, please—"

"Please what? Tell me, Jane. Tell me what possible means I have to occupy my time besides drinking myself into a stupor at some disreputable establishment."

"Hush," Jane hissed, reaching for his sleeve. "This is neither the time nor the place for such an outburst."

He wrenched himself from her grasp, his anger increasing. "Isn't it? I must say, I don't give a bloody farthing what anyone thinks anymore. Besides, if I don't provide sufficient fodder for the gossip mill, they'll just make it up instead."

Jane's eyes flashed angrily. "Just go, Colin. Go." She waved a hand in dismissal. "Do what you must. If you can drag yourself from your bed tomorrow, come by Rosemoor House and I'll share what news I have from Brenna."

"I'll do that," he muttered, suddenly feeling contrite. He reached for Jane's hand. "You *are* a gem, you know."

Her frown gave way to a weak smile. "As are you, Colin. You've only just forgotten it."

He watched as she turned and strode confidently

*Take A Trip Into A Timeless World*
*of Passion and Adventure with*
*Kensington Choice Historical Romances!*
## —Absolutely FREE!

Enjoy the passion and adventure
of another time with Kensington
Choice Historical Romances.
They are the finest novels of
their kind, written by today's
best-selling romance authors.
Each Kensington Choice
Historical Romance transports
you to distant lands in a bygone
age. Experience the adventure
and share the delight as proud
men and spirited women
discover the wonder and
passion of true love.

# Get 4 FREE Books!

We created our convenient Home Subscription Service so you'll be sure to have the hottest new romances delivered each month right to your doorstep—usually before they are available in book stores. Just to show you how convenient the Zebra Home Subscription Service is, we would like to send you 4 FREE Kensington Choice Historical Romances. The books are worth up to $24.96, but you only pay $1.99 for shipping and handling. There's no obligation to buy additional books—ever!

## Save Up To 30% With Home Delivery!

Accept your FREE books and each month we'll deliver 4 brand new titles as soon as they are published. They'll be yours to examine FREE for 10 days. Then if you decide to keep the books, you'll pay the preferred subscriber's price (up to 30% off the cover price!), plus shipping and handling. Remember, you are under no obligation to buy any of these books at any time! If you are not delighted with them, simply return them and owe nothing. But if you enjoy Kensington Choice Historical Romances as much as we think you will, pay the special preferred subscriber rate and save over $8.00 off the cover price!

We have 4 FREE BOOKS for you as your introduction to
**KENSINGTON CHOICE!**
To get your FREE BOOKS, worth up to $24.96, mail
the card below or call TOLL-FREE 1-800-770-1963.
Visit our website at www.kensingtonbooks.com.

## Get 4 FREE Kensington Choice Historical Romances!

💚 **YES!** Please send me my 4 FREE KENSINGTON CHOICE HISTORICAL ROMANCES (without obligation to purchase other books). I only pay $1.99 for shipping and handling. Unless you hear from me after I receive my 4 FREE BOOKS, you may send me 4 new novels—as soon as they are published—to preview each month FREE for 10 days. If I am not satisfied, I may return them and owe nothing. Otherwise, I will pay the money-saving preferred subscriber's price (over $8.00 off the cover price), plus shipping and handling. I may return any shipment within 10 days and owe nothing, and I may cancel any time I wish. In any case, the 4 FREE books will be mine to keep.

NAME_____

ADDRESS_____APT._____

CITY_____STATE_____ZIP_____

TELEPHONE (_____)_____

E-MAIL (OPTIONAL)_____

SIGNATURE_____

(If under 18, parent or guardian must sign)

Offer limited to one per household and not to current subscribers. Terms, offer and prices subject to change. Orders subject to acceptance by Kensington Choice Book Club. Offer Valid in the U.S. only.

KN066A

ǀǀ...ǀ..ǀǀ....ǀǀ.ǀ.ǀ.ǀ.ǀ.ǀ.ǀ.ǀ..ǀǀ.ǀ.ǀ..ǀǀ.ǀ.ǀ..ǀǀ...ǀ

**KENSINGTON CHOICE**
Zebra Home Subscription Service, Inc.
P.O. Box 5214
Clifton NJ 07015-5214

*Take A Trip Into A Timeless World
of Passion and Adventure with
Kensington Choice Historical Romances!*

## —Absolutely FREE!

Enjoy the passion and adventure
of another time with Kensington
Choice Historical Romances.
They are the finest novels of
their kind, written by today's
best-selling romance authors.
Each Kensington Choice
Historical Romance transports
you to distant lands in a bygone
age. Experience the adventure
and share the delight as proud
men and spirited women
discover the wonder and
passion of true love.

# Get 4 FREE Books!

We created our convenient Home Subscription Service so you'll be sure to have the hottest new romances delivered each month right to your doorstep—usually before they are available in book stores. Just to show you how convenient the Zebra Home Subscription Service is, we would like to send you 4 FREE Kensington Choice Historical Romances. The books are worth up to $24.96, but you only pay $1.99 for shipping and handling. There's no obligation to buy additional books—ever!

## *Save Up To 30% With Home Delivery!*

Accept your FREE books and each month we'll deliver 4 brand new titles as soon as they are published. They'll be yours to examine FREE for 10 days. Then if you decide to keep the books, you'll pay the preferred subscriber's price (up to 30% off the cover price!), plus shipping and handling. Remember, you are under no obligation to buy any of these books at any time! If you are not delighted with them, simply return them and owe nothing. But if you enjoy Kensington Choice Historical Romances as much as we think you will, pay the special preferred subscriber rate and save over $8.00 off the cover price!

We have 4 FREE BOOKS for you as your introduction to
**KENSINGTON CHOICE!**
To get your FREE BOOKS, worth up to $24.96, mail
the card below or call TOLL-FREE 1-800-770-1963.
Visit our website at www.kensingtonbooks.com.

## Get 4 FREE *Kensington Choice Historical Romances!*

♥ **YES!** Please send me my 4 FREE KENSINGTON CHOICE HISTORICAL ROMANCES (without obligation to purchase other books). I only pay $1.99 for shipping and handling. Unless you hear from me after I receive my 4 FREE BOOKS, you may send me 4 new novels—as soon as they are published—to preview each month FREE for 10 days. If I am not satisfied, I may return them and owe nothing. Otherwise, I will pay the money-saving preferred subscriber's price (over $8.00 off the cover price), plus shipping and handling. I may return any shipment within 10 days and owe nothing, and I may cancel any time I wish. In any case, the 4 FREE books will be mine to keep.

NAME_____

ADDRESS_____ APT._____

CITY_____ STATE _____ ZIP_____

TELEPHONE (_____)_____

E-MAIL (OPTIONAL)_____

SIGNATURE_____

(If under 18, parent or guardian must sign)

Offer limited to one per household and not to current subscribers. Terms, offer and prices subject to change. Orders subject to acceptance by Kensington Choice Book Club. Offer Valid in the U.S. only.

KN066A

PLACE
STAMP
HERE

ǁ..ǁ.ǁǁ....ǁ.ǁ.ǁ.ǁ.ǁ.ǁ...ǁǁ..ǁ.ǁ..ǁǁ.ǁ..ǁǁ..ǁ

**KENSINGTON CHOICE**
**Zebra Home Subscription Service, Inc.**
P.O. Box 5214
Clifton NJ 07015-5214

up the front walk, looking as elegant and regal as always. As she rapped on the door, he leapt into the curricle and took up the reins, suddenly uncertain of where to go.

Bloody hell, as always, Jane had cut right to the heart of the matter. With a flick of the wrists, he flapped the reins across the horses' backs, and they started off. But where to? Despite Jane's cutting words, a part of him wished to head to Covent Garden, to some nameless establishment where he could get blissfully and mindlessly drunk on cheap gin. Yet another part wished to prove himself better, though the devil only knew why.

Mandeville House. Yes, that's where he would go. If Mandeville was absent, he could await him in his study and enjoy the marquess's fine brandy, or, better yet, his smuggled whisky. Lucy would no doubt be busy entertaining Colin's mother. Hadn't she said she meant to call on Lucy? Still, just being in Lucy's home brought him peace he could not find elsewhere. Perhaps there was something to be said for acceptance, after all.

And then perhaps he'd return to Rosemoor House for dinner, to the promised side of beef and to Jane's news from Brenna. An unexpected rush of hope surged through his veins, quickening his breath. *Let my mother's information prove to be false.* The desperation sliced through his heart, nearly cleaving it in two.

Last night he'd lain awake in his bed till dawn, tossing and turning beneath twisted bedclothes as he'd recalled Brenna's eager response to his kiss, his touch. Just the memory alone of her fingers sliding beneath his shirt, raking across his bare torso, had been enough to force him to hastily and efficiently see to his own needs. Still, even after he'd found release, he hadn't found sleep. Instead he'd continued to savor the memory of her kiss, of her breasts beneath his hands, beneath his mouth.

She was exquisite. The thought that that bastard Sinclair might soon possess her made bile rise in his throat. Sinclair didn't deserve her.

Not that he deserved her, either. No, in his current state, he would only bring her sorrow and shame. She should be allowed to return to Scotland, to the home she loves, free to marry some brawny, bearded Scotsman in kilt and sporran. Someone who loves the Highlands as she does, who shares her passions and convictions. She deserved that and no less.

He looked up from the street, surprised to see he had accomplished Mandeville House while lost in his thoughts. Reining in the horses, he leaned back against the seat and took a deep, calming breath. As he did so, a movement caught his eye in the house's front window and he squinted against the sun. It was Lucy, her golden hair unbound. She stood framed in the glass, her back toward the street. As he watched, a shadow moved in front of her, arms encircling her slender waist. Lucy's head tipped back, her arms reaching up in an embrace. In seconds, Mandeville swept her off her feet and carried her away, out of Colin's sight. In the middle of the afternoon, for God's sake.

Couldn't they cool their ardor, especially when standing in plain view of the street? He shook his head, a decidedly foul mood descending upon him. Damn it all to hell.

His first instinct had been correct. He needed a drink—a strong one. "To Covent Garden," he said aloud, slapping the horses' backs with the reins and setting off once again.

Toward further ruin, no doubt.


"Like this?" Brenna tucked a single delphinium behind one ear, then sat on the white wrought-iron chair Jane had placed beside the rose-covered trellis.

Jane nodded. "Exactly. There, drape one wrist over the chair's arm, as if you're in a state of repose."

Brenna did as she'd requested, feeling quite foolish.

"Perfect," Jane said.

The scented breeze stirred, fluttering the hem of Brenna's gauzy gown. Two birds chirruped gaily as they fluttered overhead, dipping and darting through the trees' canopy. "Do ye really enjoy such an activity as this? On such a lovely afternoon?"

Jane dipped her brush into the paints she held on her palette, then tipped her head to one side to more carefully observe her subject. "It isn't something I've turned my hand at often, which is why I thought to practice. You have an interesting face; quite lovely, really. Can you tilt your chin down a bit? There." Jane tentatively made her first strokes on the canvas as Brenna considered far better occupations for such a fine day.

Of course, here in London her options were limited. There were no fields to ride, no fences to check, no tenants to visit. The closest thing to a loch was the long water they called the Serpentine in Hyde Park. It paled in comparison.

On the other hand, Jane's company was exceedingly pleasant. Brenna had no close female friends her age near Glenbroch now that Elsbeth had married and gone off to Edinburgh. In fact, most of the women her age, save servants, had married and dispersed throughout the countryside. Many had families by now. 'Twas not something she had particularly envied—till now.

Much as she hated to admit it, Colin had stirred something within her. A longing of sorts, one she'd never before felt but now made sleep elusive. After Colin had left her there in the garden last night, she'd been restless, unable to finish charting the skies. Instead, she'd retired, long before her parents' return from Lady Welbourne's musicale. Yet she'd lain abed for several hours, staring at the moon and wishing she could feel Colin's arms around her once more. She'd allowed herself to wonder what it might be like to share his life, his bed, what their children might look like. Scandalous thoughts, aye. He wasn't even a Scot.

Besides, 'twas irrelevant. She would return to Glenbroch soon enough, and she had plenty to worry her as it was, what with Lord Danville's insistence that she wed Sinclair.

"Don't scowl," Jane admonished from her seat before the easel. "You've a dreadful furrow in your brow."

"Oh?" Brenna endeavored to force her features into a pleasant expression. "I'm verra sorry. I was distracted by some disagreeable thoughts."

"Oh?" Jane laid down her brush. "Nothing too terrible, I hope."

"'Tis dreadful, really." She considered unburdening herself to Jane. 'Twas what a friend was for, after all, and perhaps Jane could offer some much-needed advice. She nodded, her mind made up, then took a deep breath before speaking. "My father has signed a betrothal agreement with Lord Thomas Sinclair."

Jane sighed, her mouth curving into a frown. "Oh, dear. I'd hoped the rumor was false."

Brenna sat up sharply. "Ye mean to say you've heard the news already?"

"I'm afraid so. Mama had it from Lady Cowper this morning. I must say, we were all shocked. Colin took off in a huff of indignation and—"

"Colin?" Dear Lord, what must he think of her? After last night? She should have told him, before he'd had the chance to hear it elsewhere. Only she hadn't imagined that anyone would speak of it so soon.

"Yes, Colin seemed more than a trifle disturbed by the news. I confess, I'm worried about him. He's not been himself lately, and he's become far more self-destructive than ever. He blames Lord Thomas for his fall from grace, and now this . . ." Jane trailed off, shaking her head. "You see, I believe my brother to be fond of you."

A flush heated Brenna's cheeks.

"*Quite* fond," Jane added. "It's only natural that he would not wish to see you wed to his sworn enemy. Might I be so bold as to ask if you've formed an attachment to Lord Thomas?"

"Quite the opposite. 'Tis fair to say I dislike him

immensely. I've opposed the match, though my father makes it seem as if I have no say in the matter. He insists this is the way 'tis done here in England. If that is so, 'tis a barbaric practice, indeed."

"You have my agreement on that count. Did Lord Danville not consult you, ask your thoughts, before accepting Lord Thomas's suit?"

Brenna shook her head. "Nay. He simply sat me down and produced the contract that he'd already signed, waving it before me like a victory. Worse still, it seems that Lord Thomas claimed to have had my consent before going to my father."

"No!"

"Aye. Dreadful, isn't it? I've told Lord Danville I won't honor a bargain made under such false assertions. Still, he insists I'll marry him by Christmastime."

"That's outrageous. I suppose it means Lord Thomas fancies himself in love with you."

"Love? Nay, Sinclair's motivations are clear enough, and they've nothing to do with love. Judging by the sum named on the contract, Lord Danville has been extraordinarily generous with my dowry. Taken together with my holdings in Scotland, I suppose I'm worth a great deal to a rogue like Sinclair."

"Oh, he's worse than a rogue. Much worse. What shall you do?"

"I suppose I could simply return to Glenbroch and pretend the contract does not exist. I canna imagine that Sinclair would pursue me across the border and force me to wed him against my will. But I'd feel much better about it if I could see the contract broken before I left. I dinna want him to have any claim on me."

"I agree."

"Aye, but how?"

Jane nibbled on her lower lip, her brow furrowed in thought. Brenna waited, holding her breath in expectation.

"Well," Jane said at last, "there *is* one way, though it will surely cause a scandal."

"Tell me," Brenna entreated. "Nothing ye suggest can possibly be worse than being forced to wed that despicable man."

"If you were found in a"—Jane looked around furtively, then lowered her voice an octave—"a compromising position with another man, Sinclair's pride would force him to withdraw his offer."

Brenna leaned forward in her chair, her hands gripping the curved arm. "A compromising position? I dinna ken what ye mean."

"If you allow a gentleman to . . . well, take liberties." Jane arched her brow. "Make it seem as if your virtue is in question."

Brenna recoiled at the words. "But . . . but," she sputtered, "what of the gentleman I allow such liberties? Won't I simply be forced to wed him instead?"

"True," Jane answered with a nod. "I hadn't thought of that. But, well . . . is there not a gentleman who you would consider wedding? If so, you would only be hastening it. It would not be the first time a girl used such means to hurry a reluctant groom to the altar."

Colin's face swam into focus in her mind's eye, but Brenna forced away the thought. Nay, she could never do such a thing. 'Twas far too dishonest, too calculating. Brenna shook her head. "Nay, there is no one."

Jane's hopeful expression fled at once. "No? You're certain?"

"I'm certain. And even if there were, I couldna do such a thing."

"No, of course not."

"Besides, when I do marry, I'll marry a Scot. I dinna mean that as an insult, but—"

"No, it's perfectly understandable. But there are many Scottish gentlemen here in London, you know. I can make the proper introductions. There's Angus MacDonnell, for one. A very fine man, if only a bit too old. And, let's see." She pursed her lips. "Oh, Lord Ian MacTavish. Not so handsome, but young and quite rich, I'm told."

"I dinna ken 'tis such a good idea," Brenna answered truthfully. "I'll speak to Lord Danville once more about my objections, but perhaps I should just return to Glenbroch. 'Tis best, I think."

Jane hurried to Brenna's side and reached for her hand, giving it a squeeze. "You must forgive me, Brenna. It's my selfish nature that wishes you to remain here in London, when I know your heart remains in the Highlands."

Brenna gripped Jane's hand, returning the pressure. "'Tis nothing to apologize for. Ye are a verra good friend, Jane. I've no idea how I would have survived thus far without ye."

"I vow, together we shall find a way out of this engagement. I will not see you treated so cruelly, so unfairly."

"Thank ye. Truly, I feel better just for having told ye. Now," Brenna said, peering at the abandoned easel, "will ye finish this painting? Or shall we go inside and have some refreshments?"

Jane returned to her seat before the easel and picked up her palette and brush. "Indeed I shall finish it, and it will be my finest work to date. Can you remember just how you were sitting?"

Brenna did her best to strike the same languid pose as before, tucking the fragrant bloom more securely behind her ear. "Well?"

"Perfect," Jane replied with a nod, then set to work with obvious enthusiasm.

*Nay, there is no one I wish to marry,* Brenna repeated silently, over and over again. If only she could make herself believe it.

# Chapter 13

Brenna stepped out of Hatchard's, humming a tune as she clutched her parcel tightly against her bosom. Oh, what a lovely bookshop! She'd never before been inside such a marvelous place—row after row of books, all shapes and sizes and covering every subject imaginable. She'd browsed for more than an hour and could have stayed many more. Why had no one brought her there before now? She smiled gratefully at Jane, who clutched her own parcel as she stepped lightly up into the carriage.

Brenna followed suit, her fingers itching to tear the paper off her new treasure and leisurely flip through the pages, taking all the time in the world to examine each chart, each lovely illustration.

"Shall we head to Gunter's for an ice?" Jane asked as they settled themselves against the leather squabs. "It's quite warm today, isn't it?"

Brenna looked down at the still-wrapped book in her lap, then back up to Jane. "Aye, 'tis warm, indeed, but . . . would ye mind terribly if I went directly home instead? I confess, I'm so eager to read this I can barely contain myself."

Jane laughed. "Of course I would not mind. I've three new novels myself. We'll take you home directly, but only if you promise to accompany me to Gunter's tomorrow instead."

"Verra well," Brenna said with a grin. "'Tis agreed. I should love to."

Jane spoke briefly to the driver, then returned to her seat opposite Brenna. Seconds later, the carriage lurched forward, toward Danville House.

Still smiling to herself, Brenna ran a gloved fingertip along the edge of the coarse paper, enjoying the feel of the book's weight in her lap. It had been costly, aye, but worth every pence. All the latest astronomical findings in a single illustrated volume. She had nothing like this at home. Even her books at Glenbroch were horribly outdated, and none so fine as this.

Minutes later, she bid Jane farewell and climbed down to the walk. Oddly enough, Alfred did not appear at the door, so she let herself in, still smiling happily and clutching the book to her bosom. The house was quiet; her father must be at his club and her mother out paying calls. *Thank goodness*. She could enjoy several hours of solitude, undisturbed in the sanctuary of her bedchamber.

That thought in mind, she tiptoed across the front hall, nearly holding her breath as she reached for the carved newel post at the base of the staircase.

Male voices, coming from the direction of her father's study, made her pause on the landing. Blast it, it was Lord Thomas Sinclair. She recognized the sound of his laughter.

"To marriage," she heard him say.

"To marriage," Hugh echoed. Glassware clinked together, and the men's voices grew muffled. Moving as quietly and stealthily as possible, Brenna hurried to the closed door, pressing her ear against it.

"Though I still believe I got the better end of the bargain," Hugh said, his voice now clear and distinct even through the heavy door. "Honoria is positively delectable. Perhaps I'll have no need for a mistress once I have her in my bed. I think it might be time to send Josephine packing."

"I wouldn't act so rashly, Ballard. Not till you've sampled Honoria's wares. One can never tell, you know."

"True, true. Still, I've grown bored with Josephine, and she's become far too costly to keep in the manner in which she aspires to, greedy fool. Anyway, how did Belinda take the news of your own upcoming nuptials? Have you any intact dinnerware left, or did she toss it all at your head?"

"Oh, every plate, bowl, and glass is smashed to bits. She was in quite a pique this time. I've never heard a woman carry on like that, howling and weeping for hours on end. I finally placated her with promises of a cottage in the country for her and her brats. Another one on the way, if you can believe it. And she wonders why my interest fades."

"Not for too long, I'd say, judging by the number of bastards you've managed to sire."

Brenna's blood ran cold. More than anything, she wanted to flee. She didn't want to hear any more. Yet she forced herself to remain, listening to such coarse, vulgar talk. Perhaps she would learn something of value to Colin.

"What am I to do?" Lord Thomas asked, his tone

light. "The slut has the most marvelous tits I've ever seen, and she can perform miracles with her mouth. Ah, well. I'll keep her around a bit longer. She's not quite used up yet."

Hugh had the audacity to laugh—actually laugh—at such a vile statement. Brenna's stomach pitched uncomfortably, and for a moment she feared she might begin to retch. Clamping one hand over her mouth, she swallowed the bile that rose in her throat.

"Anyway, where is that sister of yours?" Lord Thomas continued, his voice now sounding bored. "I've a few things to discuss with her regarding our betrothal."

"She's not likely to return for several hours. She's gone out with Jane Rosemoor of all people, her constant companion these days. They've become near inseparable. I've no idea why my mother has allowed it."

"I'll have a word or two with my bride-to-be about the company she keeps. I won't stand for having my name tarnished by association with that family."

Hugh grunted his agreement.

"Besides, I never liked Jane Rosemoor. She's nothing but an uppity little cocktease. I think it's high time she earned her comeuppance."

"Well, why not ruin her while we're at it?" Hugh asked with a chuckle. "All in the family, I say. Cocktease or not, she *is* an exquisite little minx. Ruining her might prove enjoyable."

Rage surged through Brenna's veins, heating her skin and making her pulse leap. *The bastard.*

"Perhaps I'll let you have the pleasure, but first

things first. I'm not yet entirely satisfied with our current bargain."

"And why not? I've done my part. My father signed the agreement several days ago; soon everything she has will be yours. From what I hear, her estate in Scotland will fetch an enormous sum, especially if you first clear the land. Together with her inheritance and her sizable dowry, you'll be a very rich man."

"Ah, but you've left out the best part, the icing on the proverbial cake. I had no idea I'd get a comely little tigress in my bed as part of the bargain. What fun I shall have taming her."

"You'll have a time of it, that's for certain."

"Perhaps, though it's not necessary that she come willingly to my bed."

"No?"

"No, it'll be good sport to drag her there by her hair, kicking and screaming all the while. Nonetheless, she must come willingly to the altar, and that's where you've failed. I can't very well hold her before the vicar in chains. Betrothal contract or not, she must consent to the nuptials. She needn't be pleased about it."

"What would you have me do? Short of drugging her, I've done all that I can on your behalf. Perhaps you should have done a better job seducing her. I must say, I'm disappointed in you. That she would allow Colin Rosemoor to sniff about her skirts but not you—"

"I did what you asked me to do, Ballard," Lord Thomas spat out. "The card was planted in Rosemoor's pocket, wasn't it? It was no simple task, finding someone at White's to accomplish it, yet it was done with aplomb. Rosemoor was tossed from White's, cast from polite society, and now you've won the hand of the pretty little Honoria. Everything you desired has come to pass, exactly as planned. Now I expect you to make good on your part. Just as you promised, your sister's hand is worth far more than our original bargain, and I will accept nothing less than her full compliance as payment. Do whatever is necessary to get her to agree. Do I make myself clear?"

"Perfectly," Hugh answered. "Have no doubt, she *will* acquiesce."

The devil she would! Brenna had heard enough. Slowly edging away from the door, she made her way back toward the staircase. She removed her slippers and carried them along with her wrapped parcel up the stairs. Holding her breath, she made her way down the corridor and into her bedchamber. Only when the door was closed and latched behind her did she exhale, her cheeks aflame as she leaned against the door, her shoulders heaving with rage.

It was true; Colin had been right all along. How dare Hugh do something so despicable? How dare either of them—vile bastards, the pair. Yet her brother's betrayal pained her most of all. His crime went far beyond plotting to ruin an innocent man. As if that alone weren't bad enough, he'd then bartered off his sister to a cruel, deceitful, and monstrous man in payment. Was this Honoria worth so much to him? More so than family, a sister?

She bit her bottom lip so savagely that she tasted blood. Now what was she to do? Confront him? Confess that she'd overheard their wretched conversation? Tell Lord and Lady Danville? Would they even believe her, or would they take the word of their son, the child they'd always known, over hers? She was naught but a stranger to them, after all.

She wanted to scream, to keen with rage. Instead, she stormed over to the bed, peeling off her gloves as she did so. She deposited them, along with her slippers and the package, there on the coverlet, then viciously punched a pillow, wishing it were Hugh's head instead. The pillow tumbled to the floor, and she kicked it with her stocking feet, ruthlessly, repeatedly, until feathers flew in the air.

Hera came screeching out from under the bed, leaping into the air and swatting at the feathers as they floated back down to the floorboards.

She had to tell Colin straightaway. But how? She hadn't any idea where he lodged, and even if she did, she knew enough of the *ton*'s ways to know she could not go there herself, unchaperoned.

"Stop it, Hera," she whispered, watching as the cat began to chew on a feather. "'Tis not a bird, just a pillow." She scooped up the cat and held her in her arms like a babe, tossing the half-chewed bit of feather to the ground. Hera regarded her with a steady, green gaze, her nose twitching in the air. If only Hera could offer advice. How sad that there was not a single other soul in the house she could trust. Only a cat.

She set Hera on the bed while she attempted to collect the feathers from the floor. Hearing the familiar purr, she looked up, arms full, and watched as the cat rubbed the side of her face against the corner of the still-wrapped parcel. She'd all but forgotten about the new book, about her morning spent perusing the shelves at Hatchard's with Jane.

*Jane.* Of course. She'd have to enlist Jane's help. 'Twas no other way to get word to Colin, really.

If she snuck out now, no one would even know she had been home. Quickly, she retrieved her gloves and slippers, casting one last glance at Hera before reaching for the door's latch.

"Just don't eat them all," she whispered. "'Twill make you sick, no doubt."


"I thought you were coming by Rosemoor House days ago," Jane scolded as she untied her bonnet and tossed it to the credenza. The twin green silk ribbons resembled serpents, lying there on the polished wood, regarding him. His vision slightly blurred with sleep, Colin squinted, examining them more closely. Ah, just harmless ribbons, after all.

At last he turned his gaze to his sister with a scowl, simultaneously glad to see her and wishing she hadn't come. What was this, some dashed sort of female conspiracy? He'd just sent Lucy on her way, and now he had Jane to contend with. Devil take it, but his head throbbed.

"Don't tell me you've only now just arisen? Have you any idea how late the hour is?" Her voice was unusually shrill to his ears.

He groaned, one hand reaching up to his temple. "Must you come barging in here, scolding me like a fishwife? Have a care for my head, will you?"

"Too much to drink last night, I suppose."

"A likely assumption, indeed. Yet wholly incorrect. This time, at least." God, if only he were suffering the ill effects of over-imbibing. He'd give his eyeteeth for a bottle of brandy right now. He'd had no spirits whatsoever for a full three days now, and it was near enough killing him. He was a damnable bloody mess.

Jane eyed him critically, her sapphire gaze sweeping from his mussed head to his bare feet. "Whatever happened to you, then? You look dreadful."

"And you look beautiful as always." Besides Lucy's brief visit just moments before, he hadn't laid eyes on a single soul save his valet and butler since his self-imposed exile several days ago, and he had to admit his sister was a sight for sore eyes.

"Don't change the subject," she said crisply. "Shall I summon the physician?"

"No, you most definitely shall not," he grumbled, feeling peevish. "You just missed Lucy, by the way. In fact, she left her reticule here." He pointed to the pale blue silk pouch that lay on the marble table beside the door. "So I assume she'll soon return. Anyway, I'll tell you just what I told her. I am perfectly well and in no need of a physician. Just tell me why you're here, and then go on about your merry way, spreading cheer throughout Mayfair."

"Very amusing, Colin. Really. What do you think I'm doing here? No one has seen nor heard from you in days. You said you'd come by Rosemoor House to hear what I'd learned from Brenna about her betrothal, yet you never came. And now you stand there, in your bare feet, your face bruised, looking as if you've just crawled from bed even though it's long past midday." Her voice rose, and Colin resisted the urge to cover his ears with his hands. God help him, she was angry.

If only she knew the truth—that he'd stumbled home from the East End at dawn three days past, his pockets empty and his clothing reeking of smoke and vomit. He'd had no memories whatsoever of what had transpired over the course of the night, but one of his eyes was blackened, and he had a cut on his right shoulder two inches in length, caked in dried blood. He might have slept in the street for all he knew. Perhaps he'd been robbed by some ruffians, and that would explain his missing ebony walking stick and pair of gold cuff links. Or perhaps he'd gambled away his valuables at the public house where he'd first gone after leaving Jane at Danville House.

Either way, he had crawled into his bed as the sun rose and sworn he would never again touch spirits of any kind. He'd remained abed, alternately dozing and dreaming about Brenna and then awakening to wish desperately for a drink. His valet, after returning to the public house Colin had named and retrieving his employer's curricle and horses, had silently and patiently cleaned up Colin's vomit without summoning a chambermaid, and Colin had been grateful for the man's discretion.

Today he had risen from his bed, though his head still ached miserably, and he'd had some coffee and toast for breakfast. It was a good thing Jane had chosen this day for her unexpected visit. He might look dreadful now, but he no doubt looked a far cry better than he had the day before.

"Well?" he asked. "Why don't you tell me your news, then?"

"First, you should sit. Really, you look as if you're about to topple over. Whatever is the matter with you?"

"I've been rather indisposed for the past few days."

"Indisposed?"

"One might say. You're right, though. I should like to sit. Should I ring for tea?"

"No, don't bother." She reached for his arm as if he needed assistance. "Come, let's sit, and then I will tell you my news."

He tugged his arm from her grasp. "Really, Jane. Despite appearances, I assure you I'm not an invalid."

"If you say so." She followed him into the salon, a room he seldom used. He stood, leaning against the mantel, watching as Jane took a seat in one of the broad leather chairs that flanked the fireplace. It was a good thing he hadn't grown too fond of these accommodations, as he could no longer afford the rent. By the end of the week, he'd either have to return to Rosemoor House with his tail between his legs or find himself some cramped apartments elsewhere.

"Colin?"

"Yes?" he snapped, running one finger along the face of an ivory clock. Perhaps he could get a fair price for it.

"Sit," she ordered, pointing to the chair opposite hers.

With a sigh of defeat, he complied. "Well?" he prompted, slumped in the chair with his gut clenched in anticipation.

His sister didn't mince words. "It's true, I'm afraid. Brenna's father signed a marriage agreement with Sinclair."

"Damn." He struck the arm of the chair with his fist, then met Jane's steady gaze. "If you'll pardon my language. And what are her thoughts on this arrangement?"

"What do you think?" Jane snapped. "She's furious, of course. She says she won't do it, that she'll flee to Scotland before she honors the agreement."

"Why would Danville do this to her if she's so opposed to the match?"

"It seems that Sinclair wanted her badly enough to lie to Lord Danville. He told him he had already secured Brenna's acceptance. I can only suppose Sinclair wants her money."

"Her money? Surely her dowry isn't that large." Colin picked up an intricate piece of blown glass from the table between the chairs, turning it over in his hands to check the maker's mark. He wondered just where he had acquired such a piece as this, and then he wondered how much blunt it might fetch.

"Apparently her dowry is more than generous. Together with her estate in Scotland and the inheritance she has from the Maclachlans, she is a very wealthy woman, indeed."

"I had no idea. She's a sitting duck for fortune hunters, then."

"I suppose that, given her age and upbringing, the Danvilles feared being unable to secure any match at all. A short-sighted and baseless fear, of course. And no doubt that wretched Hugh Ballard spoke up for Sinclair, shielding his parents from the truth about the man's character. All they know of Sinclair is that he is well-connected, the son of a duke. I'm sure they see this as an accomplishment."

"Only a fool could remain blind to Sinclair's true character. He uses women for sport."

"Perhaps," Jane said softly. "But unless Brenna can find a way out of the agreement, I'm afraid she will be the next woman used."

"Damn it to hell." Colin stood on unsteady legs. He needed a drink. He began to pace, his hands in fists by his sides. "You should go, Jane."

"Why? So you can drink yourself sick, Colin? I beg of you, don't do it."

"I have no idea what you mean." He was seething with rage, near blinded with agony over the thought of Brenna's inevitable mistreatment at Sinclair's hands. Just a finger of brandy, no more. Just a taste, to soothe his stomach.

Jane stood and grasped his arm, turning him to face her. "You know exactly what I mean, Colin Rosemoor. Don't do it. You don't need to lose yourself in the drink. Help me instead. Help me find a way for Brenna to escape this awful fate."

"How?" he bellowed, knocking over the table holding the piece of blown glass, which fell to the floor and shattered into a million tiny bits. "How do you expect me to do that? Should I kidnap her? Is that what you think I should do? Spirit her off to Gretna Green? I doubt she wants to marry me any more than she wants to marry Sinclair. I'm not received anywhere respectable, I haven't a bloody farthing to my name, and I'm to be tossed to the street with nowhere to live by next week. Is that what you want for your friend? Do you think that preferable to marrying Sinclair?"

A small gasp parted Jane's lips. "Is it really as bad as that, Colin?"

"Yes, by God, it really *is* that bad. Have you any idea what it's like to have women you've known all your life give you the cut direct? To have men you went to school with cross the street in order to avoid you? Struck from each and every respectable guest list? Do you think marrying Brenna would help my situation in any way?"

"I don't—"

"No," he cut in. "The only chance I have, save exposing those who set me up, is marrying a woman in the *ton*'s good graces, someone they wouldn't dare snub. Not someone like Brenna, an outcast like myself. Any alliance between us simply hurts us both, don't you see?"

"I . . . I suppose you are right. I hadn't thought of it that way. I only wanted to save her the heartache of marrying an animal like Sinclair."

Colin ran a hand through his hair, silently cursing the way his fingers shook. "I realize you only mean to help her, Jane. You are a kind and unselfish woman. Yet your matchmaking efforts are misguided in this case. If you want to help Brenna, you should advise her to make haste for Scotland and hope he doesn't come after her."

"I'm ashamed to admit I suggested that she should find herself in a compromising position with someone more appealing than Sinclair. Of course, she would not even consider it. She still hopes to convince Lord Danville to break off the agreement. He might do it, I suppose. I wonder if Papa would speak with him? Or Lord Mandeville? Do you think it might help?"

"He might listen to Mandeville, but I doubt it. Danville is a staunch Tory, and he strongly opposes many of Mandeville's reform efforts. Probably a wasted effort."

"I'm sure you're right."

The clock chimed the hour, and Jane looked up in surprise. "Oh, no. The time. I must be going, as

I promised Mama I would return within the hour. She'll be on pins and needles, waiting to hear what has become of you. But truly, Colin, perhaps I should send for the apothecary. Or, better yet, you should go straightaway to Rosemoor House and let Mama tend you. Cook makes a wonderful tonic—"

"I don't need Cook's tonic, nor do I need Mother's coddling. Will you rest easy if I vow to you that I will not drink myself into a stupor after you take your leave? In fact, I won't drink anything stronger than coffee. Like a good Quaker."

"Oh, Colin. I *do* worry about you."

He reached down to pat her head, trying not to muss her carefully arranged hair. "Don't worry yourself on my account, sister dearest. Really, I'm not worth it."

"Don't patronize me, Colin Rosemoor." She smiled even as she chastised him.

"Really, you offend me." He thumped his heart with a fist. "I wouldn't dare patronize you."

"Hmm, yes. I suppose I have no choice but to trust your vow. Will you come to supper tonight? Susanna and Richard will be there."

"No, not tonight." He couldn't, not just yet, despite the disappointment in Jane's face. Especially not if his youngest sister and her husband would be there. He loved Susanna, but her silly chatter wore on his nerves. "Tomorrow. I promise you."

"Susanna will be disappointed."

"I doubt that." He followed Jane to the foyer where she retrieved her bonnet. "Unlike Lucy, she has little time for me now that she's wed. Besides, I think Richard now fears my company, lest his own reputation should suffer by association."

"If Richard Merrill had any backbone whatsoever—"

"Then he probably wouldn't have done us all a favor and married Susanna. Remember that."

"Excellent point." She tied the green ribbons under her chin, then pulled on her gloves. "Tomorrow, then. I'll tell Mama to expect you for dinner."

"Very well."

"Until then, I expect you to keep your word. Nothing stronger than coffee."

"You have my word," he said with an exaggerated bow.

He just hoped to God he could keep it.

# Chapter 14

"I'm afraid Miss Rosemoor is not home at present. Would you care to leave your card?" The Rosemoors' butler held out a gloved hand, but Brenna shook her head.

"Nay, that won't be necessary. 'Tis imperative I locate her straightaway. Have ye any idea where she might have gone to?"

The butler regarded her with narrowed eyes. "Is something amiss? Miss Rosemoor's not in danger, I hope."

"Nay, nothing like that. I simply must speak to her, that's all."

He raised one bushy brow in reply but said nothing. Blast it, she must think of some excuse. But what? Her mind cast about frantically for something, anything, to placate the man. "Ye see, I must . . . that is, I've a ball to attend tonight," she dissembled. "A verra important ball, and . . . and I'm not certain which gown to wear. 'Tis imperative I wear just the right sort of thing because . . ." Because why? What possible reason could she name? She wrung her hands, wishing desperately for inspiration. And then it struck. She took a deep breath and hurriedly continued. "Because Prinny himself shall be there, and—"

"Stop." The butler held up one hand. "That's quite enough, miss. I believe Miss Rosemoor said she was off to Mr. Rosemoor's lodgings."

Perfect. "Verra well, I'll be on my way, then. Thank ye ever so much." The only problem was she had no idea where Colin's lodgings were.

"Good day," the butler said in dismissal, reaching to close the door.

"Wait," Brenna called out, bracing one hand against the heavy wooden panel. "I don't mean to be a bother, but can ye tell me where I might find Mr. Rosemoor's lodgings?"

With a disapproving scowl, he named an unfamiliar direction.

Brenna repeated the direction aloud, wondering how she would locate it. She shook her head, defeated. 'Twas useless. If only she had found Jane at home, they could have traveled there together. Or had she taken the Danvilles' carriage, the driver could no doubt locate it. But sending round for the carriage would have alerted Hugh to her presence, and she couldn't have taken such a risk. Instead, she had come alone, on foot, and without a chaperone.

Nay, she had no choice but to leave word for Jane to seek her out immediately at Danville House, and then return there to await her. If she were lucky, Lord Thomas would have tired of waiting for her and departed by now. Off to his mistress's house, perhaps—where his passel of illegitimate children resided.

She looked up and noticed the butler still standing there, staring at her quizzically.

"Have you a conveyance to see you there safely, miss?"

"Nay, I . . . I came in haste. On foot, I'm afraid."

"Perhaps I can see if we've something to spare. I would not want to be responsible for your wearing the wrong sort of gown in Prinny's presence, after all. If you'll excuse me one moment."

Less than a quarter hour later, Brenna found herself seated in a light barouche, being driven toward Bloomsbury at a brisk clip. Thank goodness Jane had chosen this same afternoon to call upon her brother. 'Twas perfectly respectable to remain in his company while Jane was there. Forbidden by her family, aye. But respectable. At least she hoped it was. She would quickly tell him what she'd overheard and be on her way again, and no one would be the wiser.

Her pulse began to race when the carriage slowed, stopping before a small, rather unremarkable gray stone town house. Not what one would call fashionable.

"Shall I wait for you, miss?" the driver asked as he handed her down to the walk below.

"Nay, 'tis not necessary." She would accompany Jane home.

The man tipped his hat in reply and clambered back to the driver's seat. In an instant, he headed the carriage back in the direction from which he'd come.

Without glancing back, Brenna hurried up the steps and reached for the brass knocker. The door swung open at once, and she found herself facing yet another stone-faced butler, this one slightly more aged and stooped than the last.

"Forget something, Lucy?" a familiar voice called out, and Brenna started in surprise as a disheveled Colin appeared beside the butler, a blue reticule dangling from one long, aristocratic finger.

Brenna gasped, taking a step backward. Her slipper caught on the landing's edge, and her ankle twisted painfully. Instantly, Colin's arms were around her.

"Devil take it, are you hurt?"

"Nay, I've only twisted my ankle. Och!" she cried out, trying to put weight on the affected limb.

"You *are* hurt." He lifted her off her feet and swept her into the entry hall, his arms warm and strong around her. "What in God's name are you doing here? I thought you were Luc—Lady Mandeville."

"'Twas obvious," she said through gritted teeth, squirming in his grasp. Blast it, but her ankle hurt.

"Here, you must lie down." He carried her into the front parlor and deposited her on a long sofa covered in moss-green velvet, worn in several spots. "You should remove that slipper at once."

"Nay, I'm quite all right." She looked up at him, and her eyes widened with astonishment. Her pulse leapt, her blood a deafening roar in her ears.

Dear Lord, but he was only half-clothed. His feet were bare, his linen shirt unbuttoned at the neck, and he wore no stock or waistcoat. Her eyes were involuntarily drawn to the smooth planes of his muscled chest, exposed by the open neck of his shirt. Swallowing a lump in her throat, she averted her gaze.

He'd thought she was Lady Mandeville. "Forget

something?" he'd asked, holding up a ladies' reticule. 'Twas obvious Lady Mandeville had been here, and he'd entertained her in this state of undress. Or, she conjectured, perhaps this was all he'd bothered to put on following their illicit entertainment.

And where the devil was Jane? "I . . . I thought I'd find Jane here," she stammered, unable to look him in the eye. "The Rosemoors' butler said she'd come to pay ye a call."

"She was here. She left just minutes before you arrived." He knelt on one knee beside the sofa and reached for her ankle, probing it with gentle fingers. "Does this hurt?" he asked, his brows knitted.

She bit her lip and nodded. "Aye. Not terribly, though. I should go at once." She struggled to rise, but Colin stood and reached for her shoulders, pressing her back to the sofa.

"First you'll tell me what brings you here, all alone, unchaperoned. Someone might have seen you come in, you know."

"Well, then, ye should have left me there on the walk," she snapped.

"In this state?"

She ignored the question. "I believed Jane to be here, else I would not have come. I'm not daft, ye know."

"A fact I'm very much aware of. You still haven't answered my question. Here, raise the ankle on this pillow."

Bending over her, he removed her slipper and placed a tasseled silk pillow beneath her foot. He ran his thumbs along the arch, where a small amount of swelling was quickly becoming visible. The touch sent a shudder up the length of her body. She must tell him her news and then leave at once. Remaining here alone with him was far too dangerous.

"I had to see ye straightaway. I've just overheard a private conversation between my brother and Lord Thomas." Her stomach roiled at the memory of their vile words. "Ye were correct all along, Colin. I canna believe Hugh would do such a thing, yet 'tis true. They plotted your ruin. Lord Thomas arranged to have that card planted in your pocket that night at White's, at Hugh's urging. 'Twas all their doing."

Colin moved to the fireplace, one hand braced on the mantel. His chin dropped toward his chest. "I knew it, the bloody bastard."

"It would seem ye were correct that he coveted the hand of the woman ye had hoped to wed. Honoria."

"I assumed as much." He raised his head, staring blankly at the wall above the mantel. "But what did Sinclair get from the bargain, besides the pleasure of seeing me ruined? Money? I hadn't thought him in need of funds."

Brenna struggled to swallow, her throat feeling suddenly parched. "Me," she answered, her voice breaking. "'Twould seem *I* was his prize. Hugh Ballard cares naught for me, his twin. I was simply something to barter. If he thinks I'll let Lord Thomas get his filthy hands on Glenbroch, he's gravely mistaken. 'Tis my land, my estate. My da worked long and hard to make it prosper, as have I. I would kill Lord Thomas with my own hands before I'd let him clear it."

Dropping his hand from the mantel, Colin whirled around to stare at her. A moment passed before he spoke. "Let us hope it will not come to that."

"I believed Lord Danville to be an honest and caring man, the best of the lot. I will speak with him further on the matter. I canna imagine that he will force me to wed against my will, once he understands how completely opposed I am to the match. But what of ye? How will ye use this knowledge?"

He shook his head. "I'm not sure. Would you be willing to sign a statement, attesting to what you heard?"

"Aye. Why not? I owe my brother nothing."

"You realize it will cause a stir, a scandal? That they will deny the truth and call you a liar?"

"I dinna have a care about that. Let them call me what they wish," she said with a shrug. "'Tis not as if I have any friends here in London save Jane. My only fear is that I'm an outsider—what we call a *Sassenach.* They think me beneath them, the ladies and gentlemen of the *ton.* Who will believe me?"

"Perhaps no one." He moved to the side of the sofa, sitting on the curved arm beside her, and reached for her hand. "But you'd do this for me, all the same?"

Brenna nodded mutely, unable to reply. Colin was peeling her kidskin gloves from her hands. Folding the pair, he set them carefully on the sofa beside her, then took one bare hand in his grasp. His skin was hot, burning hers with his touch, and she noted that his hand shook ever so slightly.

"Why?" he asked, his voice a hoarse whisper beside her ear. "Why would you do this for me?"

Was he trying to seduce her? Like he'd seduced Lady Mandeville? She moistened her lips before she spoke. "Because it is the truth. 'Tis reason enough for me."

"You said you have no friends in London, none but Jane. What of me, Brenna? What am I to you?"

Her breath hitched in her chest. "I . . . I'm not certain. I thought ye were my friend, but then ye said yourself ye were not a man of character, that ye had deceived me. I dinna ken what to think."

In an instant he was beside her on the sofa, tugging her into his lap, cradling her like a child against his chest. She could feel his heart slamming against her own breasts, his mouth moving against her hair. She squeezed her eyes shut, her heart torn in several directions at once.

Colin clasped her small body tightly against his. Why had she chosen this time to appear on his doorstep? Why not a quarter hour earlier, while Jane had remained? All Colin could think about was carrying her upstairs to his bed and having his way with her, doing all the things he'd imagined doing to her since the day he'd met her. His whole body burned with unruly lust, his sudden erection pressing uncomfortably against the flap of his trousers.

"God's teeth, Brenna," he said with a groan, struggling to rein in his desires. "Have you any idea how much I need someone . . . a friend . . . right now? I need you. I need you to say you'd do this for me because you believe in me, because you care for me."

Her whole body quivered against his. "Nay, I canna say it."

"You can," he commanded, reaching for her chin and tilting her face upward, forcing her to meet his gaze. Her round, aquamarine eyes met his, blinking repeatedly, the threat of tears dampening her lashes. "You tremble at my touch, go weak when I kiss you. Tell me it's true, that I'm not losing my bloody mind. You want me as much as I want you."

"Did ye ask the same of Lady Mandeville?" she answered, her voice steady and cool. "Before she left her reticule behind?"

"Certainly not. What do you think, that Lucy and I . . ." He trailed off, shaking his head. "Of course you do, and of course I cannot tell you the truth, either." To tell anyone the truth of his relationship to Lucy would endanger her reputation, her standing in society. He hadn't even confided in Jane, for God's sake, difficult as that had been.

"As I have indicated, Lucy is like a sister to me," he said, carefully measuring his words. "No more, no less. To suggest that there is anything improper between us is preposterous, and that's all I will say on the subject."

"Let me go." Brenna struggled against him, but he tightened his grasp.

"No." He couldn't. He needed her. Today more than ever. If she left now, he knew he'd have to find a drink somewhere. He couldn't bear it, not now. "Please," he said, his voice a ragged growl.

She went immediately still in his arms.

"I realize I can't . . . that I'm not the sort of man—"

She silenced him with her mouth.

"Oh, Colin," she murmured against his lips, her arms reaching around his shoulders. She kissed him, tenderly at first, then far more hungrily as he opened his mouth against hers. Her tongue slipped inside, moving in tentative exploration.

His hands moved to her hair, removing pins in a

desperate attempt to run his fingers through the glossy, reddish-gold locks that he'd dreamt of each night. At last her hair spilled haphazardly down her back. He raked his fingers through the silky waves, cupping the back of her head with both hands, drawing her closer still. He wanted to devour her; he'd thought of nothing else for days on end, and now, here she was, in his arms. For a moment he thought he might weep with relief.

Instead, he moved his mouth lower, to the slim column of her pale neck, where her pulse leapt wildly beneath his lips. A crest of desire coursed through him, and he suddenly had to see her breasts, to see if they resembled the ones he'd imagined in his dreams.

Inhaling sharply, he hooked his thumbs into the edge of her bodice, where the rose-colored gauze met the gentle swell of her breasts. Near viciously, he tugged on the fabric, taking her chemise with it. She moaned against his throat as he freed her breasts, exposing them to his hungry eyes.

Devil take it, they were beautiful, more so than he'd ever imagined. Pale, round globes the color of almond milk, crested by delightfully erect nipples the same shade of rose as her frothy gown.

"Don't," Brenna cried out softly, even as she guided his head toward them with her hands, arching her back in anticipation. A flame licked at his groin as he flicked his tongue over one straining peak. How would he ever stop, now that he'd tasted the forbidden fruit? This was what he needed to lose himself in, not the drink. This nectar was far, far more intoxicating than the finest brandy. He captured her nipple in his mouth, suckling her till she moaned and squirmed in his arms.

He resisted the urge to carry her upstairs, knowing if he did so, he'd never stop, never abandon her lush little body till it was far too late. Right now, it was all he could do to keep his rogue hands from removing her gown entirely, baring her to his lustful gaze. Pausing to catch his breath, he felt her fingers move against his chest, tugging at his shirt, freeing it from the band of his trousers. Suddenly her hands were on his bare skin, lighting a fire up his torso as she struggled, tugging at the folds of linen.

Realization dawned on him, nearly making him dizzy. She was attempting to remove his shirt. Skin against skin—he could suddenly think of nothing else. Leaning back, he reached for his shirttails and pulled the linen over his head in one fluid motion, not caring where it landed. With a sharp cry, she pressed herself against him, her bare breasts flattened against the muscles of his chest.

For several seconds, neither moved, their hearts pounding in rhythm. She was so very beautiful, flawless in every way. Their bodies molded perfectly. At once he hungered for more. He needed more, as much of her as he could have. Reaching for her gown's hem, he drew her skirts up to her waist, his fingers gliding along her thigh, skimming the silky flesh and drawing gooseflesh in their wake. She leaned into him, her breathing becoming shallow and ragged against his neck.

At once her entire body tensed against his. "Nay, ye must stop this at once, Colin."

Remorse washing over him, he released her skirts and clutched her to him. If he let her go now, he might never have the opportunity to hold her like this again. He wasn't yet ready to give her up. Yet he must. He had no claim on her. None. He'd allowed himself to get carried away, to use her like he would a whore. "I'm sorry, Brenna. So very sorry. I *will* make this right. I won't take advantage of you and then—"

"I must go," she said, her breath warm against his bare chest.

He knew he must let her go. He hadn't a choice, even if it nearly killed him to do so. He nodded, forcing his fingers to tug her bodice back to its rightful place, covering her breasts, shielding them from his view, perhaps forever. "Can you stand?" he asked, silently cursing the tremor in his voice.

"I . . . I think so," she answered, sliding off his lap, away from his persistent erection. "But my hair." She looked about wildly at the pins scattered across the carpet. She took one tentative step, then faltered, her injured foot buckling beneath her.

Frozen, Colin watched in horror as she crumpled to the ground. At last springing to action, he tore himself from the sofa and knelt beside her, gathering her in his arms.

"My ankle," she said, looking up at him sheepishly.

"Let me see it." He pushed up her skirts and took her still-bare foot in his hands, massaging gently. Nothing appeared broken, and the swelling was minor. He grasped her foot firmly and rotated it, making small circles in the air, first clockwise, then counterclockwise. "How does that feel?"

"Better, actually. Dear Lord, Colin, look at us." She plucked his shirt off the carpet and dropped it into his lap. "Just imagine what people would think were they to see us like this."

"Well, they wouldn't be that far off the mark. Can you ever forgive me, Brenna? I've not been myself lately, and these past few days have been difficult. I meant to hold you, to kiss you, perhaps, but I never meant to take advantage of you like that."

"'Tis my fault as much as yours," she said, studying him sharply. "Truly, Colin, I didna notice it before now, but ye look terrible. Whatever has happened to ye?" She reached out to touch his bruised eye, then the bandage on his shoulder.

He swallowed hard before answering. He could not tell her the entire truth—that he'd drunk himself senseless, spent the night God knew where, and then spent the past few days withdrawing entirely from alcohol. "A rough night in the East End is all. I've been . . . recuperating."

"Well, whoever he was, I hope ye got the best of him. Ye look as if ye could use a bit more recuperation."

"Hmm, perhaps. I could say the same of your ankle. You should stay off it a bit, at least till the swelling goes down. A fine pair we make, don't we?"

She laughed then, an easy, gentle laugh, and the tension he'd felt began to melt away. "Wretched," she answered. "I'm ashamed to tell ye I have no means to return to Danville House. Your family's butler sent me here in an old barouche to locate Jane. I think I gave the man an apoplexy, appearing on his doorstep like a madwoman, raving about ball gowns and Prinny himself and insisting I must speak with your sister at once."

"Prinny and ball gowns? I'm almost afraid to ask. Here, let me help you up." Just as he extended a hand to her, the front door slammed shut, startling him. "What the—"

"Colin, dear," a voice called out. *Damnation*. His mother. He attempted to scrabble to his feet, taking Brenna with him, but he slipped on his shirt, which still lay in a heap on the carpet.

"Jane said you were gravely ill, so I brought you one of Cook's tonics. Mrs. Butler and I were just on our way . . ." His mother appeared in the doorway, Mrs. Butler at her side. Both women goggled at the sight before them, their mouths open and their faces white with shock. "Dear Lord in heaven," his mother said, finding her voice. "I think I'm going to swoon." Without further warning, she slumped against the moldings and slid to the floor with a resounding thud.

Colin almost laughed aloud at the comical horror of the situation. Brenna gasped, gazing up at him with pleading eyes, as if there were anything he could do to right the current state of affairs. It was hopeless. They were trapped, plain and simple.

For how could he possibly explain why Brenna was sprawled on his carpet, her skirts bunched around her knees? Worse still, her bodice had slipped so low that one rose-colored half-moon peeked over the edge of the fabric, the skin surrounding it bruised by his mouth. And if that alone weren't bad enough, there was also the fact that he was wearing nothing save his trousers and was nearly straddling her at the present.

No, he could do nothing but watch in horror as Mrs. Butler crouched over his mother, waving a vinaigrette before her nose in an effort to revive her. She came around with a moan, the back of one hand pressed to her forehead.

Devil take it, why was it that whenever he thought things couldn't possibly get any worse than they were, they found a way to do just that? And what a grand way to illustrate the point.

He returned his gaze to Brenna, a stricken expression darkening her features. Did she fully understand the implications? There was no question he'd be forced to marry her.

Had this been Brenna's plan all along, a desperate ploy to extricate herself from the marriage agreement with Sinclair? Hadn't Jane just confessed to suggesting such a scheme to her? Blast Jane and her bloody brilliant ideas.

His head swam in confusion, his thoughts nothing but a muddled mess. Of *course* he should marry her. He'd taken unforgivable liberties, after all. He'd tried to say as much, but she'd silenced him, unwilling to hear it.

Never had he expected to be coldly manipulated into marriage, careful as he'd always been with ladies of virtue. And now, here he was, manipulated by the one woman whose affections he yearned for. Married—not for who he was, but instead for who he was *not*. That miserable, emasculating thought alone sliced through his gut, made his lungs burn as if he were suffocating.

"Good afternoon, Mother, Mrs. Butler," he said at last, rising to his feet and bowing toward the two gaping women. "It looks as if you're just in time for an offer of marriage, aren't you?"

# Chapter 15

Stone-faced and silent, Brenna sat perched on the edge of the sofa, absently twisting a handkerchief in her lap. Beside her, Lady Danville wailed into her own handkerchief, lowering it now and again to cry out, "Why, Margaret?" or "How could you do such a thing?" till Brenna thought she might go mad.

Worse still were the angry sounds coming from her father's study. Furniture crashed, glassware shattered. "That brazen little bitch!" she heard Hugh roar just before another loud crash. "I'll wring her neck," he added, sounding as if he meant it.

"You'll do no such thing," came Lord Danville's voice as Lady Danville's sobs grew louder beside Brenna. "And I'll ask that you watch what you say about your sister. She is my daughter, after all. She acted foolishly, yes. Terribly so, and our family's name will no doubt suffer. Still, it could have been worse, much worse. Dissolute or not, at least Colin Rosemoor is the heir to a viscountcy, and he has already agreed—"

"Already agreed? You mean to say you've already spoken with him? What of your agreement with Sinclair?"

"Come now, Mrs. Butler is a known gossip-monger. Do you honestly think Sinclair would honor the agreement, now that your sister has been so publicly compromised? I'll offer him a generous settlement, as we're in breach of promise, but—"

"She will marry Sinclair!" Hugh bellowed, sounding near-crazed.

"She will marry Colin Rosemoor, scoundrel or not." Lord Danville's voice was remarkably calm. "She might carry his child, for God's sake."

Another crash made Brenna flinch. One hand slipped from her lap to the sofa beside her, her nails digging into the velvet's deep nap.

"Goddamn that little bitch to hell." The study door splintered as Hugh flung it open against the wall. He stormed out, toppling a chair in his path as he headed toward the front door.

Brenna closed her eyes and sighed deeply. Lord, but she'd wreaked havoc with her behavior. She'd never forgive herself such foolishness. *Never.* In the course of one day, she'd been reduced to a witless twit, no better than the women who populated the silly, romantic novels her nursemaid Jenny had favored.

"She'll pay for this," Hugh warned before throwing open the door and disappearing into the night.

Lady Danville's sobs increased as a weary-looking Lord Danville came to stand before them. He sighed, his face drawn and taut. "Well, daughter, I hope you are satisfied. Breach of promise, public scandal." He ticked off her transgressions with his fingers. "At least I can take comfort in the fact that I cannot claim responsibility for your upbringing. You've made your bed, young lady, and now you must lie in it, uncomfortable though it may be. You'll marry Colin Rosemoor in a fortnight."

Her mouth fell open. "A fortnight? Surely you're not serious?"

"I assure you, I am entirely serious."

"Nay, sir. 'Tis too soon. I must speak with him first. I canna just—"

"You can and you will. You've disappointed me greatly, Margaret. Despite the fact that those . . . those *people* raised you, I thought you to be a virtuous woman. That you would defy my specific instructions and associate with such a man, well . . ." He shook his head once more. "I misjudged you. And now we must all suffer for it."

"How shall I face my friends?" Lady Danville wailed. "Mrs. Butler said he was near enough mounting her there on the carpet, both of them half-clothed—"

"Shush, Harriet, that's more than enough. She knows what she's done. No use rehashing it over and over again."

Brenna only stared at her hands, unable to reply in the face of such criticism. Never before had she disappointed those who claimed to care for her. She'd been naught but a source of pride and joy to the Maclachlans, a loving and dutiful daughter above all else. What would the Maclachlans think of her now—a fallen woman by all accounts? It didn't matter that her virginity remained intact. By all appearances she was ruined, and appearances were what mattered to the *ton*.

"Come now, Harriet," her father said, reaching for Lady Danville's shoulder as she continued to sob, quietly now. "You'll make yourself ill, carrying on like this. Besides, there's much to be done. A trousseau to be bought, a wedding to be arranged, and only a fortnight to accomplish it."

"A fortnight?" Lady Danville snuffled, at last ceasing her weeping. "No, that simply will not do. I cannot make such arrangements in a fortnight alone."

"Oh, but you'll find a way, I'm certain. It needn't be a large affair. Something intimate, a small ceremony in the drawing room followed by a wedding breakfast. Certainly not the circumstances for a lavish affair."

Lady Danville's trembling mouth curved into a smile, despite her damp eyes. She turned toward Brenna, laying a hand on her wrist. "Your father is right; there is so much to do. Tomorrow we will go to Madame Vioget for your trousseau. We must be quick about it, as there isn't much time. And oh, the menu! I wonder if Cook is still about. I must consult with her at once." She rose, her eyes darting toward the drawing room. "Fifty guests, perhaps, and a string quartet should suffice. A rib roast and those pastries stuffed with lobster and prawns. Perhaps an aspic, too, and turtle soup." She drummed her fingers together, her mouth pursed thoughtfully. "Gunter's for a tiered cake, of course. We must arrange for that at once, as well. La, so much to do. I simply don't know how I'll manage. Mrs. Tupper?" she trilled. "Oh, fustian. Where is the bell? Mrs. Tupper!"

Brenna watched as Lady Danville hurried off in

search of the housekeeper, whistling a wedding march as she did so. However did the woman accomplish such a transformation—from utter despair to utter delight—in so short a time? 'Twas astonishing.

"Well, now," Lord Danville said, stroking his whiskers. "You must excuse me, as I've some unpleasant business to attend to with Lord Thomas Sinclair. I only hope he takes the news better than your brother did. Best not go in my study right now, not till the staff sweeps up the damage. I suppose you should get some rest. Heaven knows, your mother will run you ragged in the days to come."

Again, Brenna only nodded. She was afraid to speak, afraid she might begin to weep. Her emotions were naught but a muddle. Not since the Maclachlans' deaths, one right after the other, had she felt so lost, so frightened and utterly alone. She bit her bottom lip to keep it from trembling.

Lord Danville stepped closer, his eyes narrowed as he regarded her sharply. "He did not hurt you, did he, Margaret? If that rogue forced himself on you, I'll—"

"Nay, sir, I assure ye he did not," she said, finding her voice at last. "I know ye have no reason to believe me, but 'twas not at all as it appeared. Truly. I only went to his lodgings because I believed Miss Rosemoor to be there, and I wished to speak with them both. I would have left straightaway once I found Mr. Rosemoor alone, but I twisted my ankle on the steps, ye see." She lifted the hem of her skirt, exposing her still-swollen ankle. "He was only trying to be helpful."

"Hmm, perhaps," he said, sounding tired, defeated. "Even if what you say is true, there's no alternative save marrying him. You must see that."

"Not really," she muttered.

"I only hope you do not fancy yourself in love with him." He patted her on the shoulder. "Nothing but trouble would follow such imprudence as losing your heart to a man like him. You must remember that. I fear I'm partly to blame for this fiasco, and the burden weighs heavily on me. I should have taken more seriously your objections to marrying Sinclair. Still, I had no idea you'd act so rashly, so irresponsibly, in order to extricate yourself. Jane Rosemoor is your friend, and I suppose you thought . . . Well, you shall have her as a sister now, won't you? Let that thought comfort you."

Brenna could only wonder how Jane felt about the circumstances forcing the marriage. Would she think less of her now? Her cheeks grew warm at the thought of Jane's disapproval.

"The Rosemoors are highly esteemed," he added, "despite young Rosemoor's attempts to ruin them."

Och, if only Lord Danville knew the truth. 'Twas his own son's efforts that had ruined Colin's reputation. *I should tell him so,* Brenna thought. She didn't owe Hugh protection, especially after his violent little outburst in Lord Danville's study. Lord Danville wouldn't believe her, but she'd try, nonetheless. "There's something I must tell ye, sir."

"Yes? Go on."

"About Hugh. Think what ye will of Colin Rosemoor, but he is no cheat. 'Twas Lord Thomas Sinclair who arranged to have that card planted in Colin's pocket. He did so at Hugh's direction."

"Rubbish. Wherever would you get such a ridiculous notion as that? From Rosemoor himself, I suppose."

"Nay, Lord Danville. I heard them—Hugh and Lord Thomas—speaking of their plot to ruin him. Today. 'Tis why I had to speak with Jane so urgently."

"Enough. I will not listen to such outlandish tales."

"But, Lord Danville, 'tis true. Hugh hoped to gain the hand of Miss Lyttle-Brown and needed Colin discredited so that she might—"

"I said enough, Margaret." Lord Danville held up one hand. Just as she'd suspected, he would not entertain the truth, not when it spoke so unflatteringly about his only son and heir. "No more. Go on, up to bed now. You'll need every ounce of your strength in the coming days. Dressmakers, milliners . . ." He shook his head. "Wherever else it is young ladies must go to see to their needs before marriage. Don't fret yourself over Hugh. He'll get over it soon enough."

Would he? She'd destroyed the terms of his bargain with Lord Thomas, after all. She only hoped Colin wouldn't suffer for it. Hadn't he suffered enough at the hands of the scheming pair? She did not care if Hugh ever forgave her, so long as he left her in peace.

"Good night, Lord Danville," she said quietly, rising and heading toward the stairs with only the slightest limp. Her father was right—she needed some rest. The day's events had exhausted her, both physically and mentally. Her ankle still smarted, though it was the least of her worries. She could no longer hide from the decision she must make. She knew she must choose which course of action to take: flee to Glenbroch within the fort-night, or stay and accept the consequences of her actions.

'Twould be a sleepless night, no doubt.

"The yellow lawn is lovely, Margaret. Don't you agree?"

Brenna glanced up at the bolts of fabric draped across the long wooden table and nodded distract-edly. "Aye, Lady—Mama," she corrected. "The yellow lawn is lovely."

"Perhaps the lilac silk as well?" Her mother ran her fingers across a bolt of fabric the color of heather. "For an evening gown, I think. A turban to match might do nicely. I've some lovely feathers we could trim it with. Hmm, what else?"

"*S'il vous plait,* madame, I highly recommend the blue crepe." Madame Vioget held up a length of filmy fabric so sheer that the sunlight shone through it. "It will look positively charming with her coloring. For her wedding gown, *non?*"

*My wedding gown.* Brenna gulped. Was she really here to purchase her trousseau? It hardly registered in her numb mind. She shook her head. No, the blue crepe wouldn't do. It was far too . . . *celebratory.* This hasty marriage felt more like a duty than a cel-ebration. Something simpler, more serviceable, felt right. A shade of gray silk, perhaps, or ecru satin.

Madame Vioget pushed her spectacles up her thin nose. "And I was thinking this pearl-colored silk for a nightdress and matching dressing gown. For your wedding night, mademoiselle."

Brenna could only stare at the sumptuous fabric.

Wedding night? Dear God, she hadn't even allowed herself to think that far ahead.

"Perhaps with Spanish lace trimming the bodice. *Oui?*" The modiste smiled wickedly. "I think your young monsieur will find it appealing. *Très belle.*"

Brenna covered her mouth with one hand. Would he really expect . . . ? She swallowed hard. Aye, of course he would. But so soon? 'Twas not as if he had spoken of love or affection, and yet she'd already allowed him to bare her breasts to his gaze, to touch her in intimate ways she'd never imagined would bring her such pleasure. Her cheeks warmed uncomfortably at the memory. He would think her eager, willing to be bedded. Her legs began to tremble, and she grasped the edge of the table for support.

Her mother patted her hand reassuringly and turned toward the modiste with drawn brows. "You're certain you can complete the order in less than a fortnight?"

"*Oui*, of course, madame. I'll have every seamstress available put right to work."

"This one," Brenna blurted out, pointing to a bolt of dove-gray silk. "For my wedding gown."

Her mother shook her head. "No, dear, not for your wedding gown. It's much too simple, too solemn. The blue crepe is better suited."

"Nay," Brenna pressed. "I like the gray silk. I will make at least one decision myself, as far as my wedding is concerned." A bleak gray, like her future.

The bell in the shop's door sounded. Brenna looked up as Lady Brandon, together with a silver-haired companion she remembered as Mrs. Appleton, headed their way.

"Good day, Lady Danville, Lady Margaret," Mrs. Appleton said. "Why, you must be here buying your trousseau. How positively delightful." She clapped her plump hands together.

"Good day, Mrs. Appleton, Lady Brandon." Her mother nodded. Brenna tipped her head but said nothing.

"What a happy coincidence," Mrs. Appleton chirped. "Why, not a half hour past we ran into Lady Cowper, and she told us the news. Stunned I was, I tell you. Simply stunned. Not a match I would have predicted. I'm sure you've heard of his reputation, the rapscallion? Turned out of White's, they say."

Lady Danville's eyes narrowed, her mouth set in a hard line. "Nothing more than the impetuosities of youth, I assure you, Dolly."

"Hmph." Lady Brandon eyed Brenna severely.

It took every ounce of Brenna's fortitude not to squirm under such scrutiny, yet she managed to stand erect, her head held high.

"Cat got your tongue, gel?" Lady Brandon asked.

"Nay, Lady Brandon. As ye can see, I'm still fully capable of speech." *Horrible woman.* "'Tis a pleasure to see you, as always."

"Impertinent, as always," Lady Brandon answered. "Say what you will, Harriet, but everyone knows Colin Rosemoor's troubles are far more serious than boyish mischief. I can't say I'm at all surprised by the match. Seems fitting, indeed."

Mrs. Appleton had the good grace to look uncomfortable. "Still," she offered, "Lord and Lady Rosemoor are lovely people, and Jane Rosemoor has always been a darling of the *ton*, has she not?"

"Indeed," Brenna's mother answered coldly.

"Anyway," Mrs. Appleton continued breathlessly, "Colin Rosemoor is a wicked one, isn't he? Never without a beautiful woman on his arm, and I've always wondered about his relationship with Lady Mandeville, even though she and the marquess *do* seem very much in love. Why, it's even rumored that Mr. Rosemoor was seen at the opera recently with Mrs. Trumball-Watts."

"That is no rumor," Lady Brandon said. "It's the truth. I saw the pair with my very own eyes. Simply scandalous."

"Well, perhaps our girl here can set him to rights, hmm?" Mrs. Appleton chucked Brenna under the chin. "Wanted your dowry, I suppose. All those debts to pay, Mr. Appleton says. Well, who could blame the young buck? At least he had the brains to choose sensibility over beauty when selecting a bride. I hear you're smart as a whip, Lady Margaret. There are worse things, I say. Well, we must be on our way. We've much to do today, haven't we, Lady Brandon?"

"Indeed," her companion answered. "Best of luck, gel. You'll need it."

"I thank ye for your kind felicitations," Brenna ground out through gritted teeth, wishing the earth would open up beneath her slippers and swallow her whole.

At last the women took their leave. Brenna watched them make their way back through the bolts of cloth, not releasing her breath until the bell jangled in the door, signaling their exit. Only then did she chance a glance at her scarlet-faced mother.

"Why, I never!" Lady Danville huffed. "I would

expect such treatment from Lady Brandon, but Mrs. Appleton? Her own daughter is married to a wastrel—the most lascivious rake for miles about. Forced to live in Cheapside now, from what I hear. We'll strike her off our invitation list, won't we, Margaret? Serve her right, the old tabby." Her lips pursed, her mother returned her attention to the blue crepe.

Brenna dropped her gaze to the dusty floor. *Her dowry.* Of course. That explained why Colin had come immediately to Danville House to face her father's wrath instead of fleeing the district at once. He needed her dowry—not to mention her inheritance—to pay off his gambling debts. Why had she not thought of it before?

A heated flush climbed up her neck as she silently cursed her loose tongue. She hadn't thought twice about telling Jane the surprisingly large sum she'd seen named as her dowry on the marriage contract. Had Jane repeated the sum to Colin? If so, Jane had no doubt meant well. Still . . .

She reached up to rub her temples, still smarting at Mrs. Appleton's unkind words. She was well aware she paled in comparison to the elegant young ladies who gathered in Lady Brandon's drawing room; she needn't the blunt reminders. Certainly her own appearance did not measure up to Lady Mandeville's, she thought, calling to mind the woman's golden hair, emerald-green eyes, and delicate features. Despite her small stature, Lady Mandeville appeared womanly, curved in all the right places. She glanced down at her own small bosom, fiddling with her pelisse as her mother finished her business with Madame Vioget.

Brenna reached one hand up to stifle a yawn while she waited. She was tired, having lain awake last night till dawn, deciding whether or not to go through with the marriage. To do so would drastically alter the course she'd set for her life. To have such a decision thrust upon her in so short a time frightened her terribly. Still, only a coward would refuse to face the consequences of their behavior, no matter how unpleasant those consequences might be, and she was no coward.

And perhaps the consequences wouldn't be so unpleasant, after all. She enjoyed Colin's company, she had reminded herself, and there was no denying that she desired him. The thought that she might have foolishly allowed herself to fall in love with him had even flitted uncomfortably across her mind. She'd dismissed the thought, refusing to acknowledge it. Instead, she'd tossed and turned in her bed for hours on end. As the first hazy light of dawn had cast an eerie glow on her bedchamber, she had at last made peace with her decision to remain. Only then had she been able to drift off into a restless sleep.

Looking back now, she realized that perhaps she'd made the wrong decision after all.

# Chapter 16

Colin paced before the Danvilles' pianoforte, trailing his fingertips along the smooth rosewood case while he waited for Brenna to join him. He had no idea what he'd say to her but felt they should speak privately before their wedding, which was now only days away. Perhaps seeing her would set his mind at ease. Even if it did not, it didn't seem right that he should next see her standing beside him as they became man and wife. Damnation, it still didn't signify.

Jane had claimed responsibility. She hadn't imagined that Brenna would actually take her ill-conceived advice and attempt to entrap him, she said. Yet he detected a gleam of triumph in her eyes whenever she spoke of it. Which, of course, only made him feel all the more manipulated. Had he been nothing but a pawn in an elaborate game of chess? It certainly felt that way. Yet, at the same time, he felt a sense of relief. Despite his chafing at the female maneuverings, he was glad to save Brenna from marrying Sinclair. Now she would not be misused at Sinclair's hands. She would be safe under his protection, of that he would make certain.

He ceased his restless pacing, looking toward the empty doorway. What was keeping her? It seemed he'd been waiting an interminable time, though in truth it couldn't have been more than a quarter hour. He was impatient. Distracted. Scanning the room, his gaze fell upon the long sideboard against the far wall. A cut-glass decanter of brandy, nearly full, sat there on a silver tray. A pair of snifters sat invitingly beside the decanter. Damn, but he needed a drink. How many days had it been? He'd lost count. Hadn't he proved himself no longer dependent upon it? What harm could come from indulging in just a taste, no more?

He crossed the room in several strides, pausing before the sideboard. He could almost taste the smoky, rich liquid sliding down his parched throat. *Just a taste,* he reminded himself. Reaching for the stopper, he froze. Horrified, he withdrew his hand with a silent curse. What the hell had happened to his self-control? He'd only now reached the point where he didn't crave the blasted stuff on an hourly basis. No good would come from indulging now. He rammed his hands into his pockets, turning his back on the decanter before he changed his mind.

A rustling sound in the doorway captured his attention, and he opened his eyes to find Brenna standing there, watching him. Devil take it, but his heart began to race. In the silence, he allowed himself a moment to study her. She wore a frothy gown of pale blue, generously trimmed with girlish ribbons. In stark contrast, her hair was pulled back into a severe knot, without even a single softening curl to frame her face—a face that appeared drawn, pale, her eyes hollow.

"Mr. Rosemoor," she murmured at last, offering him a slight curtsy. She did not meet his eyes, yet he could sense hers flashing angrily as she brushed past him and took a seat on the sofa.

"Rather formal today, aren't we?" he drawled, moving to stand opposite her, leaning indolently against the windowsill. "I rather think you might call me Colin. We *are* to be married soon, after all."

"A fact I'm well aware of. I've done naught but prepare for it for more than a sennight now." Her voice was cold, clipped.

What reasons could she have for her anger? Hadn't he played right into her hands? "I'd expect you to sound more pleased about it."

"Would ye, now? I canna for the life of me imagine why."

"Your sharp tongue alone could wound a man, you know." He rapped on his chest. "Straight through the heart."

"Have ye a quip for every occasion, Colin?"

"I *do* try."

"Aye, ye make light of everything. Dinna ye realize how very serious this matter is? We're to be joined in matrimony, in four days time. Till death do us part? Surely you've heard the phrase."

"I'm quite aware of the gravity of the situation," he snapped. "You can rest assured that I won't take our vows lightly."

"Every vow? Or simply the ones ye choose to honor?"

"What are you implying, Brenna? That I'm not a man of my word? That I will abandon you, abuse you? Tell me, precisely which vow do you fear I might fail to keep?"

"All of them . . . none of them," she corrected, shaking her head. "I dinna ken what I mean."

He hadn't thought it possible, but somehow her pale face became paler still. He studied her countenance again, more closely this time. Dark shadows rimmed her eyes, eyes that practically knocked the air from his lungs with their look of desperation. He could no longer bear to look into their turbulent depths.

With a groan, Colin turned toward the window and leaned against the sill, his palms damp. It was hard to remain angry at someone who was clearly in such a state of despair—a state brought on by being forced to marry him against her will. Was she really so horrified by the prospect? The thought sent his mind reeling.

He closed his eyes and took several deep, calming breaths before opening them again to gaze out the window at the neat grounds of Danville House. The garden appeared orderly, well manicured. Nothing like the rambling, wild gardens his mother preferred at Rosemoor House, and, on a larger scale, at Glenfield. He shivered as a breeze heavy with the sweet scent of honeysuckle rippled the drapes. With a sigh, he dropped his chin to his chest. However had he gotten himself into this?

His life was about to change—irrevocably—and he wasn't in the least prepared for it. Now evicted from his bachelor lodgings, he hadn't anywhere to live with his bride save Rosemoor House, together with his family. Until his father chose to give him one, he had no country estate of his own, and he could not afford to lease one. He had nothing to offer her; nothing besides his name. And, of course, the betrothal ring he carried with him now. One hand moved to his pocket, his fingers tracing the outline of the velvet pouch that held a precious Rosemoor family heirloom, one he'd chosen especially for Brenna.

Would she accept the token with pleasure? Or would she slip it on her finger with reluctance? He was almost afraid to find out. With a silent curse, Colin pressed his forehead against the glass, cool against his burning skin. Bloody hell, what a mess. This was not the way in which he hoped to begin his married life. God help his foolish romanticism, but he'd imagined tender feelings, heartfelt declarations of love. Not this. Not tension, distrust. Anger.

He turned to Brenna, who sat where he'd left her, absently twisting a handkerchief on her lap. He did not wish to be drawn into an argument with an obviously distraught and exhausted woman. "Come now, must we continue to snap at each other like this?" he asked, his tone light. "It isn't helping the situation. You look unwell, you know. Perhaps you should go lie down."

Her eyes narrowed perceptibly before she spoke. "I'm well enough."

"I beg to differ. If I might say so, you look exhausted. You're not yourself today, besides. Not the Brenna I've come to know."

"Perhaps ye dinna ken me as well as ye supposed," she answered, glowering at him.

"I know you well enough," he said, his voice tight.

"I suppose knowing the size of my dowry would suffice."

"Is that what you think?" Something inside him snapped at the mention of her dowry—the dowry he'd given his word not to touch. He'd been surprised to learn just how generous a portion she had behind her, one which Lord Danville had insisted be put in trust. So that he couldn't get his hands on it, of course, and risk losing it at the gaming tables. That stipulation had been humiliating at best, yet he'd accepted it without hesitation. No matter how pressed for funds he might become, he'd never take his wife's money. "How can you sit there accusing *me* of being a fortune hunter, when you were the one who brought about this marriage?"

"However did I bring about this marriage? By succumbing to your practiced seduction?"

"I don't remember you offering the slightest resistance to my efforts."

She rose to face him, her cheeks stained strawberry and her hands balled into angry fists by her sides. "How dare ye, Colin Rosemoor. 'Tis bad enough ye treated me like . . . like a common harlot," she sputtered. "Like your Mrs. Trumball-Watts. Aye, I've heard all about her, about your relationship with her."

Relationship? Colin drew back in surprise. He'd escorted Mrs. Trumball-Watts home from the opera one night, at her request. Deposited her at her doorstep and taken his leave, nothing more. That single, unexceptional event summed up his entire so-called relationship with the woman. "Nothing but trumped-up lies and innuendo," he protested. "You must believe I've nothing to do with her—"

"Nay, I dinna want to hear it." Her eyes darkened to a stormy hue, the color of roiling seas. "But to suggest that I allowed ye to seduce me in order to bring about this . . . this *scandal*. Ye think I enjoy hearing the hushed gossip about me everywhere I go? Ye think I would bring this upon myself, simply for the pleasure of marrying ye?"

No. Why would she? *To escape the horrible fate of marrying Sinclair,* his mind supplied. He was a lesser of two evils. Yet her anger seemed genuine, her indignation valid. Colin felt the blood pound in his temples. He no longer knew what to think. All he knew was that she stirred his blood, stoked his desire, even as she stood there glaring at him.

"Well?" Brenna asked, clasping her hands in front of herself. "Have ye not anything more to say on the subject? Another quip, perhaps?" He was silently watching her, an altogether strange look upon his features. She could almost swear she saw desire in his eyes. Did he think her clay in his hands, so easy to manipulate? A look, a touch, and she would bend to his wishes?

He raked a hand through his hair, leaving it decidedly more mussed than before. "Yes, well. Actually, I did come here today with a purpose in mind." He reached into his pocket, rummaging around with a frown. Pulling out a black velvet pouch, he withdrew something from within, closing his fingers around it.

Brenna's breath caught as he reached for her hand, then sank to one knee beside her.

"I know we've had a . . . well, an unfortunate start to our betrothal. Still, I'd hoped to do this properly."

He held up a ring—an exquisite oval aquamarine set with diamonds—and smiled up at her uncertainly.

Despite her resolve to resist his charm, her heart soared at the sight of him kneeling before her, looking so very hopeful and vulnerable. So devastatingly handsome.

"I very much hope you'll do me the honor of becoming my wife, Brenna. Though God knows I don't deserve you."

Brenna covered her mouth with one hand, temporarily rendered speechless. Her gaze briefly met his questioning one, then slid back down to the ring he held out between his forefinger and thumb like an offering. It was exquisite, really. Far more beautiful than any jewel she'd ever owned. "Oh, Colin, 'tis lovely."

He rose to stand before her. "It was my great-grandmother Rosemoor's. As soon as I saw it, I knew you must have it. The stone is exactly the same shade as your eyes." Again, he reached for her hand. "A perfect match to your beauty, your strength, your brilliancy. Will you have me, Brenna?"

His words touched her heart. Still, she couldn't help but notice he made no mention of love. Why did the omission bother her so? She was a sensible girl, a practical girl. Before coming to London, she'd never entertained the notion of marrying for love. Love was for silly, foolish girls, for those at leisure to fritter away their days, lost in lofty daydreams. Yet here she stood, her heart near to breaking for the lack of that very same emotion. Her desire for him was surely leading her down a path toward love, a journey on which she feared Colin would not join her.

She sighed deeply, knowing there was naught she could do about it now. "Aye, Colin. I will have ye."

He nodded, then slipped the ring on her finger. Brenna stared at it in amazement, a smile tipping the corners of her mouth. 'Twas a perfect fit. "I think I may need my head examined, but I do accept ye willingly."

"As do I," Colin said at last, his expression solemn.

"Accept yourself?" Brenna teased. "And willingly, too?"

"Hmm, very amusing. I was striving to be serious, you know. Now you see why I don't often bother." He held her hand in his, examining the ring on her finger with a satisfied smile. "You'd never have accepted me under normal circumstances, would you?"

"Truly, Colin, there's no telling what I might have done. Even I canna say for certain where ye are concerned."

His eyes began to twinkle with mischief. "Do I really have that effect on you? Fascinating."

"Isn't it?" she replied wryly. "'Twill be the undoing of me yet."

"Might I test the theory with a kiss? For the sake of science, of course."

She shook her head. "'Tis perhaps not the best idea." Heaven forbid she might end up on the carpet, half-clothed again. Being discovered once in such an embarrassing fashion was quite enough for a lifetime. Even now, her cheeks grew warm at the memory.

"Still, I'm tempted all the same." He moved closer, his purely male scent suddenly overpowering her.

Sandalwood, tobacco. For once, the smell of brandy was absent. Curious. She hadn't time to consider it before he gathered her in his arms, his touch gentle as his mouth found hers. Her arms stole around his neck, her body pressing feverishly against his.

Yet his usual sense of urgency was gone. Instead, his kiss was slow, tender. His lips brushed against hers in a tantalizing fashion, his tongue parting her lips with such controlled restraint that she feared she might cry out with longing. Instead, a small moan of pleasure escaped her lips, and she felt him go rigid against her in response.

Regrettably, his mouth abandoned hers, his breath coming fast against her ear as he buried his face in her neck. "I must stop. Otherwise, I might . . . well—"

"Aye, you must."

"You're trembling," he said, pulling away to peer down at her anxiously.

"I dinna ken why. I'm a wee bit nervous, perhaps. The wedding . . . 'tis so verra soon. What must your mother think of me now? How can I face her, after—"

"Do not trouble yourself about that, Brenna. Despite the initial shock . . ." He cleared his throat, no doubt remembering that his mother had seen her with one breast nearly half-exposed, the effects of his mouth still visible on her bare skin. "Despite that," he continued, "she's delighted about the marriage. Jane speaks so very highly of you, and my father holds Lord Danville in esteem. Like any mother, she's dedicated her days to marrying off her children, one by one. This is her final triumph. She'll take it however she can get it; trust me. After that unpleasant business at White's and all that followed, I'm sure she despaired of ever seeing me honorably wed."

"Which reminds me, what are we to do about that? About Hugh and Lord Thomas? When shall I make my statement?"

Colin's jaw flexed. "There will be no statement."

"Whatever do you mean? We canna let them get away with such despicable behavior."

"As much as I detest the notion, I'm afraid we will."

"But why? I dinna understand. Just because we are to be wed—"

"I will not put my wife in a position to be called a liar in public."

"But—"

"No buts. Your family will soon be mine. I will not cast aspersions on their name, not now. Nor will I give Lord Danville further reason to detest me. We will simply move forward and try to forget the past."

"We canna do that. 'Tis not fair. I canna abide by it, not when I know the truth."

"You can, and you will."

"Ooh," she huffed. "Now ye sound like Lord Danville, telling me what I can and canna do."

"Have no fear, it's not something I'll attempt often. But in this case, you must see it's the only way."

"So ye will just accept it, then? Being expelled from your club? Falsely named a cheat?"

His features hardened, his eyes regarding her warily once more. "It's the price I must pay for marrying you."

Brenna's mouth fell open, and she could only stare at him in surprise. The *price* he must pay? And what of her costs?

"Blast it," Colin said, his hands clenched into fists by his sides. "I did not mean to phrase that so poorly. It's a price I pay willingly, and without regret. I say—"

"I think we've said enough for one day," Brenna snapped. "I'm sure ye must have business of some sort to attend to."

"Not particularly," he muttered. "But, alas, I'll leave you to your rest. You look as if you sorely need it." He strode toward the doorway, then paused. "Oh, and Jane said she'd likely pay you a call this afternoon. She's been unwell these past few days. Wanted me to tell you that's why she's not called since the betrothal was announced. Anyway, I said I would relay the message."

"And now ye have."

"I have, indeed. Well, then. Good day." He offered her a stiff bow. As he straightened, his gaze fell upon her hand, to the ring adorning her finger. A slow smile spread across his face. "It looks lovely on you, doesn't it?"

Seemingly involuntarily, her hand rose to her breast, her fingers running along the edge of her bodice. "It does, Colin. I canna thank ye enough."

"You like it, then?"

"I do. Verra much."

"I'm glad. You didn't notice the inscription, did you?"

"Inscription?" Brenna asked, her eyes wide with surprise. "Nay. Whatever does it say?"

Colin only quirked a brow in response.

She tugged the ring from her finger. Holding it up, she squinted at the single word engraved in script inside the band.

*Unbidden.*

"Unbidden? Whatever does it mean?"

"Hmm, let's see." He stroked his chin. "Unbidden. An adjective, I believe. Something that isn't bidden, that comes uninvited, of its own will."

Brenna could not help but laugh. "I know verra well what the word means, Colin. I only meant, why? Whatever does it mean to us?"

Colin opened the door and stepped out into the corridor, then turned to face her once more. "You'll understand its meaning soon enough, my sweet."

# Chapter 17

"I say, it all went rather well, didn't it? Lady Danville did a remarkable job, in so short a time."

"She did, didn't she?" Brenna answered, self-consciously arranging her personal articles on the vanity while her husband stood behind her, languidly leaning against the bedpost, his coat thrown carelessly over one shoulder and his cravat untied and hanging about his neck. In the glass, her eyes skimmed his reflection as he reached up to undo the top buttons on his shirt, revealing the firm, muscular planes of his chest. She swallowed hard at the sight.

*Her husband.* She dropped her gaze to her hands and, despite her rational thoughts, nearly gasped at the sight of the simple gold band encircling her finger. The morning's ceremony was nothing but a blur in her mind. She'd stood there beside Colin in her pale gray silk gown, thinking how very sorry she was that the Maclachlans hadn't lived to see her made a bride. She'd never imagined her own wedding like this, surrounded by people she'd known for so short a time. When it had been her turn to repeat her vows, she'd stood there like a fool, lost in her thoughts, staring at the floor beneath her slippers. Jane, standing beside her as her sole attendant, had to reach out and pluck her sleeve to gain her attention.

Afterward, they'd enjoyed a lavish meal, one that had gaily continued on for hours. At last the sated guests had departed, and Brenna's trunks had been loaded onto the carriage. They'd driven the short distance to Rosemoor House—her new home—in silence, Hera in her traveling case between them.

"I apologize that we cannot take a wedding trip right away," Colin said, drawing her from her ruminations. "I must first settle some matters here in Town."

*Financial matters, no doubt,* Brenna thought.

"Later, perhaps, once we are more settled," he continued. "In the meantime, is this bedchamber to your liking?"

"'Tis lovely, Colin." Brenna's voice sounded unnatural to her own ears. She set down her brush and met Colin's eyes in the looking glass. A shiver began at the base of her spine and worked its way up to her neck, and she clasped her arms about herself in an attempt to quell it.

"I'm glad to hear it. You mustn't get too comfortable, though. It seems my father has purchased us a town house on Henrietta Street as a wedding gift."

"Indeed? How verra generous of him," she murmured.

"Yes, quite a turnabout," he answered, his voice laced with bitterness. "It wasn't so long ago that the man was threatening to cut me off without a shilling. Anyway, tomorrow you shall go with my mother and Jane to order some furnishings and whatever else we might need to set up housekeeping."

Brenna's palms grew damp at the thought. Furnishing a London town house was not something she had ever aspired to. In fact, she'd never given it a single thought nor paid overmuch attention to her surroundings at Danville House. "I've no idea what will be required, ye know," she said, panic rising in her voice. "'Tis not as if I were raised in such surroundings."

"And that's precisely why my mother and Jane shall accompany you. No doubt Lucy will tag along, too. You'll manage well enough."

They'd all think her an incompetent ninny. Such domestic duties were simply not among her strengths, and she disliked engaging in activities she did not succeed at. She'd have a better time of repairing a dwelling's roof than she would of suitably furnishing it.

"And it also seems we'll have use of one of my father's lesser estates, a modest country house in Kent. If you'd like, we can take a brief wedding trip to Brighton at the close of the Season, and then retire immediately to Kent. I think that perhaps I'll begin raising hunters. I'll look to acquire some breeding stock from Lucy's stables—"

"Nay, I must go to Glenbroch at the Season's end," Brenna cut in, her chest tight. "Besides, I thought ye might wish to see Hampton's lands, now that they are rightfully yours. Get to know your tenants and—"

"I've already dispatched my man of affairs there

to see to it. It isn't necessary for us to travel there right away."

"But I've much to do at Glenbroch. I've been away far too long as it is. I must speak with Mr. Moray about the harvest, discuss the spring crops. We've much to do before winter's arrival. I thought ye would understand that I must return home—"

"This is your home now, Brenna," Colin said, his voice firm.

"Nay, 'twill never seem like home to me," she said, her voice hoarse.

Colin regarded her silently for several seconds. When he spoke at last, his voice was gentle, placating. "It's late, and you must be weary. Can this discussion not wait till tomorrow?"

Nay, she wanted it settled now. She reached up to stifle a yawn, her lids growing heavy. Blast it, but she *was* exhausted—perhaps too much so to make a persuasive argument. Colin was a worthy opponent in a match of wits, and this was a match she must win. She would not yield. Perhaps now was not the time to press the matter.

"Verra well," she conceded, yawning again. "But we *will* speak of it soon." Her gaze was drawn to the bright green eyes peering out from under the bed. Hera. Poor cat, she'd lived her whole life at Glenbroch and now had been uprooted twice in so short a time.

Colin cleared his throat, drawing her attention away from Hera. He pulled off his cravat and unbuttoned his waistcoat before fixing his gaze most uncomfortably on her burning face. "Perhaps I should give you a moment to prepare, and then you will join me in my chamber?"

*Prepare?* At once her mind snapped into focus, her cheeks growing warm with the significance of his words. To consummate their vows, he meant, and Brenna wasn't certain if he meant it as a request or a command. Either way, 'twas expected on their wedding night. Besides, she could not deny that a part of her burned with curiosity, desperate to finish what they'd begun only a fortnight ago in his parlor. Her mouth suddenly too dry to speak, she simply nodded her assent, her stomach fluttering nervously in anticipation as she watched him disappear through the doorway that connected their chambers.

Colin paced on the other side of the door, wondering just what was taking her so bloody long. His coat, cravat, and waistcoat lay discarded in a heap on the chair beside him, his valet long dismissed. It had been more than an hour since he'd left her, sitting at her dressing table, blushing furiously.

He forced his restless feet to still and paused before the door, staring at the panel while his resolve swung wildly to and fro. He reached for the handle, then reconsidered. Shaking his head, he retreated. He clasped his hands behind his back and resumed his anxious pacing. A moment later he stopped again, eyeing the door suspiciously.

Did she fear sharing his bed? She seemed a passionate woman, yet he could not forget she was a virgin. She would likely be frightened, and the expression on her face when he'd left her there in her room confirmed as much. The day had been long and tiring, besides. As much as he longed to make love to her, he didn't want to rush her, to force her. More than anything, he wanted her to come willingly and eagerly to his bed.

He could wait. It might kill him, but he could wait. A day or two, at most, until she felt more comfortable. He took a step forward, intending to go and set her mind at ease, then stepped back in surprise as the door swung open.

"Och, I didn't mean to startle ye." Brenna's head appeared in the doorway, her cheeks crimson.

He stepped aside, watching in fascination as she glided into the room, her hands clutching together the neckline of her wrapper. Her hair shone like amber in the candlelight, cascading across her shoulders in rippling waves, and her skin was flushed a delicate pink. From a warm bath, he surmised, noticing the scent of lavender that emanated from her person, stirring his blood as it always did. Her cream-colored dressing gown appeared to be made from the finest silk, enticingly skimming her subtle curves, and Colin could only wonder what lay beneath the fabric.

Her carriage and countenance formed a vision of virginal reticence, of fear mixed with curiosity. But she had come to him, after all. His heart began to pound furiously in anticipation.

"I . . . I'm sorry for taking so verra long. Celeste seemed overly enthusiastic in her ministrations tonight. I hope . . ." Her voice trailed off, and the silence was deafening.

"Don't make yourself uncomfortable, Brenna. You look lovely."

She ignored the compliment. "I didna realize it

had grown so late. I think perhaps I might have dozed off while Celeste attended my hair."

"It has been a long day, hasn't it?" Truth be told, he was exhausted himself.

"I confess I am a wee bit nervous."

As was he. He'd never felt so emasculated in his life—actually nervous to bed a woman, something he'd done many a time with much pleasure and usually without much thought. Why did tonight seem so different? *Blast it.* He was surely over-thinking the matter.

He cleared his throat and tried to affect a mask of ennui. "A touch of nerves is to be expected, I'm sure. Has Lady Danville not—"

"Aye, of course she has, and I was well aware of the . . . of my marital duties before then."

His brows rose in surprise. An informed virgin. That certainly made things a bit less complicated.

With trembling hands, she reached down and untied her dressing gown. It slipped to the floor with a swish, and his curiosity was instantly satisfied. His bride stood before him in a silk gown the same creamy color as the wrapper. The fabric was delicate, near transparent, and trimmed in rich lace. A single tie held the gown together between her breasts, breasts that were fuller than he'd remembered. Rose-colored peaks crowned their fullness and strained against the fragile fabric. Just above each gently curved hip, a tie held together the wisps of front and back panels. Even in the candle-light he could clearly see the tantalizing dark shadow at the point where her thighs joined. He felt the pull of his breeches across his groin and drew in a sharp breath.

In one quick movement, he swept her off her feet, into his arms. He heard her gasp at the contact, her body trembling against his as he carried her to the bed and deposited her gently on the pillows.

She lay there provocatively, the hem of her gown tucked up to her thighs and her breasts splayed out as he turned from her, removing his boots and stockings. Hastily, he pulled his shirt over his head.

*His gift.* His thoughts were drawn at once to the long velvet box lying on his dressing table, holding the piece of jewelry he'd commissioned for his wife—a delicate rope of oval aquamarines, separated by diamonds and held together by a gold filigree clasp. It was truly a magnificent piece, a perfect match to the betrothal ring he'd given her. He'd had to put himself deeper into debt to pay for it, but it would be worth every last pence to see it on her neck, lying in the hollow above her collarbones, just below her fluttering pulse. The image of her wearing the necklace and nothing else sent flames of desire lapping at his groin, and he nearly groaned aloud. He had to present it to her, *now.*

"I've something for you," he said, turning toward her.

The color in her cheeks rose, and she tugged down the hem of her nightdress in an attempt to cover her bare limbs.

Colin swallowed hard, wanting nothing more but to ravish her. Immediately. "Wait there," he managed to say. "I'll only be but a moment." He picked up the silver candelabra beside the bed and hurried through the doorway to his dressing room, intent on finding the gift and hastening back to his bride as expeditiously as possible. Holding the candelabra aloft, his gaze scanned the top of his oak dressing table, seeing nothing but a pair of silver cuff links and a watch.

Blast it, where was it? He could have sworn he left it sitting right there. Had he put it away? He opened the top drawer, pushing aside monogrammed handkerchiefs and cravats as he rummaged through the drawer's contents, all to no avail.

It took him a full quarter hour to locate the box, lying on the mantel beside the ebony clock, whose pendulum rhythmically marked the minutes he'd been away from her. He frowned, having no recollection of having put the box there. Perhaps the chambermaid had moved it? He flipped open the case, smiling at the jewels that lay there against the folds of velvet, sparkling in the candlelight. Perfect. Snapping shut the case, he retrieved the candelabra and hurried back to his bedchamber, as eager as a schoolboy. He would fasten the jewels about her neck, then remove her nightdress, lowering it inch by tantalizing inch till she was entirely bare save the gems at the base of her throat.

His erection pressing fervently against the flap of his trousers, he stepped into the bedchamber and stopped short, his gaze drawn immediately to her small form, lying in his bed where he had left her.

One of her slender hands lay across her breasts, the other arm above her head, her fingers splayed out against the pillow. Her head was turned to one side, her lashes resting against her flushed cheek where a few auburn tendrils lay damply against her skin. Her rose-tinted lips were parted, her chest rising and falling regularly.

Colin looked heavenward, emitting a sharp

groan of frustration as he cursed his ill-begotten fate.

She was fast asleep. On their wedding night, no less.

"Oh, look. Here he is now. Colin, dear, wait till you see the drawing room furnishings we've chosen. Delightful, just delightful. Your wife has impeccable tastes," his mother said, beaming at Brenna.

*His wife.* The words still startled him, a full twenty-four hours after they'd pledged their troth before God and family. He peeled off his gloves as he strode into the salon, a smile playing at the corners of his mouth. What a happy sight—his wife perched on the curved arm of the settee, obviously engaged in a lively conversation with Jane and Lucy, wrapped parcels and squares of fabric strewn about the room. No doubt enough furnishings and fabrics had been ordered to outfit a palace. The expense made him shudder. He supposed they thought her dowry was paying for such things. Instead they would quickly bleed him dry.

Out of habit, Colin made his way toward the sideboard on the far wall, reaching for an empty glass that sat beside a decanter of his father's favorite claret. He turned the glass over in his hand, holding it up to the sunlight as if to admire the cut. Mercifully, he remembered himself just in time. Setting the glass back down with a thump, he returned his attention to the women.

"Impeccable tastes, you say?" he drawled.

"Doesn't surprise me in the least. You mustn't forget she married me."

"Well," Jane interjected, "everyone is entitled to a lapse in judgment now and then. Perhaps one day she'll realize her folly."

"As always, Jane, you wound me. Truly. Isn't there some gentleman out there for you to toy with instead? A heart to break? Who's your next victim, now that you've chased poor Nickerson off?"

"Now, Colin," Lucy said, "you know she had every right to refuse him. Though I still can't fathom why she would," she added under her breath.

Lady Rosemoor clapped her hands together. "Squabbling like children, all of you. Enough, I say. Goodness, what will poor Brenna think of her new family? Come now, Colin. You must look at the fabric samples we have here. Lovely, just lovely."

"Speaking of lovely," Mandeville said, stepping into the room beside him, "there is my wife. I thought I might find you here, Lucy."

Colin sighed in relief, appreciating Mandeville's impeccable timing. God knows, he hadn't relished admiring fabric as a form of entertainment. As always, Lucy's emerald eyes became luminous as she gazed adoringly at the marquess from across the room.

"Has Parliament closed for the day?" Jane asked.

"Indeed, and quite fortuitous timing, too. It's a fine afternoon," he said, moving to Lucy's side and placing a kiss on her cheek. "Perhaps we should all adjourn to the park for a stroll. Are you up to it, Lucy?"

"Of course I am. I'm not an invalid, you know. My father said exercise was perfectly appropriate in my condition." She turned toward Brenna. "My father is a physician, you see, and . . . Wait, I nearly forgot. You don't know, do you?"

Brenna shook her head.

"I'm with child," Lucy answered, near beaming. One hand moved to her abdomen. "Soon my confinement will begin, much as I dread it. I'd hoped to stay in London till the end of the Season, but my stubborn husband will not hear of it."

"I'd feel better with you tucked safely away in the countryside." Mandeville planted a kiss on the top of Lucy's head. "Certainly not too much to ask."

"How exciting for ye both," Brenna said. "My heartiest felicitations."

Though Brenna smiled as she congratulated them, Colin couldn't help but notice that she looked from Lucy to him with carefully guarded suspicion. Surely she didn't still believe that he and Lucy . . . He couldn't even bear to think the words. Wasn't it obvious just how much in love the Mandevilles were? It wasn't as if they made any effort at all to hide it, a fact that alternately warmed and annoyed him, depending on his mood.

"Really, Lucy, isn't it vulgar to speak of such things?" he said, brushing an invisible speck of lint from his lapel. "I'm sure you're breaking some iron rule of etiquette here."

"Don't be so priggish, Colin." Lucy frowned at him. "Honestly, you're a married man now. You'd best get used to such talk."

*Not at the rate my wife and I are proceeding,* Colin thought irritably.

Brenna dropped her gaze to her slippers, her cheeks reddening. Clearly she, too, was remembering their wedding night. The fact that they had not consummated their vows hung heavily between them, a topic they'd both avoided since awakening in his bed together that morning.

She'd stirred beside him at dawn, her eyes widening in surprise when she'd seen him lying there awake, watching her. "Did we . . . that is to say . . ." she stuttered, clutching the bedsheets about her. "Have we—"

"I assure you that, had we done so, you would remember it," he'd answered dryly.

With a satisfied nod, she slid from his bed. Retrieving her wrapper from the floor, she hurried to her own bedchamber, leaving him there alone in the suddenly cold bed, his body aching for her. They'd not spoken of the matter since.

"I say, what of that stroll Mandeville suggested?" Colin asked, changing the subject to something far more comfortable than marriage and childbearing.

"A fine idea," his mother said.

"Indeed." Jane flashed Brenna a bright smile, linking her arm through hers. "Come, Brenna. Let's join your dashing husband for a stroll."

The sky was a dazzling blue, an almost surreal color, the air unusually cool and refreshing for late summer. Lucy and Mandeville took the lead, leaning into each other intimately. Lady Rosemoor and Jane followed a discreet distance behind the pair, while Colin and Brenna brought up the rear.

The party ambled down Upper Brook Street and made their way across Tiburn Lane. The park was bursting with activity, welcoming and bright. Smiling broadly, he guided his wife onto the walking path, headed toward the Serpentine.

He glanced down at Brenna, her face upturned toward the warming sun, its rays casting a golden glow upon her fair skin. He was relieved to see her looking more relaxed than he'd seen her in quite a while, yet he was disappointed that the delightful smattering of freckles that had previously dusted her nose were now beginning to fade. The constraints of Town, no doubt—never allowed outdoors without the protection of a bonnet.

The nagging thought that she'd been right, that she did not belong in London, or even in oh-so-civilized Kent, disturbed him. She'd been removed from her element, and he was forcing her to remain there indefinitely. She would be far happier at her beloved Glenbroch, riding through fields of heather, freckles on her sun-browned skin.

He shrugged away the unpleasant thoughts, forcing himself to consider their future there in London instead. "It sounds as if your shopping expedition was a success."

"Oh, 'twas a grand success. Your mother was indeed an enormous help. She is verra kind, and her guidance is most welcome."

"She is kind, indeed. A very fine woman, my mother. Just don't let her tire you. She can prove to be relentless when it comes to shopping."

"Is that so? Hmm, I didna notice." Her eyes sparkled like gems beneath the arch of her brows.

"Point taken. Did I hear Jane mention that Lady Alderson's annual ladies' luncheon is taking place tomorrow?"

"'Twould seem so."

"And I suppose you've spent the better part of the day deciding just which frock will suit the affair?"

"Nay, of course not." She shook her head, her bonnet trimmings dancing in the breeze.

"I'm surprised. I thought all females—"

"But I wasna included in the invitation."

"Whatever do you mean? Didn't I hear Jane say that both she and my mother had been invited?"

"Perhaps."

His heart began to thump against his breastbone. "And Lucy—"

"Truly, 'tis not so important, is it, Colin? I was often excluded from such things, even while I resided with Lord and Lady Danville. I dinna expect it now."

His pulse quickened as his anger rose a pitch. How could Lady Alderson—a long-time friend of his mother's—snub Brenna in such a fashion?

"But . . ." he sputtered, his lungs burning, "but I thought that . . . that . . ."

"That what?" She turned to face him, her eyes full of understanding. "That once we married, everything would be set to rights? Even I know it doesna work that way. Ye are my husband, and your status, your station, becomes mine."

"I suppose," he muttered, his throat constricting most uncomfortably. "But it isn't at all fair to you. You've done nothing wrong."

"Neither have ye, Colin. Ye must remember that, even if they willna see it."

"Even if I had, even if I were the worst sort of cheat, it doesn't give the *ton* any excuse to treat you as if you are not worthy of their notice."

"Besides, they have all declined the invitation. Your mother and Jane; Lucy as well. 'Twas not necessary, but I do appreciate their show of support."

"Bloody right they should decline the invitation. In fact, I'd like to take the blasted card and shove—"

"Shh, Colin. Ye should lower your voice. Isna that Lord Barclay up ahead with Lord Mandeville?"

"I don't give a damn if it's Prinny himself," he barked, and then quieted as the pressure on his arm increased.

Up ahead, Lord Barclay moved away from the Mandevilles, tipping his hat toward Colin's mother and Jane. After a brief exchange of pleasantries, he headed their way. Colin looked over at Brenna, saw her fix a forced smile on her face, and then he looked up again, just as Barclay drew abreast of them. Colin reached for his hat. "Good day, Lord Barclay," he called out cheerily in greeting.

Barclay's eyes met his, then narrowed perceptibly before moving away, his gaze fixed upon the horizon. The silence was deafening.

As the arrogant man moved past them, Colin went blind with rage. How dare he? How dare he cut them so directly, particularly Brenna? He stood, rooted to the spot, his heart hammering and the rush of blood deafening his ears.

"How dare you, sir?" he roared.

Beside him, Brenna started in surprise. "Nay, Colin," she whispered. "Don't. He'll hear ye."

"I hope he does hear me, the bloody bastard."

His mother and Jane hurried over, wringing their hands.

"Do you hear me, Barclay?" Colin clenched his fists by his sides, his gaze fixed on the man's retreating form. "I'm calling you a bastard!"

"Truly, Colin, 'twill only make matters worse," Brenna said, her voice level.

Mandeville appeared at Colin's side, Lucy following close behind. "What the devil are you shouting about?"

"The bloody bastard gave us the cut direct, that's what. Didn't have the decency to acknowledge a lady's presence. Why, I ought to—"

"That's enough, Colin," Lucy said, reaching for his arm. "Though you're absolutely right. He's no longer welcome in our home." She looked up entreatingly to her husband, who nodded his agreement.

"Damn implacable Tory, anyway," Mandeville muttered.

"But this is not the place for such talk," Lucy continued. "Come now, we'll accompany Brenna back to Rosemoor House. Henry, please . . ."

"Of course. Come, Rosemoor. Perhaps a drink or two in my study will settle you down."

# Chapter 18

Brenna watched as Lord Mandeville led Colin away, a knot in the pit of her stomach. She reached for Jane's arm with trembling hands. Her heart was beating erratically, her breath coming dangerously fast. She knew that Lord Barclay was an important man, an influential man. An acquaintance of Lord Danville's. She'd been welcomed into his drawing room on more than one occasion, and yet today he'd looked right through her as if she didn't exist.

Truly, she didn't give a fig what Lord Barclay thought of her; she did not require his approval. Such things meant very little to her. And while Colin had been anxious to restore his honor, and rightfully so, he hadn't seemed to have minded terribly that he'd been cast from polite society. Yet she'd never before seen him so angry, so bitter. Did her own acceptance by the *ton* matter so much to him? 'Twould seem that it did.

Walking beside her, Lucy patted her arm sympathetically. "Oh, Brenna, I know it's dreadful. But please, try not to take it to heart. There are still some who will believe the accusations against him, but, well . . . With Colin married now, things will surely begin to change. If only . . ." She trailed off, shaking her head.

"Please, go on," Brenna urged.

"If only he'd try a bit harder," Jane supplied. "Stubborn fool. After the disaster at White's, Mandeville offered to use his influence to have him restored there. But no, Colin just thumbed his nose at the efforts. Instead of White's, he simply turned his attention to undesirable gaming hells, places where his name wasn't so sullied. It's a shame, really. But we thought perhaps now . . . now that he's married, he would settle down and try to set things to rights."

Lady Rosemoor nodded her head. "The *ton* just needs a bit more time, more distance. Another scandal will surely come along soon enough, and all will be forgotten. By next Season, I'm sure everything will be as it ought."

Brenna wasn't so certain. Colin should face the accusations directly, allow her to make her statement to the club's manager and expose Hugh and Sinclair for what they were. "Colin is a proud man," she said at last. "'Twould seem he wishes to restore his honor himself, without the aid of others."

"Hmm, I suppose you're right," Jane said, nodding. "But how? I know that despicable Lord Thomas Sinclair is behind this."

Brenna turned sharply toward Jane. "'Tis true. I . . . I know for certain because I overheard Sinclair boast about it to . . . to his accomplice. He arranged to have the card planted in Colin's pocket himself."

"Does Colin know this?" Lucy asked, a heated flush suddenly staining her cheeks.

"Aye. 'Twas why I had gone to his lodgings that day, to tell him. I went to Rosemoor House, looking for Jane, and was told she had gone to pay a call on Colin."

"So that's why . . . never mind." Jane blushed furiously. "And to think, here I'd thought you'd actually taken my silly advice and tried to . . . well . . . Oh, I'm such a fool, Brenna. How will you ever forgive me?"

"Goodness, Jane," Lucy said, pausing on the walk. "Whatever did you do? You didn't tell Colin that you had suggested that Brenna . . . well, attempt to entrap him, did you?"

Jane raised one gloved hand to cover her mouth, looking stricken.

Brenna's heart began to pound. Had she? Dear Lord, no wonder Colin had thought she'd manipulated him into marriage.

"Well," Jane mumbled, tears threatening the corners of her eyes, "I didn't specifically suggest Colin. I think I might have put forward several eligible Scotsmen instead."

A bubble of laughter welled in Brenna's breast. "Dear Jane," she said, laughing aloud. "Please, dinna fash about it. I only wish Colin would let me expose Sinclair and"—she swallowed hard—"and his accomplice." She was embarrassed to admit to Hugh's part in the scheme. Her brother, of all people.

Lucy shook her head. "But they'd only think you supplied the story in order to clear your husband's name. Everyone knows there is no love lost between Colin and Sinclair. No, I fear it wouldn't help at all. It would only expose you to criticism."

"Lucy's right," Lady Rosemoor said, her brow

furrowed. "We cannot subject you to such scrutiny, not even to clear Colin's name. If it is true that Sinclair arranged to have the card planted in Colin's pocket, then that information must come from a source outside the family. Otherwise, it won't help matters in the least."

Brenna nodded. "Colin has said as much. Perhaps you're right. Still, it angers me to know he's been falsely accused and that I canna do anything to help him."

"You're a fine woman, Brenna." Lady Rosemoor patted her on the cheek. "I'm honored to call you daughter."

Brenna smiled warmly at her. "'Tis an honor to be part of your family, Lady Rosemoor," she answered, surprised to realize that she meant it with all her heart.

"Oh, come now." Jane dabbed at her eyes with a handkerchief. "You're both making me cry."

Lucy sniffled her agreement. "Aren't I weepy enough already these days? No more, or my eyes shall be red and swollen."

Their party continued on in companionable silence, their boots clicking rhythmically against the walk. At last back at Grosvenor Square, Brenna stepped inside the front hall of Rosemoor House and removed her shawl and bonnet.

The butler entered carrying a silver tray laden with the day's correspondence. "The post, my lady," he said to Lady Rosemoor, bowing stiffly before laying down the tray on the sideboard and disappearing from whence he had come.

"Thank you, Penwick," Lady Rosemoor trilled, thumbing through the stack of thick cards. "Oh, the gossip page." She pulled out a long sheet and unfolded it. "I'm finding it more and more unpalatable these days. Nothing but malicious supposition and innuendo. I declare, the author takes great pleasure in ruining reputations on a daily basis. Only fit for the fire, if you ask me." She set it down on the sideboard and headed down the hall toward the drawing room. "Shall I ring for tea?" she called out over her shoulder, Lucy close on her heels.

"Yes, Mama. We'll be right in," Jane answered, then tapped the discarded page with a frown. "I wonder whose reputation has been ruined today?"

With a sudden lurch of trepidation, Brenna reached for it and smoothed the page flat. "Only one way to find out," she said, and handed it to Jane who began to read aloud:

*"It has been noted that the former Lady M—— has now been relegated to the unenviable position of Mrs. R——. How heartbroken her poor parents must be! It has been rumored, of course, that the pair was forced to wed after being discovered in a compromising situation. So, gentle reader, one can only surmise that innocent appearances can be misleading and that even the best families have their bad seeds, particularly when such a seed has been cultivated in inferior soil. . . ."*

Jane's voice trailed off, her cheeks stained an angry red.

"Aye, I suppose that answers your question," Brenna said, her voice a mere whisper. *"Mine."*

* * *

Hours later, Colin stumbled up the front steps of Rosemoor House. *Blasted expensive brandy,* he thought, reaching up a hand to his aching head. He'd meant to refuse the snifter Mandeville had slid across the table toward him, but dammit, he'd needed a taste. Desperately. One draught of the forbidden liquid had led to several, and, before he'd known it, he'd been nearly drunk. Now he would pay the price, tonight of all nights. He'd yet to bed his bride, and now another day would pass without accomplishing it. He'd drunk nearly an entire pot of coffee, wishing to sober up before returning home, yet it was all for naught, as Brenna had no doubt long since retired.

As he entered the front hall, he noted a light from his father's study. He fished out his watch and flipped open the case. It was well past midnight. Curious, as his father usually retired at ten. What was he doing up so late?

As Colin stood there pondering the question, a door creaked open and a masculine voice called out to him. "There you are, Colin. I'd like a word with you before you retire."

"Of course, sir." With a grimace, he headed toward the study, returning the watch to his pocket.

His father stood in the doorway with a cheroot, motioning for him to take a seat. "I've been trying to get a private word with you ever since the wedding, but it's near enough impossible to drag you away from all those hens flapping about you."

"I suppose," Colin muttered noncommittally.

"My solicitors were here today, and the Henrietta Street town house and Kent estate are all settled now, in your name."

"Thank you, sir. I appreciate your generosity." Inwardly, he chafed at the charity, but what choice had he? He had a wife now to think of.

"Just don't muck it up, Colin. That's all I ask. I've settled most of your debts, but I won't bail you out again, mark my words. You've got a chance now to start anew, and I suggest you make the most of it."

Colin could only nod, his chest uncomfortably tight.

"Well now, son. What do you have to say for yourself, a married man? You've done quite well, haven't you?" His smile was one of smug satisfaction. He reached across the table, the cheroot in his outstretched hand.

Colin leaned forward and took the cheroot, wincing as his head throbbed painfully. "I suppose so, Father. Though I'm certain Brenna might not think so highly of the bargain."

"Well, when one plays with fire . . ." He waggled his brows suggestively.

"What do you mean by that?" Colin straightened sharply, groaning aloud as his stomach began to churn.

His father chuckled. "Your mother told me just what state she found you in with your future bride. A bold little chit, I must say. Going alone, unchaperoned, to your bachelor lodgings. A brilliant plan. I'm glad to see you heeded the siren's call."

"I'll have you know it wasn't like that at all," Colin bit out through clenched teeth. "She did not come to my lodgings intent on seduction. Instead, she came to deliver some important information, information that I had requested. Furthermore, I can assure you she was *not* compromised, despite the state in which we were discovered. I agreed to marry her because it was the honorable thing to do, given the circumstances."

"Hmm, quite a speech there, son. You'll do well in Parliament one day, won't you? Well, no matter. The long and short of it is you managed to snare quite a catch. Largest dowry this Season I'm told, with a generous inheritance of her own from those Scots who raised her."

"Fat lot of good it does me," Colin mumbled under his breath.

"I suppose you'll also be in need of a town house in Trevor Square in which to set up a mistress?"

"Why would I want such a thing? As you've mentioned, I'm a married man now."

"Married, son. Not dead. Often a man has needs that go beyond the marital bed. No shame in slaking them with a woman of your choosing, so long as you're discreet."

Colin's face grew hot. He rose from his seat and leaned against his father's desk, eyeing him coldly. "Are you suggesting I 'slake my needs' with some cheap tart, Father? Or do you only suggest dallying with one's wife's dearest friend, as you did? Were you so discreet with Lucy's mother?"

His father's face turned scarlet, his jowls wobbling in indignation. "I told you I would never again speak of that business, Colin, and I meant what I said."

"That *business*? Is that what you call it? Lucy is your daughter," Colin spat out. "Did you ever think what *that business* might have done to Sarah's life if Oliver Abbington hadn't married her? What would have become of Lucy? Have you ever considered how Mother would feel were she to find out? You betrayed her in the worst way, you bastard, and you sit there telling me—"

His father rose to face him, his face merely inches from Colin's. "How dare you?" he bellowed, pounding one fist on the desk. "How dare you speak to me this way?"

Two full years of outrage sputtered to the surface, brimming over the precipice of Colin's tightly guarded control. "How dare you put such a burden on our family? You think I carry around this knowledge with pleasure? I can barely stand to look my own mother in the eye, keeping such a secret from her. And Lucy—"

"Lucy does not know, nor will she." His father's eyes glittered coldly as they met Colin's.

"Of course she knows," Colin retorted before he thought better of it. "And it near enough killed her to learn such a horrible truth about the mother she remembered so dearly."

The color drained from his father's face. "Goddamn you, Colin. Told her, did you?"

"I hadn't a choice."

His father looked near apoplectic as he shook a fist at his son. "I ought to—"

"To what, Father?" Colin taunted. "Disown me? Disinherit me? If I correctly understand the laws of primogeniture, you can do nothing. I am your heir, and there's nothing you can do to alter that fact. I am your only son, besides. At least your only *legitimate* son. Are there any other clandestine correspondences of yours I should be privy to? More packets of letters awaiting me at your solicitor's office? Any other children born on the wrong side of the blanket who did not fare so well as Lucy did?"

"Get out of my sight, Colin." He pointed to the door, his arm visibly quaking. "Go, until you can speak to me with the respect a father deserves from his son."

"With pleasure," Colin said, turning away from the man so violently that a wave of nausea washed over him. "And you can keep your town house and estate in Kent. I'll make my own way, thank you." On shaking legs, he stormed to the door.

Just as he reached for the handle, an oddly strangled, choking sound behind him forced Colin to turn back toward his father, who was as white as a specter and clutching frantically at his chest. His blue-tinged mouth was grotesquely agape as he struggled desperately for a breath.

At once it seemed as if the earth stood still. "Father!" Colin cried out, his voice muffled to his own ears. He lunged across the room and reached for his father's sleeve, just as the man slumped to the floor, his eyes staring, unseeing, at the ceiling above him.

He knew in an instant that his father was dead. A cry of anguish rent through the night as Colin sank to his knees beside his father's crumpled form. He'd killed him, as surely as if he'd run a blade through his heart.

# Chapter 19

"Have the solicitors left?" Brenna asked as Jane stepped into the drawing room, her eyes red-rimmed and swollen.

With a nod, Jane hastened to Brenna's side and took a seat beside her on the sofa, reaching for her hand. Brenna was grateful for Jane's warm, soothing touch. She attempted a weak smile as Jane gave her hand a gentle, reassuring squeeze.

"They left more than an hour ago, yet Colin remains in my fath—" She choked on the word. "In the study. He hasn't eaten anything all day. I had Mrs. Millington send in a tray, but he sent it away, untouched." Jane's chestnut brows drew together.

"And how is your mother?" Brenna asked. "Will she get any rest tonight?"

"She's doing as well as can be expected. She's a strong woman. She finally accepted the laudanum the physician ordered, so she will sleep well tonight, at least."

"I'm verra glad to hear it. And Susanna?"

"Susanna is in a bit of a state. She, too, is now enjoying the effects of the laudanum."

Brenna nodded. "Mr. Merrill seemed verra worried for her."

"Like Lucy, Susanna is increasing. I vow, her husband acts as if she's the first woman to find herself in such a condition. I have no doubt she'll get through this well enough, as her disposition is naturally cheerful."

"And ye, Jane, how are ye faring?"

"Well enough. I sometimes wish I could allow myself to cry and carry on like Susanna does. But, alas, it's not in my nature I'm afraid."

"Nor mine," Brenna said, remembering the sorrowful months that followed the Maclachlans' deaths. "Holding back the tears is surely more painful than allowing them to fall freely. But we must each grieve in our own way."

Jane nodded. "If only my brother didn't worry me so. I hate to see him in such a state as this. Did you hear him bellowing at the solicitors when they first arrived? Saying he refuses my father's title?" Jane shook her head, her eyes so full of sadness that Brenna's breath hitched in her chest. "He's convinced that Papa's death was his fault, and he won't be persuaded otherwise."

"Och, 'tis dreadful."

"Isn't it? Have you tried to speak with him since he shut himself away? Perhaps you can talk some sense into him."

"Nay, but I thought I saw Lucy go to him." Brenna's stomach lurched uncomfortably at the thought.

"Lucy tried her best, but he sent her away." Jane

dropped her gaze to her lap. "I've never seen him so despaired, so broken. To be quite frank, my brother has a . . . well, a propensity for engaging in self-destructive behavior. Someone must save him from himself at a time like this. I know you're only newly wedded, but still . . . Someone must try to get it through that thick skull of his that he's not to blame for Papa's death."

Brenna nodded her assent, her throat aching. Poor Colin. "I canna promise anything, Jane, but I will do my best. He should not suffer through this alone."

Both women rose. "I'll go to him now," Brenna said with a nod, then headed toward the study on wobbly legs.

Seconds later, she stood in front of the heavily carved door, her heart pounding in trepidation. Would he turn her away? And even if he did not, could she bring him a measure of comfort? She took a deep breath and exhaled slowly. She'd promised Jane she would try, and she owed it to her husband, besides. Without allowing herself to think upon it further, she rapped on the door.

Silence.

She tried once more, rapping more forcefully this time. "Colin?" she called out, her voice betraying her hesitancy. "May I come in? I'd like to speak with ye."

Again, no response. She felt her palms dampen, but she reached for the door handle nonetheless. It turned easily, and she stepped inside, closing the door softly behind her.

Brenna crept into the room and stopped in its center, her hands clasped together in front of her breasts. Colin sat slumped in his father's chair, his shoulders hunched over and his head cradled in his hands. His hair was in disarray, and his cravat lay untied against his linen. Most worrisome was his silence. Not a single sound emanated from his person.

Brenna hurried to his side, filled with anxiety and uncertainty.

After several seconds, he looked up at her, and the unmasked pain, the raw anguish, she saw there in his countenance tore at her heart, taking her breath away.

His jaw was clenched, his brow creased, but worst of all were his stormy, tormented eyes, glistening with unshed tears. No, of course he would not weep, and she knew just how dreadful it felt to hold in such grief, to refuse to give in to the tears that must be blinding him. She forced herself to breathe as he dropped his gaze, cradling his head in his hands once more.

"Oh, Colin," she whispered, her throat so tight it ached. She reached out to him, tentatively stroking his hair with her fingers. He reached up and clasped her hand to his face, pressing her palm against his stubbly cheek. Brenna held her breath as Colin turned his face into her hand. She felt his lips press into her palm, and she shuddered violently. "'Tis not your fault. Truly, ye mustn't think that it is."

He looked up at her sharply. "But it *is* my fault, don't you see?" His voice faltered. "We should never have taken up residence here."

She reached for his hand, but he pulled it from her grasp. He rose, pacing the floor like a caged animal. Abruptly he stopped, leaning into the wall, one arm flung above his head. Brenna could only stand motionless, staring at his back in confusion.

Suddenly he pounded his fist against the plaster, rattling the portrait of some ancestor that hung from the moldings above. "Dammit, Brenna, I killed the bloody bastard, as sure as if I'd squeezed the life from him with my own hands."

She hurried to his side and reached for his sleeve. "Nay, Colin. Dinna say it. Ye canna think that way. 'Twas only . . . the physician said . . . 'twas his heart. His heart was weak; it simply gave out."

"No!" he bellowed. "No, you don't understand. We were arguing."

"Arguing?"

"Yes, about Lucy—"

"Lucy?" Brenna interrupted, a coldness settling in the pit of her stomach. "Why ever would ye be arguing about Lady Mandeville?"

Colin stalked to the window, his hands balled into angry fists. He leaned against the sill, staring out into the inky night. "I cannot tell you. Devil take it, Brenna." He shoved himself away from the window, flinging himself back into his father's chair. "How can I live with myself? How can I take his title when it is my fault that—"

"Stop," she ordered. "Ye mustn't blame yourself." Kneeling on the carpet at his feet, she stroked his head, tears burning the corners of her eyes. "Please, Colin, I cannot bear it. I cannot watch ye suffer more than ye ought."

She rose and gathered his head to her breast, stroking his hair as if he were a boy. His body trembled violently and then stilled. She pulled away and looked down into his tortured face. A vicious pain tore through her gut. Almost involuntarily, she moved her lips to his temple, her hands threading through his hair, so soft and silken. He didn't move a muscle as her lips trailed lower, across his strong jawbone, where the taut muscles quivered beneath her mouth.

Whatever was she doing? 'Twas not the time for such things. She drew away in panic, but not before he pulled her down into his lap, his mouth slanting over hers. She sucked in her breath as his mouth possessed hers, his hands clutching at her bodice in desperation, tugging her sleeves from her shoulders. The room began to spin, and she struggled to her feet.

She looked down and saw the surprise on his face, coupled with hurt and any number of other painful emotions. She shook her head, confused, as a quiver of fear shot through her.

"Colin, I—"

"Don't apologize, Brenna. I understand perfectly." He rose, hastening to the cart that held his father's brandy.

"No!" she cried. "No, you dinna understand. Your father is not even yet laid to rest, and your family is just down the corridor. 'Tis neither the time nor the place for such things."

"Pray tell me, then, just when will the time be right? How many nights will you feign sleep while—"

"Feign sleep? Ye think I was playacting to avoid ye? I waited up till near midnight last night, hoping to—"

"Did you forget?" He picked up a tumbler and poured a small amount of the amber-colored liquid into it. "I was far too busy murdering my own father last night."

"Ye didna murder your father, Colin, but ye might tell me why ye were arguing."

"As I said before, I cannot tell you."

"I am your wife, Colin. Have ye forgotten that? I know that we . . . that we have not yet . . ." She trailed off, the now-familiar question once again nagging at her mind: Was Lady Mandeville his mistress? She had to know. "Lady Mandeville," she whispered, "ye love her, don't ye?"

He whirled around to face her. "Of course I do."

Brenna sucked in her breath sharply.

He hurled the half-empty glass across the room. Brenna flinched as it crashed against the mantel, shattering into a million tiny bits and sending a spray of golden liquid across the room.

"Don't you see?" he bellowed. "Isn't it obvious?"

At once the door flew open, banging loudly against the wall. "I heard a crash," Jane called out breathlessly, standing framed in the doorway. Her gaze flew from Brenna to Colin and back to Brenna again.

Brenna looked down and saw that the front of her black crepe gown was damp, spattered with brandy. A tiny shard of glass had nicked her forearm, a thin trail of dark red blood tracing a path toward her hand.

"Dear Lord, Colin! Whatever have you done to her?" Jane hurried across the room to Brenna's side, plucking out the sliver of glass and pressing a handkerchief to the wound.

"'Tis nothing, Jane. Just a nick, nothing more."

The color drained from Colin's face. Without a word, he hastened to her side, pushing away Jane's handkerchief and examining the cut with worry-filled eyes. "Are you hurt?" he asked, his voice hoarse.

"Nay, Colin. As I said, 'tis nothing."

"What have I done?" he muttered, pressing his hands to his temples. "God help me, Brenna, I didn't mean to hurt you."

"Of course ye didna mean to hurt me." She reached for his sleeve, hot tears threatening her eyes. "Dinna fash about it, Colin. I'm perfectly well."

"I must go," he said, his voice wavering. "I must get out of here."

"Colin, don't."

"Nay, Colin." Both women spoke at once, but he didn't heed their pleas. Shaking off Brenna's hand, he hurried through the open doorway. Seconds later, they heard the front door slam shut.

Brenna reached for Jane's hand. "I've only made matters worse," she said, her voice a mere whisper. "Much worse."

Hours later, Brenna awoke with a start. It was nearly dawn; a murky gray light was beginning to filter through the drapes, casting heavy, slanted shadows on the floor. She had stayed awake half the night, awaiting Colin's return. Yet she'd never heard the fall of his footsteps, never heard the sound of the connecting door snapping shut. Had she slept through it? She rubbed her eyes and swung her legs over the side of the bed.

Dare she?

With a lump of dread in her throat, she crossed the room and reached for the door that connected their chambers, still slightly ajar as she'd left it. She held her breath and listened carefully. Silence. Slowly, she pushed open the door and peered inside. The bed, draped in midnight blue velvet, was empty.

"Looking for me?"

Brenna jumped in surprise, her heart pounding furiously in her breast. Colin sat in the wing chair facing the window, shirtless, wearing nothing but his trousers.

"Dear God, Colin. Ye just about frightened me to death."

"And what a shame that would be, dear wife. No, I've been the cause of enough death and mayhem this week. I fear you are safe enough tonight."

She swallowed hard. Just what was he about? His tone was cold, clipped. She'd never heard him speak this way, and it unnerved her. "When did ye arrive home?" she finally managed.

"Not a half hour ago."

"But . . . but it's nearly dawn. Ye stayed out all night?"

"Why, yes, I did. How clever of you to deduce that."

A pang of jealousy stole across her heart. Had he been with another woman? Had he spent the night in some woman's bed, some woman's arms? Lady Mandeville's, perhaps? The thought gnawed on her nerves, nipped at her chest uncomfortably. He'd been just about to tell her something about Lady Mandeville when Jane had burst into the study. What sort of confession had Jane interrupted? The pressing question had been burning in her mind for hours now, near enough driving her mad.

Oh, why did the man always make her feel things she didn't wish to feel? She swallowed hard, endeavoring to make her voice as steady and cool as possible before speaking.

"Ye must excuse me, then. Undoubtedly ye wish to be alone." She stumbled back through the open doorway.

"Get back in here at once, Brenna!" he bellowed.

Gooseflesh rose on her arms. This man was a stranger, not the affable, wry Colin she knew. She stood motionless, unable to obey his command yet unwilling to flee.

In one quick motion, he rose from the chair and closed the distance between them, angrily reaching for her hand and pulling her toward him. "You are my wife, whether you like it or not, and you will do as I say." His voice wavered slightly, his words starting to slur.

Brenna wrinkled her nose. He reeked of cheap gin, and . . . Was it a woman's perfume—cheap perfume at that—she smelled intermingling with the scent of liquor?

"You're drunk," she bit out in disgust. "I'll ask that ye unhand me at once."

"And I'll ask that you remain right where you are." He pulled her more tightly against him, and she could feel the evidence of his arousal pressing against her. "Yes, I am drunk. What have you to say to that?"

"I . . . I . . ." she stammered, unsure of her response. She couldn't think clearly, not with him so close, holding her like this. "Just where have ye been all night? I dinna think it an appropriate time for ye to be out drinking and . . . and—"

"Drinking and what? What were you going to accuse me of? Gambling? Whoring?"

"You're not yourself, Colin. You're still in some sort of state, and I dinna think—"

"I don't give a horse's ass what you think, Brenna. But just to put your mind at ease, I'll confess I haven't been with another woman tonight. I'm a married man, and unlike my dear old father, I honor my vows. Difficult as it may be for you to believe."

"I . . . I never said—"

"But gambling . . . now that's altogether another story. I'm afraid you'll have to forget about the new furnishings you've ordered for the town house. I went through quite a bit of blunt tonight and—"

"How dare ye?" She shoved against his steely chest with all her might. *"How dare ye?"* Her voice rose a full pitch in indignation. "Haven't ye enough troubles as it is?" She reached up a hand to strike him, but he caught it in midflight.

"Don't do it, Brenna."

She dropped her hand, forcing her anger to abate. "You're drunk and in no way fit for civil conversation, Colin. I'm going to bed." She turned on her heel, headed for the door, but he reached for her waist and spun her around to face him.

"Why did you pull away from me earlier, Brenna? Am I so very repulsive to you? So unappealing that you can't bear my touch? My kiss?"

"I . . . It didna seem right, is all. Ye were hurting; ye were out of your mind with grief."

"That's it?" His eyes scanned her face, and then he shook his head. "No, I don't believe you. You think Lucy is my mistress, don't you?"

"I've no idea what to think." Her heart was racing, making her feel at once dizzy and queasy. "Ye yourself admitted ye were in love with her."

"I didn't say I was *in* love with her. I said I loved

her. There's quite a difference there. I was going to tell you the truth, just before Jane barged in."

"Tell me now, then," she commanded, "and be done with it."

"Very well. Lucy is my sister, my father's illegitimate daughter. Lucy's conception was the result of my father's affair with his wife's dearest friend."

Lady Mandeville was his sister? Dear Lord, of course. Now it all made sense. Perfect sense. Their easy camaraderie, his protectiveness toward her. However had she been so blind?

"All the anger I've held in," he continued, his voice rising, "the displeasure I've known since I found out the truth, just came spilling forth the night he died. There I was, railing at my father about something he did more than twenty years past as if it had happened yesterday, as if I myself were more moral, more ethical than he."

"But . . . but why? What brought it up now?"

"He was being flippant about our marriage. Congratulating me for snaring a woman with such a large dowry and saying how the bonds of matrimony don't restrict a man's appetite for—" He broke off abruptly.

Brenna only stared at him, wide-eyed.

"What's more, Jane does not know about Lucy. Nor does Susanna or my mother."

"I assume Lucy knows?"

"You assume correctly. I had no choice but to tell her two years past. It would seem Lord Mandeville jumped to the same conclusion as you did."

"Well, of course he did. 'Twould not surprise me if a number of the *ton* think the same."

"Really?" he asked, his eyes wide with surprise. "I confess, I never really considered—"

"Ye should have considered it, and ye might have told me earlier, besides. 'Twould have spared quite a bit of suspicion on my part."

"I told you, quite plainly I might add, that there was nothing but friendship between Lucy and me. Have I ever given you any reason to doubt my word?"

"Nay, but—"

"No, and yet this isn't the first time you've doubted me."

Remorse washed over her as she realized the truth of his statement. Never had he given her any reason to doubt him. He'd always spoken the truth, as frankly as possible, from the moment they'd first met. Yet doubt him she had, on more than one occasion.

His gaze met hers, forcing her to acknowledge his sincerity. "As I stand before you, Brenna Rosemoor, I vow I will never break my word to you. *Never.* I cannot say it any plainer than that. I want you to believe in me, when no one else will." His voice broke. "Is that really so much to ask?"

At once Brenna saw his bravado fade. She recognized the vulnerability in his countenance, the pain that shadowed his eyes. She knew she should be angry; he'd stayed out all night, drinking and gambling, his losses no doubt funded by her dowry. She had every right to be furious.

But she wasn't angry. Raw, painful emotions flooded her consciousness, but anger was the least of them. She had failed him. Rather than continue with recriminations, she reached for the hem of her night rail instead. Surprising herself as she did so, she pulled the garment up and over her head, depositing it on the floor at Colin's feet in a puddle of shimmering silk.

Boldly, she raised her gaze to meet his. Utter shock and surprise played across his features. Then desire. Raw, primal desire. Brenna shuddered in anticipation, her own desire matching his.

# Chapter 20

Colin stood entirely mesmerized, rendered mute by the sight of Brenna standing there before him, completely and gloriously bare. All rational thought fled him as he allowed his gaze to leisurely glide across her body, taking in every delicious inch of her.

At last, he found his voice. "You really are exquisite," he stated simply, his voice thick with desire.

She blinked rapidly but said not a word. Instead, she reached for his trousers, fumbling with the fastenings. Colin groaned as he felt her hand reach for his shaft, which was growing painfully swollen as the realization of what was happening sunk in. However did she know . . . With a sharp hiss, his thought trailed off. God help him, if he let her continue to stroke him, this encounter would end abruptly before it even began.

Perhaps a bit too roughly, he pulled her into his embrace. Together they stumbled back to the bed, their mouths finding and devouring each other's like two starving souls. His fingers tangling in her hair, he cried out her name against her lips, the delicious feel of skin against skin near to overwhelming his senses as he deepened the kiss, his tongue slipping into her warm, welcome mouth. Still clutched together, they rolled over and over again until they tumbled to the floor in unison.

Without even the slightest pause, their kiss resumed, more ardent than ever, their tongues touching then retreating, exploring, tasting. Colin nipped at her lower lip, moving his mouth to her throat as her nails skated down his back, to his backside. As she cupped his buttocks, his tongue found the spot where her pulse beat wildly, fluttering against her skin like butterfly wings.

Reaching down between their bodies, his fingers traced the inside curve of her silky thigh. Slowly, tantalizingly, his fingers inched toward the apex of her thighs, searching for the place where their bodies might join. At last he found his prize. His heart leapt, skipping a beat in anticipation. She was damp with desire, ready for him. As he stroked her, she cried out. Yet she did not clamp her thighs together in denial. Instead she opened them to him, allowing him access.

*Beautiful, so very beautiful,* he thought. His whole body shuddered with desire as his fingers slipped into her wetness, stroking her. She cried out, her body writhing beneath his. She would not stop him this time—not tonight. At last she would be his. Entirely his.

*Not yet,* he told himself, despite the proof that she was ready enough for him, eager for him, perhaps. Such knowledge nearly made him weep with relief.

He rolled over and pulled her atop him, onto his lap. She looked up in confusion, her face flushed a delicious pink. Combing his fingers through her hair, he fanned the silky tresses across her shoulders, then drew his finger across her collarbone, eliciting a shiver. Slowly, teasingly, he trailed his fingertips lower still, across the gentle swell of one rose-tipped breast. Then he stopped, watching her.

Her eyes flew open at once. "Dinna stop now, Colin."

"No?" he drawled, the restraint nearly killing him.

"Nay. Though I must confess, so far this is naught like I've heard marital relations described. Are ye sure ye know what ye are doing, Colin?" she asked, her eyes dancing mischievously.

"Oh, I know exactly what I'm doing, my sweet," he answered, encircling one engorged nipple with his thumb and forefinger, kneading it.

"I suppose I must take your word, then. Still, perhaps the tales I heard were greatly exaggerated."

"Do you think so?" Dipping his head, he took the nipple between his teeth, ever so gently. An almost-primitive sound escaped her lips as she tipped her head back.

He leisurely drew the taut skin into his mouth, suckling gently at first. "What do you think now?" he asked, drawing away.

"Nay, perhaps 'twas no exaggeration." She moaned softly as he took her in his mouth once more, suckling her more insistently now.

"Oh, Colin!" she cried out, squirming against him and working him to a fever pitch as her bottom rubbed teasingly against his swollen shaft.

He could hold out no longer. He had to have her—*now*. He rolled over, braced above her, his eyes meeting hers, seeking permission. The desire he saw in their depths nearly took his breath away.

Gently, he brushed a stray lock of damp hair from her cheek, her skin hot and moist beneath his fingers. "Brenna. I . . . This is sure to hurt you. I'll do what I can to—"

"Quickly," came her breathless reply. "I canna wait any longer."

He squeezed his eyes shut, grinding his teeth in an effort to gain control of his rampant lust. For if he did not, her words alone were likely to push him over the edge. Forcing himself to breathe deeply, to take his time, he pressed the tip of his phallus against her entry. Her soft moan of reply was nearly his undoing, yet slowly, carefully, he entered her. Hot, wet, tight—a multitude of exquisite sensations rushed over him, stealing away his breath.

His eyes scoured her face, wanting to memorize every detail, every expression. Her gaze met his, showing no fear, no reticence.

Trailing his fingertips along the side of her face, he pressed forward a measure until he met the proof of his wife's innocence.

She gasped as he pressed against the barrier. Before he had the chance to react, she clasped him to her, tilting her hips so that he was fully sheathed inside her in one single stroke. "Oh!" she cried out sharply, then went still beneath him.

Clutching her to him, he rolled onto his back, taking her with him. He studied her face, his heart near to bursting. If he'd hurt her, if—

Her eyes flew open, and a smile spread slowly across her face, dimpling her cheeks. At once she was moving atop him, her eyes glowing with determination.

"Say my name," he growled between thrusts,

suddenly desperate to hear his name on her lips. "Please."

"Colin," she responded breathlessly.

He felt himself move closer to the edge. "Say it again."

"Colin. Oh, Colin, what's happening, I . . ."

He couldn't help but increase the speed, pulling her onto him with as much force as he could, her name tumbling from his lips, over and over again.

At once she cried out, and he felt her begin to quiver. She threw back her head and moaned—and then he felt it, her body pulsating against his deeply buried shaft, carrying him over the edge into mindless ecstasy. He clutched her body to his as his seed spilled into her, their bodies slick with sweat, burning with the heat of the fire they'd stoked.

Brenna gasped for breath, gazing down at her husband in wonderment. "Oh, my. That was . . ." She trailed off, shaking her head in astonishment. *Lovely,* her mind supplied. Extraordinary. Yet she couldn't seem to make her lips form the words.

He kissed her forehead, then pulled her closer still, his heart beating furiously in rhythm with her own. "You're trembling," he said. "Did I hurt you?"

"Only for the briefest moment, Colin. 'Twas worth it, I assure ye."

She rolled off him, shivering as the cool air swept across her skin. Colin reached across her and plucked up the folds of her night rail from the carpet. "Here," he said gruffly, helping her pull it over her head, then gathering her into his lap. "A bit cold this morning, isn't it?" He reached up to the bed and pulled a blanket down across them. "I'd carry you to bed, but I'm afraid my legs won't support me right now."

Brenna's easy smile disappeared. He'd been drunk. Angry. She'd nearly forgotten, so lost was she in the pleasure of their coupling. "We ought not to have done that, ye know."

"And might I ask why not? We are husband and wife. I daresay it's perfectly acceptable. High time, in fact."

"Must I list the reasons? You're drunk, for one."

He smiled wickedly. "Obviously not *so* drunk, eh?"

"And two," she continued, ignoring his remark, "because we were both so verra angry."

"True," he said, grasping her chin and forcing her gaze to meet his. "And yet I do not regret it, making love to you. Not the slightest bit."

She considered his words, then shook her head. "Nay, nor do I."

"Good. Truly, Brenna, I was near enough sober by the time I came home."

She swallowed hard, gathering her courage for what she was about to say. "Colin, I think perhaps . . . perhaps ye drink too much." She felt him stiffen beneath her, his whole body rigid against hers. "'Tis nothing to be ashamed of, but some men canna handle their spirits, and—"

"Enough, Brenna."

"But ye must see that—"

"I will not discuss this." He drew away from her as if he wished to distance himself. "I'm near enough exhausted, and I will not allow you to draw me into an argument. Not now."

Brenna's brows drew together in annoyance. "If ye hadna stayed out all night, gambling away our living, ye might not be so exhausted."

"Touché," he muttered. "I'll keep that in mind next time."

She tipped her chin in the air. "Nay, there willna be a next time. No more gambling."

He actually smiled down at her, his eyes heavy lidded. "You're a bossy little thing, aren't you? No wonder Glenbroch has fared so well." His hands slid up her sides, moving to cup her breasts, his thumbs massaging her still-sensitive nipples through the fabric of her nightdress. "Speaking of next time . . ." he trailed off, his smile a lascivious one.

Brenna marveled at the way in which he skillfully changed the subject. Still, her body could not help but respond to his touch. He sent shivers of delight racing down her spine, gooseflesh rising on her skin in the wake of his deft fingers. There was no doubt he knew just what to do to make her bend to his wishes. She had to admire such skill.

Her husband was an experienced lover, 'twas expected, of course. Still, the knowledge sent a pang of jealousy straight through her heart. Was she not the first bride who couldn't help but imagine her husband with the lovers who had come before her? Imagining them far more beautiful, more skilled, than she was?

She sighed, tipping her head back to allow him further access as his mouth moved to her throat, trailing hot, wet kisses across her skin.

"Have you any idea how very beautiful, how very desirable you are, Lady Rosemoor?" he asked, his voice a husky whisper beside her ear.

Her worries slipped effortlessly away, replaced by the wondrous sensations now coursing through her as he lifted her night rail, his mouth following the trail of the silk up her body.

"A girl? Are you certain? How lovely." Colin heard Lucy's soft laughter coming from Brenna's bedchamber, and he stopped short in the hallway. Amazing. Nothing like baby talk to forge a solid bond between two females. With a smile, Colin moved toward the door, which had been left slightly ajar, and peered inside.

*What the devil?* Lucy was reclined on the blue velvet settee by the window with Brenna kneeling before her, something shiny clasped in her hand and suspended above Lucy's abdomen. Whatever the object was, it was swinging back and forth like a pendulum.

"Thank you," Lucy said, reaching for Brenna's hand. "I cannot tell you how much this means to me. A daughter!"

"I only hope I'm right." Brenna stopped the object's movement and clutched it in her palm. "I'm woefully out of practice."

"Do you think we could ask the babe's date of birth? I'd like to be prepared."

"Why not?" Brenna dangled the object before Lucy's reclining form once more.

Colin shouldered his way through the doorway. "What the devil are you doing to her, Brenna?"

Whatever Brenna had been holding aloft clattered to the floor.

"Colin!" Lucy called out, sitting up in haste and smoothing her skirts. "You startled us."

Brenna shook her head and blinked rapidly,

reaching for the object and clutching it in her palm. "I was just . . . that is, we were only—"

"Dowsing," Lucy supplied with a smile.

"What the h—" he broke off, reining in the curse. "Pardon me. What in God's name is *dolsing?*"

"Not dolsing, Colin." Lucy waved a hand at him. "Dowsing, you fool."

He looked to Brenna, whose cheeks had pinkened considerably.

"Pray, enlighten me."

"The ancient art of divination," Brenna said brightly. "Ye use a pendulum. . . . Well, in this case I'm using Lucy's wedding ring." She opened her hand to reveal a shiny gold band attached to a thin black cord. "Normally one would use a pendulum of some sort—I've a drop of amethyst at home—to find sources of water, lost objects, or even to foretell the future. I was just . . . well, 'tis also used to determine the sex of an unborn child, and Lucy was curious, so—"

Colin's eyes widened in surprise. "So you were employing some sort of witchcraft on Lucy? Some type of ancient sorcery?"

"Nay, not witchcraft. 'Tis not magic, not really." Brenna tilted her head to one side and bit her lower lip, as if she were carefully considering his suggestion. "Well, perhaps a bit of white magic, but nothing more. 'Tis harmless, really. Just a useful skill passed from one generation to the next. My nursemaid Jenny taught me, much to my mam—much to Lady Maclachlan's despair. Lady Maclachlan refused to believe in such things, ye see."

"Lady Maclachlan sounds like a reasonable woman."

Lucy rolled her eyes. "Colin, you *do* realize you sound like a horse's arse, don't you?" she asked.

"I sound like a . . ." He broke off, shaking his head in amazement. "Does your husband allow you to speak in such a manner?"

"My husband allows me to say and do as I please, Colin Rosemoor." Lucy's emerald eyes flashed angrily. "He doesn't make silly judgments and pronouncements based in ignorance. Well, not anymore, that is," she corrected. "Nor does he slink about, eavesdropping on private conversations conducted behind closed doors."

"I wasn't slinking, and I'll have you know the door was open," Colin retorted, reaching up to loosen his cravat.

Brenna's eyes narrowed a fraction. "Perhaps a quarter of an inch, no more." Both women advanced on him, their hands planted on their hips.

Bloody hell, they were ganging up on him. "I'll leave you to your counsel, then." Colin took several steps backward toward the door.

"Aye, ye shall," Brenna said. "Didna ye say ye had urgent business to attend to?"

"Er, yes. I do."

"And you won't breathe a word of this to Henry," Lucy added with a scowl. "I'd like to surprise him. Let him wonder how it is that I can accurately predict the gender of our children."

"Just chalk it up to female intuition," Brenna suggested.

"Exactly. Good day, Colin." Lucy dismissed him with a nod.

Colin took another step backward, catching his

boot on the bedpost and stumbling awkwardly before catching his balance.

Both women turned their backs to him, laughing softly as they linked arms and glided back toward the chaise. Brenna cast one last glance over her shoulder, her aquamarine eyes shining as she smiled sweetly at him.

Colin turned and strode out, more gracefully this time, his boots tapping the floorboards as he hurried down the corridor toward the stairs, grinning like a fool.

At last, everything seemed perfectly right in his life. Perhaps fate was finally on his side.

Colin's step was light as he headed down Gracechurch Street toward Cheapside's strand of shops, whistling a happy tune as he made his way through the boisterous crowd. He was in love— truly in love this time. He could no longer deny it. The sentiment had been there, lurking in his heart all along. Only he'd dared not name it, fearing he could never have her. Only now, now that she was his, could he acknowledge such feelings. Welcome feelings, indeed.

His heart sang with pleasure at the memories of their coupling. Not surprisingly, Brenna had been an enthusiastic lover, willing and eager. She'd displayed no virginal shyness, despite the evidence he'd seen of her innocence, now staining his bedsheets. She'd left him no doubt she'd enjoyed their lovemaking as much as he had. What man wouldn't long for a woman like her—passionate, intelligent, amusing?

Together, they would start anew, a fresh beginning. And, by God, he wouldn't destroy it this time.

He hurried his step, eager to meet with Nigel so that he could return posthaste to his wife's side. He could hardly bear to be apart from her, yet it was time to tell Nigel to cease his efforts as far as Ballard and Sinclair were concerned. Colin had lost the urge to expose the men for what they were. Despite a hint of rumor that a waiter at White's was somehow involved, no further information had come to light. He couldn't allow Brenna to come forward with the information she'd overheard, and, without a confession, they were at an impasse.

Time to move forward, to forget the unfortunate past and create their own future. Time would prove him trustworthy again, and, until that time, they'd remain busy building a life together. He would take his place in Parliament, stay away from gaming hells, and prove himself worthy once more—worthy of his wife's respect. Her trust. Her forgiveness. And, dare he hope it? Her love.

If only he hadn't imprudently lost so much blunt at the tables last night. What piss-poor timing on his part. Worse still, his losses were likely heavier than he imagined, as he had nothing but hazy memories of the evening's conclusion. He vaguely remembered sitting across from Harold Mifflin, cursing the ever-fickle Lady Luck. Next thing he remembered he was in a hired hack with Staunton, headed toward Rosemoor House at the first light of dawn. He only hoped Brenna would forgive him his foolishness. He would make it up to her, make it right. Somehow.

At last reaching his destination, he ducked beside

the same curiosities shop where he and Nigel had last met. One of these days he'd actually have to step inside the shop and inspect the wares. If the oddities in the window were any indication, it certainly looked to be an interesting establishment.

"Well, it's Viscount Rosemoor now, isn't it?" Nigel said, clapping him on the shoulder. At once his joviality faded as he no doubt remembered just how Colin had come into the title. "My deepest condolences on the loss of your father," he added soberly.

"Thank you," Colin muttered.

"Yet my heartiest felicitations on your marriage." Nigel brightened once more. "I should have been there, you know. Standing up for you. I've grown weary of this blasted business, this pretense."

"As have I, Nigel. Which is precisely why I asked to meet you today. I'm through with this."

"Whatever do you mean?"

"I mean what's done is done. Enough searching for evidence against Ballard and Sinclair. I'm willing to let it be."

"You would let them get away with this, the bloody bastards? I cannot believe you would simply give up."

"I'm not giving up, Nigel. I'm simply moving forward. I have a wife now, parliamentary duties, estates to manage."

"And a mark on your honor. Can you forget that?" Nigel reached into his breast pocket and withdrew a handkerchief, then dabbed at his brow.

Colin shoved his hands into his pockets. "Time will prove me honorable again. Besides, in many ways they've done me a favor. Kept me from marrying Miss Lyttle-Brown, didn't they? If not for them,

I might have made the single biggest mistake of my life, and I wouldn't be married to Brenna now. I say, I'm almost grateful to the bastards."

"But we're so close to exposing them. I've obtained some new information, a new lead."

"Go on," Colin urged. "Though it's not likely to affect my decision."

Nigel nodded. "One of Sinclair's employees. Correction, *former* employees. A footman. He overheard several mentions of a bargain the pair had struck. The two apparently got in quite a row when you managed to . . . ahem, after your engagement to Danville's daughter was announced. It would seem that your wife played some role in the bargain."

"This is old news. Brenna herself discovered as much."

"Your wife?"

"Precisely." Colin nodded. "I won't go into detail, but Brenna overheard a conversation between Sinclair and Ballard, one in which they openly discussed having the card planted and their motivations behind such a move."

"This is marvelous news, old man. Why don't you bring her down to White's straightaway to make a statement, then?"

"Because she is my *wife*," Colin ground out.

"This is not a trial, Rosemoor. It's not as if you're asking her to testify on your behalf. This is only a matter of honor, and I'm certain Mr. Montgomery will take her claims seriously."

"No." Colin shook his head. "I won't allow it. Ballard and Sinclair will simply call her a liar and attempt to impugn her veracity. Her reputation is tenuous enough as it is, considering the fact that we were forced to wed rather hastily. No, I won't put her under such scrutiny."

Nigel shuffled his feet, his gaze on the littered ground. Several seconds passed as he stroked his whiskers thoughtfully, considering Colin's words. "I cannot say I agree with your decision," he said at last, meeting Colin's eyes. "But it is your decision to make. You know, Rosemoor, you might have told me you possessed the deed to such a valuable parcel of property in Scotland. You might have sold it and used the coin to pay for a Bow Street runner's services. Someone trained in ferreting out the truth might have had better luck with it than you and I together."

Colin shook his head. "I cannot sell that land."

"Well, man, of course you can't, not now. I ran into Ian Staunton this morning, and he says you've gone and lost it at the tables. I've no idea why you never thought of it before—"

"What did you say?" All breath left Colin's body in a rush.

"I said I've no idea why—"

"No," he said, his voice strangled. "Before. Staunton said . . ."

"That you've gone and lost it at the tables. Last night, I believe. A terrible waste."

Nigel continued to speak, but Colin could hear nothing save the roar of blood in his ears. God help him, no. *No.* He couldn't have. He'd given her his word that he would secure the land, that it would never fall into careless hands.

"Are you certain those were Staunton's exact words?" he asked, desperation lacing his words. "That I'd lost the property?"

"Fairly certain. Lost to Harold Mifflin in a hand of cards, he said. Still can't imagine why you never . . . I say, Rosemoor, you don't look at all well. You're suddenly white as a ghost."

Colin's stomach began to roil, the ground swaying beneath his feet. Brenna would never forgive him. *Never.* Struggling toward the side of the building, he fell to one knee and unceremoniously cast up his breakfast, there on the cobbles.

When the painful retching subsided, he reached for his handkerchief and mopped his mouth with it. Closing his eyes, he summoned the strength to rise.

"Good God, Rosemoor," Nigel said. "Whatever is the matter with you?"

At last Colin stood on unsteady legs. Nigel eyed him curiously, his eyes full of concern while he dug in his coat pocket.

"Here." He withdrew something from his pocket and held it out to Colin. "Have a peppermint drop."

"Thank you," Colin muttered, taking the offered sweet and popping it into his mouth. "Do you suppose word of this . . . this loss has traveled around Town by now?" His stomach lurched once more in anticipation of Nigel's answer.

"Likely so, I'd think. Does it matter so much? It's not as if—"

"I will lose her." His throat ached, the words nearly stealing his breath away.

"What do you mean, you'll lose her?"

"I must go." Colin took two stumbling steps away from Nigel, his vision slightly blurred.

"I say, you still don't look quite right. Perhaps we should find somewhere to get you a cup of coffee. Somewhere we won't be recognized."

"No, I must find a hack at once and get home to Rosemoor House posthaste. I must find her and tell her what I've done, before she hears it elsewhere." Without a word of farewell, he turned from his friend, hell-bent on finding Brenna as quickly as possible. Before it was too late; before his whole world came crashing down around him.

Even if he did get to her first, would she ever forgive him? After he'd given her his word; after he'd accused her, just last night, of not believing in him, not trusting him?

*Not bloody likely.* The certainty of it near enough killed him.

# Chapter 21

Brenna stepped into Lord and Lady Danville's sitting room, a forced smile upon her lips. In truth, she was uneasy. Why had they summoned her there? Couldn't they have simply called on her at Rosemoor House if they'd been so eager to see her?

"Margaret, dear, you must have a seat," Lady Danville said.

Brenna paused a beat before replying. "I confess I'm finding it increasingly difficult to answer to such an unfamiliar name. I really do wish ye could call me Brenna instead."

Her parents simply frowned in reply.

After an uncomfortable silence, she cleared her throat. "I'm verra glad to see ye both, but I must ask why ye summoned me here."

"Only to see how you are faring, daughter," Lord Danville said. "You look well enough."

"I am well. Could ye not have come to Rosemoor House to see for yourselves? I'm certain you'd be most welcome there."

"But perhaps I would not be."

Brenna looked up in surprise as Hugh strode into the room, looking as smug and arrogant as ever. She rose from her seat and turned to face her brother. "Nor should ye be welcome in their home."

"What a dreadful thing to say to your brother, Margaret," Lady Danville said, her eyes narrowed to slits.

"'Tis deservedly so, Lady Danville. If I'd known *he* would be here, I wouldna have come."

"Whatever rift has come between you, I hope you will set it aside," Lord Danville said, a frown creasing his brow. "You are bound by blood, after all."

Brenna looked her father in the eye. "I told ye what has come between us, Lord Danville. Only ye did not wish to believe it so."

He shook his head. "I've no idea what you mean. Anyway, Hugh asked that we call you here this afternoon. Begged us, really. He, at least, would like to see the peace restored and feared being refused admittance at Rosemoor House."

"By all rights they should refuse him admittance. After what he's done to Colin—"

"I've done nothing more than he deserved," Hugh snapped.

"How can ye say such a thing? Ye caused irreparable damage to an innocent man's reputation, Hugh."

"Perhaps you'll reconsider whose word to believe when I tell you what I've learned today," Hugh added mysteriously, his eyes glittering.

"'Tis not likely. I've listened to your lies before. Nothing ye say can be taken as the truth, especially where Colin is concerned."

Lady Danville rose, her cheeks flushed scarlet. "Are you calling Hugh a liar?"

Brenna met her gaze, her chin tipped into the air. "Indeed I am."

"Oh!" Lady Danville exclaimed, sinking back to the sofa.

"Say what you will, dear sister, but I have this as fact. From Ian Staunton, a close associate of your husband's. It seems Rosemoor spent the entire night out last night, drinking and gambling in some seedy East End establishment. His losses were severe."

"As much as I hate to deprive ye of the enjoyment of telling me these things, I'm already well aware of how my husband passed the night."

"Oh? Confessed his sins, did he?"

"'Tis really none of your business, but aye. My husband and I have no secrets between us. I'm well aware of his recent losses."

"I'm surprised you're taking the news so calmly, then. He'll no doubt clear the land. Mifflin, I mean. And so near your beloved Glenbroch, too."

Brenna's breath hitched in her chest. "Whatever are ye talking about?"

Hugh took out his watch and flipped open the case, studying its face intently as he spoke. "Perhaps your outrage about the Clearances was all an act. Now that you're an English viscountess, perhaps you no longer care overmuch what happens in the Highlands. Perhaps you'll even see fit to clearing your own land one day." He shut the watch and returned it to his pocket, his gaze meeting Brenna's once more. "No doubt your husband could use the funds," he added.

Brenna could not speak. She could not force her mouth to form a single syllable. Her blood ran suddenly cold, and for a moment she could barely catch her breath.

"What *are* you talking about, Hugh?" Lord Danville asked. "I thought you meant a reconciliation with your sister today?"

"Perhaps once she sees that I've been correct about her husband all along, we shall be able to reconcile our differences. It's only too bad she didn't listen to me before it was too late."

Finally, Brenna found her voice, however tremulous. "I havena any idea what you're speaking of, Hugh, but I suggest ye get on with it and tell me. 'Tis nothing but another lie, no doubt."

"If only it were. A few inquiries will surely confirm it, if you doubt my word. Anyway," Hugh said, smiling maliciously, "in addition to losing a shocking amount of blunt at the tables last night, it seems the newly made Viscount Rosemoor wagered a deed to some property in Scotland. Land he'd only recently acquired at the tables himself from the Marquess of Hampton."

Brenna inhaled sharply. "Nay," she whispered.

Hugh nodded. "Yes, wagered and lost, I'm afraid. So very careless. The deed now rightfully belongs to Harold Mifflin, a man known to have no scruples. A mercenary, really. Anyway," he said, waving one hand in dismissal, "if there are no secrets between you and your husband, then I'm sure I'm not telling you anything you don't already know."

Could it be true? Nay, she refused to believe it. 'Twould not be the first time Hugh had told a blatant and outright lie about Colin. She would not make the same mistake all over again, doubting Colin in the face of Hugh's lies.

She rose, her head held high. "If ye will excuse me, Lady Danville, Lord Danville. I've much to do today at Rosemoor House." She did not spare a glance for Hugh.

"Must you go?" Lady Danville asked. "Tea hasn't even yet arrived. We've some delightful new cream cakes, too."

"Perhaps next time," she murmured.

"If you must go, I'll see you out," Lord Danville said, offering his arm.

Brenna took it, grateful for the support as her fingers trembled against his coat. "Good day," she said, offering her mother a nod.

Minutes later she was on her way back to Rosemoor House, walking so briskly that Celeste, trailing behind her, could barely keep up.

"Please, mum," Celeste called out, her voice near breathless. "You must slow down. What will people think, you racing down the walk like there's a fire at yer back?"

Brenna paused just long enough for Celeste to catch up. "I dinna care a fig what people think." She quickened her gait once more, the heels of her boots tapping against the walk in rhythm to her heart. *It isna true,* her mind repeated, over and over again. *It canna be true.*

Jane was standing in the front hall of Rosemoor House when Brenna stepped inside, her cheeks warm and her breath coming far too fast.

"There you are," Jane said with a sigh, relief evident in her wide blue eyes. "Is Colin with you?"

"Nay, why ever would Colin be with me?"

"He came home not an hour ago, looking quite pale. He asked after you, and Mama told him you had gone to Danville House for tea. I vow, Brenna, his face went entirely white. He flew out in a rage, off to find you. I don't mean to pry, but—"

"I'm verra sorry, Jane. But I canna speak of it yet, not till I find Colin."

"Oh, dear." Jane wrung her hands. "I cannot imagine what my brother has done now. I hope it's nothing too serious."

"'Tis likely nothing, Jane. Dinna fret about it, not just yet."

Just then the front door burst open, startling her. Colin took two steps forward before he spied her, standing there with Jane. He froze, his gaze searching hers. He looked dreadful, his hair mussed, his cravat horribly askew. Worse still was his expression—the raw guilt she saw darkening his features, shadowing his eyes.

"Nay, Colin," she cried out. "Please. It canna be true."

"Ballard told you, didn't he?"

"Told her what?" Jane asked, her voice rising. "What's going on, Colin?"

"Aye, he told me. Such awful things. I refused to believe them. But now . . ." Brenna shook her head in despair, continuing to study his expression. Dear Lord, his countenance said it all—the look of defeat that haunted his eyes when he looked at her. "'Tis true, isn't it?"

"Jane," Colin said, his voice steady, "if you'll excuse us, I need a moment alone with my wife."

After a pause, Jane nodded. Without another word, she left them. Brenna closed her eyes, the disappointment almost too painful to bear. Lies, all lies. He'd sworn he always kept his word when he'd known full well it was a lie. He'd broken his vow, and for what? A hand of cards. And he hadn't even had the decency to own up to it before he'd . . . She let the thought trail off, her cheeks flushing uncomfortably. She couldn't stand to look at him, to remember the way he'd held her last night, the tender words he'd spoken as he'd made love to her.

At last she opened her eyes and met his unflinching gaze. "How could ye, Colin? How could ye do such a thing?" she repeated.

"I was too far in the cups, Brenna. Too much so to realize what I was doing."

"Nay, 'tis no excuse. Ye canna blame the drink. Ye hypocrite," she tossed out. "Ye bloody hypocrite, accusing me of not trusting ye."

"You asked how I could do such a thing, and I'm answering you in all honesty. I'd no idea what I'd done, none whatsoever. Not till Nigel told me just now."

"Have ye any idea what you've done, even now?" she asked, shocked by the shrillness in her voice. "Have ye? He'll clear the land. They'll be driven off. I sent word that their fate was secure in your hands, and now you've proven me a liar. They trusted me, Colin. And now 'tis my husband, my own *husband*," she repeated, her voice rising, "who will cause them to lose their land." She slumped against the wall, her legs suddenly unable to bear her own weight. "Jenny isna well. Where will she go when she and her husband are turned out? Where will any of them go?"

Colin's heart hammered so violently in his breast that he feared it might burst. The anguish in her eyes was tearing him apart, bit by bit. He wanted to make it right, but God help him, he didn't know how. "I . . . Perhaps he won't clear the land. It's far too early to know his intentions."

"I must go home at once."

"You *are* home, Brenna," he said in desperation. "This is your home. Right here, with me."

"With *ye?*" She nearly spat the word, her hands balled into angry fists by her sides. "To think I actually felt badly that I hadn't trusted ye, hadn't given ye a proper chance. What a fool ye must think me, believing ye a man of honor." She began to weep, deep, gulping sobs. He moved to her side, reaching for her arm, but she backed away, shrugging off his hand as if repulsed by his touch.

"Tell me what to do, Brenna. What can I do to make it right again?" *Anything*. He would do anything to turn back time, to right the wrong.

"Ye canna make it right, don't ye see? Your word . . . Your word means nothing now. A drink or two and you're willing to forget any promises you've made, even to me."

"I made one mistake, Brenna, terrible though it is. Only one."

"And people will suffer for it, dinna ye see? I trusted ye, Colin. I cared for ye—nay, I loved ye."

"And now?" he asked, barely able to breathe. A wave of nausea washed over him, making his palms dampen. She loved him. She *had* loved him. And he'd ruined it. He'd gone and bloody ruined it.

"I feel nothing for ye."

Exquisite pain tore through his gut, ripping his heart to shreds. He raked a hand through his hair, wondering if he might vomit for a second time in one afternoon.

"I must go and pack my trunks," she said, turning toward the stairs.

"No!" he bellowed, his thoughts growing muddy. He could not lose her. He would not. Springing into action, he caught up with her, reaching for her hand and spinning her around to face him. "You remain steadfastly loyal to the Maclachlans' memory, despite the fact that they damn well snatched you from your home, your family. Your tenacity knows no bounds as far as your people at Glenbroch are concerned. Yet your love for me—your husband, I might remind you—is fleeting. Strange, as you've never before had a fleeting thought or feeling in your life. You're a fraud, Brenna Maclachlan. A coward. You don't love me; you never did. You only married me to extricate yourself from the contract with Sinclair, didn't you? I'll wager you planned to run off to Scotland without me all along."

"And what if I did?" she flung at him cruelly, her cheeks scarlet. "'Twould be no more than ye deserve."

"You are on English soil now, Brenna, where English law prevails. You are my wife. This is your home, and you will go nowhere without my permission."

She snatched her hand from his grasp and met his gaze, her chin tipped defiantly in the air. "Just watch me," she bit out, her eyes flashing angrily.

Up the stairs she flew in a flash of muslin, taking Colin's hopes and dreams with her. She was lost to him, forever. And he'd no one to blame but himself.

His reeling mind could suddenly think of nothing save finding a drink, and fast.

\* \* \*

A weary Brenna sat forward on her seat in the coach, straining to see through the familiar heavy mists that blanketed the rolling countryside, both brown and green this time of year. A light drizzle was falling, the air decidedly chilly. Wrapping her shawl more tightly about her shoulders, she peered through the wet glass, desperate for a glimpse of home. *Home,* at long last.

"Nearly there, Hera," she whispered to the cat who slept in the traveling case beside her. She glanced over at Celeste, dozing with her head tilted in what appeared to be a terribly uncomfortable angle, her lips parted slightly. Thank goodness the girl had agreed to accompany her to Glenbroch; she'd never have been able to endure the long journey alone. Besides, she'd grown used to her company, the nearest thing she had to a friend, besides Jane.

Her heart wrenched painfully at the memory of Jane, begging her not to leave, pleading with her to give Colin another chance. Yet she couldn't, not even for Jane. She'd no choice but to travel home, to tell those who lived on what had been Hampton's lands that she'd been wrong, that the lands were not secured, that she'd no idea whether or not the current landlord would allow them to retain their crofts. She would offer Jenny Cannan and her husband a place at Glenbroch, but she could do little else. There were far too many of them to burden Glenbroch with. She would do what she could to help, but she could make no promises.

The coach hit a rut in the road, and Celeste snuffled loudly, her chin dropping to her breastbone. What ever would Mrs. Campbell think, her bringing along a lady's maid to Glenbroch? Brenna nearly laughed aloud at the thought. She'd no doubt think her time amongst the English had addled her brain, that's what. And perhaps it had.

Beside her, Hera awakened with a loud meow, as if sensing they neared home. Brenna watched the cat stretch languorously, arching her back while reaching forward with each slender paw. For several minutes, the cat smoothed her fur with her tongue. Her ablutions at last complete, Hera sat looking out the case expectantly, her pink nose twitching as she sniffed the air.

Brenna quickly glanced back out the window, sucking in her breath at the sight that greeted her tired eyes. There, just beyond the next rise, the gray stones of Glenbroch rose from the mists. The untidy pile of stones had never before looked more beautiful, more welcoming, than it did at that very moment, and Brenna feared she might begin to weep. Instead, she took several deep, calming breaths, then reached over to pluck at Celeste's sleeve.

"Celeste," she whispered, her voice quaking with emotion. "Wake up. There's Castle Glenbroch, just ahead."

The maid's head snapped upright, her eyes flying open. "Wha . . . what?" she stammered, then licked her lips.

"We've reached our destination. Look." Brenna pointed toward the window on her right. "There it is. Och, 'tis the most beautiful sight I've seen in ages."

Celeste blinked several times. "But . . . but that's no castle."

"Nay, the original castle fell on hard times many generations back. Much of it burned after Culloden.

'Twas rebuilt as a manor house, with only the original south tower remaining. Yet the name endured."

"Hmph. Seems misleading," Celeste muttered. "Calling it a castle when it ain't."

"Ye will find it far more comfortable and less drafty than a true castle, I think. And Mrs. Campbell, the housekeeper, ye will adore her."

Celeste looked skeptical, at best.

*Soon,* Brenna thought, watching Glenbroch's walls loom larger as they approached. Brenna allowed herself to feel the first twinge of happiness she'd felt in days, temporarily lifting the oppressive heaviness from her heart.

Soon, in the familiar surroundings of Glenbroch, she'd put Colin from her mind, forget his betrayal—forget that she'd ever loved him. And then she'd decide what to do about their marriage. One day, perhaps sooner than she'd supposed, she'd have to face him again, perhaps even forgive him. But not now. Now while the pain of his betrayal was so fresh, so raw. So painful.

She pushed the unpleasant thoughts from her mind as the coach turned off the main road and began to slow. She'd figure it all out later, once she was settled, once the wound began to heal a bit.

At last, the coach jerked to a halt. The door swung open, and the cool, damp Scottish air assaulted her senses at once, bringing a bittersweet smile to her lips.

Glenbroch! Home at last, where she belonged.

# Chapter 22

Brenna stepped into the front hall, peeling off her buff gloves and depositing them on the long wooden table by the door. She sighed heavily, glad to have settled back to a familiar routine. More than a fortnight had passed since her arrival, and she was back to her usual duties as the Maclachlan of Glenbroch. The day had been long, yet pleasant, visiting tenants and hearing their complaints and concerns.

As she began to unbutton her overcoat and shrug out of it, Jenny Cannan rushed in, a smile brightening her narrow, gaunt face.

"There ye are, mistress. Here, let me help ye out of that."

Brenna smiled at the reed-thin woman, allowing her to remove the garment from her shoulders. "Now, Jenny," she scolded. "I told ye, didna I? Ye are a guest here, not a servant. I no longer require a nursemaid."

"Bah." Jenny dismissed her comment with the wave of one hand. "Never too old for a wee bit of coddling, especially a fine lass like yerself. And look at ye, mistress, out with no bonnet. Ye'll be freckled by morn."

"And what if I am?" Brenna answered with a shrug. "Perhaps I like the freckles. Some might say they lend character to my face."

Jenny shook her head, clucking noisily like a mother hen.

"Besides, there is no sun today. Look"—Brenna gestured toward the window—"'tis damp and gray as can be."

"Well, dinna stand there catching a chill, wearing naught but that silly little frock. Go, find your woolens."

Brenna glanced down at her muslin gown, the hem now stained with mud. Jenny was right—it *was* a silly garment, utterly ill-suited to her life there at Glenbroch. What had she been thinking when she'd slipped it on that morning, then allowed Celeste to dress her hair as if she were setting out for Mayfair's finest drawing rooms rather than the manor's modest tenant farms?

"I'll go and change, Jenny, if ye will grant me one favor."

"Anything, mistress."

"Would ye find Mrs. Campbell at once and tell her that Angus Ferguson's boy has taken ill? Poor Mrs. Ferguson is busy enough with an infant at her breast. Mrs. Campbell should have Cook make her special broth and have it sent round to the Fergusons' croft straightaway, along with any fruits and vegetables she can spare."

"Verra well, mistress. I'll tell her straightaway."

"Oh, and how is Mr. Cannan getting on with Mr. Moray?"

"Quite well, quite well. I canna thank ye enough for givin' him such an opportunity, lass." She reached for Brenna's hand and squeezed it.

"Dearest Jenny, I'm only sorry—"

"Nay, 'tis not yer fault, wee one. Besides, naught has come of it yet. Mayhap ye were mistaken."

"I truly wish I were." There had been no word yet of a new landlord at Hampton's estate, though Brenna knew that soon enough the man would make his position known. Give him time, she reminded herself. After all, it hadn't been a month since . . . Brenna shook her head, unwilling to remember the night in question.

"Go on, off with ye." Jenny hooked her thumb toward the stairs.

Brenna obeyed with a sheepish smile, becoming suddenly aware of the cold dampness that permeated the folds of her gown. Goodness, after the warm, pleasant weather in London, it seemed she would never get warm here at Glenbroch.

Wearily, she climbed the stairs toward her room. Hera came racing up beside her, following closely at her heels.

"And where have ye been off to? I havena seen ye since this time yesterday, Hera. Out enjoying yourself? Glad to be home, I suppose?"

The cat raced ahead, darting into her bedchamber. Brenna followed suit, closing the door softly behind her. A pang of guilt shot through her, catching her suddenly off guard. She should be glad to be home, and yet she wasn't, not entirely. As loath as she was to admit it, she missed her newfound family—Jane and Lady Rosemoor, even Lucy. A part of her even missed Lord and Lady Danville, despite their awkward attempts at familial relations. While she'd never entirely felt as if she'd belonged in London, a new, uncertain feeling had crept into her heart here at Glenbroch. She didn't entirely belong *here,* either.

Had she imagined it, or had the tenants looked at her slightly differently today? Now that they knew the truth about her—that no Maclachlan blood flowed through her veins—did they no longer think her worthy of their fealty, their respect? The easy camaraderie she'd once felt with them was gone. They now seemed slightly uncomfortable in her presence, as if they were entertaining a near stranger rather than the woman they'd known since she was naught but a girl. Of course, this fancy frock hadn't helped matters, she thought, glancing down at it with a scowl. They'd no doubt supposed she thought herself better than them now, decked out in her finery from Madame Vioget's shop while they entertained her in their homespun.

She tugged the damp dress down, not caring if she ripped the fabric or fastenings. She had no need for such fine things now. Reaching up, she viciously tore the pins from her hair, allowing it to spill across her shoulders. She had no need for such elaborate hair arrangements, either. A simple plait, coiled and pinned against her head, would suffice as it always had. She would be sure to speak with Celeste about such matters.

Sighing heavily, she moved to the window, peering out the drapes wearing naught but her shift. Dear Lord, but she'd hoped he would come for her. As each day dawned, she'd lain in bed thinking that perhaps *this* would be the day that Colin would appear on the front steps, begging her forgiveness. Declaring that he could not live without her.

She'd confided in no one save Jenny about her marriage, though she assumed that Celeste had let the news slip below-stairs—that Brenna was in fact a married woman, the Viscountess Rosemoor, estranged from her husband less than a sennight after they'd wed. Shocking news.

'Twas what she deserved for marrying an Englishman, they no doubt whispered amongst themselves.

With each passing day, it became more and more clear that Colin did not love her. To be fair, he'd never claimed such tender feelings. Still, she'd thought . . . Well, she'd thought that perhaps he had. She was made hopeful by her own imprudent feelings, like a silly, foolish girl. 'Twas exactly why she'd never wished to marry for love. She'd never wished to be made a fool of, mooning after someone who did not return her affections.

Aye, if Colin had loved her, he would have come for her by now. At the very least, he would have sent a letter. After all, she'd received two such missives from Jane, cheerful letters that were careful not to mention Colin at all.

She shook her head in confusion. Was she ready to forgive him? How could she, after the words he'd spoken just before she'd left? A coward, he'd called her. A fraud. Cruel words. Had she let her desire for him outweigh his betrayal? How else could she explain the fact that she yearned for him, despite his actions? She glanced down at the betrothal ring she still wore on her finger, along with her wedding band. *Unbidden*.

A knock sounded on the door, startling her.

"Mum? Lady . . . Rosemoor?"

Brenna sighed. She'd so many different names that poor Celeste didn't know what to call her anymore. "Aye, Celeste. Come in."

The maid came in on silent feet, closing the door behind her. "Shall we start preparin' you for dinner now?"

"Nay, I'm not . . . not feeling well. I think I might go up to my observatory instead."

"Again? The mists are so thick, yer not likely to see a thing tonight."

"The moon, perhaps," Brenna answered. It didn't really matter what she saw through her telescope. Just sitting there, in her favorite spot in the tower, would bring her the peace she could not seem to find elsewhere.

"Mrs. Cannan will be sorely disappointed, mum. You've not been down to dinner more than three times in a sennight."

'Twas true. While she still took great pleasure in the day-to-day duties of managing Glenbroch, evenings were a whole different matter. She simply wasn't good company, and the strain was too much for her to bear.

"I . . . Ye must send my regrets, Celeste."

"Shall I at least have a tray sent up?"

"Something light, perhaps. Truly, I'm not hungry."

"If you say so, mum." With a nod, Celeste turned toward the door. "If only the Rosemoors' cook were here," she said, glancing back over her shoulder.

"You dinna think the cook here at Glenbroch is sufficiently talented? Why, I've always thought—"

"No, mum, it's not that. She's a fine cook, indeed. I only meant that the Rosemoors' cook makes a tonic that is known to cure anything from the ague to gout. Even heartbreak, I'm told," she added, boldly meeting Brenna's gaze.

A tonic to cure heartbreak? If only it were true, 'twould be worth its weight in gold. "Well, no matter. I suppose I shall have to make do without, won't I?"

"I should have asked for a vial before we left, is what I should have done. Well, good night, mum."

"Good night, Celeste," Brenna answered, reaching for her dressing gown. She shrugged into it and tightened the belt around her waist as the maid scurried out.

"Come, Hera," she called to the cat who sat perched on the wide stone sill, watching her. "I would verra much like your company tonight in my observatory." The cat, at least, didn't ask questions. Or expect her to carry on cheerful conversation, something she no longer seemed capable of. *Time*, she reminded herself. She needed naught but time.


"Must you come in here and begin banging around like that?" Colin muttered, keeping his gaze firmly trained on the *Times* he held in his hands, even though the words were nothing but a grayish blur.

"Must you continue to snap at me like that?" Jane retorted, thumping a book on his desk for emphasis. "I'm not the enemy, you know. Just because you managed to make a veritable mess of things—"

"I suggest you hold your tongue, Jane." The all-too-familiar rage welled within him, nearly suffocating him.

"Or what, Colin? I'm tired of tiptoeing around you, not allowed to so much as utter her name. She was my friend, and you've driven her away. I *must* know why."

"In case you have forgotten, she's the one who left me."

"Hmph. I'm sure she had her reasons. What I cannot understand is why you have not gone after her."

"You think I should chase after her like a spurned schoolboy?"

"Well, she *is* your wife, after all."

"Believe it or not, I do have a measure of pride left."

"You would allow yourself to suffer so for the sake of pride? Look at you, Colin." She planted her fists on her hips. "Just look at the state you're in. You look as if you have not slept or bathed in days—nor eaten, judging by the fit of your waistcoat. Neither have you joined us for dinner in more than a fortnight. Instead, you sit here for hours on end, in Papa's—in your study," she corrected, "doing"—she waved her hands in the air—"something." She eyed him suspiciously. "I have no idea what it is you're doing in here." Her gaze slid toward the cart where their father had kept his spirits.

Now empty. The day Brenna had left, he'd poured it all out. Every last drop.

"Not that it's any of your concern, but I've been familiarizing myself with the Rosemoor estates and holdings." Going over the books was all he could do to take his mind off the constant, excruciating suffering. If he allowed himself one moment of peace, of rest, he'd go mad with it. Still, he refused to permit himself to dull the pain with spirits. No, he'd suffer through every last torturous second—sober.

This was his penance, his punishment, for allowing the single best thing in his life to slip through his fingers. "Quite interesting, really," he lied, his voice betraying him by breaking on the last syllable, revealing him to be the weak fool that he was.

Jane did not miss it. "Oh, Colin. Colin," she repeated, her voice full of anguish. "You must do something. I cannot stand to see you sitting there, acting as if nothing is wrong when it is clear your heart is breaking."

He neatly folded the paper before responding. "Don't be so melodramatic, Jane. It isn't becoming."

With a sigh, she perched on the edge of his desk, inadvertently toppling the stack of books she'd deposited there only moments before. Colin bent down to retrieve them, his gaze drawn to an unfamiliar, leather-bound volume.

"What's this?" he asked, flipping open the cover.

Charts. Page after page of them. Stars, planets, constellations, all labeled in what must be Brenna's surprisingly childish scrawl. His breath hitched, burning his lungs. Dampness threatened his eyes, making his neck warm with mortification. He couldn't speak, not a single word. Instead, a strangled cry escaped his lips as he slammed the book shut.

Jane leapt to her feet, her brows drawn. "What is it?" She snatched the book away, quickly flipping through the pages. "It's only one of Brenna's chart books. She must have left it behind. Why do you look so stricken?"

Colin's heart thumped painfully against his ribs. "Leave me, Jane. Now."

"No, I can't. I won't. Besides, Lucy and Mandeville will be here shortly, and—"

"I said leave me," he said, his voice a strangled whisper.

"You're frightening me, Colin. You're pale and trembling, and—dear God, no. Not like Papa . . ." She hurried to his side, reaching for his hands.

He snatched his hands away, turning from her so that she would not see the tears pooling in his eyes. "Devil take it, Jane, just leave me be."

His stubborn sister held her ground. "No. You must go after her. Whatever you've done, tell her you're sorry; tell her that you were wrong."

"I can't, don't you see?" he shouted. With the sweep of one arm, he pushed everything from the desk to the floor, sending papers and books flying through the air. "There's nothing I can do to make it right again. She's better off without me."

"She's your wife, Colin. Your wife!"

"And I do not deserve her." Bloody hell, he could no longer hide the shameful tears.

"How can you say such a thing? You, the most honorable man I know; the kindest, the gentlest, most protective of brothers."

"You needn't bother saying things you don't mean simply to placate me, Jane. I'm a grown man. A viscount now, for God's sake. And look at me." He spread his arms wide. "Just look at what a mess I've made of myself."

Jane shook her head so vigorously that one chestnut lock escaped its binding and fell across her flushed cheek. "I see a man who's suffered ill fortune, who's been falsely accused and maligned. Yet through it all, you've maintained your dignity, your honor. You've married an exceptional woman—a woman who loves you, Colin."

"She doesn't love me."

"Of course she does. Are you really so blind?"

"She might have loved me once, but no more."

"Balderdash. Surely you've not done anything quite so egregious as to—"

"But I have." He rose on unsteady legs, despising his weakness. "If you only knew what I've done. . . ." He shook his head.

"Tell me, Colin," Jane urged, her voice soft. She clasped both his hands in her own warm ones. "Tell me just what you've done, and let me be the judge."

He swallowed the lump in his throat. "The night I was tossed from White's, I'd won a parcel of land in Scotland from the Marquess of Hampton. Land that borders Brenna's Castle Glenbroch, it turns out."

"That would seem quite fortuitous, then."

"No, hear me out. I promised Brenna, long before we wed, that the land would remain safe, that I'd never clear it. I gave her my word as a gentleman, and she passed on my assurances to Hampton's tenants."

Jane's eyes widened in horror. "No, Colin. No. Please say you did not."

"Clear it? No. I hadn't the chance. Just after Father died, I managed to find myself gambling in the back room of some seedy East End establishment. Lost an appalling amount of money that night, and then, when I was all but done up, it seems I offered up the land in Scotland. I don't even remember doing it, I was so foxed."

"And you lost it," Jane hissed, dropping his hands. "You lost it, didn't you?"

"It would seem so. As I said, I have no memory of it, none whatsoever."

"You stupid, stupid fool." Jane pounded one fist on the desk.

"I appreciate the sentiment, Jane. Harold Mifflin is now the rightful owner of the property, and he'll no doubt clear it. Right under Brenna's nose. She'll never forgive me, never trust me again. And who could blame her?"

Jane sighed heavily. "But you love her."

"Of course I bloody love her."

"And she loves you, I'm sure of it. You must go to her, beg for her forgiveness. Grovel if you must."

"No."

"God's teeth, Colin, she might very well be carrying your child, your heir. Did you ever think of that?"

*No.* No, he hadn't. It was unlikely at best, as there had been only that once. "No, but it's very unlikely. Despite what it seemed, I can assure you we did not get a head start on . . . er, on such matters. I can't believe I'm discussing this with you."

"It would seem I'm all you have right now, Colin. You've acted abominably, it's true. Still, I cannot help but love you."

He rose, enfolding his sister in his embrace. "You're a generous woman, Jane Rosemoor. Kind and giving, and I would not trade you for the world." He nearly choked on the words.

"Nor I you, Colin," Jane said, her voice muffled against his coat. "But I beg of you, give Brenna a chance. Let *her* decide if you are worthy of her love."

"Jane?" a voice called from the hall.

*Lucy.* Jane stepped away from Colin, wiping her eyes with the back of one hand. "In here," she called out cheerily.

Colin reached down to straighten his waistcoat just as Lucy strode into the room, Mandeville behind her.

"Oh, Colin, I'm so relieved you're here." A smile spread across Lucy's face, lighting her emerald eyes. "Have you heard?"

"Heard what?" Jane asked, mercifully allowing Colin to remain silent while he attempted to rein in his emotions.

"Tell him, Henry. Oh, it's marvelous news, simply marvelous."

Mandeville nodded. "I've just come from White's, where I spoke at length to Mr. Montgomery. Some interesting facts have come to light, it would seem."

"Go on," Jane urged, settling into the wide wing chair Colin had only recently vacated.

Mandeville continued. "It would seem a waiter came forward just last night and confessed his involvement in a scheme perpetrated by Thomas Sinclair. Said he was paid to plant a card in your pocket, if I remember correctly, by none other than Sinclair. Apparently he had sufficient evidence in the form of payments made to him to convince Mr. Montgomery that he spoke the truth.

"Being a gentleman's gentleman, Mr. Montgomery went to Sinclair at once with the evidence. Sinclair, of course, refused to take the blame alone. He claimed Hugh Ballard to be the mastermind behind the plan, even going so far as to assert he'd been threatened with physical harm had he not complied with Ballard's demands."

"I cannot believe it," Jane exclaimed, her eyes shining brightly.

Colin only nodded, though his heart began to accelerate.

"Tell the rest, Henry," Lucy prodded.

Mandeville straightened his cravat. "Thoroughly annoyed that such a deception had played out in

White's hallowed halls, Mr. Montgomery called upon the Duke of Glastonbury at once, informing the man that he had, in fact, *not* been cheated by you, but that Sinclair and Ballard had been the perpetrators of mischief. Suffice it to say, Sinclair and Ballard have both been permanently removed from White's, and you, Rosemoor, have been reinstated. The Duke of Glastonbury wasted no time in publicly declaring his disdain for Ballard and Sinclair, and, as we speak, the news is now making its way around Mayfair."

"You've been cleared," Lucy said, clapping her hands together delightedly.

Colin let out his breath in a rush. Dear God, could it really be true? "Why would this waiter come forward now, after all this time?"

Mandeville shrugged. "Seems he'd required further payment from Sinclair in order to keep his silence, and Sinclair eventually got tired of paying. Figured no one would take the word of a mere waiter over his, anyway, so he cut the man off. Clearly, Sinclair underestimated Mr. Montgomery. Who, by the way, has requested that I pass on his deepest apologies and who will no doubt be calling upon you shortly. He's prepared to make a public acknowledgment of your innocence."

Jane turned toward Colin, nearly grinning. "It's just as Colin said it was, and now everyone will know the truth. I must go tell Mother at once."

So it was true. He'd been entirely cleared. Sinclair and Ballard had been exposed. He'd expected to feel joyous at this moment—relieved, vindicated. Instead, he felt nothing. Numb.

# Chapter 23

Colin sat, in his shirtsleeves, slumped in the leather chair behind his desk, staring unseeing at the walls of his study. Mr. Montgomery had come and gone, and Colin was now officially reinstated at White's. Yet the pleasure of his vindication was fleeting. What was he to do now?

Pretend the events of the past few months had never transpired? Return to the life he left behind? No, it would never do. He was not the same man he had been then. The very idea of whiling away his days at his club no longer appealed to him. Without the distraction offered by drinking and gaming, how would he spend his days while awaiting his wife's return?

He could, of course, heed Jane's advice and go after her, demand that she accompany him home. Only she was quite likely to refuse him, and he was far too big a coward to face that certainty at the present.

With a heavy sigh of defeat, he dropped his head into his hands. Damn it all to hell, he had been cleared, his honor restored. His life was finally turning about. He was a peer of the realm now, his finances solvent. He had property, prestige. A name without blight. A wife he adored.

Yet she despised him, he reminded himself. With good reason.

"Lord Rosemoor?"

Colin looked up in surprise at the butler standing in the doorway, a white card in his outstretched hand.

"Pardon me, Lord Rosemoor, but you have a visitor."

Colin nearly looked over his own shoulder, expecting his father to be there, before it dawned on him that *he* was Lord Rosemoor now.

He shook his head. "I'm sorry, Penwick. A visitor, you say?"

"Indeed. A Mr. Randolph Lyttle-Brown."

Lyttle-Brown? What the deuce could he want with him? For a moment he thought to refuse him an audience. Yet curiosity got the best of him, and he found himself shrugging into his coat and following Penwick across the entry hall and into the sitting room.

Mr. Lyttle-Brown had helped himself to a glass of port and stood leaning against the sideboard with glass in hand when Colin entered.

"Ah, Mr. Rosemoor. How very good to see you. I must apologize for our last meeting. Shameful business what Sinclair and Ballard did to you. Shameful, indeed."

"Quite so," Colin agreed coldly.

"I vow, I never truly believed it of you." He took a hearty swig of port, then wiped his mouth with his sleeve. "Not Colin Rosemoor, I said, on more than one occasion."

"Is that so?" Colin asked. "Interesting, as my memory of our last meeting would prove otherwise. I distinctly remember you forbidding me from keeping your daughter's company ever again."

Lyttle-Brown waved one hand in dismissal. "Oh, that. You must understand, I had my daughter's reputation to think of, and with what they were saying about you . . ." He shook his head as he stroked his whiskers. "My only daughter, you know. A true gem."

"Ah, yes," Colin said, his voice laced with sarcasm. "A diamond of the first water."

"I'm glad you think so, son. Oh, but you must excuse me. I should no doubt call you 'sir' now that you have been made a viscount, shouldn't I?"

Colin shrugged, remaining silent and fixing the man with a glare. He didn't care what he called him. He only wished he'd state his business and be on his way.

Lyttle-Brown cleared his throat. "Ahem, yes. Well. You must see what a bind I'm in now, my precious daughter promised to Hugh Ballard. Falsely impugning a gentleman's honor." He shook his head. "He's done up for certain, never to be trusted again. I've come to you with a proposition, one that I hope you will consider."

"Pray, go on," Colin bit out.

"I've heard rumors that your wife has abandoned you."

A flush climbed up Colin's neck. "Abandoned me? Is that what they are saying? That she abandoned me?"

"You'll pardon me if I've been misinformed. I heard it from Lady Brandon not two days ago. Anyway, I spoke with my solicitors at length this morning, and they tell me there might be a loophole in which to extricate yourself. Your wife signed your marriage license as 'Brenna Maclachlan,' did she not? Brenna Maclachlan of Glenbroch, Scotland."

"That's how she wished to sign it. She was raised at Glenbroch. A Maclachlan all her life." Even as Colin said the words, an uncomfortable sensation washed over him. Had this been a calculated move on Brenna's part? So that she could legally end their marriage if she so desired?

"Yes, yes," Lyttle-Brown said, waving one hand. "I see why she would wish to do so, though I do not understand why you would allow it. By the laws of England, she is Margaret Danville of Sussex, is she not? You will have no resistance to a legal annulment, and you've every right to seek one. Annul your marriage and marry Honoria. Take her to Gretna Green and be done with it as hastily as possible. I will pay you handsomely. Triple her original dowry, plus I will settle all of your debts."

Colin blanched. "Good God, man. Are you that desperate to rid yourself of your daughter?"

"I am that eager to see her married well," Lyttle-Brown corrected. "She is distraught—terribly distraught—with her current situation and is angry that I forced it upon her. It's *you* she wants, you she wanted all along. Besides, I'm well aware you could use the funds, despite your recent inheritance. Rid yourself of this so-called wife, this barbaric Scotswoman who left you mere days after your wedding. Marry Honoria, a fine, gently bred

English girl, a favorite of the *ton*. It will be as if this whole dreadful business with Ballard and Sinclair never happened, and you will have exactly what you desired all along. Say you'll at least consider it."

Colin stared blankly at the man standing before him. An annulment? Blast it, but the man was correct. There *were* grounds for an annulment, if the courts decided she had signed a false name and place of residence. The thought had never before crossed his mind.

"Well?" Lyttle-Brown prodded. "What say you?"

"Leave me." Colin took a step back from the man, unable to say any more. He needed time—time to sort out his thoughts, to decide what course his life might take.

"Of course, you'll need some time. A day or two, no more. I'd like this settled as soon as possible."

"Leave!" Colin shouted, pointing toward the door.

With a nod, Lyttle-Brown set down his glass. "I'll expect to hear from you shortly," he said, then bowed sharply before taking his leave.

Blast the man. Colin struck his palm against the sideboard. A barbarian he'd called Brenna, while his own daughter was a gem—a gently bred English girl, exactly the type Colin had always pictured by his side. *Everything he'd ever desired,* Lyttle-Brown had said. His honor restored, his coffers full, acceptance into the most hallowed social circles in Mayfair. A viscountess adored by one and all. Yes, that had been what he'd always wanted, hadn't it? Perhaps Lyttle-Brown had the right of it.

His chest tight with anger, he made his way back to his study, slamming the door behind him. Shoving his hands into his pockets, he paced a circuit before the cold fireplace. Back and forth he strode, thinking of nothing save the fact that Brenna had left him. *Left him*. He had all but begged her to stay, and she had left, anyway.

At once his gaze fell upon a large, rectangular package wrapped in brown paper, leaning against the wall behind his desk. *What the devil?*

He bent down to retrieve it, his brows drawing together as he noted his name written on a white card attached to the parcel. Jane's neat, precise hand. Ripping the card from the paper, he turned it over in his palm. Nothing. He shrugged. Picking up the parcel, he measured its weight with his hands. Light. It felt like a canvas. He set it back down on the desk and stared at it for several seconds, oddly fearful of what the paper might hide.

Unable to bear the suspense, he at last nodded to himself. Tentatively, he reached for one edge of the paper and pulled. White canvas peeked out, exposed at the corner. Had Jane bought him a painting? *Curious*. And more curious still, why did he feel as if his life hung in the balance as he exposed it? Shrugging away the sense of unease, he reached down and ripped away the paper in one long stroke.

He gasped, unable to do anything but stare at the sight before him. *Brenna*. His heart began to race; his palms dampened. He blinked several times, the image swimming in and out of focus before his very eyes. A painting of Brenna, and a remarkable likeness at that. She reclined in a white wrought-iron chair, surrounded by greenery, a deep blue flower tucked behind one ear. A faint smile tipped the corners of her mouth—a mysterious smile. Her eyes, the color of the sea, appeared sleepy, bored, perhaps. The pose was languorous, alluring; her expression nothing if not sensual. Bloody hell, but she was beautiful. Much more so than Honoria, despite her classic pert, blond looks. Truly, there was no comparison as far as he was concerned.

Barbaric? No. Rough around the edges, perhaps. Intelligent. Capable. Accomplished in ways that went far beyond the talents suited to the drawing room alone. Brenna was far more loyal, more civilized than those of the *ton*—those who changed their allegiance on the whim of gossip, who cared more for appearance than for substance, who would betray a friend or sister to satisfy their own desires.

Yes, perhaps a woman like Honoria would once have satisfied him, would have represented everything he'd ever wanted in life. But that was the old Colin. The Colin who drank too much, who gambled too recklessly, lived too carelessly. Then Brenna had come into his life and set his very existence on end. She'd made him want to be a better man, a stronger man. A man of substance.

Almost reverently, he picked up the painting and set it on the mantel, then took several steps backward, his gaze never leaving the image of her face. He realized at once he would do anything to earn her love. It mattered not where they lived, Scotland or England. As long as they were together, he could be that man he aspired to be.

His eyes filled with tears, and yet he felt no shame for them, not this time. He would set things to rights with his wife—now. Not tomorrow, not in a fortnight. On this very day he'd begin to right the wrongs. He knew what he had to do. Mandeville would no doubt aid him in any way he could. Hell,

Mandeville owed him. Colin had helped Mandeville and Lucy find their happy ending; now Mandeville would return the favor.

Taking one last, longing look at the painting, he nodded to himself, then turned and headed for the door, smiling broadly. First things first. There was a deed to some property in Scotland to buy back. Oh, it would no doubt cost him dearly. He'd sell off every last thing he owned if it came to that. But the end result would surely be worth it. *She* was worth it.

There were no guarantees, of course. He'd be forced to risk his heart once more. God only knew she had every reason to reject him—again. To flay open his heart and trample it. But for once in his life he'd do something utterly brave, completely courageous.

He reached for his tall beaver hat and tipped it onto his head, then let himself out onto the walk where the sun shone down brightly upon him. This time Colin Rosemoor would win his fair maiden. He'd make damn sure of it.

And as for Randolph Lyttle-Brown and his offer . . . The man could go to the devil for all Colin cared. And he could take the *ton* and their hypocrisy with him. Colin had other fish to fry.

Of the *Scots* variety.


"Goodness, Hera, look how quickly this storm moved into the glen. Perhaps we should go back inside." Brenna glanced up, watching as dark, ominous clouds raced across the sky, completely obscuring Ben Nevis in the distance. At once a brilliant flash of lightning illuminated the night. She braced herself, awaiting the clap of thunder that would surely follow.

*Boom!* The sound echoed off the walls of the tower, rattling the floor beneath her. Hera wailed pitifully, crouching as low to the ground as possible as she attempted to hide behind Brenna's skirts.

She should go inside. Now. And yet she felt reckless, somehow enlivened by the storm's power. 'Twas silly, of course. She'd come to her observatory to look for falling stars, which were always abundant this time of year. She'd hoped to glimpse a few despite the patchy cloud cover. Then the storm had rolled in with such a violent ferocity that she'd been mesmerized, compelled to remain in the tower, exposed to the elements even while the parapet shielded her from the worst of the storm's impending onslaught.

Another bright flash of lightning zigzagged across the sky, raising gooseflesh on Brenna's arms. The accompanying crack of thunder followed almost immediately, again rattling the tower's old stone walls. A wave of fear washed over her. She should have returned to her room long before the storm gained its strength. Now, with the winds howling and rattling the shutters, 'twas too late. The rain swept under the parapet, stinging her skin as it sluiced across her. At her feet, poor Hera keened, trembling in fear. Quickly, she gathered her charts and ink pot and prepared to flee down the uneven stairs, likely now wet and slippery.

Another bright flash of light. In the moment before the thunder shook the walls, Brenna could have sworn she heard the pounding of hooves in the distance, drawing closer. What fool would be out riding in this storm? Hera meowed as the thunder crashed, and Brenna reached down to scoop the cat up into her arms, dropping her charts and ink as she did so.

"Poor Hera. Dinna worry, I'll get ye in before ye blow away. Och, dinna put your claws in me."

At once the fur on Hera's back rose. An eerie silence followed, and then a blinding flash of light lit the sky, accompanied by a crack so loud that Brenna screamed. The floor beneath her feet seemed to shake. Almost immediately, Brenna smelled scorched wood.

*Smoke.* Dear Lord, she smelled smoke. Had the tower been struck by lightning? Though the main structure was made of stone, the crumbling stairs had been reinforced with oak planking in several places, and a wooden railing had been installed along the walls. If the stairs were burning, how ever would she get down?

Smoke began to drift into the observatory, billowing out on the wind and making her eyes water. She coughed, the smoke burning her lungs. *No. Oh, no.* She was trapped. Clutching Hera tightly against her bosom, her mind cast about frantically for a solution. Her gown; she was soaked through. She glanced down at her skirts, stuck wetly to her chemise. Perhaps she could use her gown to beat out the flames once they began to threaten her. Gently, she set the quivering Hera down at her feet and, with shaking fingers, reached around herself to unfasten her gown. She stepped out of the heavy, wet woolen folds and looked about wildly. What now?

Help. She must call for help. If no one came to her rescue, then she would attempt to make her own way down. But perhaps if she screamed loudly enough, someone would hear her. Celeste had known her destination, after all. She must hurry. The smoke was making her light-headed and dizzy. Taking a deep breath, she began to scream as loudly as possible, praying she would be heard above the din of the storm and the crackling of the fire below.

Near-blinded by the driving rain, Colin leapt from the horse's back, pulling his hat low on his brow in a useless effort to keep the water from his eyes. Just as he'd ridden up at Glenbroch, lightning had struck the structure with a terrifying crack, and now the smell of smoke mingled with the scent of rain and earth. Thick, black smoke billowed from a round stone tower's windows, on the south side of the property. Thankfully the tower appeared disused; it didn't seem large enough to serve any purpose, other than perhaps as a lookout in the days of clan warfare. He must get inside the main house at once and find Brenna, ensure her safety.

He wrapped his cloak about himself and had taken two steps toward the house when he heard someone screaming. A woman's voice, coming from the direction of the tower. His heart dropped to his knees, leaving him momentarily breathless. Bloody hell, the tower. A lookout spot. No doubt Brenna would favor such a place, where she could gaze at the sky unfettered. Another scream sliced through the night. *No.* Dear God, no.

Mercifully the rains began to recede. He sprang

into action, sprinting toward the base of the tower. "Brenna?" he yelled, his lungs burning with the effort.

A thin woman, her face lined with age, rushed around the side of the house, holding up her skirts as she plowed through the mud. "Saints preserve us, the mistress is up there," she said breathlessly, pointing toward the parapet at the top of the tower. Flames could now be seen licking at the windows halfway up.

"Brenna! Can you hear me?" His heart was pounding so loudly that he could barely hear over it. He cupped his hands to his mouth and tried once more. "Brenna?"

"Colin?" came her disembodied voice from above, nearly making him weep with relief. "Is that ye, Colin?"

Her amber-colored head appeared over the edge of the parapet. "The stairs," she called down. "I'm trapped. You must . . ." The rest of her words were drowned out by the sounds of the crackling fire.

Colin turned toward the woman at his side. "Go inside at once and gather buckets. As many as you can. Send out every man, woman, and child with a bucket of water."

"Aye, sir." With a curt nod, she lifted her skirts and hurried back in the direction from whence she had come. Colin ripped off his now-soaked cloak, holding the wet folds in front of his mouth. He pulled open the heavy wooden door at the tower's base and rushed inside, coughing as the smoky air entered his lungs, even through the fabric. Up he flew, up the steep steps till the snapping fire became louder, the smoke so thick he could barely see. At once he began to beat at the flames that struggled to thrive in the damp environment. His arms

aching, he brought down his cape over and over
again until he was able to pass through the worst of
it. His feet nearly flew up the remaining steps.

At last he reached a wide corridor, which was
filled with smoke. He stumbled through the arched
doorway at the end, his eyes burning and his hands
raw and blistered.

"Colin!" Brenna cried out, her voice thick with
tears. In a hazy blur, she threw herself into his arms,
and he stumbled backward under the weight.

"You're safe, my love. But we must hurry." He
swept her into his arms, only barely cognizant of the
fact that she wore nothing save a thin chemise.

She struggled against him. "Nay, I must find
Hera. I canna leave her."

"Let me first take you down to safety, Brenna.
Then, I vow, I will come right back up for the beast."
He had to get her down straightaway. There was no
telling how long the stairs would remain safe.

"Hera? Where are ye, Hera?" she called shrilly,
still struggling against his iron grasp.

He heard a low mewl from the corner, beneath
a small table.

"There," Brenna said, escaping his arms at last. In
a flash, she was on her hands and knees, pulling the
frightened cat out from under the table and clutching her tightly against herself.

Colin quickly unbuttoned his coat, also soaked
through, and shrugged out of it. "Follow close
behind me," he commanded. "I will beat out the
flames as we go down, but we must hurry. Here, take
my coat. Use it if you must."

Brenna nodded mutely. In seconds they were in
the smoke-darkened corridor leading down, feel-

ing their way along the rough stone walls. Brenna clutched the back of his shirt with her fingers, coughing and sputtering behind him. As they reached the height of the flames, the space seemed to become void of air. The walls danced with orange and red, the roar near deafening. Tirelessly, he beat away the flames, his cloak slapping wetly against the crumbling wood and stone, over and over again. Behind him, Brenna did the same with his coat, somehow still managing to clasp the cat in one hand as she did so. Inch by agonizing inch, they made their way past the worst of it.

At last they reached the gaping door, just as a half-dozen people rushed past them, carrying buckets of water that sloshed over the ground as they hurried toward the flames.

Out in the damp air at last, Colin reached for his wife, scooping her into his arms. Still clutched tightly to Brenna's breast, the cat hissed, swiping at Colin's face with an outstretched paw. Claws made contact with his skin, and he felt the sting of blood on his cheek.

Mercifully, the ungrateful beast leapt from Brenna's arms and raced away toward the house, apparently unscathed.

With a sigh of relief, he pressed Brenna against his chest, cradling her in his arms as he buried his face in her smoke-scented hair.

"Brenna, oh, Brenna, my love," he murmured. "Thank God you're safe."

"Colin," she rasped, and he gazed down at her soot-covered face.

His happiness turned to horror as her eyes suddenly rolled up in her head, and her body went limp in his arms.

*No!* his mind screamed, his heart nearly stilled. He could not lose her now. Still clutching her small form, Colin sank to his knees in the mud, crying out like an injured animal.


*Thirsty. So verra thirsty.* Brenna swallowed, her throat dry and parched, as her heavy eyelids fluttered open. It was night, and naught but hazy moonlight lit the room. Clearly the storm had abated, but whatever had happened to her?

At once the memories came flooding back to her—smoke, heavy acrid smoke. Fire below her in the tower's stairs, and then Colin . . . Nay, her mind countered, and she shook her head. A dull, throbbing ache accompanied the movement, making her wince and reach a hand up to her temple. Her mind must be playing tricks on her. Cruel tricks. Colin wasn't there at Glenbroch. He couldn't be.

Her gaze flitted across the room, her eyes stinging dreadfully with the effort. Yet the vision remained. There, in a chair beside the bed. Someone was dozing, the moon reflecting off unruly golden hair.

Her heart began to drum against her ribs. Could it be? Nay, she'd wanted him there so verra badly that her mind had simply conjured up his image, sleeping there in her chair. And looking so verra real. "Colin?" she tried to call out, her voice hoarse. "Is it really ye?"

He sat upright at once. And then he was on his feet, moving to her side in a blur. "Brenna? Oh, thank God. Here, drink this." He lifted a glass to her mouth. Some sort of spirits, by the smell of it. She took a sip. Whisky. The liquid brought tears to her eyes, burning her throat as it scorched a path down to warm her stomach.

Relief flooded through her veins, nearly taking her breath away. It *was* him, in flesh and blood, there in her bedchamber. Her husband. "'Tis really ye," she said, her voice gravelly. She felt his lips in her hair.

"I should have come long before this. Will you ever forgive me?"

She struggled to sit, leaning back against the carved headboard. "Light a candle. I must see your face. 'Tis been far too long."

In moments, he complied, moving toward her with a single taper. Brenna inhaled sharply, shocked by her husband's appearance as the soft flicker of light illuminated his features. His face was far thinner than she'd remembered, his eyes darkly shadowed. Gone was the easy, wry expression, the sardonic tip to his lips. Instead, his mouth was taut and pinched, his brow creased. The scar on his eyebrow seemed to stand out in stark relief on his pale skin. A red, angry scratch, caked with what appeared to be fresh blood, ran the length of one gaunt cheek. He looked as if he hadn't slept in days. However did a man age ten years in little more than a moon?

She found her voice at last. "Hold me." 'Twas all she could manage.

"I don't deserve to," he choked out.

"Ye saved my life, Colin Rosemoor."

He swallowed with obvious difficulty. "I love you

more than life itself. I'd give mine in a heartbeat to save yours."

"I know ye would, Colin. 'Tis what kind of man ye are." She reached for his hand, drew it toward her, then gasped in surprise as she saw the bandages wrapped around his palms.

"Your hands," she said, her voice tremulous.

"Not nearly as bad as they look, I assure you. Mrs. Cannan put a balm on them."

Ever so gently, she raised his trembling fingers to her mouth, kissing them one by one. "Do they pain ye terribly?"

"Not anymore they don't."

"My hero," she murmured. "'Tis the stuff of romantic novels, is it not?"

"I'm no hero," he said sharply, shaking his head. One wavy lock fell across his forehead. "God knows I don't deserve you, but if you'll give me one more chance, I'll show you what kind of man I can be. No more drinking. No more gambling. No false promises. When I'm a better man, a stronger man, perhaps then you can love me. Perhaps you'll understand just how much I love you."

Her vision blurred by the tears that filled her eyes, she reached down and pulled the heavy aquamarine from her finger. She held it up to the light, reading aloud the single word cut into the gold band. "Unbidden. An adjective. Something that comes uninvited. A love that steals into your heart before ye realize ye wanted it. A love that finds ye when ye weren't even searching for it. Perhaps even when ye least wanted it. And yet perhaps the greatest love of all, a love that comes unbidden."

A slow, easy smile spread across Colin's face. "So

now you know. I think I began to fall in love with you the day I made your acquaintance, just after I trounced you in Lady Brandon's garden." He moved to her side, reaching out to stroke her cheek with his bandaged hand. "I've loved you from the moment I heard you talk about the stars and the moon, about Glenbroch and the pride you have in running it. I knew then that you were extraordinary. I married the single most magnificent woman in the world, and I will do anything to keep her."

"Then hold me, Colin, if it willna pain your hands too badly. That's all I ask of the man I love above all else."

She watched as he stripped down to his trousers, his eyes never leaving her face as he did so. Seconds later, he was beside her on the bed, his arms wrapped protectively about her. As the sun began its slow ascent into the sky, she laid her cheek against his hard, muscled chest, listening to the rhythmic beating of his heart.

*Home,* Brenna thought as Colin leaned down to kiss the top of her head. She was home at last, in Colin's arms.

# Epilogue

"Ye don't have to do such a thing, Colin. Truly, 'tis not necessary." Brenna's gaze swept appreciatively over her husband, the bright sun shining down on his gleaming fair head like a halo as he leaned against the tall standing stone, one of an ancient circle there in the glen. "We're already lawfully wed, ye know."

"And yet Mrs. Cannan and your friends, your staff, your tenants, they all missed seeing the Maclachlan of Glenbroch made a bride, didn't they? No, I cannot deny them the pleasure. Forget the formal ceremony. In true Scots tradition, we will simply clasp hands on the steps of the church and I will declare you my wife. And then we will invite everyone from miles about to our home for a feast in honor of our marriage. At Castle Glenbroch."

Brenna nodded, smiling up at her handsome husband with delight. Amazing how his health, his vigor, had restored so quickly there at Glenbroch. Only a fortnight had passed, and yet his cheeks were no longer gaunt, his eyes no longer shadowed.

A smile danced upon his lips once more, his good humor at last restored.

"London is our home, too," she said, reaching down to pluck up a stem of heather. She brought it to her nose, inhaling the familiar sweet scent. "Already I find myself missing Jane and your dear mother. I suppose I miss Lord and Lady Danville a wee bit, too, though I don't care if I ever lay eyes on Hugh Ballard again," she added with a scowl.

Colin nodded, running one hand along the stone's smooth, stark-white surface. "Oh, don't worry. Ballard has hightailed it out of London by now, I'm sure. Sinclair, too. The pair will no doubt bide their time in the country till the scandal fades away. I was thinking, what if we make our home in London during the summer months, whilst Parliament is in, and Glenbroch for the remainder of the year?"

"But what of your family seat in Essex? Glenfield, 'tis called?"

"Jane and my mother can remain at Glenfield during the winter months. It shall be their home to live out their days in, just at the top of the road from Lucy at Covington Hall. I've no need of it, after all. I like it here at Glenbroch. This is perhaps the finest land I've ever laid eyes on."

"Och, next thing I know, ye'll be wearing a kilt and sporran and speaking with a brogue."

"Hmm, perhaps I will," he teased, his eyes dancing mischievously. "Only I worry so about the drafts."

Brenna laughed, rising up on tiptoe to kiss his smiling mouth. "So this is why ye brought me here, Colin? To tell me that ye plan to wed me once more, here on Scottish soil?"

"That," he said, reaching into his coat pocket,

"and to give you this." He held out a heavy piece of folded parchment.

"What is it?" she asked, reaching for it.

"Open it and see for yourself. It's a belated wedding gift. I managed to obtain it just before I left London. You said this circle of stones was special to you, so I thought it the perfect place to present it to you."

Curiously, Brenna broke the seal and unfolded the page, her eyes quickly scanning it. "A deed? I dinna understand." She looked up and met Colin's gaze. The love she saw shining in their depths nearly took her breath away. It had been there all along. However had she missed it, doubted it?

"Hampton's estate," he said, brushing a lock of hair from her forehead. "The land neighboring Glenbroch to the east, Mr. Moray tells me. I was able to buy back the deed from Harold Mifflin, and now I've deeded it to you. The land is yours."

Brenna swallowed the lump in her throat. Tears burned behind her eyelids—happy tears. Joyful tears. "However did ye do this?"

"With some help from Mandeville. Mifflin didn't want to give it up, that's for certain. Tightfisted bastard. Anyway, it's yours now, to merge with Glenbroch. I somehow imagine you a far better manager than I could ever be, and perhaps you can set up Mr. and Mrs. Cannan in the main house. As caretakers, so as not to hurt their pride."

A tear fell from the corner of Brenna's eye, coursing down her cheek. Lord, but she'd become so emotional lately, so quick to tears. She reached up to wipe it away, but Colin beat her to it, brushing it away with his thumb. Encircling her waist with his hands, he drew her toward him, claiming her mouth with his own.

After several pleasant minutes, Colin's mouth retreated, leaving her breathless. "Did you feel that?" he asked, his brow furrowed.

"Feel what?" Brenna asked, still attempting to regulate her breathing.

Still grasping her shoulders, he took a step away from the standing stone he'd been leaning against. "I could swear I felt . . . something. In the stone. Like a vibration or something."

"Hmmm, and perhaps if ye look behind it, you'll see a fairy," she teased.

"Very funny, indeed. Fine, have a laugh, but I vow I felt something."

"Did ye really?" Brenna asked, serious now. "Surely ye have heard the legend of these stones?"

"No. There's a legend?"

"Aye. 'Tis said that this is the place where the ancient Pict priestesses came to conceive a child, for it 'twas known to be fertile ground. They'd bring a lover here, and make love right in the center of the circle. And then they'd come to stand, well . . ." She trailed off, biting her lower lip to keep from laughing. "Right there, I think. Right where ye are standing." Brenna couldn't help but smile as Colin took two steps away from the stone. "And if a child had been conceived by the act the stones had borne witness to, then the stone would vibrate."

"How very strange," Colin said.

"'Tis strange, indeed. Stranger still that it would vibrate whilst ye leaned against it. I'm fairly certain that ye are not with child, after all." Brenna endeavored to keep a straight face. 'Twas difficult, as the puzzled look on his face was near priceless. "Hmmm." She tapped one finger against her chin, pretending to consider the situation. "Do ye think that perhaps since I was leaning against ye whilst ye were in turn leaning against the stone . . ." She shook her head. "Nay, perhaps not." Her mouth curved into a smile as Colin seemed to finally grasp the full meaning of her words.

His eyes grew wide as he reached for her, one hand splayed against her stomach. "Are you trying to tell me something, Brenna Maclachlan?"

"Lady Rosemoor to ye," she retorted. "And aye, I am. With child, I meant. A son, if my dowsing pendulum is correct."

The expression on his face was pure rapture. Brenna had never before seen her husband look so happy, so utterly delighted as he did at that very moment. "Thank you, Brenna," he said, his voice husky, and then he sank to his knees, his mouth pressed against her stomach. She stroked his hair, the soft waves slipping through her fingers like silk.

"No, thank *you*, my love," Brenna responded, growing teary-eyed once more, blast it.

He rose, peering down at her curiously. "Did you hear that? You said 'you.'"

"Well, of course I did. What else would I say?"

"Ye. Usually you pronounce it 'ye.' Only just now, you said 'you.'"

"I think *ye* are losing your mind, Colin Rosemoor. I dinna say any such thing."

"I make you a viscountess and next thing I know, you're speaking like an Englishwoman. It won't do at all. And while I'm on the subject, I've yet to see you swim in the river in nothing but your undergarments and then lie on a rock while you wait for them to dry. You would deprive me of that? I've carried that mental image in my mind for so long now it's nearly driving me mad."

"I dinna know it meant so much to ye," she said with an easy laugh. "I knew I shouldna have said such a thing to a gentleman."

"Oh, I'm no gentleman," he said, tossing his coat to the ground. His fingers flew over the buttons of his waistcoat, and then it joined his coat in the grass at his feet. Quickly, he slipped down his braces before untying his cravat and unbuttoning his linen.

"What on earth are ye doing?"

"Undressing," he said with a shrug, then pulled the shirt over his head. "I suggest you do the same."

"'Tis fairly obvious what ye are doing, Colin. I only meant why." Good Lord, he was unfastening his trousers now. She looked about wildly to make sure no one was about. Mercifully, the glen was silent but for the birds chattering gaily as they flitted through the sky above them.

Colin cleared his throat to gain her attention. "Lady Rosemoor? You really should get undressed. I feel quite silly standing here like this. Alone. Drafts, you know."

She returned her gaze to her husband. He really *was* naked, his skin cast a golden yellow from the bright midday sun above. And he was aroused. Heavens above, but he was aroused.

*As am I,* she realized with a start, reaching around to unfasten her gown as expeditiously as possible.

"It's only fair to the stones, you know," he said, standing there watching her like a Greek god, all hard planes and corded muscle. "We've deprived them of the first part of the ritual, after all. Bearing witness to our lovemaking. I suppose we must put forth our most impressive effort. Wouldn't want to seem unworthy, you know. Not after they vibrated for us and all that."

At last Brenna's gown fell to the grassy carpet with a swish. She stepped out of it, quickly undoing her stays. They, too, fell to the ground. In seconds, she'd removed her stockings and slippers. Her hands shaking with anticipation, she pulled her shift over her head and deposited it with the rest of her garments. Undressed at last, she stood before her husband, waiting for him to take her into his arms.

Instead, he frowned. "What's that there, on your leg?" he asked, moving toward her with narrowed eyes.

"What?" Brenna looked down. "Oh, ye mean my birthmark?"

"I can't believe I've never before noticed it. Right there." His fingers brushed her thigh, sending ripples of delight racing across her skin.

"Aye, it's been there all along," she said. She'd always despised it. And yet, if it weren't for the birthmark, they might never have identified her as Lord and Lady Danville's daughter, setting in motion the chain of events that had led her to Colin. For the first time in all her years, she looked at the mark with affection.

"I say, it almost looks like . . . No, it must be my imagination." He shook his head.

A *fleur-de-lis*, Brenna added silently, smiling to herself as she reached up to embrace her husband. *Flower of the lily.*

He shrugged, his hungry mouth finding hers and

claiming it with unrestrained passion. Hands moved against bare skin in unabashed exploration as they sank to the soft, springy grass in the center of the stones.

She'd made up the legend, of course. Surely a wife was allowed one secret from her husband, wasn't she?